BLACK RAVEN

A MAX RYKER THRILLER

JACK HUNT

DIRECT RESPONSE PUBLISHING

ISBN: 978-1-0690069-0-5

For my father, February 4, 1948 – June 29, 2024. From your military service to your work on the mission field, you lived your life in service to others. Rest easy, Dad. I miss you and love you always.

ALSO BY JACK HUNT

If you haven't joined ***Jack Hunt's Private Facebook Group*** just do a search on facebook to find it. This gives readers a way to chat with Jack, see cover reveals, enter contests and receive giveaways, and stay updated on upcoming releases. There is also his main facebook page below if you want to browse. facebook.com/jackhuntauthor

Go to the link below to receive special offers, bonus content, and news about new Jack Hunt's books. Sign up for the newsletter. http://www.jackhuntbooks.com/signup

Max Ryker Thrillers

Black Raven

American Asset (out in 2024)

Coming soon...

A High Peaks Mystery Thrillers

In Cold Blood

Vanish From Sight

Her Final Hours

The Smart Killer

The Catcher

Twice Missing

After it Turns Dark series

When the World Turns Dark

When Humanity Ends

When Hope is Lost

When Blood Lies

When Survivors Rise

Ring of Fire series

Those Who Survive

Those Who Fall

Those Who Defend

The Great Dying series

Extinct

Primal

Species

A Powerless World series

Escape the Breakdown

Survive the Lawless

Defend the Homestead

Outlive the Darkness

Evade the Ruthless

Outlaws of the Midwest series

Chaos Erupts

Panic Ensues

Havoc Endures

The Cyber Apocalypse series

As Our World Ends

As Our World Falls

As Our World Burns

The Agora Virus series

Phobia

Anxiety

Strain

The War Buds series

War Buds 1

War Buds 2

War Buds 3

Camp Zero series

State of Panic

State of Shock

State of Decay

Renegades series

The Renegades

The Renegades Book 2: Aftermath

The Renegades Book 3: Fortress

The Renegades Book 4: Colony

The Renegades Book 5: United

The Wild Ones Duology

The Wild Ones Book 1

The Wild Ones Book 2

The EMP Survival series

Days of Panic

Days of Chaos

Days of Danger

Days of Terror

Against All Odds Duology

As We Fall

As We Break

The Amygdala Syndrome Duology

Unstable

Unhinged

Survival Rules series

Rules of Survival

Rules of Conflict

Rules of Darkness

Rules of Engagement

Lone Survivor series

All That Remains

All That Survives

All That Escapes

All That Rises

Single Novels

The Aging

The Haze

The Delay (Sequel to The Haze)

The Last Sound

15 Floors

Blackout

Defiant

Darkest Hour

Final Impact

The Year Without Summer

The Last Storm

The Last Magician

The Lookout

Class of 1989

Out of the Wild

Mavericks: Hunters Moon

Killing Time

PART I

PROLOGUE

Croatia

The blade glided past Max Ryker's rib cage, narrowly missing him. He counter-attacked, driving his elbow into the assailant's jaw. The man staggered back, slamming into one of the round tables outside the café. Chairs toppled, and drinks shattered. No one paid attention — tourists were already screaming and running for safety. The distraction had worked. The fight would have been the focus without it, but now it blended into the city's chaos.

Ryker's attacker recovered quickly, more determined, slashing wildly. The blade nicked Ryker's cheek, but he swiftly grabbed the man's wrist, twisted it, and drove the knife deep into his gut, pushing it upward until the man struck the wall behind him.

Ryker glanced to his right. His target, Carol Kingsley, thirty-four, cowered, her handbag in hand, dark hair windswept across her face. She searched for a way past but was trapped by chairs, tables, and people hurrying for the stairs.

"The exchange was compromised," he said.

"My contacts are dead?"

He nodded. Over his comms unit, Max heard a teammate speak.

"Let's go!" Ryker extended his hand to Carol. She hesitated too long, so he grabbed her wrist and yanked her away from the wall. "The others will be here in minutes."

"How many?" she yelled, looking over her shoulder.

He didn't answer, his focus locked on the crowd ahead. They elbowed their way through, Ryker's grip on her hand unyielding. Weeks, months, even years had led to this moment. National security was just the tip of the iceberg—far more was at stake. Behind his sunglasses, Ryker scanned the scene, noting the countless cell phones capturing the chaos.

Had anyone recorded him? He didn't care. There were more pressing concerns.

Unfazed, he adjusted his baseball cap and shades, partially hiding his features. The earlier gunshots had cleared most people from the wall. The same shots would have been a distraction for what should have ended with Carol dead and highly sensitive material confiscated.

"We move to plan B," he said.

"Wait. What?"

"We have no choice. Down this way," he directed, starting down the concrete steps. He noticed another agent hurrying up through the crowd. Ryker watched as she slipped a hand into her jacket, knowing she concealed a silenced Glock 17. They turned on a dime, continuing along the wall.

The defensive stone wall, stretching 1.2 miles, encircled

the city. On a good day, it was a forty-minute trek. Every bend and view below was steeped in history. Wide, marble-paved streets fanned out into the heart of the Old Town, a testament to the careful reconstruction after the 1667 earthquake. Onofrio's Fountain stood at one end, and the Clock Tower at the other, bookending the historic thoroughfare.

To thousands, the city's walls were relics of a fortified era. To them, they were a trap.

Ryker glanced down at the Adriatic Sea, nearly eighty feet below. Waves crashed against the rocks. The thought of leaping crossed his mind but quickly vanished.

Another gunshot rang out, closer this time.

Ryker and Carol burst through a weathered wooden door onto a terracotta rooftop, the faded orange tiles warm beneath their feet. The Adriatic Sea glimmered in the distance.

"This way," Ryker hissed, guiding Carol across the uneven surface. They scrambled over the sloping roofs, their footsteps echoing off the ancient tiles. Carol's breath came in short gasps as she struggled to keep up.

Suddenly, Carol slipped on a loose tile. She cried out, pitching toward the edge. Ryker spun around and grabbed her jacket. For a heart-stopping moment, Carol dangled over the narrow street below, held only by Ryker's iron grip.

"I've got you," he grunted, straining to pull her back up. As he did, he saw their pursuer — a lithe woman with steely eyes — closing in fast.

"Move!" Ryker shouted, pushing Carol ahead. They raced across the rooftops, leaping over narrow gaps between buildings. The woman behind them moved with fluid grace, gaining ground.

Spotting a balcony below, Ryker made a split-second decision.

"Jump!" he commanded, launching himself off the roof. Carol followed, landing less gracefully. Ryker yanked open a sliding glass door and ushered Carol inside.

"Wait here," he said, pushing her into the kitchen. He positioned himself beside the door, waiting. Seconds later, the female agent burst through. Ryker exploded into action, driving his shoulder into her midsection. They slammed against the wall, but she countered with a vicious knee to his ribs. Using Krav Maga techniques, she spun around him, landing several rapid uppercuts.

Ryker staggered back, then surged forward, grabbing the woman and hurling her through the glass door. Shards exploded outward, raining down on the street below. As she scrambled for her weapon, Ryker charged, shoving her off the balcony. Her scream faded, cut short by the impact below. A gunshot cracked above him.

"Another one," Ryker growled, dashing back inside.

He grabbed Carol's arm, pulling her toward another window.

They clambered onto another rooftop, the warm tiles scraping their palms. Ryker led the way, guiding them across interconnected roofs. The Old Town spread out beneath them, a maze of narrow streets and historic buildings.

They reached St. Margaret Bastion, the southernmost part of the wall, a section that extended into the sea. The circular structure stood like a sentinel, its weathered stones bearing witness to centuries of vigilance. The bastion's thick walls offered momentary cover from their pursuers. Gunshots rang out behind them.

"What about the original file?" Carol gasped, eyes wide with fear.

"It's taken care of."

"Where is it?"

Another gunshot.

Carol stumbled, her sandals ill-suited for the sprint. Ryker caught her arm, steadying her without breaking stride.

"No time. Keep moving," he said, eyes darting for any sign of pursuit.

"How will I find you again?"

He didn't answer. They rounded a corner, the breathtaking view of the Adriatic momentarily stealing their attention. The deep blue waters sparkled under the intense sunlight.

A bullet whizzed past, chipping stone near Ryker's head. He instinctively ducked, pulling Carol down with him.

"Stay low!" he commanded, drawing his weapon.

The narrow walkway atop the wall left little room for maneuvering. Tourists, moments ago enjoying the views, now pressed against the inner wall, faces etched with terror. "Go down those steps," Ryker urged, his voice strained.

"I won't make it out," Carol protested, her face pale with fear.

"Head out the eastern gate."

He shoved her towards the stairs and held off the attacker with multiple rounds before backing up to the wall. He didn't have time to decide on an alternative. As he clambered up to jump, a gunshot clipped him, spinning him and sending him plummeting toward the churning waters.

The Adriatic Sea, usually a serene backdrop to the city's beauty, now waited to claim Ryker. Its deep blue waters, which had long protected Dubrovnik from invaders, seemed poised to become his final resting place. The waves crashed against the walls, their rhythm unchanged by the drama. His body landed hard. Then, nothing but pain, blackness, and the swirl of water.

As Ryker's consciousness faded, his last glimpse was of the city — a living museum of stone and history, now scarred by modern-day intrigue and violence. The file, the reason for all this chaos, was lost to him, its secrets gone along with its protector.

1

Chicago

It was a strange kind of hell.

Darkness surrounded him, a horrifying inky black that pressed against his eyelids. For a moment, Max Ryker floated in this void, disconnected from time and space. Then, with a jolt that sent pain ricocheting through his body, he snapped back to consciousness.

Laying on his back, he forced his eyes open. The sky above was out of focus, a dull mix of black smoke and ash swirling in lazy patterns. Weak rays of sunlight strained through the haze, bathing his face in an eerie, diffused glow. He gasped, struggling to draw a breath, his lungs burning as if he'd inhaled fire. Pain coursed through him, each nerve ending screaming for attention. His mouth felt like sandpaper, his tongue swollen and useless. One nostril was plugged closed, the other barely able to pull in the acrid air.

For what felt like an eternity, Max lay motionless on the snow-covered concrete. The biting cold seeped through his clothes, numbing his skin. All he could do was blink with every wave of pain that washed over him, each one threatening to drag him back into the comforting darkness of unconsciousness. But something kept him tethered to awareness — a primal instinct, perhaps, or years of training kicking in.

Slowly, the world around him began to take shape.

Behind the curtain of gray, a cacophony of sounds built gradually, as if someone was turning up the volume on a nightmare. The shrieking of twisted metal, the hiss of escaping steam, and a chorus of honking and bleating car alarms ushered the world back into focus. Layered between these mechanical wails were human sounds — cries of pain, groans of despair, shouts for help. The sounds of desperation attacked his senses, a terrifying jumble that brought the stark realization that he wasn't alone in this hellscape.

As his hearing sharpened, so did his other senses.

The rancid smell of burning flesh and sulfur assaulted his nostrils, making his stomach churn. The taste of blood and ash coated his tongue. Disoriented and overwhelmed, Max struggled to understand if he was dead or alive. Was this some kind of afterlife punishment for past transgressions? Had he finally crossed a line that couldn't be uncrossed?

He blinked hard, forcing himself to focus. Taking a couple of deep, painful breaths, he summoned the strength to roll onto his side. The movement sent fresh waves of agony through his body, but it also brought clarity. As he pushed himself up on one elbow, Max was confronted with untold devastation that stretched as far as he could see.

Rubble spread in every direction, a sea of broken concrete

and twisted metal shrouded in a cloud of gray dust. The front of a large 45-story building was gone. Among the debris lay the scattered remnants of ordinary life turned extraordinary — destroyed office equipment, shattered picture frames, and a lone shoe. And then there were the bodies. Some moved, writhing in pain or struggling to stand. Others lay still, broken and mangled beyond recognition.

People staggered aimlessly through the chaos, coated in thick ash and snow that turned them into ghostly figures. The scene was hauntingly familiar, stirring memories of images he'd seen of Ground Zero after 9/11. But this wasn't New York, and it wasn't 2001. This was happening now, and he was in the middle of it.

Water sprayed from broken pipes, creating treacherous ice patches. Some of the liquid turned to slush as it hit the blanket of snow covering the ground, adding to the hazards of the terrain. In the distance, flames licked at the skeleton of what must have once been a towering building, sending plumes of black smoke into the wintry sky.

What the hell happened? Max thought, trying to piece together the fragments of memory floating just out of reach. Where am I?

As if in answer to his unspoken questions, fleeting images of Croatia bombarded his mind. Sun-drenched coastline, ancient stone buildings, the glint of a scope in the distance. But how had he gotten from there to... here?

Gritting his teeth against the pain and cold, Max slowly turned his head to his other side. His gaze fell upon an intact window, miraculously spared from the destruction. In its reflective surface, he caught sight of himself, and his brain started to assimilate the information.

The man staring back at him looked to be in his mid-thirties, with piercing green eyes that seemed to hold more questions than answers. His hair was an unruly long dark mess, matted with dust, snow, and what might have been blood. He had a beard with pieces of debris embedded in it and a shard of glass. His disciplined physique, honed by years of training and fieldwork, was lean and taut, pressed tightly against unfamiliar clothing.

Max's skin was dark and weathered, bearing signs of too much time spent under the harsh sun in far-flung locations. His expression was a mixture of wariness and confusion, mirroring the tumult of emotions churning inside him.

He squinted, focusing on his attire. Gone was the tactical gear he last remembered wearing. Instead, he wore blue workman overalls, the kind of uniform donned by industrial workers or maintenance staff. With a trembling hand, he brushed a thin layer of gray dust and snow from his breast, revealing a company patch that read: "Jan Pros - Chicago Cleaning Professionals."

Chicago? The realization hit him like a physical blow. How had he ended up in the Windy City? And why was he dressed as a cleaner? None of it made sense, yet here he was, amid what appeared to be ground zero of some catastrophic event.

Max's head swam with unanswered questions as he pushed himself to a sitting position. But one thing was clear — he needed to move, to understand what had happened, and to figure out his role in all of this. With a grunt of effort, he began the painful process of standing up, ready to face whatever this strange new reality had in store. He rose from the ground, spitting a wad of phlegm.

As he staggered away from the immediate chaos, the full extent of the devastation began to unfold before him. The smoke and burning materials assaulted his nostrils, making his eyes water. He blinked fast, trying to clear his vision as he took in the horrifying scene around him.

Twisted metal and shattered glass littered the street blanketed in snow. The once-bustling business district had been transformed into a war zone. Office buildings that had stood tall and proud just moments ago now bore gaping wounds, their facades crumbling and windows blown out. Papers fluttered like macabre confetti, carried by the hot currents rising from smoldering debris before settling on the ground.

As he moved further from ground zero, Max's ears were assaulted by a cacophony of sounds. The wail of approaching sirens pierced through the din of panicked voices and the groans of the injured. Car alarms blared incessantly, their owners long since fled or incapacitated. In the distance, he could hear the ominous creaking and groaning of damaged structures threatening to collapse at any moment.

His gaze was drawn to a woman kneeling on the icy sidewalk, cradling something in her arms. As he drew closer, his stomach lurched as he realized it was a body — small, lifeless, and covered in dust and snow. The woman's anguished sobs cut through the chaos, a haunting reminder of the human toll of this catastrophe.

He stumbled onward, his mind reeling as he tried to make sense of his surroundings. Suddenly, a sharp pain in his wrist caught his attention. Max looked down, noticing for the first time a digital watch strapped to his arm. His breath caught in his throat as he saw the numbers on the display: 61:48:43, 61:48:42, 61:48:41... A countdown, ticking away relentlessly.

"What the heck?" he muttered, his voice hoarse and barely audible over the commotion.

Max's eyes widened as he noticed a gold band encircling

his ring finger. He held his hand up, staring at the unfamiliar jewelry in disbelief. When had he gotten married? And to whom? His thoughts surged, desperately trying to conjure any memory of a wedding, anything — but came up blank.

As he lowered his hand, something on his palm caught his eye. Scrawled in faded ink were two words: "Black Raven." Max's brow furrowed as he tried to decipher their meaning. Was it a code? The more he pondered, the more his head ached with the effort of remembering.

Instinctively, he patted himself down, searching for a cell phone or identification. His pockets were empty, save for a few crumpled bills and some loose change. He had no wallet, no phone, and no clues beyond the mysterious watch, ring, and cryptic message on his palm.

A piercing scream cut through his thoughts, snapping his attention back to the present. Through the thinning smoke and swirling snow, Max spotted a young woman on her knees, her hands clawing desperately at a pile of rubble.

"Help! Please, somebody help me!" she cried out, her voice raw with panic.

He rushed over, momentarily forgetting his own confusion. As he approached, he saw tears freezing on her cheeks, cutting clean trails through the dust on the woman's face.

"Are you hurt?" Max asked, kneeling beside her.

The woman shook her head frantically. "My daughter! She's trapped under there. Please, you have to help her!"

His eyes widened. He could see a small hand protruding beneath a large concrete slab and twisted metal.

"Okay, just wait here. We'll get her out," Max said, trying to sound more confident than he felt. "What's your name?"

"Sarah," the woman choked out between sobs. "And my daughter is Clara. She's only six."

He nodded, his mind in overdrive as he assessed the situation. "Alright, Sarah. I'll try to lift this, but I need your help pulling Clara out. Can you do that?"

Sarah nodded vigorously, wiping her tears with the back of her hand. "Yes, yes, of course. Just please, hurry!"

Max scanned the area, looking for anything he could use as a lever. His eyes landed on a long piece of metal, likely part of a support beam from the collapsed building. He grabbed it, ignoring the sharp edges that bit into his palms and the cold metal. Max wedged it under the edge of the concrete slab.

Gritting his teeth, he pushed down on the makeshift lever with all his might. The debris shifted slightly, but it wasn't enough. Sweat beaded on his forehead, cooling almost instantly as he strained against the weight.

"It's too heavy," he grunted. Max looked around frantically, spotting a man stumbling through the wreckage nearby. "Hey! You! Can you help me over here!"

Dazed and covered in dust and snow, the man turned towards Max's voice. After a moment's hesitation, he jogged over.

"What do you need?" the newcomer asked, his voice rough.

"There's a little girl trapped," Max explained quickly. "Help me lift this while her mother pulls her out."

The man nodded, clamping hold of the metal beam.

"On three," Max said. "One, two, three!"

He and the other man pushed down with all their strength. Slowly, agonizingly, the slab of concrete began to rise.

"Now, Sarah!" he shouted through gritted teeth. "Pull her out!"

Sarah didn't hesitate. She reached into the small opening, her hands grasping for her daughter. "I've got her!" she cried out. "Clara, baby, come on."

With a final tug, Sarah pulled her daughter free from the rubble. The moment Clara was clear, Max and the other man let the debris crash back down.

Sarah clutched her daughter to her chest, peppering her dust-covered face with kisses. "Oh, thank God. Thank God," she repeated, rocking back and forth.

Max slumped to the ground, his muscles burning from the exertion. He watched as Sarah checked her daughter for injuries, relief washing over her face as she found only minor scrapes and bruises.

The man who had helped turned to Max. "That was close," he said, offering a hand to help Max.

Max took it, rising to his feet. Still trying to catch his breath, he looked around, the surreal nature of the situation hitting him anew. "What... what was this place?"

The man gave him an odd look. "Did you hit your head or something? It was a federal building."

Max's brow furrowed. "Where?"

"Downtown Chicago," the man replied, suggesting Max might be in shock. "Look, maybe you should sit down. The paramedics should be here soon."

Max staggered back, his mind reeling. Another flood of memories rushed in — but they weren't of Chicago. They were from Croatia. The mission. The target. How had he ended up here?

"Do you have a phone?" Max asked abruptly.

The man nodded, pulling a smartphone from his pocket and handing it over. Max's fingers trembled as he dialed a number he knew by heart — his home number. It rang once, twice, three times. Each unanswered ring increased his anxiety.

"Come on, pick up," he muttered. But there was no answer. After several more rings, the call went to voicemail.

Confused and increasingly worried, he tried another number — his work contact. This time, a robotic voice informed him that the number was no longer in service.

His heart thumped as he stared at the phone in disbelief. How could both his home and work numbers be unreachable?

Max handed the phone back to its owner. Nothing made sense. He walked away from the man, his eyes scanning the debris-strewn street. A crumpled newspaper, half-buried in a nearby snowdrift, caught his attention.

He pulled it out, his eyes immediately drawn to the date. December 29th. Less than three days before New Year's Day. But that was impossible. Just yesterday — or what felt like yesterday — he had been in Croatia on a mission.

Max let the newspaper fall from his hands, his world spinning. He staggered away from the chaos of the bombing site, his feet carrying him on autopilot. He needed to get home and find something familiar that made sense.

The sounds of sirens grew louder. Emergency vehicles were arriving now, their flashing lights reflecting off the snow and adding to the surreal atmosphere. Ryker barely noticed as he passed them, his mind consumed with questions.

He knew who he was, but why couldn't he remember how he got here? What did the countdown on his watch mean? And most pressingly — what the hell had happened between his last clear memory and now?

His pace quickened as he moved further from the blast site, his breath forming small clouds. He needed answers and had a sinking feeling that time was not on his side. Whatever was going on, whatever had brought him to this moment, Max knew one thing for sure — his life as he knew it had been blown apart just as surely as the federal building behind him. And he had less than 62 hours to piece it all back together.

2

The Chicago field office of the Federal Bureau of Investigation buzzed with frenetic energy, a marked difference compared to the chaos unfolding just 3.5 miles away. Supervisory Special Agent Meredith Jansen strode through the corridors, her mind struggling to process the fragments of information trickling in from the blast site. Her colleague, Doug Erikson, struggled to keep pace, his arms laden with hastily printed reports and a tablet displaying real-time updates.

As they approached the main operations room, the din of ringing phones, urgent conversations, and the constant hum of computers grew louder. Jansen paused at the threshold, taking in the scene before her. The large, open-plan office was a hive of activity, with agents and analysts hunched over workstations, their expressions illuminated by the blue glow of multiple screens.

The far wall was dominated by a massive display showing a map of downtown Chicago. A pulsing red dot marked the location of the John C. Kluczynski Federal Building, surrounded by concentric circles indicating the blast radius. Smaller screens flanked the main display, cycling through live news feeds, social media updates, and incoming data from various agencies. One screen showed footage of emergency vehicles struggling through snow-draped streets.

Jansen's eyes darted from screen to screen, her mind cataloging each piece of information. She absently took another bite of the sandwich in her hand, barely tasting it as she chewed. She tossed the remainder into a nearby trash can as she entered the room, focusing on the task.

"Listen up, folks," she called out, her voice cutting through the cacophony. The room fell silent, all eyes turning to her. "We're still unsure if this will be the only attack or who is responsible," she continued, her tone clipped and authoritative. "Chicago's bomb squad is on scene at the blast site. Initial indications point to an act of terrorism, not an accident."

A young agent near the front raised his hand, his tie askew and forehead glistening with sweat. "How can they be sure?"

Jansen's eyes narrowed slightly. "Experience, Anderson. Experience," she replied, her voice tinged with impatience. "The target was the Kluczynski Federal Building. Surrounding buildings have been damaged within an 8-block radius. Initial indications point to a remote detonation or a timer."

Another voice piped up from the back of the room. "And casualties?"

Jansen's expression tightened. "Extensive," she answered, her tone grave. "Emergency services are at ground zero. Police are securing the scene. 911 is overwhelmed." She paused, surveying the room. "Our job is to find who is responsible and fast. Now, the window is closing. We have no way of knowing if another location will be attacked."

She began pacing, her energy palpable. "I want the CTA system temporarily put on hold. I need CCTV footage from every public space, traffic intersection, public transportation hub, ATM, sister agency, and private sector camera within an eight-block radius before and after the explosion. Let's go!"

As agents scrambled to carry out her orders, Jansen turned on her heel and headed towards her office. Doug followed close behind, his eyes fixed on a spot on her blouse. He cleared his throat, pointing discreetly.

Jansen glanced down and cursed under her breath. A dollop of mustard had escaped her sandwich, leaving an unsightly stain on her crisp white shirt. She grabbed some wipes from a nearby desk and began dabbing at the spot, but her efforts only seemed to make it worse.

Without a second thought, she unbuttoned her blouse and shrugged it off, revealing a simple tank top underneath. The office full of agents pointedly averted their eyes, focusing intently on their screens as Jansen rummaged in a drawer for a fresh shirt.

Doug raised an eyebrow. "You know you're spending too much time here when you bring your wardrobe to work."

"Doug, I don't have time for this now," Jansen snapped, buttoning up the clean blouse.

He hesitated for a moment before speaking again. "You sure you don't want Ricardo handling this?"

Jansen's hands stilled on the buttons. "And why would I do that?"

Doug's eyebrow inched higher.

"My son is the reason I do this, not the reason not to," Jansen said firmly, her voice low but intense.

With that, she grabbed her jacket from the back of her chair and headed out, leaving Doug to hurry after her once again.

As they re-entered the main room, the energy had shifted. The initial shock had given way to focused determination. Agents moved with purpose, their conversations now hushed and urgent. The large screens were alive with activity, displaying a constant stream of incoming data.

One section of the room had been hastily converted into a makeshift command center. A group of senior agents huddled around a table strewn with maps and satellite images, their fingers tracing potential escape routes and secondary targets. The satellite images showed a city blanketed in white, the snowy streets creating a striking juxtaposition against the destruction at the blast site.

Nearby, a team of tech specialists furiously typed at their keyboards, their eyes darting between multiple screens as they combed through surveillance footage and social media feeds. The air was thick with the smell of coffee and the faint odor of stress-induced sweat.

Jansen made her way to the center of the room, her presence drawing attention without her having to say a word. "What do we have?" she asked, her voice carrying across the space.

A young analyst stepped forward, tablet in hand. "Preliminary reports suggest the explosive device was significantly larger than anything we've seen domestically in years..." he trailed off, swallowing hard.

Jansen nodded. "Keep digging. I want to know what was used, how it was transported, and who had access to those materials."

She turned to another agent, this one older, with graying

hair at his temples. "Thompson, what's the status on evacuations?"

The agent consulted his notes. "We're coordinating with local law enforcement and emergency services. The immediate area is being cleared, but there's concern about structural integrity in the surrounding buildings. We're looking at potentially thousands of displaced individuals. The winter weather is also complicating matters."

Jansen's jaw tightened. "Set up a liaison with the Red Cross and local shelters. We need to account for everyone in the affected area and ensure they have warm places to go."

As she continued receiving updates and issuing orders, a commotion near the entrance caught her attention. A group of men in dark suits had entered, their expressions grim. Jansen recognized several of them immediately — representatives from Homeland Security, NSA, the Bureau of Alcohol, Tobacco, Firearms and Explosives (BATFE), and the National Counterintelligence and Security Center (NCSC).

She excused herself from the group and made her way over to the newcomers. "Gentlemen," she greeted them, her tone professional but wary.

The tallest of the group, a man with a closely cropped beard and piercing blue eyes, stepped forward. "Agent Jansen," he said, his voice low. "Is there a place we can talk privately?"

Jansen's eyes narrowed slightly, but she nodded. "Of course. This way." She led them towards a small conference room off the side of the main office.

As they walked, Doug appeared at her elbow. "Meredith," he murmured, his voice barely audible. "Your daughter's school called. They're initiating lockdown procedures and want to know if you'll be picking her up."

For a brief moment, Jansen's carefully composed expression faltered. She closed her eyes, took a deep breath, and when she opened them again, her resolve had hardened. "Tell them she's to remain at the school until further notice. I'll send someone when it's safe."

Doug nodded, understanding the weight of her decision. As he turned to make the call, Jansen squared her shoulders and pushed open the conference room door. Whatever information these men had, whatever was coming next, she knew it would change everything.

3

Smoke and dust filled Charlie Prescott's nostrils as he crouched behind a parked car, his heart pounding. Just moments ago, he had been trudging towards Lake Park, his camera bag slung over his shoulder, resigned to covering yet another mind-numbingly dull assignment. A ribbon-cutting ceremony for a park bench. It was a far cry from the hard-hitting journalism he'd dreamed of when he'd graduated, but at least it beat fetching coffee and lunch orders for the entire newsroom.

Now, the world around him had erupted into chaos. The thunderous explosion had shaken the ground beneath his feet, sending him stumbling for cover. His eyes widened at the scene before him as he peered over the car's hood. The Kluczynski Federal Building, once a towering symbol of government authority, now stood partially collapsed, a gaping wound torn into its side. Smoke billowed from the structure, obscuring the sky and casting an eerie, apocalyptic pall over downtown Chicago. Snowflakes mingled with the ash, creating a surreal, almost haunting atmosphere.

Charlie's hands trembled as he raised his camera, but years of practice kicked in. He steadied himself, framing the shot, and began to capture the unfolding nightmare. The rapid-fire click of his shutter seemed absurdly quiet against the cacophony of screams, sirens, and the ominous groaning of damaged buildings.

A woman stumbled past, her face streaked with blood and tears, clutching a child to her chest. Charlie's finger hesitated on the shutter button for a split second before he took the shot. This was it, he realized. This was his moment. The big break he'd been waiting for since he'd first stepped foot in the newsroom.

As he snapped photo after photo, a small voice in the back of his mind whispered that he should be running and helping. But a louder voice that sounded suspiciously like his hard-nosed editor urged him on. This was news. This was history. And he was right in the middle of it.

The shrill ring of his phone cut through the chaos. Charlie fumbled in his pocket, nearly dropping the device as he answered it, his eyes never leaving the viewfinder of his camera.

"Charlie?" It was Victoria Blackwell. His superior's voice crackled through the speaker. "I hope you're getting all of this."

"Everything," Charlie replied, his voice steadier than he felt.

"Look, all the staff will be working on this, but I'm not well enough to work. This flu is worse than I thought." A violent sneeze punctuated her words. "I'll send you my current calls. Just get back to me with anything important."

Charlie ducked lower as a piece of debris whistled overhead. Sirens wailed around him, their urgent cries coming from every direction at once. People ran past, their faces masks of terror and confusion. In the air, papers and smaller bits of debris swirled like grotesque confetti, a mockery of celebration in the face of tragedy.

"You know," Charlie said, a hint of desperation creeping into his voice, "I was thinking perhaps I should call in sick."

"Don't dodge this. Man up. You said you wanted a stab at a piece," Victoria's voice was sharp, brooking no argument. "This is yours. Don't mess it up as my name will be on it."

The line went dead before Charlie could respond. He stared at the phone momentarily, shaking his head in disbelief. She was off sick and had been forwarding most of her calls and emails to him for days so she could "stay on top of work." It was just another one of the downsides to being a recent graduate, he thought bitterly. He was at the bottom of the ladder, expected to handle everything without complaint.

Charlie grimaced, pushing the thought aside as he raised his camera again. This was his chance, he reminded himself — his opportunity to prove that he was more than just the office gofer.

Through his lens, he captured the raw human drama unfolding before him. A group of office workers, their once-pristine suits now covered in dust, helped a limping colleague away from the devastation. First responders rushed towards the building, their faces set in grim determination. In the distance, he could see more emergency vehicles arriving, their lights flashing uselessly against the smoky gloom.

As he worked, Charlie's journalistic instincts began to kick in. Questions raced through his mind. Who was behind this? Was it a terrorist attack? An accident? How many were injured or...? he swallowed hard, not wanting to complete the thought.

He needed to get closer, to see more, to document everything. Cautiously, he began to edge out from behind the car, keeping low to the ground. The air was full of dust, making it hard to breathe. Charlie pulled his shirt over his nose and mouth, his eyes watering as he moved forward.

A sudden aftershock sent him scrambling back to cover. For a terrifying moment, he thought there might be another explosion. But as the rumbling subsided, he realized it was likely just part of the damaged building shifting.

Charlie's phone buzzed again. A text from Victoria: "Need eyewitness accounts. Get quotes."

He looked around, spotting a shell-shocked man sitting on the curb nearby. Taking a deep breath, Charlie approached him, camera at the ready.

"Excuse me, sir?" His voice sounded strange in his own ears, too calm, too professional for the chaos surrounding them. "I'm from the *Chicago Tribune*. Can you tell me what you saw?"

The man looked up at him, his eyes unfocused. "It... it just exploded. One minute, everything was normal, and then..." He trailed off, shaking his head.

Charlie snapped a quick photo, then pressed on. "Were you inside the building when it happened?"

"No, I was just walking by. On my way to get food." The man's voice cracked. "If I'd left five minutes earlier..."

As Charlie jotted down notes, a commotion near the building caught his attention. Firefighters were emerging from the smoke, carrying someone on a stretcher. Without thinking, Charlie raised his camera, zooming in on the scene.

Through the lens, he could see the injured person clearly. It was a woman, her face covered in soot and blood. One of her arms hung limply off the side of the stretcher. As Charlie watched, her eyes fluttered open, meeting his gaze through the camera.

For a moment, time seemed to stand still. Charlie felt a wave of guilt wash over him. This wasn't just a story. These were people's lives shattered in an instant. His finger hovered over the shutter button, suddenly unsure.

But then he remembered Victoria's words. "Don't mess this up." With a silent apology, he took the shot.

As he lowered the camera, Charlie noticed a man in a cleaner's uniform stumbling away from the scene, looking dazed and confused. There was something about his expression, a mix of shock and... was that guilt? Charlie frowned, raising his camera again to get a better look.

Just then, his phone buzzed once more. Another text from Victoria: "Anything on the perpetrators yet? Police statements?"

Damn, she was pushy.

Charlie glanced back to where he'd seen the janitor, but the man had vanished into the crowd. He shook his head, trying to clear it. He was letting his imagination run wild. Right now, he needed to focus on the facts.

With a deep breath, Charlie steeled himself and began to move closer to the police cordon that was rapidly forming around the blast site. This was his chance to prove himself.

4

The taxi weaved through the Chicago streets, its progress slowed by the chaos that had engulfed the city. Max sat in the back, his body tense, eyes constantly scanning the surroundings. The smell of smoke still clung to his clothes, a constant reminder of the devastation he'd left behind. Outside, the snow-lined streets added an eerie calm to the otherwise chaotic day.

"Man, can you believe this?" the driver said, shaking his head. He was an older man, probably in his sixties, with graying hair and worried eyes that kept darting to the rearview mirror. "I've been driving these streets for thirty years and never seen anything like it."

Max grunted in response, not really in the mood for small talk. But the driver seemed determined to fill the silence.

"I was picking up a fare downtown when it happened," he continued. "The whole building just... exploded. Like something out of a movie, you know? The ground shook, windows shattered. People were screaming, running everywhere."

"You see anything suspicious before the explosion?" Max

asked, his professional instincts kicking in despite his exhaustion.

The driver shook his head. “Nah, nothing out of the ordinary. Just another day in the city, until it wasn’t.” He paused, then added, “You were there too, weren’t you?”

Max didn't respond, instead focusing on the street signs. They were roughly five minutes from his home now, and he could feel the tension in his muscles increasing with each block they passed.

“It’s scary, you know?” the driver continued, oblivious to Max’s unease. “Makes you wonder if we’re safe anywhere anymore. My daughter works in one of those big buildings downtown.”

He was about to ask if the driver’s daughter was okay when the sound of shattering glass filled the cab as the driver’s head snapped back, a spray of red misting the windshield and seat. The taxi swerved violently. Max leaned forward, struggling to control the wheel from an awkward position in the back seat.

Time seemed to slow as the vehicle careened across the lanes. Max could see the horrified faces of pedestrians on the sidewalk and hear the blaring horns from other cars. He'd avoided a head-on collision with an oncoming SUV, but the sudden wheel jerk sent the taxi into a spin.

With the sickening crunch of metal on metal, it slammed into a parked car. The impact was jarring, but Max had managed to brace himself. The taxi wasn’t done though — its momentum carried it further, until it crashed into a lamppost with a resounding bang.

For a moment, everything was silent except for the hissing of the taxi’s engine and the incessant blaring of the horn where the driver’s lifeless body slumped against the steering wheel. Then, as if someone had turned the volume back up, the world erupted into chaos once more.

Max didn't waste any time. He knew he was exposed, vulnerable. Whoever had taken the shot at the driver — and he was certain now that he had been the intended target — would be moving in to confirm the kill.

He kicked open the door, ignoring the sharp pain in his ribs as he stumbled out onto the street. Traffic had come to a standstill, and a crowd of onlookers was already gathering, their faces a mix of shock and morbid curiosity.

Max's gaze darted around, taking in every detail. Windows, rooftops, alleyways — any place a shooter could be hiding. He needed to move, to disappear into the crowd before the assassin could get another clear shot.

"Hey, are you okay?" a woman asked, reaching out to him. "You're bleeding!"

Max touched his forehead, his fingers coming away red. He must have hit his head in the crash. "I'm fine," he replied, moving past her.

He merged into the growing crowd, using the crowd around him as cover. His heart was pounding, adrenaline surging through his veins. This was no random attack. Someone knew he had survived the explosion and knew he was heading home. The question was, who?

As he moved, Max felt a flurry of ideas take hold. He couldn't risk another taxi — too exposed, too easy to track. His home was about two miles away now. He could make it in about ten minutes on foot, running at full tilt. It wasn't ideal, but it was his best option.

Max broke into a run as soon as he cleared the crowd, ignoring the startled looks from passersby. He stuck to side streets and alleys, constantly changing his route, doubling back occasionally to check for tails. The exertion made his head pound and his ribs ache, but he pushed through the pain.

As he ran, the events of the day swirled in his mind. The explosion. Waking up in the debris. The confusion, the gaps in his memory. And now this — a professional hit attempt. None of it made sense, but one thing was clear: he was in the middle of something big, something deadly.

5

From Virgil's vantage point on the rooftop, the chaos on the street far below looked like a child's playground. People scurried about like ants, their panicked voices a distant hum carried on the wind. Sirens wailed in the distance, growing closer with each passing moment. Virgil allowed himself a small smile as he methodically disassembled his rifle, each piece finding its designated spot in the sleek black suitcase.

He'd always prided himself on his efficiency, his ability to blend into the background and disappear without a trace. But today, something had gone wrong. His target, against all odds, had survived.

With practiced ease, Virgil snapped the suitcase shut, the sound barely audible over the commotion below. He pulled a burner phone from his pocket, his fingers dancing across the keypad as he dialed the backstop number he knew by heart.

The line rang twice before a crisp, professional voice answered. "Broadstreet Telecommunications. How may I help you?"

Virgil's jaw clenched as he gave his credentials. "R12 Agent 92 Victor Alpha Echo. He escaped."

There was a pause on the other end, heavy with disappointment and barely concealed anger. "You mean you failed."

Virgil's eyes narrowed, his gaze fixed on where he'd last seen Ryker disappearing into the crowd. "Ryker must have known," he said, his voice low and controlled.

"That's impossible," the voice on the other end snapped.

"Any more impossible than him surviving the bombing?" Virgil countered, a hint of frustration creeping into his tone. He paused, considering his following words carefully. "Maybe someone's helping him."

The silence that followed was thick with tension. Virgil could almost hear the gears turning in his handler's mind as he considered the ramifications.

"Which way was he heading?" the voice finally asked.

Virgil's eyes scanned the streets below, mapping out the most likely route. "Northwest. Home? Do you want me to activate the team?"

"No," came the swift reply. "There are other ways to make problems go away."

The line went dead, leaving Virgil with the distant sounds of chaos. He pocketed the phone, his mind shifting gears, analyzing the situation from every angle. Ryker's survival complicated things, but it wasn't insurmountable. In his line of work, adaptability was key.

As he made his way to the roof access door, Virgil had an unsettling impression this was just the beginning of a much larger game. Ryker had proven himself a formidable opponent, one not easily eliminated. And if someone was indeed helping him... Virgil shook his head, pushing the thought aside. His job was to follow orders, not speculate. Whatever came next, he would be ready. After all, there was no room for failure in the shadows where he operated. Not again.

With one last glance at the snow-dusted street below, Virgil disappeared into the building, leaving no trace of his presence save for the chaos he'd unleashed.

6

Max's lungs were burning by the time he turned onto Hutchinson Street. He slowed his pace, trying to look casual as he approached his house. The serene, snow-blanketed street seemed surreal after the chaos he'd just escaped. An oasis of normalcy in a world that had turned upside down.

Standing on the icy sidewalk in front of his modest two-story home, he took a breath. The sun cast long shadows across the lawn. For a moment, he stood motionless, trying to reconcile the peaceful winter scene before him with the turmoil in his mind.

Shaking his head to clear it, Max made his way up the short, slippery path to his front door. His hand trembled slightly as he reached for the doorknob, relieved to find it unlocked. He stepped inside, his mind so preoccupied that he didn't notice much around him. Without a second thought, he headed straight for the stairs, taking them two at a time as he hurried to the bedroom to change out of his dust-covered clothes.

"Rachel?" he called out as he pulled off his shirt. "You home?"

Silence greeted him as he quickly changed into fresh clothes. A sense of unease began to creep over him as he buttoned up a clean shirt. Why wasn't she answering?

Max made his way back downstairs, his movements slowing as he finally began to notice the state of the house. The living room came into focus, and with it, the first signs of disturbance became apparent. The coffee table was askew, and magazines were scattered across the floor. A floor lamp lay toppled, its shade cracked. Max's heart began to race as his eyes darted around the room, taking in more details. A half-empty mug of coffee lay on its side, its contents forming a dark stain on the beige carpet.

"Rachel?" he called again, louder this time, his voice tinged with concern.

The silence that greeted him was oppressive, broken only by the soft ticking of the antique grandfather clock in the hallway. He moved further into the house, his senses on high alert.

He moved quickly towards the kitchen, his footsteps echoing loudly in the eerie quiet. As he rounded the corner, the scene that greeted him made his blood run cold. The kitchen was in complete disarray. Cabinet doors hung open, and contents spilled across the countertops and floor. Shards of broken plates and glasses crunched under his feet as he entered the room.

Something on the floor caught his eye as he moved into the kitchen. Rachel's phone lay nearby, the contact screen lit up, showing the last call made to Eve Collins. He remembered Rachel often speaking of Eve, one of her colleagues and a good friend. The sight of the phone, left behind in the disorder, made his skin prickle with unease.

And then he saw her.

Rachel lay crumpled behind the kitchen island, surrounded by a tangle of pots, pans, and the broken shards of her favorite vase. But it was the dark, sticky pool of liquid spreading around her head that made Max's heart stop.

"No," he whispered, his voice barely audible. "No, no, no."

Max dropped to his knees beside Rachel's body, his hands hovering hesitantly over her still form. Her eyes, once so vibrant and full of laughter, now stared vacantly at the ceiling. The gash across her throat was raw and angry in contrast to her pale skin.

With trembling fingers, he reached out to touch her hand. It was cold, unnervingly cold. The warmth that had always drawn him to her was gone.

As the weight of the situation settled over him, Max's mind rebelled, overwhelmed by a flood of memories. He was no longer in the blood-streaked kitchen but lost in a montage of happier times.

Rachel, smiling at him over a steaming mug of coffee before he left for work. Her laughter ringing through the house as they painted the living room, her nose dusted with pale blue paint. The way her eyes sparkled as she shared a particularly terrible joke, relishing his groans. The feel of her skin against his as they shared a passionate moment in the shower, water cascading around them.

"Rachel," Max murmured, his voice thick with emotion. He blinked, and the memories vanished, leaving him once more in the harsh reality of the present.

Before he could process the situation, the splintering of wood shattered the stillness. The front door crashed open, and the house was instantly filled with shouting voices and heavy boots pounding.

"Police! Get your hands up!"

Max's head jerked up, eyes wide with shock as a team of heavily armed officers stormed into the kitchen, their weapons trained on him.

"Back away from her! Now!" an officer ordered, his voice sharp and commanding.

"You've got it wrong," he said, rising slowly to his feet with his hands raised. "I didn't do this. I just got home. I found her like this."

His protests were ignored. Two officers moved in, roughly pinning him against the wall. Max felt the cold snap of handcuffs around his wrists as another officer patted him down.

"Max Ryker, you're under arrest for the murder of Rachel Turner and a taxi driver," the lead officer announced, his tone devoid of sympathy.

Max's brain went into overdrive as the officers began reading him his rights. How had they known? How had they arrived so quickly? And most pressing, who had killed Rachel?

As they led him out of the house, he couldn't tear his eyes away from Rachel's body. Passing the kitchen island, he glimpsed her face one last time. At that moment, a chilling realization struck him: Rachel's expression wasn't one of fear or pain. It was one of surprise. She had known her killer.

As he was pushed into the back of a waiting police car, Max's training kicked in. He forced himself to breathe slowly, fighting the tide of emotions threatening to overwhelm him. He needed clarity. Someone had set him up, and they had done it expertly.

The car pulled away from the curb, its tires crunching on

the white-cloaked street. Max closed his eyes, his mind already formulating his next move. He had been framed for Rachel's murder — and possibly for the bombing downtown. But why? What was the connection?

As the police car sped through the wintry streets of Chicago, Max made a silent vow. He would uncover who was behind this and make them pay — for Rachel, for the victims of the bombing, and for himself. But first, he needed to escape. And for that, he needed a plan.

7

Special Agent Jansen gripped the steering wheel of her black Chevy Tahoe, her knuckles white with tension. The streets of Chicago, usually a bustling network of organized chaos, had devolved into gridlock. The aftermath of the bombing had turned the city into a maze of blocked roads, panicked civilians, and overwhelmed emergency services. Snow piled up on the sidewalks added to the sense of disarray.

"Get the hell out of the way!" Jansen shouted, slamming her palm against the horn. The shrill blast joined the cacophony of sirens and car horns. Her emergency lights flashed, painting the surrounding vehicles in red and blue, but it made little difference. There was simply nowhere for the traffic to go.

Jansen's heart raced, a mix of adrenaline and frustration coursing through her veins. She had been en route to a police station seven minutes north of the arrest site in Portage Park. That's where Ryker should have been taken — the closest station, per protocol. From there, he would have been transported to the FBI headquarters on Roosevelt Road for questioning. That was how things were supposed to go.

But nothing about this day was going according to plan.

Her cell phone rang, the sound barely audible over the cacophony outside. Jansen tapped the accept button on her steering wheel, her eyes never leaving the sea of vehicles before her.

"Doug, this better be good," she barked, recognizing the caller ID.

Doug Erikson's voice came through the speakers, tense and apologetic. "He's been transported to a department in downtown."

Jansen's brow furrowed. "What? Who authorized that?"

"No idea. We just received the update." Doug reeled off an address on State Street.

Jansen's mind was flooded with urgent thoughts. She was at least ten minutes away from that location, assuming the traffic miraculously cleared. "Damn it. Make sure they hold him. I'm on my way." She paused, glancing at the immobile vehicles surrounding her. "Well, if I can get through this traffic." Another thought struck her. "And Doug, find out who authorized that switch."

She ended the call and immediately laid on the horn again, holding it down as she maneuvered the Tahoe into a tight U-turn. The large SUV groaned in protest as she gunned the engine, forcing her way south against the traffic flow.

As she drove, Jansen's mind whirled with possibilities. Why move Ryker downtown? Who had the authority to countermand her orders? And more importantly, what did it mean for their investigation?

The bombing had thrown the entire city into chaos. Every

agency was scrambling to take the lead, to be the one to crack the case and bring the perpetrators to justice. But this was her investigation. She had fought tooth and nail to maintain control and wasn't about to let it slip away now.

Jansen weaved through the gridlocked streets, using sidewalks and alleys when necessary. She ignored the angry shouts and honks from other drivers. Her only focus was getting to Ryker before something went wrong.

Her phone rang again. This time, it was her superior, Assistant Director Jim Carlson.

"Jansen, where are you?" Carlson's voice was sharp, cutting through the ambient noise.

"En route to the station on State Street," Jansen replied, swerving to avoid a delivery truck that had decided to make an ill-timed turn. "Sir, did you authorize the transfer?"

There was a pause on the other end of the line. "Negative. I thought you had."

Jansen felt a chill race through her, leaving her momentarily breathless. "Sir, something's not right here. I'm pushing through to get there as fast as I can, but this traffic—"

"I don't want excuses, Jansen. Get to Ryker, secure him, and get him to our facility. We can't afford mistakes on this one."

"Understood, sir." Jansen ended the call, her jaw set in determination.

As she approached the heart of downtown, the full impact of the bombing became apparent. Smoke rose from several buildings, and the streets were filled with a mix of emergency vehicles and shell-shocked civilians. Jansen's trained eye picked out several unmarked vehicles she recognized as belonging to various intelligence agencies. Everyone wanted a piece of this investigation.

She was still several blocks from the station when her phone rang again. It was Doug.

"Talk to me, Doug," she said, not bothering with pleasantries.

"You're not going to like this, boss," Doug's voice was tense. "I've been making calls and trying to trace the authorization for the transfer. Nobody seems to know anything."

"What do you mean nobody knows anything?" Jansen snapped, her frustration mounting.

"I mean, there's no record of the transfer order. The station downtown claims they received a call from our office, but no log of any such call was created."

This wasn't just a mix-up or a miscommunication. This was something else entirely.

"Doug, I need you to listen carefully," she said, her voice low and urgent. "I want you to put out an alert. All channels, highest priority. Ryker is to be considered dangerous. No one and I mean no one, is to move him or have any contact with him until I get there. Understood?"

"Yes, ma'am," Doug replied. "What do you think is happening?"

Jansen grappled with the possibilities, each more troubling than the last. "I don't know."

She ended the call and pressed harder on the accelerator. The Tahoe surged forward, weaving through the thinning traffic with urgency.

As the police station came into view, Jansen felt a knot of apprehension tighten in her stomach.

She pulled to the curb, the Tahoe's tires protesting with a screech. Something was wrong, and she had a sinking feeling that she was approaching a situation far more dangerous than a simple bombing investigation.

Taking a deep breath, Jansen straightened her jacket and walked towards the station entrance. Whatever awaited her inside, she was determined to uncover the truth. Ryker was the key to this entire mess, and she wasn't about to let him slip through her fingers.

8

The fluorescent lights buzzed incessantly overhead, their harsh glare reflecting off the metal table in the center of the small, windowless room. Max shifted uncomfortably in his chair, the cold metal digging into his back. He'd lost track of how long he'd been sitting there, waiting. The camera in the corner of the room blinked steadily, its red light a constant reminder that he was being watched.

His thoughts tumbled, trying to piece together the events that had led him to this moment. The bombing, waking up in the debris, finding Rachel — it all felt like a nightmare he couldn't wake up from. He glanced down at his hands, both wrists secured to the table by a sturdy chain. The weight of it felt alien, wrong.

The sudden sound of the door opening snapped Max back to attention. A woman in a crisp suit entered, slightly out of breath, holding a tablet in one hand and a steaming cup in the other. She moved with purpose, her hazel eyes sharp and assessing as they swept over him.

As she took a seat across from him, Max leaned forward, the chain clattering against the table. “Miss, there has been some kind of mistake here.”

The woman didn’t respond immediately. She set her cup down and settled into her chair, flipping through screens on her tablet. “The traffic is absolute chaos out there,” she said, finally glancing up at him. “Well, look at that. Another thing they screwed up.” She shook her head, tapping out a few notes on the tablet.

“What?” he asked, confusion evident in his voice.

With a nudge of her head, she gestured towards him. “They took your prints but didn’t process the rest. The watch and ring—they usually remove them. Don’t worry; we’ll be transferring you to our facility shortly, and we’ll get everything squared away.”

Max glanced down at the items in question, a fresh wave of confusion gripping him. He pushed it aside, focusing on stating his case. “Look, I don't know what you think you’ve got, but I didn’t kill my girlfriend, and I certainly didn’t harm that taxi driver.”

“Of course not,” the woman replied, her tone neutral. “So you ran because...?”

“What would you do if someone took a shot at you? I wasn’t thinking straight.”

She locked eyes with him for a moment, her gaze intense and searching. “Uh-huh. So, did she find out? Is that why you killed Rachel?”

“What? Found out what?”

The woman glanced down at her tablet, reeling off information. “Max Ryker, enlisted in the U.S. Army, served as a helicopter pilot before eventually going through a rigorous selection and training process for the Special Forces. You were discharged as a survivor of Operation Crimson Dawn in Afghanistan's Kunar province. Suffering from PTSD, you ended up on the streets for a time. The courts established you got into a bar fight. Almost killed a man. Court-ordered treatment. You attended the Stand Down event. Sometime around then, you met your girlfriend, Rachel Turner." She paused, looking up at him. "Tell me something. Who do you work for now? Because it certainly isn't Jan Pros - Chicago Cleaning Professionals. They don't exist."

"Of course they don't," Ryker replied, his jaw tightening.

"And yet you were seen on surveillance at ground zero of the bombing of a federal building wearing a uniform."

Max stared back, processing it all. "Are you suggesting I had something to do with that?"

"Let me just cut to the chase," the woman said, leaning forward. "Since you've been here, we've established multiple things. Not only are you on CCTV fleeing the scene of the taxi driver shooting, a driver that picked you up from the bomb site. But your DNA was on a remote detonator found inside a van rented in your name, the same van that had traces of explosive material, the same explosive material that was found at your home — probably found by Rachel. Your prints have also been found on a knife that killed Rachel Turner, along with a cell phone in your name with times, dates, and a map of the federal building. And then, of course, there is a recent deposit of over five million in an offshore bank account in your name."

"Woah," Max said, backing up slightly in his chair. "What?"

"Who deposited the five million?"

"I don't know."

"Well, let me clear that up. It originated from a bank in

Switzerland. It was transferred from a corporation called Baldar, a front for Hamas."

Max's mind reeled. None of this made sense. He took a deep breath, trying to stay calm. "You've got this all wrong. Look, I told the cops to get hold of Langley."

"Right, right, you said you work for the CIA."

"A division of the CIA."

"Black book operations."

"Something like that."

The woman's expression remained skeptical. "See, here's the thing: there's no record of you working for the CIA."

Max leaned forward, his voice low and urgent. "I'm listed as working for Veritage Wealth Advisory. A company that has a global presence. It's an off-the-books cover organization. It allows us to travel, gives us an excuse to handle financial data, meet with individuals and businesses, and it's seen as a respectable profession to avoid suspicion."

"Hmm, yes, Veritage," the woman nodded, glancing down at her tablet. "You said they were global, based out of Chicago." She looked up, her eyes narrowing. "You said it was a two-story industrial red building next to the railway tracks off Leavitt Street. You see, there are only two problems with that. There is no global branch that goes by that name. As for the building, it's been sitting empty for the past eight years and is available for lease. We spoke with the leasing company."

Max felt a cold sweat breaking out on his forehead. "Like I said, it's a cover. We operate without congressional oversight. Look, I swore an oath to serve and protect the American people. Why on earth would I put them in danger?"

"I have some theories," the woman replied, her tone dry.

"Listen, if you think I killed my girlfriend, why would I return there?"

"You tell me."

Frustration bubbled up inside him. "This is bullshit. I'm being set up."

"Set up? Okay." She looked back down at her tablet and swiped the screen several times. "You said you don't remember how you ended up outside the federal building. That your last memory was of a mission in Croatia to target a woman wanted for espionage and that you woke up at the scene of the bombing wearing overalls without any memory of how you got there."

"That's right."

"Mr. Ryker, there is no record of you exiting the country or entering."

"You won't have it. We flew privately."

"Obviously." She shook her head as if finding something amusing. "So this woman wanted for espionage. Does she have a name? What had she taken?"

Max had some fleeting memories. "A drive."

"And this drive, what was on it?"

"Sensitive material."

The woman leaned forward, her voice taking on an edge of impatience. "What are we talking about? Strategic plans, weapons, communications data, nuclear capabilities, locations of missile sites, safe houses, cryptographic machines, NATO and U.S. war plans, Max?"

"I don't know."

"Because you never saw what was on the drive?"

"I don't remember." His memory of the mission was getting harder to piece together. Had the blast affected him? Or had he even been there? He glanced at his watch, still ticking down.

She nodded, her expression a mix of frustration and

something else—pity, perhaps? "I want to believe you. I really do. But place yourself in our shoes. You say you know who you are, who your girlfriend was, where she lived, and who you worked for. Yet, you can't remember much about a mission to Croatia, the drive, the woman you were after, or how you wound up back on U.S. soil. Specifically, you were seen at the scene of a bombing of a federal building that killed hundreds, and evidence directly connects you to it. Add to that the fact that there is no record of you working for the CIA. You see where I'm coming from?"

Max felt a growing sense of desperation. "Look, I'm telling you the truth."

"Or maybe you're bending the truth."

"I told you, I'm being set up. Don't you understand?"

The woman sighed, shaking her head. "Unfortunately, no. But what I do see is a troubled person with PTSD looking for a way to snap back at the government after being discharged. Listen to me carefully; you are being charged with domestic terrorism and mass murder."

Panic gripped his chest. "No. Speak to Langley. Get someone down here from the CIA. There is someone else behind this. I'm innocent."

"We're going to transport you to our federal facility for further questioning before your arraignment."

As she got up to leave, Max rose, his chains holding him in place. "Listen to me. I didn't do this."

The woman paused at the door, turning back to look at him. For a moment, Max thought he saw a flicker of doubt in her eyes. But then it was gone, replaced by the cool professionalism she'd maintained throughout the interview.

"Mr. Ryker, I've been doing this job for a long time. I've heard every excuse, every plea of innocence. But the evidence... it's overwhelming. If you have anything else to add, anything that might help your case, now's the time."

Max's thoughts raced. What could he say that would make her believe him? He glanced down at his watch again, the numbers still ticking down. Suddenly, an idea struck him.

"The watch," he said, his voice urgent. "This watch. I woke up wearing it after the bombing. I don't know where it came from. It's counting down to something. And this ring — I don't remember getting married. There's something going on here, something bigger than me. Please, you have to believe me."

The woman's eyes narrowed, focusing on the watch. For a moment, Ryker thought he saw a flicker of interest in her expression. But then she shook her head, her professional mask slipping back into place.

"We'll look into it during processing at the federal facility. For now, Mr. Ryker, I suggest you start thinking about getting yourself a good lawyer. You're going to need one."

With that, she turned and left the room, the door closing behind her with a final-sounding click. Max slumped back in his chair, the weight of his situation crashing down on him. He was alone again, with nothing but the buzzing lights and the blinking camera for company.

As he sat there, his mind whirled with possibilities. Who was behind this? Who had the power and resources to frame him so thoroughly? And why? The gaps in his memory frustrated him. He knew who he was and knew what he did for a living, but the details of the past few days were a blur.

He thought about Rachel, her lifeless body on their kitchen floor. The image sent a fresh wave of grief and anger through him. Someone had killed her, someone who wanted to frame him. But who? And why go to such elaborate lengths?

The watch on his wrist continued its steady countdown. To what, he didn't know, but he had a sinking feeling that when it reached zero, something terrible would happen. He needed to figure this out, and fast.

But how? He was chained to a table in an interrogation room, about to be transferred to a federal facility. The evidence against him was overwhelming. Even he had to admit that if he were in the investigator's shoes, he'd have a hard time believing his own story.

Max closed his eyes, forcing himself to think. There had to be something he was missing, some detail that could help prove his innocence. He thought back to his last clear memory before waking up at the bombing site. Croatia. The mission. The woman with the drive.

As he concentrated, fragments of memory began to surface. A face — the woman he'd been sent to track. Dark hair, sharp features. She looked familiar, but he couldn't place her. And the drive — he remembered holding it, feeling the weight of it in his hand. But what had been on it?

Max's eyes snapped open. The drive. That had to be the key. Whatever was on it must have been important enough for someone to go to these lengths to cover it up. But where was it now? Had he managed to complete his mission before somehow ending up back in Chicago?

He looked down at his hands, noticing a small scab on his left arm for the first time that he didn't remember having before. Had he been injured during the mission? Or was it from the bombing? The uncertainty of his own memories was maddening.

The sound of footsteps in the hallway outside pulled Max

from his thoughts. They were coming to transfer him. He knew that his chances of proving his innocence would become even slimmer once he left this room. He had to do something, and fast.

As the door began to open, Max made a split-second decision. He might not remember everything, but he knew who he was. He was a trained operative, and he'd be damned if he was going to let himself be railroaded for crimes he didn't commit.

The chain on his wrist suddenly felt less like a restraint and more like a potential weapon. Ryker tensed, ready to move. Whatever happened next, he knew one thing for certain — he wasn't going down without a fight.

9

It had become an unconscious habit. Jansen snapped the rubber band against her wrist twice as she strode out of the interrogation room. The sharp sting momentarily grounded her racing thoughts. The simple behavioral technique had been suggested by her therapist years ago after losing her son to a terrorist attack.

The interview weighed heavily on her mind.

“Who authorized Ryker’s transfer to this precinct?” she asked the police sergeant on duty, her jaw clenched, barely containing her frustration.

The sergeant blinked, clearly caught off guard. “I’m not sure, ma’am. The order came down from above.”

Jansen’s eyes narrowed. “Someone must know. I want a name.”

Before the sergeant could respond, a voice called out from behind her. “Agent Jansen?”

She turned to see a man in a crisp suit approaching, his badge already out. “Thomas Reeves, National Counterintelligence and Security Center.”

"NCSC." Jansen suppressed a sigh. "I've already spoken with one of your colleagues."

"As the incident at the federal building could be related to a foreign intelligence operation and pose a threat to U.S. intelligence assets, I've been called in to coordinate information shared between our agencies. I will be working with you. I would like to speak with the suspect," Reeves said, falling into step beside her as she continued down the hallway.

"And you will," Jansen replied, her tone clipped, "once he's transferred from here to our secure headquarters for further questioning before his arraignment." She looked at him with a puzzled expression. "Don't you communicate between your colleagues?"

Reeves ignored the jab. "We were told he believes he works for the CIA."

"He believes many things, none of which can be substantiated," Jansen said, shaking her head, beginning to walk. "The evidence against him is overwhelming. I'm sure in the coming days, he'll let that CIA story slide, and we'll find out his connection to Hamas."

"And the taxi driver?"

She paused, turning to face Reeves. "What about it?"

"That's where I was initially sent," Reeves replied. "A gun was found in the vehicle."

Jansen frowned. "Ryker told the cops the driver was shot through the windshield."

"Well that should be easy enough to establish. Ballistics will be able to confirm he fired from behind."

"But why?" Jansen mused, more to herself than to Reeves.

"These things rarely make sense."

Jansen shook her head. "No, I mean why kill a random taxi driver?"

"He could identify him," Reeves suggested.

"As could all the CCTV cameras we have throughout the city," Jansen countered.

She was about to press further when a commotion erupted down the hall. Shouts and the sound of gunfire echoed through the precinct.

"What the hell?" Jansen muttered, her hand instinctively moving to her weapon.

She and Reeves exchanged a quick glance before breaking into a run towards the source of the disturbance. As they rounded a corner, they saw a group of officers converging on the rear exit.

"He's gone!" one of them shouted. "Ryker's escaped!"

Jansen felt a chill sweep through her. How could this be happening? She had left him secured to the table less than five minutes ago.

Ryker's escape was too convenient, too well-timed. But if he wasn't working alone, who was helping him? And why?

MINUTES EARLIER, Max had sat in the interrogation room, chewing over the conversation with Agent Jansen. The door opened, and an officer he didn't recognize stepped in. He uncuffed him from the chain but kept the cuffs on him.

"Mr. Ryker, your legal representative has arrived," the officer said.

He hadn't requested any legal assistance. Nonetheless, he followed the officer down the hall and into a conference room, where a sharply dressed man in his forties greeted him with a firm handshake.

"Mr. Ryker, I'm James Holloway," the man said, his voice smooth and assured. "I'm here to represent you."

Ryker eyed him warily. "I didn't arrange for any attorney."

Holloway smiled. "The court has assigned me to ensure your release. I've arranged for bail to be posted."

The officer nodded. "While we've received a court order for his release, we'll have to process some paperwork first."

Holloway's demeanor shifted subtly as he spoke. "Understood. I need to speak with Mr. Ryker privately. Could you remove the handcuffs for the duration of our discussion?"

The officer hesitated, then sighed. "Only in here. Make it quick."

As the officer went to unlock the handcuffs, Holloway suddenly pulled out a concealed weapon and shot the officer, who collapsed with a muffled thud.

"What the...?" Ryker shouted, stunned.

Holloway quickly grabbed the key from the fallen officer and freed Ryker from the remaining restraints. "We don't have much time. Move!"

They exited the room.

Another officer rounded the corner, eyes widening at the scene. He reached for his weapon, but Holloway was faster, firing a round that grazed the officer's shoulder. The officer staggered back, crying out in pain.

"Let's go!" Holloway ordered, shoving Max towards the exit.

They burst into the alley behind the precinct, where a police cruiser waited, engine running. Holloway shoved him into the back seat and slid into the front passenger side. The driver, another man Max didn't recognize, slammed the cruiser into gear and sped out of the alley with a screech of tires.

"I'm guessing you're not a lawyer," Ryker said, his voice tight with tension.

Holloway's expression was grim as he turned to face him. "I'm with the Division. We're here to extract you."

AGENT MEREDITH JANSEN strode purposefully towards the interrogation room, Reeves at her side. She pushed open the door, expecting to see Ryker restrained. Instead, the room was empty.

"Where is he?" she exclaimed, her eyes scanning the startled officers in the hallway.

Chaos erupted as an officer with a bloodied shoulder stumbled forward. "He's gone," he gasped, "a man in a suit... shot Officer Davis... and took Ryker."

"Show me the surveillance!"

Minutes later, they had footage showing Ryker being loaded into a police cruiser. Jansen memorized the vehicle's number.

"Let's go," she ordered Reeves, heading for the exit. They jumped into her unmarked car, Jansen behind the wheel.

As they roared out of the parking lot, sirens blaring, Jansen's mind was chaotic. What the hell was happening?

MAX SAT in the back of the police cruiser, his senses on high alert as he tried to piece together the events from the last few hours. Something felt off about this rescue, and his instincts screamed at him to be cautious.

"This kind of thing isn't the norm," Max said, breaking the tense silence over the car.

James Holloway, the man who had introduced himself as Max's lawyer, turned in the passenger seat, his eyes hidden behind dark sunglasses. "What matters is you're out," he replied, his tone clipped.

Max noticed the driver's eyes flicking to him in the rearview mirror, a hint of something unreadable in his gaze. The hairs on the back of Max's neck stood up.

"Who helped you at the bomb site?" Holloway asked abruptly.

Max frowned, caught off guard by the question. "No one."

"You don't remember?" Holloway pressed.

"Nothing," Max replied, a hint of frustration creeping into his voice.

Holloway paused, studying Max's face. "And Croatia?"

"What about it?"

"Tell us about Croatia," Holloway said abruptly.

"I don't remember much." Max's heart skipped a beat. "Wouldn't my team have told you?"

"They're all dead."

"What?"

"Tell us about the mission. The target. The file."

Alarm bells rang in Max's head. This mission was classified and known only to a select few. These men shouldn't have known about it.

Trying to buy time, Max asked, "Did my handler send you?"

"That's right." Holloway nodded.

"Randall?"

"Correct."

Max's blood ran cold. There was no Randall. He'd made the name up on the spot.

In that instant, Max knew he'd been betrayed. These men weren't here to help him; they were here to silence him.

Max lunged for the door handle, but it was locked.

Holloway spun in his seat, a silenced pistol appearing in his hand. Max reacted on pure instinct, grabbing Holloway's wrist and shoving it towards the driver just as the gun went off.

The sound of the shot was muffled, but the effect was catastrophic. The driver's head snapped sideways, blood spraying across the window. His foot jammed down on the accelerator, and the car lurched forward with a sudden burst of speed.

Max and Holloway grappled in the confined space, each fighting to control the weapon. The car swerved wildly, horns blaring as they cut across lanes of traffic.

With a violent twist, Max managed to wrench the gun from Holloway's grasp. But the car hit a median at full speed before he could use it.

The world turned upside down as the vehicle became airborne. Max felt a moment of weightlessness before gravity reasserted itself with brutal force. The car slammed back to earth, metal screaming as it skidded across the pavement.

When the world snapped back into focus, Max found himself hanging upside down, held in place by his seatbelt. His head throbbed, and warm blood trickled down his face. Through the shattered windshield, he could see other cars screeching to a halt and people shouting in panic.

Holloway groaned from the front seat, stirring weakly. The driver was still.

Max fumbled with his seatbelt, his fingers feeling thick

and uncooperative. Finally, the latch released, and he fell awkwardly onto the roof of the overturned car.

Max crawled towards the rear door, ignoring the pain in his body. It was bent and warped from the impact, but it finally gave way after a few desperate kicks.

Max tumbled onto the snow, gasping as fresh air filled his lungs. His vision swam, the world tilting and spinning around him. But he knew he couldn't stay here. It was only a matter of time before more came for him.

AGENT MEREDITH JANSEN slammed her fist against the steering wheel in frustration as traffic ground to a halt. Through the windshield, she caught a glimpse of Ryker weaving between traffic.

Jansen slammed the brakes on.

"Damn it," she muttered, throwing open her door. "Reeves, call for backup!"

She took off at a sprint, her heart pounding as she pushed through the sea of stopped vehicles. Ryker was fast, but she was determined.

"FBI! Out of the way!" she shouted, shouldering past startled pedestrians.

Ryker glanced back, his eyes widening as he saw Jansen gaining ground. He veered suddenly, crashing through the door of a convenience store. Jansen followed, leaping over toppled displays of snacks and magazines.

The chase led them into a bustling street market. Ryker knocked over crates of fruit, sending apples and oranges rolling under Jansen's feet. She stumbled but kept her balance, closing the gap.

Suddenly, Ryker ducked into a Chinese restaurant. Jansen burst through the swinging doors moments later, nearly colliding with a waiter carrying a tray of dishes. The crash of shattering porcelain filled the air as she pushed past, hot on Ryker's heels.

In the kitchen, Ryker grabbed a pot of boiling water and flung it behind him. Jansen dodged, feeling the heat as it splashed past her. She vaulted over a prep table, scattering vegetables and utensils.

Back on the street, Ryker darted down an alley. Jansen followed, her lungs burning as she pushed herself to the limit. As she rounded the corner, she skidded to a stop. The alley was empty.

Breathing hard, she drew her weapon, scanning the shadows. "Ryker! Come out with your hands up!"

Silence.

She inched forward, every nerve on high alert. Suddenly, a figure burst from behind a dumpster. Before she could react, Ryker had her in a hold, spinning her around. Her gun clattered to the ground.

In one fluid motion, Ryker had her pinned, his hand reached for her weapon. Jansen tensed, waiting for the shot.

But it never came.

Instead, Ryker grabbed her handcuffs and secured her to the dumpster.

"I didn't have anything to do with that bombing or the murders," he said, his voice low and intense. Their eyes met, and Jansen saw something she hadn't expected — desperation, yes, but also sincerity.

Jansen tugged at the handcuffs, her mind a flurry of thoughts. He could have killed her, but he didn't. Why?

A seed of doubt took root in her mind for the first time since this began.

Jansen watched Ryker disappear around the corner. She tugged at the handcuffs, the metal biting into her wrist as she struggled to reach her radio.

Finally, her fingers closed around the device. She pulled it to her mouth, her voice tight with urgency.

"This is Agent Jansen. Suspect Max Ryker has escaped custody. Last seen heading east from the alley between 5th and 6th on Main Street. All units converge on this location. Suspect is considered armed and dangerous. I repeat, Max Ryker has escaped and is heading east."

As she finished the transmission, Jansen heard the distant wail of sirens. She leaned back against the dumpster, her mind replaying the encounter. Ryker could have killed her, but he didn't. And those words — "I didn't have anything to do with that bombing or the murders" — haunted her.

Suddenly, the door of the Chinese restaurant burst open. An officer came running out, scanning the alley.

"Over here!" Jansen yelled, relief washing over her.

The officer hurried towards her and quickly uncuffed her from the dumpster. Jansen rose, brushing herself off and wincing slightly at the soreness in her wrist.

Jansen continued to feel a flicker of doubt. What if Ryker was telling the truth? What if there was more to this case than met the eye?

She shook her head, pushing the thoughts aside. Right now, her job was to bring Ryker in. The truth, whatever it might be, would have to wait.

10

Max's lungs burned as he sprinted through the crowded streets of Chicago, weaving between startled pedestrians. Behind him, he could hear the shouts of pursuing officers and the squeal of tires as law enforcement swerved through traffic.

Suddenly, a voice boomed out, "Ryker!"

The sharp crack of a gunshot split the air. Screams erupted as pedestrians scattered, ducking for cover. Max glanced back to see a determined officer, gun raised skyward, his face set with resolve.

Seizing the moment of chaos, Max darted into the street. A car screeched to a halt just inches from him, the driver laying on the horn. Max's hands slammed onto the hood, using it to propel himself forward as he vaulted over the vehicle.

He barely made it across the next street before the roar of an engine caught his attention. A sleek Husqvarna 701 Supermoto motorcycle was tearing towards him, its rider oblivious to the unfolding drama.

In a split-second decision, Max stepped into the bike's path. The rider swerved, losing control. As the bike went down on the slippery, snow-dusted street, Max was already moving. He hauled the stunned rider off, ignoring the man's protests.

"Sorry, I need this," Max muttered, swinging his leg over the seat.

The bike roared to life under his touch. Max shifted gears, and the powerful engine responded instantly. He weaved through the gridlocked traffic, the wind whipping at his face as he accelerated.

BEHIND HIM, Reeves skidded to a stop, out of breath. He grabbed his radio, his voice hoarse as he called it in. "Suspect has commandeered a motorcycle. Black Husqvarna, heading north on Michigan Avenue towards DuSable Bridge. All units converge!"

MAX LEANED INTO THE BIKE, expertly maneuvering through the sea of vehicles. The DuSable Bridge loomed ahead, his gateway to escape — or capture.

AGENT JANSEN GRIPPED the dashboard of the police cruiser as it weaved through traffic, sirens blaring. Her wrist still ached from the handcuffs, a reminder of her close encounter with Ryker.

The radio crackled to life hearing Reeves. “Suspect is heading north on Michigan Avenue towards DuSable Bridge on a black Husqvarna motorcycle.”

They needed to cut him off before he crossed the river. She grabbed the radio. “Shut the bridge down. Shut it down.”

There was a moment of hesitation before the reply came. “Negative, Agent Jansen. There’s too much traffic.”

Frustration surged through her. “Raise the bridge then,” she said, her voice sharp with urgency. “That will move them.”

The officer driving the cruiser shot her a surprised look, but Jansen’s eyes were fixed on the road ahead, where she could just make out a motorcycle weaving through the sea of cars.

“Copy that,” the radio crackled. “Initiating bridge lift. All units be advised, DuSable Bridge is going up. I repeat DuSable Bridge is going up.”

Jansen leaned forward in her seat, her heart pounding. This was it. Either they’d trap Ryker on this side of the river, or...

She didn’t want to consider the alternative. “Step on it,” she ordered the driver.

Max approached the DuSable Bridge, the growl of the motorcycle’s engine echoing off the surrounding buildings. His heart sank as he saw the bridge rising, its massive steel structure slowly tilting skyward. He slowed, the bike’s engine rumbling beneath him.

His mind surged, desperately seeking an escape route. Behind him, the sirens' wails grew louder, and red and blue lights flashed in his mirrors. Cop cars were closing in, cutting off his retreat.

In a desperate move, Max revved the engine and spun the bike around, facing the approaching police vehicles. For a moment, it looked like he might charge straight at them. Then, at the last second, he veered to the side, the bike idling as he paused.

Max could see Agent Jansen through the passenger window of a nearby police cruiser. She threw open the door and stepped out, her gun drawn.

"It's over, Ryker," she called out, her voice firm. "Nowhere to go."

Max's eyes flicked from Jansen to the rising bridge and back. He inhaled, summoning every ounce of courage he had left.

"Don't even think about it," a voice shouted.

Ignoring the warning, Max twisted the throttle. The bike's engine roared to life as he accelerated, weaving through the cars lining the street. He aimed straight for the gap between the barriers, the front wheel lifting as he hit the incline.

The bridge was now at an almost 45-degree angle. Max leaned forward, willing the bike to climb higher. The world seemed to slow down as he reached the edge, the gap between the two sides of the bridge yawning beneath him.

For a heart-stopping moment, Max was airborne, the bike soaring across the divide. Time seemed to stand still as he hung suspended over the Chicago River.

Then, with a bone-jarring impact, the bike slammed onto the opposite side of the bridge. The suspension groaned under the force of the landing, but somehow, he managed to keep control. The tires squealed as he swerved, fighting to keep the bike upright.

Against all odds, he'd made it across. Max gunned the engine once more, speeding away as shouts of disbelief echoed behind him.

JANSEN GAWKED as Ryker's motorcycle landed on the other side of the bridge. She grabbed her radio, her voice tight with urgency.

"Suspect has crossed DuSable Bridge. All units on the north side converge on Illinois Street. He's heading east towards Navy Pier. Do not let him reach the waterfront!"

She could hear the squeal of tires and blare of sirens as police units responded to her call. Through the radio chatter, she caught glimpses of Ryker's progress.

"Suspect spotted on Illinois Street, still heading east."

"Roger that. Units moving to intercept."

Jansen clenched her fist, frustration and a grudging admiration warring within her. Ryker was proving to be far more resourceful than she'd anticipated.

MAX WEAVED through traffic on the other side of the bridge, the wind whipping at his face. He could see police cars converging from side streets, their lights flashing. Ahead, a roadblock was forming, officers positioning their vehicles to cut off his escape route.

But he wasn't about to give up. Max gunned the engine, the motorcycle's power surging beneath him. At the last moment, he veered onto the sidewalk, narrowly missing pedestrians who dove out of his way.

The cops scrambled to reposition, but he was already past them, tearing down Illinois Street towards Lake Michigan. Navy Pier loomed ahead, a potential dead end — or his last chance at escape.

Jansen's voice crackled over the radio again. "Do not let him reach the pier! I repeat, do not let Ryker reach the waterfront!"

The iconic Chicago landmark came into sharp focus against the winter twilight. The towering Centennial Wheel dominated the skyline, its colorful lights blinking in the fading daylight, a contrasting backdrop to the gray, ice-fringed waters of Lake Michigan.

Crowds of bundled-up tourists scattered as he tore down the main promenade, past shuttered souvenir shops and the few food stalls still open. Their warm lights a beacon. The air was crisp, carrying the scent of diesel fuel.

To his left, a row of tour boats sat idle, their decks covered in a thin layer of frost. The Chicago Children's Museum loomed to his right, its bright facade at odds with the barren landscape surrounding it.

Ahead, the Crystal Gardens greenhouse glimmered, its glass panels reflecting the last rays of sunlight. Beyond that, the Grand Ballroom's distinctive dome rose against the backdrop of the partially frozen lake.

Ryker's eyes darted frantically, searching for an escape route. The end of the pier approached rapidly — a mix of concrete barriers and metal railings separating land from the vast, icy expanse of the lake.

In a split-second decision, Max gunned the engine. The motorcycle launched off the pier's edge, sailing briefly through the air before plunging into the cold waters of Lake Michigan.

The shock of the icy water hit Max like a physical blow, driving the air from his lungs and sending needles of pain across his skin. He kicked away from the sinking motorcycle, fighting against the weight of his clothes and the numbing cold as he struggled to the surface.

As he broke through, gasping for air, a sharp pain lanced his left shoulder. A stray bullet must have found its mark and grazed him during the chase. The water momentarily numbed the pain. Max knew he was losing blood and body heat rapidly.

Darkness enveloped him as he swam away from the pier, each stroke a battle against the cold, his injury, and the chunks of ice floating on the surface. The sounds of sirens and shouting faded, replaced by the eerie creaking of ice and his own labored breathing.

Lake Michigan's vast, dark expanse stretched before him, a winter wasteland that could claim his life in minutes.

His lungs burned, and his muscles protested. The cold seeped into his bones, and the pain in his shoulder throbbed with each stroke. He knew he couldn't keep this up for long — hypothermia would set in soon if he didn't get out of the water.

Nearby, he spotted a commercial fishing boat, its running lights cutting through the twilight. It was one of a handful of vessels braving the winter waters, likely part of the year-round fishing operations. Max knew it was his only chance.

With the last of his strength, he swam towards the vessel. As he approached, he saw crew members moving about on deck, preparing their gear.

Max's heart raced — he had to time this perfectly.

Just as the boat began to move, Max reached out and grabbed a trailing rope. His muscles screamed in protest as he hauled himself up, the rough fibers cutting into his frozen hands. With a final, desperate effort, he pulled himself over the side, collapsing onto the deck.

For a moment, he lay there, gasping for air, his body shaking violently from the cold. Then, hearing voices approaching, Max forced himself to move. He crawled silently across the deck, leaving a trail of icy water, his eyes scanning for a hiding spot.

A large tarp covered a pile of nets and gear near the bow. Max slipped underneath it without hesitation, curling his body into a tight ball to avoid detection. Through a small gap in the tarp, he watched as the boat chugged further out into the lake. The lights of Chicago grew smaller behind them, disappearing into the winter haze.

As the boat rocked gently, Max spotted something nearby. Seizing a moment when the fishermen were distracted, he silently crept out from under the tarp and towards the cabin. Inside, he found a thick fishing jacket hanging on a hook. Quickly and quietly, he snatched it and slipped it on, relishing its immediate warmth. Then, as stealthily as he'd come, he returned to his hiding spot among the nets and gear, pulling the tarp back over himself.

Suddenly, the whir of helicopter blades cut through the night air. Max held his breath as a searchlight swept over the boat. The beam passed over once, twice, before moving on to scan the icy waters. The fishermen seemed oblivious to the drama around them, their voices carrying over the sound of the engine as they prepared for a long night of winter fishing.

Max allowed himself a small sigh of relief as the boat moved further from shore. He had chosen the one escape route the police couldn't immediately follow — into the treacherous winter waters of Lake Michigan. He just had to survive long enough to figure out his next move. The gentle rocking of the boat and the exhaustion of his ordeal threatened to lull him into sleep, but Max fought against it. He couldn't afford to let his guard down, not even for a moment. Every second counted.

Shivering beneath the tarp despite the added warmth of the jacket, Max tried to piece together the fragments of his memory. The mission in Croatia, the mysterious woman, and the drive had to be connected to what was happening now.

He glanced at his watch, the countdown still ticking away relentlessly. Whatever was coming, he had to be ready. Max flexed his muscles, wincing at the pain in his shoulder. He'd need to tend to that wound soon, but staying hidden was his priority for now.

Max began to formulate a plan as the boat chugged further into the open water. He needed allies, resources, and, most importantly, answers.

11

James Calloway's world spun as consciousness slowly returned to him. The smoke and gasoline filled his nostrils, and a dull ringing echoed in his ears. As his vision cleared, he found himself slumped against the dashboard of the mangled police cruiser. Pain radiated through his body, and he could taste the metallic tang of blood.

With effort, Calloway turned his head to look at the driver's seat. Michaels sat motionless, his unseeing eyes staring through the shattered windshield. A wave of nausea washed over Calloway as he registered the unnatural angle of Michaels' neck.

Forcing his gaze away from his dead colleague, Calloway's eyes darted to the back seat. Empty. Ryker was gone.

"Damn it," he muttered, wincing as the words sent a fresh surge of pain through his chest. He knew he was severely hurt — probably fatally so. But he had one last duty to perform.

With trembling hands, Calloway fumbled for the door handle. It took three attempts before he managed to push it open, nearly falling out onto the pavement. He dragged himself away from the door, leaving a smear of blood on the asphalt.

Propping himself up against the cruiser, Calloway reached into his pocket for his cell phone. The screen was cracked, but it still functioned. He dialed a number from memory, his breath coming in ragged gasps as he waited for an answer.

"Broadstreet Telecommunications, how can I help you?" a calm, professional voice answered.

"S12 285 Echo Charlie," he rasped, pausing to cough. More blood spattered his hand. "Michaels is dead. I'm badly wounded. I don't think I'm going to make it."

There was a moment of silence on the other end. Then, "And Ryker?"

Calloway closed his eyes, remembering the look in Ryker's eyes just before the crash. "Alive."

"The mission?"

"I think he knows. To what extent, I'm not sure, but he knows."

"And the file?"

"Unknown. He got away." Calloway's voice was barely above a whisper now. The effort of speaking was draining what little strength he had left.

The silence stretched on, broken only by the distant wail of approaching sirens. Calloway knew what was coming next, but he had to ask anyway.

"Sir?" he prompted.

The voice on the other end was cold, devoid of emotion. "You know what to do."

The line went dead.

Calloway let the phone slip from his fingers. He had

known this day might come and had prepared for it, but the reality of it still hit him hard. He thought of his wife, his daughter. They would never know the truth of how he died or why. It was better that way.

With shaking hands, he reached into his pocket and pulled out a small pill container. It held a single capsule — his insurance policy, his way out. Standard issue for operatives in his position, though he had always hoped he'd never have to use it.

Calloway leaned back against the car, looking up at the sky. The sun was almost gone, painting the Chicago skyline in hues of orange and pink. It was beautiful, he thought. An excellent last sight.

He placed the pill on his tongue, hesitating for just a moment. In that brief pause, his life flashed before his eyes — his childhood in rural Illinois, meeting Sarah in college, the birth of little Emily, his first day at the agency. The good and the bad, the triumphs and the regrets.

Then he bit down.

The taste was bitter, but Calloway knew it wouldn't last long. Within seconds, his mouth began to foam. His body convulsed as the cyanide took effect, shutting down his systems with brutal efficiency.

Calloway's last thoughts were of Ryker as darkness closed in around him. He hoped the man would find the truth and expose the corruption that had led to this moment. It was too late for Calloway, but maybe Ryker could still make things right.

With a final, choking gasp, James Calloway slumped to the ground. By the time the first responders arrived on the scene, he was already gone, taking his secrets to the grave.

12

The crisp winter air enveloped Washington, D.C., carrying with it the faint scent of damp earth and the ever-present undercurrent of power that permeated the nation's capital. Dan Aldridge approached the Capitol Reflecting Pool, now a solid sheet of ice, with measured steps, his polished shoes clicking softly against the sidewalk. The setting sun cast shadows across the icy expanse, transforming it into a mirror of gold and deep indigo, reflecting the last light of day.

Aldridge's eyes scanned the area, taking in the tourists snapping photos, the joggers making their evening rounds, and the occasional government worker hurrying home. His gaze settled on a figure seated on a bench near the water's edge — Marcus Sinclair, his superior, casually stroking the golden fur of a retriever at his feet.

As Aldridge drew closer, a knot formed in his stomach. This meeting was not one he had been looking forward to. The events of the past few days weighed heavily on his mind, each misstep and miscalculation — a stone dragging him down into murky depths.

He took a seat beside Sinclair, careful to maintain a respectful distance. To any onlooker, they would appear as two strangers sharing a bench, nothing more. Aldridge pulled out his phone, bringing it to his ear as if taking a call. It was a practiced move that had served him well in countless clandestine meetings.

"Beautiful evening," Aldridge murmured, his eyes fixed on the distant Washington Monument.

Sinclair leaned forward, scratching behind his dog's ears. To anyone passing by, he appeared to be speaking to the animal. "Do you know how many have died to defend the constitution of this nation?" Sinclair's voice was low, barely audible. He glanced briefly at Aldridge, his eyes sharp and penetrating. "Millions. And yet only a few have taken an oath to defend the constitution against all enemies, foreign and domestic."

The silence of the frozen expanse stretched before them, the ice of the Reflecting Pool gleaming dully in the fading light. The absence of lapping water only served to emphasize the gravity of Sinclair's words.

Aldridge felt the harsh cold of the winter evening seep into his bones. Sinclair continued, his words measured and deliberate. "What we do matters. What has been done matters. The reason we are where we are matters, Mr. Aldridge. Because of careful plans, intelligent minds, and strategic actions, we continue to be where we are. Years have gone into getting us to this point."

A group of tourists passed by, their chatter and laughter a lively counterpoint to the tension between the two men on the bench. Sinclair paused, waiting for them to move out of earshot before continuing. “So please, tell me why, Mr. Aldridge, I am only hearing about this shitstorm now?”

Aldridge swallowed hard, his mouth suddenly dry. “He had help,” he offered, knowing even as the words left his mouth how inadequate they were.

“No,” Sinclair’s voice was sharp, cutting through the evening air like a knife. "You got sloppy."

“I’m telling you, he had someone on the inside helping him,” Aldridge insisted, his free hand clenching into a fist at his side. “We tried asset recovery.”

“You mean damage control,” Sinclair paused, shaking his head. “Why is he still alive?”

“Mistakes were made.”

Sinclair’s eyes narrowed, his gaze fixed on the distant horizon. “Like Croatia? This has to do with Croatia, doesn’t it?” The pause that followed was heavy with unspoken accusations. “You told me it was handled. That the Division was secure. That you had contained the leak.”

Aldridge felt sweat beading on his forehead despite the cooling evening air. “We thought we had.”

“You thought?” Sinclair’s voice rose slightly, a hint of his carefully controlled anger slipping through. He quickly composed himself, mindful of their public setting. “No, let me tell you what you thought. You thought you could keep this all on the down low and sweep your mistake under the rug, and now we have hundreds dead, media asking questions and one of your own is being pursued by every three-letter agency in this nation!”

The words hit Aldridge like physical blows. He struggled to maintain his composure, acutely aware of the people milling around them. A jogger passed by, her ponytail swinging in rhythm with her steps. A couple walked hand in hand along the water's edge, lost in their own world.

"Is that a question?" Aldridge managed, his voice strained.

Sinclair's hand stilled on the dog's head, his fingers tightening slightly in its fur. "He could expose everything. Give me answers. Does he know about Black Raven?"

"No." Aldridge's response was immediate, but a flicker of doubt crossed his mind even as he said it.

"What about the New Year?"

"I don't believe so."

Sinclair's eyes snapped to Aldridge's face, his gaze piercing. "You don't believe, or you know for sure?"

Aldridge felt his collar tighten like an invisible noose was constricting around his neck. "He should have been dead by now."

"And yet he's not." Sinclair's voice was cold, devoid of emotion. "What happened to Kingsley in Croatia?"

The question hung between them. Aldridge became even more uncomfortable with the line of questioning but knew he had no option but to answer truthfully. Sinclair had a way of finding out the truth. Even Aldridge, who ran the Division, didn't know who Sinclair's eyes and ears were within the organization.

"The exchange was intercepted," Aldridge admitted, his voice barely above a whisper. "She's dead."

"And the file?"

Aldridge swallowed hard, the taste of failure bitter on his tongue. "Lost."

"And I'm only hearing about this now?"

"I thought—"

"If I hear you say that one more time..." Sinclair cut him off, his voice sharp enough to draw blood.

Aldridge took a deep breath, trying to steady himself. "I didn't want to burden you with what would have been a non-issue if he was dead."

Sinclair shook his head, a gesture of disappointment that cut deeper than any words could have. "If he didn't have doubts before, he does now, so you better hope you find him before the others do."

"But what about the file?"

"If he knew what was on it, he would have said something by now. Since you and I are still here, that means he hasn't said anything, if he knows anything at all."

"Do you think he will contact the old man in Washington?" Aldridge asked.

"Tap his phone just in case."

"And Ryker?"

"Eliminate him," he said.

With that, Sinclair patted his dog on the head and stood, his movements smooth and unhurried. He walked away without another word, leaving Aldridge alone on the bench, burning with embarrassment and self-loathing.

The lights around the Reflecting Pool flickered to life, casting long shadows across the ice. Aldridge sat there momentarily, watching Sinclair's retreating figure blend into the evening crowd.

Finally, he stood, his joints protesting slightly. He pulled out his phone, this time making an actual call as he began to walk away from the pool.

Someone answered on the second ring. Aldridge's voice was clipped, authoritative. "I want every ear to the ground, and eyes in the sky — hospitals, buses, trains, taxi dispatchers, motels and hotels, airlines, banks, I want Ryker found." He paused, then added, "And get hold of Virgil. Activate the team."

As he ended the call, Aldridge cast one last look at the Reflecting Pool. The frozen surface no longer mirrored the sky but reflected the city lights, a thousand pinpricks of illumination dancing on its glossy expanse. It was beautiful, in its way, but Aldridge couldn't appreciate it. All he could see was the enormity of the task ahead and the consequences of failure.

He turned and walked into the cold night, his mind working to create plans and contingencies. The hunt for Max Ryker was on, and Aldridge knew that his future hung in the balance. Failure was not an option. Not anymore.

PART II

13

Was Ryker dead?

The bitter cold wind whipped across Navy Pier. Special Agent Jansen pulled her coat tighter around her body, her breath forming small clouds. The festive Christmas lights that usually brought cheer to the pier now seemed to mock the gravity of the situation.

Her gaze swept across the expanse of Lake Michigan, taking in the vessels dotting the dark waters. Despite the winter chill, a few hardy souls of the Frostbite Fleet were out, their white sails stark against the inky blackness. Patrol boats crisscrossed the area, their lights flashing urgently. Further out, the silhouettes of larger commercial shipping vessels could be seen, their progress seemingly unaffected by the chaos closer to shore. A handful of fishing boats bobbed near the pier, their crews likely more interested in the unfolding drama than their catch.

Jansen knew that recreational boating activities were significantly reduced during the winter months, which narrowed Ryker's options if he had survived his plunge into the icy waters. Unless he had managed to commandeer one of the Frostbite Fleet dinghies or been picked up by a commercial vessel, his chances of survival were slim. Still, Jansen had a nagging suspicion that Ryker was out there somewhere, alive and on the move.

Above, two police helicopters circled like massive, mechanical birds of prey, their searchlights cutting through the darkness to sweep across the inky waters of Lake Michigan. The rhythmic thump of their rotors, the urgent wail of sirens, and the constant chatter of radios created a cacophony of urgency that matched Jansen's mind chatter.

On the water, the crews of U.S. Coast Guard and Chicago Police Department boats were scanning the waves for any sign of Ryker.

Yellow police tape cordoned off a large section of the pier, keeping back a growing crowd of curious onlookers. Some huddled together against the cold, while others held up smartphones, eager to capture a piece of the drama for their social media feeds. Jansen noticed a few news vans pulling up, their satellite dishes extending skyward like strange, technological trees.

Her phone buzzed in her pocket, pulling her attention away from the scene. She answered it, her voice terse, a puff of hot hair expelling from her mouth. "Jansen."

As she listened to the officer on the other end, her brow furrowed deeper with each passing second. "Cyanide?" she repeated, disbelief coloring her tone. "What the hell is going on?" She muttered.

"I can clear that up," a voice said behind her. Jansen turned to see Thomas Reeves from the National Counterintelligence and Security Center slipping under the police tape, flashing his badge at a Chicago cop who looked ready to stop him. Reeves approached her, his eyes darting around the scene as if cataloging every detail. "The two men found dead were part of a cell of Hamas sympathizers. Pals of Ryker's."

Jansen's eyes narrowed. "Then why was one shot in the throat and the other took cyanide?"

Reeves shrugged, his expression maddeningly calm. "Why do they strap bombs to themselves and blow themselves up?"

"No." Jansen shook her head, her instincts screaming that something wasn't adding up. "Something's not right here."

"What's not right is the FBI's ability to hold on to their man," Reeves countered.

Jansen felt a flare of anger at his words, but she pushed it down. Now wasn't the time for interagency squabbles. "You know, he got the jump on me," she said, her voice level. "He could have shot me, but he didn't."

Reeves raised an eyebrow. "A Hamas sympathizer with a conscience? Maybe he'd reached his body count for the day, or perhaps he has an affection for female FBI agents?"

Jansen shook her head again, frustration building. She was about to respond when Reeves continued.

"By the way, when were you going to share his records with us?" he asked, his tone casual but his eyes sharp.

Jansen met his gaze coolly. "If you're going to work with us, it's on you to stay up to speed. I'm not here to babysit," she said, brushing past him. "And I would appreciate it if you don't try to micromanage me."

"Where are you going?" Reeves called after her.

"To find Ryker," she said over her shoulder. "Chances are he'll return to his home or old workplace."

Reeves jogged a few steps to catch up with her. "He's gone and taken the easy way out like his pals. The temperature of the water will have killed him. They'll be dragging his body out in the next few hours."

Jansen stopped, turning to face him. "Don't assume anything."

"Assumption doesn't come into it. Facts do," Reeves insisted. "If he's alive, and that's a big if, don't think for one minute this guy isn't dangerous and won't kill you next time."

"Whatever you say," Jansen replied, making it clear she was done with the conversation.

But Reeves wasn't finished. "You're starting to believe who he said he is, aren't you?"

Jansen paused, choosing her words carefully. "It's not my job to believe. I'm tasked with bringing him in or taking him out." With that, she turned away from him and approached a group of officers huddled near a patrol car.

"Okay, listen up, folks," she said, her voice carrying the weight of authority. The officers straightened, giving her their full attention. "I want a net over the city ASAP. Set a perimeter of ten miles covering the lake. Include all waterways extending from Wilmette to Whiting and across to Melrose Park. Checkpoints at all major intersections. We'll need every bridge across the Chicago River shut down. Make sure you check hotels, motels, gas stations, hospitals, residences, transportation stations. We'll have all surveillance cameras that we can access running through our facial recognition system. I want a picture of Max Ryker distributed to the media. Prepare to work overtime until we catch this man."

Reeves, who had followed her, quickly added, "And consider him armed and dangerous."

Jansen glanced at him but said nothing, walking away. The weight of the next few hours settled on her shoulders like a physical burden.

As she returned to her vehicle, Jansen chewed over the investigation. The puzzle pieces weren't fitting together, and her instincts were screaming that there was more to this case than met the eye. Ryker's claims of being a CIA operative, the mysterious deaths of his supposed accomplices, his decision not to harm her when he had the chance — none of it aligned with the profile of a terrorist.

She reached her car and paused, her hand on the door handle. The city sprawled before her, a maze of streets and buildings where Ryker could hide. That was if he was still alive.

As she slid into the driver's seat, her phone buzzed again. It was a text from Agent Thompson. "Got a lead. You want to check it out?"

Jansen typed back a quick affirmative response. It was a long shot, but any lead was worth pursuing at this stage. She started the engine, the car's heater slowly coming to life and battling against the chill that had seeped into her bones.

As she pulled away from Navy Pier, Jansen couldn't help but glance in her rearview mirror at the scene she was leaving behind. The helicopters still circled, their searchlights dancing across the water. The crowd of onlookers had grown, held back by a thin line of yellow tape and uniformed officers. And somewhere out there, Ryker was either fighting for his life or planning his next move.

THE DRIVE to Rachel Turner's home was a blur of city lights and holiday decorations.

Jansen parked her car outside a modest two-story home on Hutchinson Street in Portage Park. As she stepped out, she noticed Agent Thompson waiting for her by the entrance, his breath visible in the cold air.

"Who called it in?" Jansen asked as she approached.

Thompson fell into step beside her as they walked up to the house. "Neighbors reported hearing the disturbance today."

They climbed the steps. As they reached the door, a uniformed officer stood guard, nodding to them as they approached.

"It's a mess in there," the officer warned as he lifted yellow tape for them to duck under.

Jansen stepped into the house and immediately understood what the officer meant. The living room looked like a tornado had torn through it. Furniture was overturned, papers were strewn across the floor, and there were signs of a violent struggle.

"Geesh," Thompson muttered beside her.

Jansen moved further into the house, her trained eyes taking in every detail. In the kitchen, she paused. A large bloodstain marred the linoleum floor, its dark color a vivid contrast to the cheerful yellow of the cabinets.

"This is where they found her?" Jansen asked.

Thompson nodded grimly. "Yeah. M.E.'s initial report suggests somebody killed her sometime yesterday afternoon. Multiple stab wounds."

"But neighbors didn't hear anything until today?" she asked.

He nodded. That struck her as strange.

Jansen crouched down, examining the bloodstain more closely. "Was there any sign of forced entry?"

"None that we could find," Thompson replied.

Jansen stood, her mind working overtime. If Ryker was

responsible, why go to such lengths to stage a struggle? And if he wasn't, who was? And what were they looking for?

She moved to the bedroom, noting the ransacked drawers and closet. Whoever had been here was searching for something specific. Her eyes fell on a framed photo on the nightstand. It showed Rachel Turner and Ryker smiling, their arms around each other. They looked happy and normal—not like a terrorist and his unwitting girlfriend.

"Here you go," Thompson said from the doorway, holding a phone in an evidence bag. "It belonged to Rachel. It was found near her. The last person she spoke to appears to have been a co-worker, maybe an hour before death. Someone called Eve Collins."

Jansen took the bag. "You get an address?"

"We're working on it." Thompson put a hand on his service weapon. "So... what do you think?"

Jansen shook her head slowly. "I think this case just got a lot more complicated."

14

The night air penetrated Max's skin as he crouched in the shadows of the harbor, his clothes still dripping from his plunge into Lake Michigan. The lights of Chicago twinkled in the distance, a reminder of the chaos he'd left behind. His teeth chattered uncontrollably, his body wracked with violent shivers as he fought to maintain his focus.

Nearby, the fishermen who had unknowingly ferried him to safety were disembarking, their voices carrying on the cold wind.

"Hell of a night, eh?" one grumbled. "You think those searchlights out there had something to do with that bombing?"

"That or the Coast Guard is running drills," another replied. "C'mon, let's get out of this cold."

Max waited until their footsteps faded before making his move. He knew he had to act fast — hypothermia was a real threat, and he couldn't afford to be caught now. His eyes scanned the harbor, searching for an opportunity.

A small building caught his attention — a changing room for the marina. It was a risk, but he had no choice. Moving as quickly as his frozen limbs would allow, he made his way to the structure, keeping to the shadows.

Surprisingly, the door yielded quickly when he turned the handle. Max slipped inside. Once in the relative safety of the interior, he quickly stripped off his soaked clothes, rubbing his arms and legs vigorously to stimulate circulation. His left shoulder throbbed where the bullet had grazed him, the wound an angry red against his pale skin.

Max rummaged through the lockers, guilt gnawing at him as he took what he needed: a pair of slightly too-large jeans, a thick sweater, dry socks, and worn boots. As he dressed, warmth slowly began to seep back into his body.

A baseball cap and a hooded sweatshirt completed his improvised disguise. He pulled the cap low over his eyes and zipped up the hoodie, knowing that every camera in the city would look for his face.

Max could hear sirens in the distance as he stepped back into the night. The manhunt was in full swing. He knew he couldn't risk going home or to his workplace — they'd be watching those places. He needed a plan, a way to clear his name and uncover the truth behind the bombing and Rachel's murder.

Rachel. The thought of her sent a fresh wave of pain through him. As he moved through the shadowy streets, keeping his head down and avoiding the main thoroughfares, a memory surfaced. A name on Rachel's phone — Eve Collins. Her friend from the bar where she worked.

The Windy Kitty Club. It wasn't much, but it was the only lead he had.

Max made his way across the city, sticking to alleys and

side streets, always alert for police patrols. The cold had settled into his bones, but the borrowed clothes and his constant movement kept him from freezing.

Finally, he found himself standing outside the gentleman's club. Neon lights buzzed, casting a lurid glow over the snow-dusted sidewalk. Taking a deep breath, he pushed open the door and stepped inside.

After the quiet of the streets, the club assaulted the senses. Pulsing music echoed, accompanied by patron chatter and the clink of glasses. Scantily clad women danced on raised platforms, their bodies gyrating in time with the beat. Max kept his head down, making his way to the bar.

A woman with dark hair and tired eyes approached him, slinging a cloth over her shoulder. "What can I get you, darlin'?"

"Haven't decided," Max replied, his voice rough. "Hey, uh, is Eve working tonight?"

The bartender nodded, motioning behind him. He turned to see a slender blonde in a bikini dancing for a group of leering men.

"When does her shift finish?" he asked, returning to the bartender.

"In a few hours. You a friend of hers?"

Max hesitated. "My..." He caught himself, remembering that Rachel's death might have made the news. "Yeah," he said instead.

"Now, about that drink?"

Max reached into his pockets, realizing too late that he had no money. "I'm good. Thanks."

Max found a spot where he could watch Eve without drawing attention to himself. The hours crawled by, and the club gradually emptied. Finally, he saw Eve heading for the exit with the other staff members.

"Night, Eve. See you tomorrow night," a large man called out as he held the door for her.

Max slipped into the parking lot, positioning himself where the shadows were deepest. He watched as Eve approached a beat-up sedan, fumbling with her keys.

Moving swiftly, Max grabbed her arm as she opened the car door. "Get in," he said, his voice low and urgent.

Eve let out a small shriek, but Max had timed it perfectly, avoiding any chance of her reaching for pepper spray or another weapon. He guided her into the car, sliding into the passenger seat beside her.

"Just drive," he instructed.

"If it's cash you want, just take it, pal," Eve said, her voice shaking.

"You changed the color of your hair," Max observed, staying low in his seat.

"What?"

"Your hair. It was blonde inside."

"It's a wig," Eve replied, confusion evident in her tone. "Who are you?"

"Rachel's boyfriend."

Eve glanced at him as she pulled out of the parking lot, the darkness of the car concealing them both. "Max?"

He nodded, relief washing over him at her recognition. "Look, I need your help. I need answers. Rachel's dead."

Eve's hands tightened on the steering wheel. "I heard. It's been all over the news. They're saying you..." She trailed off, unable to finish the sentence.

"I didn't do it," he said, his voice firm. "Someone's set me up."

Eve was silent for a long moment, her eyes fixed on the road ahead. Finally, she spoke. “Why come to me?”

Max sighed, running a hand over his face. “Because you’re Rachel’s friend. I figured if anyone might know, it would be you. I need to understand what was going on in her life. Was there anything unusual? Anyone who might have approached her?”

“You know I really don’t need this,” Eve said, her voice tight.

“Then drop me off anywhere, and I’ll disappear,” he replied. “But… right now, you’re all I’ve got.”

Eve pulled the car over to the side of the road, turning to face Max for the first time. Her eyes searched his face, looking for any sign of deception.

“Rachel talked about you often,” she said finally. “She loved you. Said you were one of the good ones.” Eve took a deep breath. “Look. I’ll listen. But if I get even a hint that you’re lying to me...”

“I understand,” he said, relief evident in his voice. “Thank you, Eve.”

“Don’t thank me yet,” Eve replied, returning to the road. “Where now?”

Max considered their options. “I just need to gather my thoughts, tend to a wound.”

“You’re bleeding?”

“It’s fine. You live nearby?”

Eve nodded slowly. “Not far. A few blocks.”

As they drove through the quiet streets of Chicago, Max chewed over the events that had led him to this point. The mission in Croatia, waking up at the bombing site, finding Rachel’s body, his escape from custody. With each fading thought, he felt a weight pressing down his shoulders. He could have sworn he could remember more than this.

As the city lights faded behind them and they headed into the unknown, a sense of foreboding settled over Max. This escape was merely the opening move in a larger, more complex game. Somewhere out there, unseen eyes tracked his every move, biding their time. And the clock on his wrist continued its relentless countdown, ticking away the moments until... what?

Max didn't know, but he was determined to find out.

15

The soft glow of the bathroom light illuminated Max's face as he stood before the mirror, his jacket and shirt peeled off to reveal the angry, bloody gash on his shoulder. The wound wasn't deep, but it stung fiercely, a constant reminder of his narrow escape. He prodded gently at the edges, wincing at the sharp pain that shot through his arm.

The sound of footsteps drew his attention to the doorway. Eve Collins entered with a small medical kit in hand. She paused momentarily, her eyes widening slightly at seeing his bare torso covered in a tapestry of old scars.

"Take a seat," she said, gesturing towards the bathtub's edge.

Max moved to comply but hesitated, glancing at the wound that needed treatment. "You know, I can take care of that," he said.

Eve shook her head, sitting beside him on the tub's edge. "Probably easier if I do it."

Her fingers traced lightly over some of his old wounds

— knife marks and bullet scars that told a story of a dangerous life. "Looks like this isn't your first rodeo," she murmured.

"Seems so," Max replied, his voice tight.

"How did you get these?" Eve asked, her voice filled with concern.

His brow furrowed. "I don't know."

Eve's hands stilled. "You don't recall how you got them?"

"No," Max admitted.

"Not at all?"

He shook his head. "Strange, isn't it?"

"A little odd, yeah," Eve agreed, unzipping the med kit and pulling out compression bandages, saline, and other supplies.

As Eve began to clean his wound, Max spoke, his voice low and troubled. "Since I woke up in Chicago, I can only remember certain things, and even those are starting to disappear."

"What do you know?" Eve asked, her eyes flicking to his face.

He nodded. "I know my name, I know I work for a division of the CIA, where I went each day, I know Rachel was my girlfriend, who my parents are, and where we lived, but the rest is a blur. The mission in Croatia, the bombing... It's like the memories can't form or just aren't there. And the little I do remember seems to be..." He paused, bringing a hand up to his face. "Fading."

Eve's hands worked deftly as she tended to his wound. "CIA? Rachel told me you worked in financing."

"That was a cover. A front for the operations," Max explained.

Eve's eyebrows rose. "A cover? Okay." She looked as if she

was trying to make sense of it all. "So... you woke up in Chicago. I wake up here daily, so what's unique about that?"

Max shook his head. "No, I mean I woke up outside the federal building that had been bombed. But I have no memory of how I got there. My last memory was of a mission in Dubrovnik, Croatia."

Eve's hands stilled. "You're telling me you don't remember traveling back to the USA?"

He nodded, his expression grim.

"So you're suffering from some form of amnesia?" Eve asked, resuming her work on his shoulder.

"Maybe," he replied. "Like I said, I know who I am and who I work for, but..." He trailed off.

"So call them," Eve suggested.

"I did. The line is no longer in service."

"Go to your work."

Max shook his head. "Too dangerous. The place will be swarming with cops. Besides, the FBI told me the building was abandoned. In their eyes, it doesn't exist. I don't exist."

Eve paused, her brow furrowed. "They think you're making it up?"

"They think I'm a terrorist and a murderer," he said, running a hand over his head.

"Stay still," Eve muttered, focusing on cleaning the wound.

As Eve worked, he asked, "So, where did you learn to patch up a wound?"

Eve's expression softened slightly. "This apartment used to belong to my mother. She passed away nine months ago from MS. In the last few years, community nurses have come in and out. Most of this is left over from when they were here."

"Sorry to hear that," Max said softly.

Eve tossed bloodied rags into the sink. "Yeah, not as much as I am." She looked at herself in the mirror, her expression distant. "You know — the gig at the club is temporary," she said as if trying to excuse her profession. "I have plans. I mean, I had plans. That was until my mother got sick and then..." She exhaled heavily and looked back at him.

"What kind of plans?" he asked.

"To become a professional dancer. Not what I do now."

Max nodded. "How long have you been working there?"

"Nine years, this September. Eight years longer than I wanted." Eve paused, her hands stilling for a moment. "After leaving a bad relationship, I came to live with my mother. She liked the arrangement. I gave her company; she gave me a way to squirrel money away. It wasn't easy. She thought I was a manager of a bar. I never told her the truth. I guess, like you, I kept my own secrets. Once she got ill, I had to eat into those savings to pay for her care. The nurses showed me a few things: how to change bandages, deal with bed sores, and whatnot." She took a deep breath. "Rachel was working on getting me a position behind the bar. An opening hasn't opened until... now." Her voice trailed off, and she returned to working on his shoulder, using a suture kit.

"What did Rachel tell you about me?" Max asked.

Eve's hands worked steadily as she replied. "Not much. A few things. That she loved you. That she didn't deserve you. I got a sense that she felt guilty."

"About?"

"I don't know. There were moments I thought Rachel would tell me something, but then she wouldn't. However, she did tell me how you met. That you stepped in when she was being mugged in the subway. Do you remember that?"

He nodded. "Yeah. That's what's odd. I remember so many things clearly, but large swaths of my memories are just non-existent."

Eve finished dressing the wound. "Well, there. That should do it. It's not ideal."

"Thank you," Max said. "Did she say anything else?"

Eve hesitated. "No, Rachel was pretty tight-lipped. We had a lot in common in some ways, but in others, we didn't. She was determined to gain custody of her son and was trying to clean up her life."

Max's head snapped up. "A son?"

Eve looked at him, surprise evident in her expression. "She never mentioned him?"

"No. I think I would have remembered that."

"Maybe not," she replied. Eve glanced down at the bloody rags in her hands. "How long have you been with Rachel?"

"About eight years."

"And she never told you about her son? That's so odd. She spoke about him all the time. She'd call him on the phone from work. She was always in tears when she got off the phone. For the longest time, I didn't know what to say. I wondered..."

"About?" Ryker prompted.

Eve got up and tossed all the rags into the garbage, including those in the sink. "Two guys visited the bar one night. I mean, this is going back, not long before she met you."

"What did they look like?"

"Office guys. Suits. They sat at the bar and struck up a conversation with her. I wouldn't have thought much of it as many guys come in and flirt with the bartenders, but she followed them outside on one of her breaks. When she returned, she looked as white as a ghost."

"Did the men return with her?"

"No."

"Did you ask what the conversation was about?"

Eve shook her head and sat on the edge of the bath as she helped Ryker ease his arm back into his shirt. "No. Listen, are you hungry?"

"I could eat," he replied, glancing at his watch, still ticking down ominously.

In the kitchen, Eve prepared a simple sandwich of salami and cheese. As she set it before him with a beer bottle, she noticed the ring on his finger. "Huh!? Rachel never said you got married."

Max raised his hand, examining the ring. "No, we didn't. At least, I don't think we did. You see, that's another thing. I've been having these memories. Flashes, you could say. I don't know if it's related to Croatia or some other time."

"What do you see?"

"I... I don't know." He shook his head, frustrated. "I woke up with this watch on my wrist ticking down, a ring I don't remember putting on, and the words *Black Raven* scrawled on my hand. The rest is just... fragmented."

Eve gave a puzzled look. "That's one of those smartwatches." She reached over and tapped a button on the side, and a slew of icons appeared on the screen. "What brand is that?"

There was no brand.

"You know about these?"

"Somewhat. I nearly bought a Garmin Forerunner. I never got it; I was too strapped for cash. It was meant for my mother because it had an SOS feature that could alert me. You know — just in case anything happened to her while I was at work. It would let me know where she was." She got up and grabbed a napkin. "Those things only last about a day before they need charging. The Garmin lasts seven days without a charge. What about yours? I haven't seen one like that."

Max noticed it was fully charged.

"Have you explored those icons?" she asked, returning.

"No, I've been a little preoccupied running from the law."

Eve raised an eyebrow, a smirk tugging at the corner of her lip. He tapped the message icon. Inside was a single message dated several days earlier. Max tapped it, and it revealed a video attachment. He tapped play.

A video loaded of an older man. A rush of memories flooded his mind, many that he was seeing for the first time and others that he could vaguely recall. The man looked nervous as if someone might walk in on him at any moment.

"Max, my name is Bob Kingsley, Carol's husband. If you're watching this, you survived, and she didn't." Bob swallowed hard, pushing back emotion. "You likely won't remember, but you and Carol worked for the Division." He appeared to be in a familiar home, but Max couldn't remember the location. The man looked over his shoulder as if he heard someone coming. It was a teenage boy.

"I got the bags, Dad," the kid said.

"Put them in the car. I'll be there shortly." The man turned back to the video. "Look, Carol purposely didn't tell us much. Maybe to protect us. Maybe to protect you." He shook his head. "But she said they would come for us. She told me that if I didn't hear from her for two consecutive days, the file exchange in Croatia was intercepted, and I was to enact a fail-safe and send this message to you. I don't know what it means, but she said you would." The video shifted to a scrap of paper with 6819000 on it. After showing it, he lit the paper in an ashtray with a lighter. "She told me to tell you the ring leads to the truth. I hope that makes sense." Tearfully, through gritted teeth, he said, "Make them pay, Max." The video went black.

"The ring?" Max looked down at his hand. He removed the gold ring from his finger for the first time. Eve sat across from him at the table as he turned the ring in the light, noticing an engraving inside. "Looks like some words."

Eve turned on another light. "That better?"

"It's too small. My eyes aren't what they used to be."

"Let me take a look," Eve offered, taking the ring and holding it up to the light. "A&E Forever. Does that ring a bell?"

Max shook his head. Eve continued examining the ring. "Oakwood Treasures. The store, perhaps?"

"Do you have a laptop?" he asked.

Eve nodded and retrieved her computer. She logged in and turned it towards him. Max did a quick online search for Oakwood Treasures. He found a jewelry store located in Sewickley, a suburb of Pittsburgh. As he clicked through images of the store, flashes of memory assaulted him — his reflection in a glass case of rings, a conversation with an older man, pointing to a specific ring.

"You okay?" Eve asked, noticing his sudden stillness.

"I think I know this place."

"Huh. That's good, right?"

"Maybe."

Max opened another tab and did a quick search on Bob Kingsley. A news article from one day earlier about Bob and sixteen-year-old Matthew Kingsley came up.

"CHICAGO FATHER AND SON KILLED IN SERIOUS COLLISION ON I-90"

His heart sank. "They were killed. Just like Rachel."

"What?" Eve asked.

Their conversation was abruptly interrupted by a hard knock at the door. Both of their heads turned towards the sound.

"Miss. Collins. FBI."

Fear shot through Max. He rose from his seat, putting a finger to his lips. Grabbing his jacket, Max slipped into the bathroom, closing the door as quietly as possible.

He approached the window, shimmying it up and looking into the cold night. The wind was blowing snow across the city. Some apartments were lit up in the darkness, while others were dark. He had no choice. Carefully, he climbed out onto the narrow ledge, lowering the window almost closed behind him.

After inching his way along the ledge, the cold wind battering his exposed skin, Max waited. The sound of muffled voices from inside the apartment reached his ears.

He strained to hear what was being said. He knew he couldn't stay out there indefinitely, but this precarious perch was his only option for now.

There was no fire escape in sight, no easy way down. Max was trapped between the cold Chicago night and the threat of capture inside.

16

The apartment door swung open, revealing Eve Collins, her expression a blend of confusion and apprehension.

"Eve Collins?" Special Agent Meredith Jansen asked, her voice crisp and professional.

"Yeah? What is this about?"

Jansen flashed her badge. She was accompanied by Thomas Reeves and several Chicago patrol officers. "FBI. We have a few questions. May we come in?"

Eve hesitated, her eyes darting between the assembled group before reluctantly nodding and stepping aside.

Jansen's trained eyes swept the room as they entered, taking in every detail. "You work with Rachel Turner," she stated, more than asked.

"I do," Eve confirmed, her arms crossed defensively over her chest.

"Are you aware she's deceased?"

Eve swallowed hard. "I am."

Jansen pressed on. "You were the last person she spoke

with by phone yesterday. Do you mind telling us what that conversation was about?"

"Nothing important. We frequently chatted."

"We saw that," Jansen replied, her gaze lingering on the open laptop on the table, its screen dark. She noted two plates and two bottles of beer. "Do you live alone?" she asked, her tone casual but her eyes sharp.

"I do. Well, it was my mother's apartment, but she passed away."

"Sorry to hear that," Jansen said, her gaze drifting down the hallway toward the bedroom.

Eve stepped in front of her, blocking her path. "Look, aren't you supposed to have a warrant or something?"

"You invited us in," Jansen countered smoothly.

Eve's nervousness was palpable as she replied, "Look, I don't know what else to tell you. Rachel and I were good friends. We worked together at the Windy Kitty Club. That's it."

Reeves stepped forward, holding up a mugshot. "So you met her boyfriend... Max Ryker?"

"Actually, no," Eve said, her voice tight. "Our friendship was work-related."

"So you haven't seen him recently?" Reeves pressed, following Eve as she picked up the two plates and took them into the kitchen.

"Yes."

"So you have seen him?" Reeves asked, his tone sharpening.

"No. I mean on the news." Eve's frustration was evident as she replied, "Look, I'm tired. I've had a long day. So unless you have any other questions, I would really like to turn in."

Jansen, who had been quietly observing, spoke up. "If you live alone, is it common for you to make two sandwiches?"

"I had a neighbor over," Eve replied quickly.

Jansen's eyes narrowed. "You know it's a crime to lie to law enforcement, even more so for harboring and abetting."

Eve's composure wavered slightly. "If I had any reason to hide, do you think I would have invited you in?"

"You might not, but Ryker does," Jansen countered.

As they spoke, Jansen's keen eyes noticed several blood spots on the floor heading toward the bathroom. "You mind if I use your washroom?" she asked, not waiting for Eve's reply before heading in that direction.

Inside the bathroom, Jansen quickly took in the scene — streaks of blood in the sink, bloody rags in the garbage, and an open med kit nearby. A slight breeze carried a few snowflakes through a gap beneath the window. "Reeves!" she called out.

Reeves hurried in, and Jansen gestured to the rags.

Jansen shimmied up the window and stuck her head out. A gust of wind blew icy flakes in her face as she turned her head and looked in all directions. She noticed prints on the ledge.

Behind her, Reeves was grilling Collins. "I thought you said you lived alone. Where is he, Ms. Collins?"

"I don't know what you're talking about," Eve protested.

"The bloody rags."

"I tended to a neighbor's wound. She cut herself."

"Must have been one hell of a cut. You want to tell us this neighbor's name and apartment number? I would really like to talk to her," Reeves pressed.

Jansen exited the washroom, suddenly shifting gears. "Reeves. Let's go."

"Let's go?" Reeves echoed, confusion evident in his voice.

"I'm sorry to have troubled you, ma'am," Jansen said to Eve, her tone suddenly polite.

As they headed out, Eve dropped one last comment. "Whatever you think this man did, he didn't do it. I knew Rachel."

"But you didn't know him," Reeves retorted. "This man has killed hundreds, and believe me, he will tell you whatever you want to hear if it means he escapes."

As soon as the door closed and they made their way down one flight of stairs, Jansen was already on the radio, updating others to surround the building and scan the streets.

"Why would you just let her go like that?" Reeves demanded.

"Because he's still nearby," Jansen replied, her voice low and intense.

"How do you figure that?"

"Prints on the ledge outside. Plus, he has nowhere else to go."

She turned to the patrol officers and instructed them to head up the east stairwell.

Reeves pointed back toward Eve's apartment. "I'm telling you, we should go back there and—"

Jansen motioned for Reeves to be quiet as they crossed to another section of the building.

They hadn't made it far when suddenly, Jansen froze, her eyes fixed on a window at the far end of the corridor. The snow flurries almost made her miss it.

Through the frost-edged glass, illuminated by the harsh glow of a nearby streetlight, she saw a figure perched precariously on the narrow ledge outside.

Ryker's back was pressed against the building's brick

facade as he inched his way along the ledge, the wind whipping at his clothes.

Jansen raised her hand, signaling for Reeves to hold his position.

She knew that any sudden movement could startle Ryker, potentially sending him plummeting to the street below.

As they watched, Ryker paused, seeming to sense their presence. His head turned slowly and briefly, his eyes locked with Jansen's through the window. In that instant, she saw something in his gaze — not the cold calculation of a killer, but the desperation of a man on the run, a man who believed he was innocent.

17

Fear gripped him.

The bitter wind howled around Max as he clung to the icy ledge, his fingers already numb from the cold. He had just rounded a bend in the U-shaped apartment complex when he heard the commotion below. Peering down, he saw several Chicago cops burst out of a door into the courtyard.

He'd been so careful, navigating the treacherous ledge to avoid detection after the FBI agent had searched the apartment. Now, his hopes of reaching the nearby telephone pole and climbing down were dashed.

The street below quickly filled with officers, their flashlights sweeping the building's facade. He knew breaking into an apartment was out of the question — they'd have cops on every floor by now.

Max shivered hard. The cold was seeping into his bones, his fingers quickly becoming stiff and unresponsive.

With no other options, he began to climb.

The wind buffeted him, icy snow pellets stinging his face like tiny needles. His hands searched for a hold on the cold brick, every movement a battle against gravity and the elements.

Halfway up, his foot slipped on a patch of ice. For a heart-stopping moment, Max dangled by his fingertips, the ground sickeningly far below. He swallowed hard, forcing down the panic rising in his throat.

"Ryker!" a voice called out.

He knew he couldn't talk his way out of this. Slowly, agonizingly, he regained his footing and continued his ascent. Each movement was a struggle, his muscles screaming in protest. The cold had numbed his extremities, making it difficult to gauge his grip on the rough bricks.

Near the top, another gust of wind nearly tore him from the wall. Max pressed himself flat against the bricks, his heart pounding. He closed his eyes momentarily, gathering his strength for the final push. With a surge of adrenaline, he hauled himself over the edge and onto the roof.

Agent Jansen's voice rang out inside the building, "Head for the roof. Go, go!"

Max scrambled to his feet, taking in his surroundings. Steam rose in the night sky. The roof was a maze of steel vents and pipes. A single door led back into the building.

Hurrying to the edge and eyeing the gap between this

building and the next, Max considered his options. It was a long jump, but he had no choice.

Backing up, he took a deep breath. The cold air burned in his lungs as he ran, pushing off at the last moment. For an eternal second, he was airborne, the yawning chasm below promising certain death if he missed. The wind howled in his ears, threatening to knock him off course. Then, his feet hit the roof, and he rolled to absorb the impact, the rough surface scraping his hands and face.

Behind him, he heard the roof access door slam open. Jansen's voice cut through the night, "Ryker! Stop!"

But he was already running, his legs pumping as he reached the edge of the second building. He leaped to the third without hesitation, his body moving on pure instinct.

As he landed, he heard a sharp crack — gunfire. The sound spurred him on, adrenaline coursing through his veins.

Risking a glance back, he saw Jansen slapping down another agents gun.

~

"WHAT THE HELL do you think you're doing?" Jansen shouted, her voice barely audible over the wind.

"You want him to get away?" Reeves retorted, his face twisted in frustration.

"I want him alive! Besides, he has nowhere to go."

~

MAX REACHED the edge of the final building, his heart sinking as he saw the drop to an L-shaped plaza two stories below.

"Shit!" he muttered, his breath coming in ragged gasps. "This will hurt."

Taking a running start, he launched himself into the void. Time seemed to slow as he fell, the roof rushing to meet him. The impact was jarring, pain shooting through his legs as he rolled across the roof. For a moment, he lay there, the world spinning around him. But the sound of pursuit spurred him on.

Staggering to his feet, he kept moving, his eyes locked on a faded blue snowplow clearing the parking lot below. It was a crazy idea, but it was all he had.

As the plow turned, Max jumped, landing hard on its roof with a resounding metallic clang. The impact sent shockwaves through his already battered body. The driver slammed on the brakes, nearly sending Ryker flying.

"What the hell?" the man shouted, climbing out.

Max was in the cab in a flash, slamming the door and throwing the plow into gear. The unfamiliar controls took him a moment to figure out, but soon, he was swinging the massive vehicle onto Kimball Avenue, heading south as sirens wailed behind him.

Two police cruisers appeared ahead, parked nose to nose across the street. Max gritted his teeth and plowed through; the cruisers' hoods crumpled like paper. The impact rattled his teeth, but he pushed on, veering onto the sidewalk. Pedestrians scattered in panic, and Ryker winced as the plow demolished everything in its path — newspaper stands, benches, and street signs flying in all directions.

A sign for the CTA Brown Line caught his eye — the subway, his best chance for escape. But cop cars were everywhere, blocking intersections and giving chase.

Max swerved down a narrow side street, the plow's blade scraping against parked cars with a horrific screech of metal. Sparks flew as he careened around a bend, barely maintaining control of the massive vehicle. A police cruiser appeared at the far end, lights flashing. He cranked the wheel hard, the plow skidding sideways and taking out a row of garbage cans before careening onto another street.

For several heart-pounding minutes, he weaved through the Chicago streets, the plow's bulk working both for and against him. He smashed through roadblocks and pushed smaller vehicles aside, but the behemoth was slow to maneuver, and the pursuing cops were closing in.

As he rounded another bend, Max spotted an opportunity. A large delivery truck was backing out of an alley, momentarily blocking the street. He gunned the engine, using the truck as cover to slip down the alley unseen.

The narrow passage forced him to slow down, the plow's sides scraping against brick walls with a deafening screech. Sparks flew as metal ground against brick. He emerged onto Spaulding Avenue, immediately spotting the CTA station ahead. It was now or never.

He floored it, the plow's engine roaring as he barreled towards the subway entrance. Police cruisers converged from all directions, their sirens wailing and lights flashing in a dizzying display. But they were too late. The plow smashed through the station doors with a deafening crash that shook the entire building.

The impact threw Max forward, his head narrowly missing the steering wheel. Glass and debris rained around him as the plow ground to a halt, half inside the station. Smoke billowed from the crumpled hood, and the smell of burning rubber dominated.

Max leaped from the cab, his body protesting after the brutal chase. His legs nearly buckled as he hit the ground, but he forced himself to keep moving. He could hear shouts and the pounding of feet as officers gave chase.

He plunged into the subway station, pushing past shocked commuters and leaping over the turnstiles. The familiar rumble of an approaching train spurred him on. He took the stairs three at a time, his lungs burning as he gasped for air.

As he reached the platform, he saw the train pulling in. Without hesitation, he sprinted towards it, squeezing through the doors just as they began to close. He stumbled into the car, collapsing onto a seat as the train lurched forward.

His heart pounded in his chest as he tried to catch his breath. He could hear the faint sound of sirens fading as the train picked up speed, carrying him away from his pursuers. But he knew he was far from out of the woods.

As the adrenaline began to wear off, the pain from his various injuries made itself known. His muscles ached, and he could feel bruises forming from his multiple impacts. But he couldn't rest yet.

Max glanced around the car, noting the mix of late-night commuters and partiers heading home. No one seemed to be paying him much attention, too absorbed in their phones or conversations. But he knew it was only a matter of time before his description was broadcast across the city.

He needed to change his appearance, find a way to blend in and figure out his next move. The watch on his wrist continued its steady countdown, a constant reminder of the urgency of his situation.

Max's thoughts spiraled as the train hurtled through the dark tunnels beneath Chicago. He had escaped for now, but he was still no closer to clearing his name or understanding the conspiracy that had ensnared him. One thing was clear — he couldn't keep running forever. Sooner or later, he would have to confront those behind this plot head-on.

18

The lighting of the subway station flickered overhead as Max emerged from the train, his heart still pounding from his narrow escape. The platform was mostly empty, save for a few late-night stragglers. He inhaled, trying to calm his nerves as he approached the stairs.

Just as he reached the bottom step, the crackle of police radios made him freeze. Two Chicago cops were descending the steps, their eyes scanning the platform. Max's breath caught in his throat as their gazes locked onto him.

"Hey, come here!" one of the officers shouted, reaching for his weapon.

Adrenaline surged through his body. He spun on his heel, sprinting back towards the train he'd just exited. But luck wasn't on his side — the doors slid shut just as he reached them, the train pulling away with a mocking hiss.

"Damn it!" Max said as he searched for a way out.

The thump of heavy footsteps echoed behind him as the officers gave chase. Max weaved through the sparse crowd, knocking over a trash can to slow his pursuers. He could hear shouts of alarm and confusion as he barreled down the platform.

Suddenly, a burly man stepped into his path, arms outstretched to stop him. Max didn't hesitate — he ducked low, driving his shoulder into the man's midsection. The impact sent them both sprawling, but Max rolled to his feet first.

Another bystander, a younger man in a business suit, made a grab for him. Max pivoted, his fist connecting with the man's jaw in a swift, brutal punch. The would-be hero stumbled back, eyes wide with shock.

"Sorry," Max muttered, genuinely regretting the violence but knowing he had no choice.

His eyes darted frantically around the platform, searching for an escape route. The pursuing officers were closing in, their shouts echoing off the tiled walls. With no other options, he made a split-second decision.

He vaulted over the platform's edge, landing hard on the tracks below. The impact sent shockwaves through his legs, but he pushed through the pain, sprinting into the tunnel's yawning darkness.

"Stop! Police!" The shouts behind him grew more urgent as the officers realized his desperate move.

Max plunged deeper into the tunnel, the dim emergency lights barely illuminating his path. The air was thick with the smell of oil and electricity. He could hear the distant rumble of an approaching train, the vibrations traveling through the rails beneath his feet.

Behind him, flashlight beams cut through the darkness, dancing wildly as the officers gave chase. Max's heart pounded in his chest, his breath coming in ragged gasps as he pushed himself to run faster.

"He's in the tunnel!" one of the officers shouted into his radio.

Max knew he was running out of time. He needed to find a way out of the tunnel before a train came barreling through.

Then, he spotted a maintenance access door set into the tunnel wall. Hope surged through him as he sprinted towards it, the officers' footsteps echoing closer with each passing second.

Max slammed into the door, twisting the handle desperately. For a heart-stopping moment, he thought it might be locked. Then it gave way, and he tumbled into the dimly lit maintenance tunnel beyond.

It stank inside of oil and damp concrete. Max's eyes adjusted quickly to the gloom, spotting a ladder leading up to what looked like a street-level access point. He didn't hesitate, grabbing the rungs and climbing.

Behind him, he could hear the maintenance door bang open, followed by cursing as the officers realized how narrow the passage was. It would slow them down, but only for a short time.

Max reached the top of the ladder, his muscles burning from the exertion. He pushed against the heavy metal cover, grunting with effort. Slowly, agonizingly, it began to move.

A blast of cold air hit him as he emerged onto the street. He was in an alley, the sounds of the city muffled by the buildings around him. Quickly, he slid the cover back into place, hoping to buy himself a few more precious seconds.

As he stepped onto the sidewalk, he looked around, searching for anything to help him blend in. That's when he spotted a homeless man slumped against a building, a nearly empty bottle clutched in his hand.

"Hey, buddy," Max said, approaching cautiously. "How about a trade?"

The man looked up, his bleary eyes struggling to focus. "What?"

Max was already shrugging off his jacket. "Your coat and hat for mine. Come on, it's a good deal."

Too drunk or too confused to argue, the man allowed Max to help him out of his tattered coat and into Max's much warmer jacket. The exchange took only seconds, but Max could almost feel his pursuers breathing down his neck.

Across the street he spotted a sign for the homeless shelter. A line of people filed in, seeking refuge from the cold night. It was perfect.

He hurried across the street, falling into line behind a group of weary-looking individuals. He hunched his shoulders, trying to mimic their defeated posture. Just as he reached the shelter's entrance, he saw the two officers emerge from the alley.

His heart rate spiked as their gazes swept the street. But their attention was immediately drawn to the drunk man wearing Max's jacket and baseball hat. Max slipped inside the shelter as they approached him, breathing a sigh of relief.

The interior was warm and filled with the smell of food. Max's stomach growled. He grabbed a tray and joined the line, keeping his head down as he shuffled forward.

"Meat and mash tonight," the server said as she plopped a generous portion onto his tray.

Max nodded his thanks, then asked in a low voice, "Is there a place I can clean up? Maybe get a razor?"

The woman pointed across the room. "Care packages are over there. It should have what you need."

Max made his way to an empty table, setting down his

tray. He grabbed the roll, wolfing it down as he walked towards the care packages. Out of habit, his eyes scanned the room, noting exits and potential threats.

Max spotted a small tin of black boot polish as he passed a row of cots. He scooped it up without breaking stride, slipping it into his pocket. He collected a care package and headed for the washroom, snagging a pair of scissors from an unattended table along the way.

Inside the washroom, Max locked the door and took a deep breath. He stared at his reflection in the grimy mirror, barely recognizing the haggard face that looked back at him. It was time for a change.

He began hacking away at his long brown hair with quick, efficient movements. Clumps fell into the sink as he worked, transforming his appearance with each snip. Next, he tackled his overgrown beard, the scissors making short work of the tangled mess.

Once the bulk was gone, he lathered with soap and used the disposable razor from the care package to shave clean. The face that emerged was younger, sharper — and hopefully less recognizable.

But he wasn't done yet. Ryker opened the tin of boot polish, rubbing a generous amount between his fingers. He raked his hands through his hair, the black dye darkening his brown locks. He even smeared a bit across his eyebrows, further altering his appearance.

As he washed the excess dye from his hands, Max heard a commotion outside. Peering through a crack in the door, he saw the two officers from earlier talking to one of the shelter staff. His heart raced — they must have figured out where he'd gone.

Max scanned the room, looking for a way out. He spotted

a staff member struggling with a large sign near the exit. The sign read "ALL BEDS FILLED — NO MORE INTAKES TONIGHT" in bold red. An idea formed in his mind.

Taking a deep breath, Max exited the washroom and strode purposefully towards the staff member. "Need a hand with that?" he asked, pitching his voice lower than usual.

The grateful employee nodded, and Max took one end of the sign. As they maneuvered towards the exit, he positioned himself so the sign blocked the officers' view of his face.

"Thanks for your help," the staff member said as they reached the door.

Max nodded, keeping his head down. "No problem. Have a good night."

And just like that, he was outside again. The cold air bit at his newly exposed skin. Max pulled up the collar of his borrowed coat. As he strolled away from the shelter, he allowed himself a small smile. He'd bought himself some time, but he knew the chase was far from over.

The city stretched out before him, a maze of possibilities and dangers. Max squared his shoulders and picked up his pace. He had a name to clear and a conspiracy to unravel. And now, with a change in appearance, he might have a chance.

As he disappeared into the night, the countdown on his watch continued relentlessly, a constant reminder of urgency.

19

His accomplice was playing games.

The air in the FBI headquarters felt tense as Agent Jansen stood outside the interrogation room, frustration mounting.

For the past hour, they'd been grilling Eve Collins, pushing and prodding for information about Ryker. Jansen could feel the weight of exhaustion settling over her, but she pushed it aside. There was too much at stake to give in to fatigue now.

Inside the room, Thomas Reeves of the NCSC was losing his patience. His voice, sharp with anger, carried through the door.

"You lied to us. Why should we believe a single word that comes out of your mouth? Now tell us the truth!"

Eve's response was tired but defiant. "I've told you everything. He approached me. I only knew his girlfriend. I want my lawyer. I'm done talking to you all."

Jansen had seen enough. She pushed open the door and

tapped Reeves on the arm. "Reeves," she muttered, gesturing towards the exit.

As soon as they were in the hallway, Jansen swept back her jacket, placing a hand on her hip. The gesture was both a sign of frustration and an unconscious assertion of authority.

"You're not going to get any more out of her," Jansen said, her voice low but firm.

Reeves' eyes narrowed. "Do you want this guy to escape?"

She stepped closer to Reeves, her voice dropping to a dangerous whisper. "Remember, you work with us. We don't work for you. Now, if you plan on pulling another bullshit move like you did on that roof, I'll have you removed. He was unarmed."

"You don't know that," Reeves shot back. "He is dangerous, and the sooner you wake up to that, the sooner we can end this."

Without another word, Reeves turned on his heel and started walking away.

"Where are you going?" Jansen called after him.

"Washington, D.C.," he replied without turning back.

"Why?"

"Ryker's parents reside there. Probably our best lead right now."

Jansen felt a twinge of unease. She didn't trust Reeves, but she couldn't deny that following up on Ryker's family connections was smart. Still, she didn't want him out of her sight.

"Get someone else to do it. We need you here," Jansen said.

Reeves paused, turning to face her with a smirk that made Jansen's skin crawl. "Make up your mind, Agent Jansen. One minute, you want me removed; the next, you want me in bed with you."

Jansen's fists clenched at her sides. "Screw you," she spat.

Reeves' smirk widened. "I'll keep you in the loop as soon as I have something. I expect the same from you." With that, he disappeared around the corner.

After taking a deep breath to compose herself, Jansen returned to the interrogation room. The door closed behind her with a soft click, sealing her in with Eve Collins.

Eve looked up, her eyes tired but still defiant. "I hope you have a phone so I can call my lawyer."

"You'll get one," Jansen assured her. "Just one last question."

Eve sighed, slumping back in her chair. The metal creaked under her weight, echoing in the small room.

Jansen leaned forward, her palms flat on the table. "What were you looking at on your computer?"

"What?" Eve's brow furrowed in confusion.

"You said you worked late; Ryker came back with you. You both had a bite to eat. On the table was an open laptop, but the screen was off."

Understanding dawned in Eve's eyes, followed quickly by a look of triumph. She leaned back in her chair, a small smile playing at the corners of her mouth.

"You didn't bring a warrant to enter my premises," Eve said, her voice taking on a note of confidence. "I might be some slutty little dancer to you all, but I know a thing or two about rights. You're going to need a warrant to search that computer."

With a theatrical gesture, Eve ran a finger and thumb across her lips and pretended to toss an invisible key.

Jansen straightened up, focusing on the next step. Without another word, she turned and headed out of the room.

"Doug!" she called out to her colleague as she strode down the hallway. "I need a warrant application. Also, get an attorney on the phone. I want Collins' laptop."

Jansen's mind whirled with possibilities as she waited for Doug to make the call. What had Eve been looking at on that computer? Was it related to Ryker? To the bombing? Or was it something else entirely?

She knew they were missing some piece of the puzzle that would make everything fall into place. The frustration of being so close yet so far gnawed at her.

As she paced the hallway, Jansen's thoughts turned to Ryker. The man was an enigma — a supposed terrorist who didn't fit the profile, a killer who showed compassion by not shooting her, a trained operative who seemed genuinely confused about his own actions.

Something wasn't adding up, and Jansen was determined to figure out what it was. She had a gut feeling that the answers they needed were hidden in plain sight.

The sound of Doug's voice pulled her from her thoughts. "Meredith? Line two."

Jansen nodded, squaring her shoulders as she prepared to make her case for the warrant. Whatever secrets Eve's laptop held, she was going to find them.

20

Charlie Prescott leaned back in his chair, rubbing his tired eyes as the glow from his laptop screen illuminated his face in the dimly lit office of the *Chicago Tribune.* The clock on the wall ticked past eleven, and an empty coffee mug sat beside him, a clear sign of the long hours he'd been putting in. He was on his fourth revision of an article about the bombing, the taxi driver murder, and the death of Rachel Turner — a story that felt like journalistic gold.

Turning back to his computer, Charlie began poring over the photos he'd snapped earlier that day. The images were haunting — debris-strewn streets, shell-shocked survivors, and first responders working tirelessly amidst the chaos. As he scrolled through, a sharp ding cut through the silence of the near-empty newsroom.

An email notification appeared on his screen. Charlie's heart raced as he saw it was from his source in law enforcement. He quickly opened the attachment — a mugshot of their primary suspect that the FBI wanted to be distributed to all media outlets.

Charlie hit print and rushed to the printer, snatching the still-warm paper. As he looked at the image, his jaw dropped. "No way," he muttered, hurrying back to his desk.

He frantically combed through the photos he'd taken at the bombing site. "Come on, come on, I know you're in here," he muttered, eyes darting from image to image. Then he saw it — or rather, him.

Charlie held up the mugshot next to his computer screen, comparing it to the first photo he'd found. The resemblance was undeniable. "Holy crap."

Not wasting a second, he grabbed his phone and dialed his superior, Victoria. After several rings, she picked up, her voice heavy with sleep and a stuffy nose.

"Charlie, this better be—"

"I got him. I mean, I snapped him," Charlie interrupted, his words tumbling out in excitement.

"Back up the train. What?"

"The bombing suspect. The guy they're looking for. Max Ryker. We just got in a mugshot they want the media to distribute. It matches the same guy in my photo that I took down at the bomb site."

"Maybe you are useful." There was a pause on the other end of the line. "Has the print run begun?"

"Not yet," Charlie admitted.

"There's still time to get it included in the print run," Victoria said, suddenly sounding wide awake. "Get both photos down to Arnold. I want them in tomorrow's paper, and the web team can now get them online. Oh, and Charlie, you better have ready one hell of an article to go with it."

"Nearly."

"Charlie!"

"I do. It will be in there," Charlie assured her quickly.

"With my name," Victoria added before sneezing.

Charlie grimaced. He was tired of running around and gaining little from it. "Right," he said, trying to keep the frustration out of his voice.

After hanging up, Charlie turned back to his laptop, fingers flying over the keys as he finalized the article. However, he paused as he was about to type in Victoria's name. "Screw it," he muttered, deleting her name and replacing it with his own, even including his profile pic.

Charlie's finger was hovering over the send button when something caught his eye. He scrolled back through the photos from the scene, this time scrutinizing each one. Several showed Ryker walking through the smoke; another captured him helping a woman and her child. But in the background of one image, Charlie spotted a figure in identical clothing to Ryker's, observing from a distance.

Intrigued, he zoomed in. The smoke obscured details, but Charlie was almost sure it was another person in a cleaning uniform. He'd need to enhance the image for a better look. His thoughts were caught in a whirlwind of anxiety. Were there others involved? And if so, why was Ryker openly helping people while this person lurked in the shadows?

Charlie's journalistic instincts kicked into high gear. This was more than just a simple bombing story — there were layers here, complexities that needed to be unraveled. He glanced at the clock, knowing he was pushing his deadline to the limit, but he couldn't ignore this potential lead.

Quickly, he opened a new document and began typing out his thoughts, theories, and questions. This would require more investigation and digging. He'd need to enhance the photos and maybe even track down some of the first responders who were on the scene.

As he worked, Charlie felt a mix of excitement and trepidation. This story could be his big break, the investigative piece that could launch a career. But it also felt dangerous.

As Charlie delved deeper, he cross-referenced timelines, examined every detail of his photos, and compiled a list of potential sources to contact. The more he dug, the more convinced he became that there was a larger story here, one that went beyond a simple act of terrorism.

He sent everything he had over to Arnold and then waited.

CHARLIE JERKED awake as the first rays of dawn peeked through the office windows, his cheek peeling away from the keyboard where he'd dozed off. Despite the crick in his neck and the fog of exhaustion, he felt a surge of exhilaration. He hadn't just met his deadline for the print edition; what he had now was potentially much bigger. This wasn't just a news story anymore — it was the beginning of an exposé.

Charlie saved his work and shut down his computer, his mind still buzzing with possibilities.

As he stepped out into the crisp Chicago morning, little did he know that his pursuit of this story would lead him down a path far more treacherous than he could have ever imagined.

21

December 30

The morning bustle had settled into the quaint town of Sewickley, outside Pittsburgh, with a light dusting of snow covering the streets. Max sat in a battered 1992 Ford F-150 pickup truck, his breath occasionally fogging the window as he observed the town's activities. Shopkeepers swept their storefronts while locals hurried along the sidewalks with coffees. The truck idled quietly, a reminder of the durability of older models — one of the reasons he'd chosen it back in Chicago.

His thoughts drifted back to the escape from the Windy City.

The decision to steal the truck had been a calculated risk. It was older, easy to hotwire, and unlikely to be reported missing for hours. In a city where vehicle thefts were common, it wouldn't immediately raise red flags. He'd opted for this over public transportation, knowing law enforcement would be scouring bus stations and train depots.

As he had navigated the streets of Chicago, slipping through gaps in police checkpoints, the falling snow had become an unexpected ally, offering an extra layer of concealment.

Now, after a night of non-stop driving, exhaustion weighed heavily on him. His gaze was fixed on Oakwood Treasures across the street as he waited for any sign of life. The jewelry store held answers — he was sure of it. The ring on his finger and the engraving inside all led back here.

A sharp rap on the window startled Max from his thoughts. He looked out, bleary-eyed, to see a parking official peering in at him.

"Can't sleep here," the man said as he wound down the window.

"Right. I was just resting. I'll move," Max replied, his voice rough from lack of use.

As the official moved on, he started the engine and drove around the town. The streets of Sewickley were beginning to stir, with early risers hurrying to work. A sense of familiarity washed over him as he navigated the quiet roads.

Flashes of memory assaulted him — laughter echoing down these very streets, a woman with a swollen belly smiling up at him, a parade with colorful floats and cheering crowds. The images were vivid but disconnected, like scenes from a movie he couldn't quite place.

He passed by a small park where children were already playing, their shouts of joy carrying on the air. A bakery caught his eye, the smell of fresh bread wafting out as a customer exited with a steaming bag. The town square boasted a picturesque gazebo, dusted with snow and wrapped in twinkling lights — a scene straight out of a Christmas card.

Max parked the truck and gathered the little change he could find in the vehicle. A nearby café beckoned with the promise of hot coffee. As he entered, several patrons glanced his way before quickly averting their eyes. He felt a prickle of unease but pushed it aside.

"What can I get you?" the barista asked cheerfully.

"Medium dark roast with cream," Max replied, then hesitated before adding, "You know what time Oakwood Treasures opens?"

"In about half an hour," she answered with a smile.

He nodded his thanks, paid for his coffee, and turned to leave. As he did, a folded newspaper on a nearby table caught his eye. Without thinking, he snatched it up and hurried back to the truck.

Once inside, Ryker unfolded the paper, his heart sinking as he read the bold headline: "FBI SEEKS SUSPECT IN CHICAGO BOMBING. WARNING: ARMED AND DANGEROUS." Below was a grainy photo of him at the bomb site — not clear, but potentially recognizable.

With trembling hands, he turned to the full story. There, staring back at him, was his mugshot in crystal-clear detail. "FBI ON MANHUNT FOR REPORTED SHOOTER IN CHICAGO," the headline blared.

Ryker's eyes scanned the article, taking in the accusations — his alleged involvement in the deaths of taxi driver Ed Hammond, and Rachel Turner. The weight of it all threatened to crush him.

He dropped the paper onto the passenger seat, his mind reeling. The entire country was about to become the eyes and ears of the FBI. His chances of staying under the radar had just plummeted.

Glancing back at the café, Max was relieved to see that no one seemed to have made the connection. His altered appearance — clean-shaven with shorter, darker hair — might buy him some time. It was a flimsy disguise, akin to Clark Kent's glasses, but it might be enough to avoid a second glance from most people.

He took a long sip of his coffee, savoring the warmth and caffeine as he considered his next move. He had roughly twenty minutes before Oakwood Treasures opened. Twenty minutes to devise a plan that wouldn't end with him being handcuffed.

As he sat there, more fragments of memory surfaced. He saw himself walking down these streets hand in hand with a woman—was it the pregnant one from his earlier vision? He remembered the feeling of nervousness and anticipation. Had he bought an engagement ring here?

The disconnect between these warm, happy memories and the accusations in the newspaper was jarring. Max knew, deep in his bones, that he wasn't a murderer or a terrorist. But with each passing hour, the evidence against him seemed to mount.

He glanced at his watch — the one he'd woken up wearing after the bombing. The countdown continued its steady march towards zero. Whatever it was ticking down to, Max had a sinking feeling it was connected to everything else.

With a sigh, he started the truck's engine. He'd circle the block a few more times, watching for any sign of police activity. The last thing he needed was to walk into a trap at the jewelry store.

As he drove, his thoughts tried to make connections. He needed answers, and he needed them fast. But more than that, he needed allies. Someone, somewhere, had to know the truth about what was happening to him.

Out of the corner of his eye, Max saw an Oldsmobile pull up outside Oakwood Treasures. An elderly man stepped out, juggling some keys as he approached the store. He watched as the man fumbled with the lock, finally opening the door and disappearing inside. He'd give the old-timer a few minutes to get his bearings before going in.

Max glanced down at the ring on his finger, turning it slowly in the weak morning light. The scrawled words "Black Raven" on his skin were barely visible now, faded from his time in the water or from the rigors of his escape and long drive. What did it mean? He racked his brain but couldn't make sense of it. It all had to mean something — the clock ticking down, the ring, the phrase scrawled on his hand. But the connections eluded him, slipping away like wisps of smoke whenever he tried to grasp them.

The man in the jewelry shop put the "OPEN" sign in the window and disappeared from view. Max took a deep breath, steeling himself for what was to come. He got out of the truck, the cold air gnawing at his face as he crossed the street and headed for the shop. A bell above the door jingled cheerfully.

"I'll be right with you," the elderly man called from the back.

Max took in the interior of the shop. It was like stepping back in time. The small space was crammed with glass display cases, each one gleaming with an array of rings, bracelets, chains, and watches. A grandfather clock stood in one corner, steadily ticking. The air was thick with the sweet, musty smell of pipe tobacco, giving the place a cozy, lived-in feel.

Antique lamps cast a warm glow over everything, making the jewelry sparkle invitingly. Framed certificates and old photographs covered the walls, telling the story of a business passed down through generations. It was exactly the kind of place you'd expect to find in a small town like Sewickley — quaint, personal, steeped in history.

The old man emerged from the back room, a pair of half-moon spectacles dangling around his neck. “Something I can help you find?”

“Yeah, actually, there is.” He removed the ring and handed it to the man. “I was in a car accident recently. I've been having trouble remembering. I think I bought this here, but I can't be sure. Would you have any record?”

“Uh, yeah, let me take a look.” The old man put on the spectacles and brought the ring over to a machine that allowed him to observe it closely. “Uh-huh. That's one of ours. We always engrave the store name and a tiny order number. You know, in the event anyone steals or loses jewelry, it just makes it easier to trace or for folks to find out the real owner. Also good for business. A lot of our custom pieces draw attention. People like to know who made them.” He looked up at Max. “You say you bought it here? Do you remember the date?”

“Sorry. No. It's all a bit of a blur.”

“No worries, we'll look it up by the number engraved.”

The man wandered into the back and re-emerged with a monstrous-sized book. “My granddaughter is in the process of inputting all this into a computer. I'm old-school. Prefer to keep hard copies of invoices and whatnot. Let me see.” He flipped through the pages, the paper rustling loudly in the quiet shop. "Ah, there we go. Andrew and Emily. I gather that's you."

Max frowned. The name summoned another memory, but it was fleeting, almost barely formed, like trying to remember a dream after waking up.

"This was bought a long time ago."

"It was?" Max asked.

"Eight years." The man studied his face as if he could recall every customer who had bought from him. The owner handed the ring back to Max. "You would have left that here after requesting the engraving and picked it up a few days later."

Max glanced down and saw an address and a telephone number beside each order. His pulse quickened. This could be the lead he'd been looking for. "You wouldn't, by any chance, have a box for this, would you?"

"Want to gift it to someone?" the old man asked, a knowing twinkle in his eye.

"Something like that," Max replied, trying to keep his voice casual.

"I'm sure I can find something. No charge." The old man turned and went out back, his footsteps creaking on the old wooden floor.

As soon as he was out of sight, Max turned the book around and used a pen on the counter to hastily scrawl the address on his hand. His fingers trembled slightly as he wrote, the adrenaline of the moment making his handwriting messier than usual.

Just as he finished, he heard the old man's footsteps returning. Max bolted for the door without a second thought; the bell jingled wildly as he rushed into the snowy street.

Behind him, he heard the old man's confused voice

calling out, but he didn't stop. He sprinted back to the truck, his breath coming in sharp bursts, visible in the cold air.

As he climbed into the driver's seat, he chewed over the information. Andrew and Emily. The names felt right, somehow, even if he couldn't fully remember why. And now he had an address — a tangible lead in the mystery that had engulfed his life.

The truck rumbled through Sewickley, carrying Ryker towards his next destination and, hopefully, the answers he so desperately sought.

22

It was maddening.

He'd spent the last hour driving in circles, frustration mounting as he tried to make sense of the hastily scrawled address on his hand from the jewelry store. Asking for help felt like a gamble, a risk he wasn't sure he could take. But desperation clawed at him, pushing him to swallow his pride. Finally, he pulled into a gas station and approached the attendant to get directions.

"Pink House Lane?" the attendant had said, scratching his stubbled chin. "Yeah, that's out in Sewickley Heights. Real fancy area. You'll want to head north on Route 65, then take a right onto Blackburn Road. Follow that until you hit Pink House Lane. Can't miss it."

He thanked him and left.

~

THE HOUSES in the neighborhood were spread out, grand, and set back from the road on large, wooded lots. He drove slowly, scanning the numbers until he found the one he was looking for.

Pulling off to the side of the road, Max parked the truck and took a moment to study the house before him. It was a traditional two-story farmhouse, its gray siding weathered but well-maintained. Dormer windows peeked out from the sloped roof, and a wrap-around porch gave the place a welcoming feel. Off to the side, a sunroom addition caught the weak winter light. Behind the house, he could make out the shape of an old barn; its red paint faded to a soft rust color.

The property was surrounded by old trees, their snow dappled branches reaching up into the gray sky. A blanket of snow covered the expansive lawn, broken only by the driveway leading up to the house. It was the kind of place that spoke of history, of generations of families living and growing within its walls.

Max took a deep breath, steeling himself for whatever he might find inside. He climbed out of the truck. As he crossed the road, the gravel crunched beneath his feet, the sound seeming unnaturally loud in the quiet morning.

He paused at the foot of the driveway, looking both ways out of habit before heading towards the house. His heart pounded, each step bringing him closer to potential answers — or more questions.

Upon reaching the porch, Max hesitated for a moment before raising his hand and knocking firmly on the door. The sound echoed through the house, but no response came. He waited, counting the seconds in his head, before knocking again. Still nothing.

Max stepped back, his eyes scanning the property. No vehicles were in sight, and there were no signs of recent activity. The house stood silent and still as if holding its breath.

Deciding to investigate further, Max stepped off the porch and made his way to the sunroom. Through the windows, he spotted a child's bicycle propped against the wall, its handlebars adorned with remnants of tinsel — a lingering reminder of the recent holiday festivities.

A swing set came into view as he continued to the back of the house. It didn't look too old, but some of the paint was chipped. Max approached it, drawn by a sudden, inexplicable pull.

The moment his hand touched the cold metal of the swing, a memory hit him with the force of a physical blow. He heard the creak of the chain and laughter ringing in his ears. A woman's face flashed before his eyes — the same one he'd seen in his earlier fragmented memories. Her smile was radiant, her eyes filled with love as she looked at him.

The intensity of the memory made Max's legs weak. He gripped the swing tightly, steadying himself as the world seemed to tilt around him. Taking a few deep breaths, he waited for the dizziness to pass before making his way to the house's side door.

He knocked again, calling out, "Anyone home?" His voice sounded strange to his own ears, too loud in the stillness of the winter morning. When no answer came, he tried the handle. To his surprise, it turned easily in his grip.

Max hesitated for a moment, weighing the risks. Breaking and entering wouldn't help his case if he got caught, but the need for answers outweighed his caution. He stepped inside.

The interior of the house was a sharp departure from the cold outside. It was warm, filled with the kind of lived-in comfort that spoke of a happy home. The kitchen, where

Max found himself, was clean but showed signs of recent use. A few dishes sat on the drying rack, and the faint smell of coffee lingered in the air.

Magnets held photos and papers to the fridge — smiling faces of people Max didn't recognize, a child's drawing, a to-do list scrawled in hurried handwriting. On the kitchen table, a stack of mail caught his attention. He sifted through it quickly, his heart rate picking up as he read the names Emily and Noah Sutton.

Max dropped the mail back onto the table, his mind whirling. Emily — the name from the jewelry store records. But who was Noah? And why did the name Andrew feel so familiar?

As he moved into the living room, Max's attention was immediately drawn to the mantelpiece. It was lined with framed photos, each one a snapshot of a life he felt he should know but couldn't quite grasp.

The centerpiece was a wedding photo. Max didn't recognize the man, but the woman... His breath caught in his throat. It was her — the woman from his fragmented memories, the one he'd seen on the swing. Emily. She looked radiant in her white dress, her smile wide and genuine as she gazed at her new husband.

Other photos showed Emily with a child — a girl with her mother's eyes and curly brown hair. There were birthday parties, Christmas, and family vacations. A whole life was documented in these frames, and Max felt like an intruder, peering into a world he didn't belong to.

He moved quietly, years of training kicking in as he navigated the unfamiliar space. He peeked into bedrooms — a master suite, a guest room, and a child's room.

The walls were painted a soft purple, with posters of

cartoon characters and bands competing for space. Stuffed animals were piled high on the bed, and a desk in the corner was covered with school books and art supplies. It was the room of a happy, loved child.

Max was about to leave when the sound of tires on gravel reached his ears. His body tensed, instincts kicking into high gear. He moved swiftly to the window, peering out to see a white Toyota SUV making its way up the driveway.

Cursing under his breath, Max headed back downstairs. He exited through a rear door, careful to close it quietly behind him. From his position at the back of the house, he could hear voices.

"Remember, only a few hours of TV," a woman's voice said, the tone warm but firm. "It might be a snow day, but I'm going to need your help cleaning the house later." There was a pause, then, "Come on, give me a hand taking in these groceries."

Max edged his way around the side of the house, his pulse increasing. Through the sunroom window, he could see a brunette woman taking bags out of the rear of the SUV. A large fir tree partially obscured his view, preventing him from seeing her face clearly.

"Just the light bag," the woman called out. "Don't try to carry the heavy one."

A young voice replied, full of determination, "I can do it."

The woman's laugh was warm and affectionate. "You are just like your father."

Max watched as the woman headed into the house, arms laden with grocery bags. A moment later, a young girl with curly brown hair appeared, struggling with a heavy paper bag. As she tried to lift it from the SUV, the bottom of the bag gave way. Apples spilled out, rolling across the snowy driveway.

Two of the apples rolled towards Max's hiding spot. Without thinking, he stepped out, bending to pick them up. As he straightened, he found himself face-to-face with the young girl. She stood frozen, her eyes wide with surprise and a hint of fear.

"It's okay," Max said softly, holding out the apples. "I'm not going to hurt you."

The girl's voice trembled as she called out, "Mom!"

"What is it, hon?" The woman's voice came from inside the house, growing louder as she approached. She appeared on the porch, her brow furrowed with concern. "Can I help you?"

Max turned slowly, his eyes meeting hers. The moment stretched out, filled with a tension he couldn't quite understand. The woman's eyes widened, her face draining of color as if she'd seen a ghost.

Her voice, when it came, was barely more than a whisper. "Andrew?"

Confusion gripped Max, his brow furrowing as he tried to make sense of the situation. His senses felt overloaded, and his brain struggled to process what was happening. At the same time, he watched as tears began to roll down the woman's face. She gripped the railing of the porch, her knuckles white, in an effort to keep herself upright.

The young girl, sensing her mother's distress, ran towards her. "Momma?"

"Go inside," the woman said, her voice strained.

"But—"

"Mia, I'm okay, go inside," she repeated, more firmly this time.

The girl looked back at Max, her expression a mix of confusion and worry, before reluctantly heading into the house. As the storm door shut behind her, the woman seemed to crumple, sliding down to sit on the porch steps. Her body shook with silent sobs.

Max approached cautiously, his hands held out in a non-threatening gesture.

"No. No, this can't be," the woman murmured, shaking her head as if trying to wake herself from a dream.

"Take a deep breath," Max said, his voice gentle.

The woman looked up at him, her eyes red-rimmed and full of disbelief. "They told me you were dead."

"Who?" he asked, feeling as if he was teetering on the edge of a revelation.

"The military," she replied, her voice breaking on the word. She reached out tentatively, her hand hovering near his face as if she feared he might disappear if she touched him. Finally, her fingers touched his cheek, warm against his cold skin. "You don't recognize me?" she asked.

Max hesitated, caught between the fragments of memory that teased at the edges of his mind and the blank spaces that still dominated his recent past. "No. Yes. I don't know," he admitted, frustration coloring his tone. After a pause, he asked the question that had been building since he'd first seen her face. "Who do you think I am?"

The woman's eyes scanned his face, confusion giving way to a softer expression of understanding and, beneath that, a deep, abiding love. "Andrew McCallister," she said, her voice steadier now. "You were my fiancé."

The words between them were heavy with implication. Max felt as if the ground had shifted beneath his feet, and everything he thought he knew about himself was suddenly called into question. He opened his mouth to speak, but no words came out. Instead, he found himself staring at this woman — Emily — as if seeing her for the first time.

Max rolled the ring around on his finger.

A&E Forever, the engraving made sense, but why could he not remember it?

At that moment, standing in the cold and hearing the young girl moving about inside the house, Max realized that he had stumbled upon something far more complex than he had imagined. The mystery of his identity, of the missing pieces of his memory, had just deepened considerably.

"I need to show you something," Emily said.

23

The charred remains of what was once a stately home in Barnaby Woods, a quiet neighborhood in the Northwest area of Washington, D.C., smoldered before him. The blackened debris scattered across the lawn stood out in the snow.

Thomas Reeves held his phone tightly to his ear, his breath visible in the morning air as he spoke to Agent Jansen. “Well, the good news is I found Ryker’s parents,” he said, his tone grim. “The bad news is, they’re in body bags.”

He watched as two EMTs carefully loaded a stretcher into the back of an ambulance. The doors closed with a dull thud, and Reeves turned his attention back to the scene before him.

“It appears we’re a day late,” he continued, looking through the debris. The smoke and burnt materials assaulted his nostrils. “I’m looking at the charred remains of their home. Whatever information could have been gleaned from the home is trash. Even with our best working on it, it could take days to extract information from laptops, if anything is even salvageable."

All around him, the scene was a flurry of activity. Firefighters in their bulky gear moved purposefully through the wreckage, their yellow helmets bobbing as they worked to ensure all hot spots were extinguished. The red and blue strobe lights of police cruisers and fire trucks painted the winter-kissed street in an eerie, pulsating glow. Neighbors huddled on their porches or behind police lines, their faces a mix of shock and morbid curiosity.

"Did anyone see or hear anything?" Jansen's voice crackled through the phone.

Reeves shook his head, even though she couldn't see him. "Neighbors called in the fire. That's all. Said it occurred in the early hours of the morning."

"Well, unless Ryker can teleport, I hardly doubt he was behind it," Jansen replied, her skepticism evident even through the phone.

Reeves' jaw tightened. "Or, he called in a favor from a friend."

"Right. To kill his parents because that makes sense," Jansen's sarcasm was palpable.

"To save them the shame for what was about to hit the media," Reeves countered. "Why do you seem so sure he wouldn't go to this extent? School shooters do it all the time."

He could almost hear Jansen's frustration through the phone. "Look, we got a lead. It appears Ryker was researching a jewelry store in Sewickley, near Pittsburgh."

Reeves paused, his brow furrowing. "Pittsburgh? Why?"

"Well, that's the part we don't know," Jansen admitted. "Eve has gone dark zero on us and called in a lawyer. She isn't saying anymore."

"You think he's escaped the city and gone there?" Reeves asked.

"Don't know," Jansen replied. "There's been no sign of him all night. We're having local PD in Sewickley swing by there."

Reeves nodded, his decision made. "I'm on my way back."

As he ended the call, Reeves looked at the devastation around him. The once-pristine neighborhood now bore the scars of tragedy. Crime scene technicians in white suits moved carefully through the wreckage, their cameras flashing as they documented every detail. A group of detectives huddled near a police cruiser, their faces serious as they discussed the case.

The weight of the situation settled heavily on Reeves' shoulders. Two more lives were lost, and they were still no closer to catching Ryker. The jewelry store lead was tenuous at best, but it was all they had. As he returned to his car, crunching through the snow, Reeves knew they were missing something crucial.

24

Agent Jansen stood over a tech analyst, her eyes glued to the computer screen as he meticulously combed through Eve Collins' laptop. The dim glow of the monitor cast a blue hue on her tired face. She clutched a cup of coffee in her hand, trying to shake off the remnants of sleep. She had managed only a few hours of rest, opting to sleep in her office at the FBI headquarters rather than go home. Her phone had remained close by, ready for any updates.

Doug, her colleague, lingered nearby, his presence a constant reminder of the urgency of their task. "For someone who is supposed to be an ordinary civilian working for a financial company, Ryker sure has a knack for staying one step ahead of us," he remarked, breaking the tense silence.

"Yeah, a real Houdini," Jansen muttered, sipping her drink.

Doug handed her a report. "Got something interesting. We received back information on the explosive material found at Ryker's home. You won't believe this, but it wasn't new."

Jansen's brow furrowed. "What?"

"It dates back to the Cold War," Doug explained.

"The explosive material was dated?" Jansen asked, surprise evident in her voice.

Doug nodded. "Not exactly. Something to do with chemical composition, manufacturing techniques, and packaging and labeling."

Jansen wrestled with the significance. "How the hell did he get his hands on that?"

"He must have purchased it on the black market," Doug replied. "The tech department is taking a fine-tooth comb over his computers from Rachel Turner's home and his finances. Besides that offshore account, there's no money trail to the explosives. This guy either knew what he was doing..."

"Or someone set him up," Jansen finished.

Just then, the shrill ring of a phone interrupted them. Doug picked it up, exchanging words before holding it out to Jansen. "Sewickley PD."

Jansen took the phone, focusing partially on Eve Collins' computer. "Yep, go ahead," she said, her tone distracted.

The voice on the other end of the line was professional. "We talked to the owner. It seems a guy was in this morning. Said he'd been in a car accident and wanted to know if he'd bought a ring from there."

"A ring?" Jansen's mind flashed back to the interview room. They had never processed Ryker's ring or watch. Based on what they knew about Rachel Turner, there had been no wedding or plans for one.

Jansen covered the phone's mouthpiece. "Doug, can you

get me some more coffee, please?" He nodded and left to fulfill her request.

Returning her attention to the call, Jansen pressed for more information. "What else?"

"The guy left in a hurry. That's all," the officer replied.

"Okay, well..." Jansen began but was interrupted by a muffled conversation in the background.

"Hold on a second," the cop said.

After a brief pause, the cop returned to the line. "The ring was made out to an A&E. Andrew and Emily. There's an address. Do you want us to swing by?"

Jansen's pulse quickened. "Are you kidding me? Of course. Let me know as soon as you have something."

She hung up, her mind already calculating. It would have taken around seven hours to get there by vehicle. Plenty of time for Ryker to have made the trip.

"Doug!" she called out as her colleague returned with her coffee. "Tell them to get the chopper ready."

Doug's eyebrows shot up. "Where are we going?"

Jansen's eyes gleamed with determination. "Sewickley."

As she gathered her things, Jansen knew that the next few hours could make or break the case.

25

A pale winter light filtered through the curtains of Emily's living room in Sewickley, Pennsylvania. Max sat on the edge of the sofa, his posture tense as he tried to process the whirlwind of emotions and memories that had assaulted him since arriving at his ex-fiancée's home.

Emily approached hesitantly, holding out a postcard with an image of Old Town Dubrovnik, Croatia, on the front. The picturesque scene of terracotta roofs and azure waters seemed to mock Max's turmoil.

"This card arrived a few days ago along with this bear," Emily said, her voice soft and uncertain. "It was unsigned. Did you send that?"

Max took the postcard, his fingers brushing against Emily's momentarily. The familiar touch sent a jolt through him, awakening more fragments of memory. He focused on the words scrawled across the back:

"Greetings from sunny Croatia! The beaches are beautiful, and

the bears are so unique. Remember when we used to say, "The bear necessities are the sweetest treasures'? Those were the days."

Max noted the misspelling of what should have been "bare necessities."

Emily's voice broke through his concentration. "You used to bring bears back from when you were overseas because you knew how much I liked them."

Max looked up, meeting Emily's eyes. The pain he saw there mirrored his own. He turned his attention back to the postcard, trying to make sense of the cryptic message. His gaze shifted to the stuffed bear sitting on the coffee table, its button eyes staring at him innocently.

He reached for it, turning it over in his hands. The soft fur felt familiar against his skin, triggering another flash of memory — a busy marketplace, the smell of spices, the sound of many people, and a foreign dialect.

The words "Press My Tummy & I Squeak" were stitched onto its belly. Max squeezed it gently, but no sound came out.

Emily watched him, her brow furrowed. "It didn't work for me either," she said. "Look, I didn't believe it was from you. I couldn't. I thought it was some mistake."

"There are no mistakes," Max muttered, his eyes darting between the bear, the postcard, and his ring and watch. Each item felt like a piece of a puzzle he couldn't entirely solve. Acting instinctually, he turned the bear over and found the Velcro opening that would typically house the sound device.

He pulled it apart with deft fingers, revealing a small black box no bigger than his palm. He cracked it open, his pulse spiking as he discovered a biometric USB flash drive inside the battery compartment.

"I must have figured you wouldn't throw it away," he said,

more to himself than to Emily. Holding the drive, Max looked up at Emily. "Do you have a computer with a USB slot?"

She nodded, leading him towards a small office at the rear of the home. The room was cluttered but cozy, with bookshelves lining the walls and a large desk dominating the space. Emily fired up the computer, the soft hum of the machine filling the silence between them.

As soon as it loaded, Max inserted the drive and placed his thumb on the sensor. His pulse quickened as the drive recognized his print and granted access. A folder appeared on the screen, containing two files. Max clicked on the first, only to find it encrypted. He tried typing in the numbers Bob Kingsley had given him, but they didn't do anything.

With a growing sense of frustration, he clicked on the second, a video file. A window loaded, revealing a bustling foreign marketplace bathed in bright sunlight. A sign in the background caught his eye — Old Dubrovnik. The scene triggered a flood of memories, some feeling like entirely new experiences, others vaguely familiar, as if buried deep in the recesses of his mind.

The camera moved erratically as if someone behind it was adjusting their position. Suddenly, Max saw himself on the screen. He was dressed in light sandy cargo pants, a green T-shirt, and a shemagh wrapped around his face. The Max in the video pulled down the shemagh, revealing a face etched with urgency and exhaustion.

Max was transfixed as his on-screen self as he motioned to a vendor selling stuffed toys. He recognized the bear — the same one on Emily's coffee table. "Keep the change," his recorded self said before turning towards the camera.

"Is it recording?" he asked, his voice tinged with anxiety.

A foreign male responded from behind the camera, "Yeah. Make it quick, they'll be here in seconds."

"Hold the camera steady," the recorded Max instructed, taking a deep breath and glancing around nervously. Sweat trickled down his temple as he began to speak. "Everything they told you about the mission in Croatia was a lie."

Max leaned closer to the screen, his heart thumping. The recorded version of himself looked over his shoulder, his breathing becoming more labored. "If you are watching this, you're probably struggling to grasp what is true. I know what you're thinking, but you must understand that you are not who you think you are. The Division is not who they say they are. They have manipulated you. You were a part of a program called Black Raven—"

The woman's voice behind the camera grew urgent. "Max, they're coming."

On-screen, Max swallowed hard, his eyes darting around. "There's so much I need to tell you, but I'm out of time, and I can't be sure you're the one viewing this. Go to Apartment 8, Millgrove Way, Washington, D.C. Red will know what to do. You have the file now."

Suddenly, the air was filled with the sound of gunfire. The camera was snatched from its holder, the image tilting wildly. More shots rang out before the screen went black, leaving Max and Emily staring at the blank monitor in stunned silence.

"Red?" Max asked, his voice tinged with confusion and frustration.

"I think you meant Harry Redding. You used to call him Red for short," Emily replied, her eyes searching his face for any sign of recognition. "He raised you."

"What? No." Max shook his head vehemently. "I was

raised by my parents, Evelyn and Keith Ryker, based out of Washington."

"No, you weren't, Andrew," Emily said softly but firmly.

"Stop calling me that. My name is Max Ryker. I was born in Johns Hopkins Hospital in Baltimore, Maryland on—"

"No," Emily interrupted, her voice steady. "You were born in upstate New York to Julia and Michael McCallister. Both died in a car crash when you were two years of age. You were adopted and raised by Red. You joined the military fresh out of high school. I know because I met you six years later while you were still in service. We were together for five years before we picked out rings to get married. That never happened because you died overseas... at least, that's what I was told."

Max shook his head, backing away from the computer. "No. This makes no sense. I would remember. I was dating Rachel Turner."

"Did you marry her?" Emily asked, her gaze piercing.

"No," Max admitted, his voice faltering.

"It's just that I saw a ring on your wedding finger." Emily pointed to the gold band. Max looked at Emily, twisting the ring. "How long were you with this woman?" she asked.

"Eight years," Max replied, his voice barely above a whisper.

Emily nodded, looking down before meeting his eyes again. "You've been gone eight years."

At that moment, Emily's daughter appeared in the doorway. Emily beckoned her over. The girl clung to her mother, looking up at Max with wide eyes.

"Mia, why don't you go out on the swing? We just need a few minutes longer," Emily said gently.

Mia nodded and headed out. Once the door was closed,

Emily stared out the window, her back to Max. "Do you see the resemblance? You should; she's your daughter."

Max was again hit with a flurry of memories: a swing, the pregnant woman, laughter, a baby's room, and a crib. His mind reeled from the onslaught of images, blurring together like a fading dream.

"You remember me, don't you?" Emily asked, turning toward him, her voice filled with hope and sorrow.

"Barely. I..." Max stumbled a little, the weight of the revelations threatening to overwhelm him. Emily moved in to assist, but he waved her off. "Stop. Please. I'm okay. I just..."

He sat at the computer and brought up the search engine, typing in the names Evelyn and Keith Ryker. He swallowed hard before hitting enter. His heart caught in his throat at the headline of a news article: "Two Dead Following House Fire in Barnaby Woods."

Max couldn't believe it. First, Rachel, then Bob Kingsley, and now his parents. They were being wiped out one by one. Every connection to him — gone.

The sound of gravel crunching under tires caught his attention. Emily went to the window and pushed aside the drapes. "It's Noah," she said, turning back to Max. "My husband. He's a good man. I thought you were dead," she said, her voice filled with a need to explain herself. She didn't need to. Not to him. Not after all these years.

Max took the USB out and shut the computer down. No sooner had he done so than a man entered. "You know the traffic is insane out there. I got you a coffee," he said when he paused, his eyes darting from Emily to Max.

Emily swallowed hard. "Noah, this is uh..."

"Max," Max said, stepping forward.

"I know who you are," Noah said, tossing down a newspaper on the table, the same one Max had read earlier that morning, the one with his mugshot. "Did he do anything to you?" Noah asked, crossing toward Emily protectively.

"No," Emily replied quickly.

"Look, I didn't bomb that federal building," Max added, his voice firm.

"I don't give a shit. You need to leave," Noah said, his tone brooking no argument.

"Okay," Max said, his shoulders slumping. "I'm sorry, Emily. I didn't want to..." he trailed off, heading for the front door. Emily was quick to cut him off.

"Wait," she said before turning to her husband. "Noah."

"No, Emily."

"Just give me a minute," she said to Max before directing him toward the rear of the house.

Max headed out the back and stood there momentarily, listening to Emily and Noah argue inside. He glanced over at Mia, who was playing on the swing. Max made his way off the deck and approached her, seeing her through new eyes, trying to see himself in her.

"Can you push me?" Mia asked, her voice filled with innocent excitement.

"Sure," Max said, getting behind her and giving her a gentle shove. "This is a nice swing set."

"Mom said Dad made it for me," Mia replied, her legs kicking out as she swung higher.

Max looked toward the house. Through the window, he could see Emily and Noah, their exchange looking heated.

"You know I can jump off this if I get high enough," Mia said, her voice filled with a child's bravado.

"You don't hurt yourself?" Max asked, a small smile tugging at his lips despite his turmoil.

"Oh no," Mia said confidently.

"You're brave. How old are you?" Max asked, his voice softening.

"Eight. My birthday was a few weeks ago," Mia replied proudly.

Max replied in a quiet, almost somber voice, "Eight years old. Well, happy birthday."

As he pushed her and she swung up higher, he felt a lump form in his throat. He'd missed so much. Birthdays, Christmases, Easters, Thanksgivings, and all the rest. They'd stolen his life. His memories. His identity. His brain couldn't comprehend it. How? Why him? None of it seemed to make sense.

Out of the corner of his eye, he saw flashing lights through the trees on the road that came around to the front of the house. No sirens were on, but he knew immediately who they were. Max took hold of the swing as the two cruisers rolled up the driveway in front of the house.

"I didn't say to stop," Mia protested, her voice filled with disappointment.

"Sorry, Mia, but we're going to have to do this another time," Max said gently.

As she shifted to get off the swing, a gun crack echoed. The wooden frame splintered near his head. In a flash, Max grabbed Mia and made a beeline for the house before the gunman could shoot again. Emily was already at the rear door, pushing it wide open. Max rushed in with Mia in his arms. His eyes flitted to the TV, where a broadcast was showing the aftermath of the bombing in Chicago. Max's mugshot was on the screen. "A massive manhunt for Ryker has already begun," the news anchor said.

"Did you call the cops?" Max asked.

"No."

"I'm so sorry," he said to Emily as she hugged her daughter tightly.

More gunshots rang out.

Through the front window, Max saw several cops coming under fire by someone to the east of the home. One by one, the officers fell, their bodies jerking grotesquely as bullets found their marks.

Then, another slew of rounds followed, each one peppering the home. How many gunmen were out there?

"Get down!" Max shouted, pushing Emily and Mia towards the kitchen. They needed cover and fast.

The remaining officers scrambled for cover behind their vehicles, but it was a losing battle. Whoever was in those trees was highly trained and ruthlessly efficient.

A lone surviving officer dashed to his cruiser, diving into the driver's seat. Max watched as the man frantically fumbled with his radio, his mouth moving as he called for backup. But his plea was cut short as a bullet shattered the windshield, striking him between the eyes. The officer slumped back, his finger still on the radio button.

"Do you have a gun?" Max asked Noah, his voice low and urgent.

"No," he said, staying low and using his body as cover for Emily and Mia. Max positioned himself near the edge of the window and peered out.

"What is going on, Max?" Emily asked. "Who is shooting?"

Right then, Max saw a gunman in black ballistic gear hurry to one of the cruisers. He reached inside, pulled out the radio piece, and spoke into it. Max could hear him through one of the open windows.

"Officers down. Officers down!"

The shooter dropped the radio and headed for the house.

"Another setup. They'll pin this on me."

Emily nodded, her face pale but determined as she got up. "There's a basement. We can—"

Her words were cut off by the sound of breaking glass. A small, cylindrical object crashed through the living room window, bouncing across the hardwood floor.

"Flashbang!" Max shouted, his body moving on instinct. He grabbed Emily and Mia, shielding them with his body as he propelled them away from it.

A blinding white light erupted, followed by a deafening bang that seemed to shake the very foundations of the house. The blast's concussive force sent waves of pressure through the air, disorienting everyone within its radius.

Max's ears rang painfully, and spots danced across his vision even with his eyes closed. He could feel Emily and Mia trembling beneath him, their bodies tense with fear. The smell of the discharged flashbang lingered, mixing with the dust kicked up by the explosion.

As the initial shock subsided, Max knew they only had seconds before his attackers would enter. Still partially blinded and deafened, he struggled to his feet.

"Move, now!" he shouted, his voice sounding muffled and distant in his ringing ears. "Stay quiet, and don't come out until I say it's safe."

Noah didn't hesitate, scooping up Mia and heading for the basement door. Emily lingered for a moment, her eyes meeting Max's. "Be careful," she said before following her family.

As soon as they were safely in the basement, Max positioned himself near the front door, his body tense and ready for action. He didn't have to wait long.

The front door exploded inward, wood splintering as a massive, ginger-haired man burst through. He was a brute, all muscle, and menace. Max didn't have time to think, only react.

He lunged at the intruder, grappling for the rifle in the man's hands. They struggled, the weapon between them, neither willing to let go. Max heard the back door kicked in — a second attacker was entering.

With a surge of strength, Max managed to turn the rifle, squeezing off a round that caught the second intruder square in the chest. The man went down hard, but Max had no time to celebrate.

The ginger-haired attacker headbutted Max. Stars exploded in his vision. Max returned the favor, slamming his forehead into the man's nose with a sickening crunch. Blood sprayed, but the brute seemed unfazed.

They careened through the house, slamming into walls. Picture frames crashed to the floor, glass shattering around their feet. The fight spilled into the kitchen, their bodies colliding with the island. Pots and pans hanging overhead clanged as their heads knocked into them.

Max's hand found a heavy skillet. He swung it with all his might, connecting with the attacker's jaw. The man's grip on the rifle loosened, and the weapon clattered to the floor.

Max dove for it, but a vise-like grip on his ankle yanked him back. The attacker was on him in an instant, powerful arms wrapping around Max's throat in a textbook rear naked choke.

Max gasped for air, black spots dancing at the edges of his vision. His fingers scrabbled desperately at the man's arms, but the hold was too tight. In a last-ditch effort, Max's hand found the hilt of a knife in the attacker's leg sheath.

With the last of his strength, Max pulled the blade free and plunged it into the man's ribs. The attacker howled in pain, his grip loosening just enough for Max to break free.

Staggering to his feet, Max lunged for the fallen rifle. He spun around just as the ginger-haired man was reaching for his sidearm. Max didn't hesitate. Two shots rang out, and the attacker crumpled to the floor, his unseeing eyes staring at the ceiling.

Silence fell over the house, broken only by Max's ragged breathing. He stood there, rifle in hand, surveying the carnage around him. The quiet suburban morning had erupted into a war zone, leaving destruction and unanswered questions in its wake.

Max knew he couldn't stay any longer. The gunshots would have alerted neighbors, and more cops or assailants could be on their way. He needed to ensure Emily, Noah, and Mia were safe, and then he had to find a way to get to Washington to meet Red.

26

Adrenaline was pumping hard, an intense, almost electric rush that heightened his senses and sharpened his focus.

Max crouched over the bodies of his fallen attackers, his hands moving swiftly through their pockets. The once-peaceful suburban home now bore the scars of violence. Shattered glass and splintered wood littered the floor.

Emily stepped forward. "Who are they, Max?"

"Hired hands."

"What are you looking for?" Emily asked, her voice tight with tension as she stood in the doorway, arms wrapped protectively around herself.

Max didn't look up as he responded, "Anything that might help." He pulled a Glock 43X from the holster of one of the men, quickly checking the magazine before tucking it into the waistband of his jeans. The weapon's weight was familiar, comforting in a way that made him uneasy.

He flipped through their wallets, taking money and scrutinizing the IDs inside. Even as he examined the licenses, he knew they were likely fake — standard procedure for operatives on covert missions. These men hadn't come prepared for the possibility of arrest, just death.

He took out a cell phone and used the dead man's thumb to open it. In settings, he turned off the need for a lock. He'd search the contacts later.

Max pocketed a set of vehicle keys. "Changing vehicles will buy me some time," he muttered, more to himself than to Emily. "The owner of the truck I took in Chicago has probably reported it missing by now. That could be how the cops found me."

As he moved to the second body, the unmistakable sound of a gun being cocked froze him in place. Max turned slowly, finding himself staring down the barrel of the rifle Noah had retrieved from one of the fallen attackers.

"Noah put it down," Emily pleaded, her voice tight with fear.

Noah's hands trembled slightly, but his eyes were hard as he kept the rifle trained on Max. "He's a wanted man. He brought this to our home."

Emily stepped between them, her back to Max as she faced her husband. She put out her hand. "Put it down. You don't understand."

"I understand enough," Noah spat. "He's dangerous."

"Noah." Emily's voice was soft but firm.

"No, he's right, Emily," Max interjected, slowly rising to his feet with his hands raised. He could see the conflict in Noah's eyes, the struggle between fear and moral uncertainty. "I shouldn't have come here. I was in trouble and needed some help. I wouldn't have sent what I did if I had known you had a child and a husband. I'm leaving now. If you want to shoot me, go ahead."

Max walked past Noah, his steps measured and calm. He could feel the tension radiating from the other man and almost saw the rapid beating of Noah's heart by a vein on his neck. But Max knew, with a certainty born of years of experience, that Noah didn't have it in him to pull the trigger.

Emily passed by Noah, shaking her head disapprovingly. Noah lowered the rifle, the fight seeming to drain out of him as Max stepped outside into the bright morning sun.

The full extent of the devastation hit Max as he surveyed the scene. Cop cars lay riddled with bullets, their windshields shattered. Bodies of officers lay where they had fallen, a grim evidence of the skill and ruthlessness of his attackers. He could already hear the sound of sirens growing louder in the distance.

"Will I see you again?" Emily's voice came from behind him.

Max paused, glancing back at her. He had no idea. The weight of their shared past, of the life he couldn't remember, hung heavy between them.

"I don't know."

"How will you get to Washington, D.C.?" she asked, concern evident in her voice.

"It's best you don't know," Max replied, his tone softening. "I'm sorry, Emily. I truly am."

Emily's following words hit him like a physical blow. "What about Mia? What do I tell her? She has a right to know you."

Max felt a lump form in his throat. The little girl on the swing, his daughter — a concept still too surreal to fully grasp. "Maybe," he said finally. "That's for you to decide." The sirens grew louder, reminding him of the urgency of his situation. "This isn't my life anymore. It's yours, and I've just opened a can of worms you didn't ask for."

Without another word, Max took off at a crouch, heading for the tree line. His eyes scanned the road beyond, quickly spotting a black-tinted Cadillac parked a few yards down. He hit the key fob, and the responding beep confirmed it was the right vehicle.

As he pulled onto the road, he saw police cars barreling towards Emily's house in his rearview mirror. He veered left onto one of the back roads, disappearing out of view, his mind already plotting his next move.

If Chicago had been hot, a small town like Sewickley was about to turn into a pressure cooker. The hiding spots and escape routes available in a big city simply didn't exist here. He was hemmed in on the west by the Ohio River, and he knew every bridge would soon be blocked.

But Max had one advantage—his changed appearance. Until an update was distributed, he had a small window of opportunity to blend in, and he intended to use it. It wasn't perfect — Noah had recognized him, but he had a reason to scrutinize him.

His decision was made in an instant. He would go where they least expected, where the sheer number of people and faces would provide cover — a place that would seem too exposed for a man on the run. It was a risk, but one he had to take.

As Max pulled away, he remembered the cell phone he had pocketed from one of the dead attackers. He fished it out, keeping one eye on the road as he checked the contacts. It was a burner phone, as he had expected, likely connected to another burner phone.

He noticed multiple calls received and made to one number. Without hesitation, he dialed it.

Someone answered. "About time."

Max listened silently.

"Did you handle it?" the man asked again.

No answer.

"Virgil?"

"I'm afraid Virgil is out of service," Max finally replied, his voice cold.

"Ryker?" the man said in a hushed tone.

Silence stretched for a moment.

"Aldridge."

"So, it's true, you do remember," Aldridge said, a note of surprise in his voice.

"You, yes."

"What else?"

"Meet me, and I'll tell you."

Aldridge chuckled. "I have to give you credit. You're like a cat with nine lives."

"If you want me dead so bad, come and extinguish them."

"I'm trying. Believe me, I am."

"Try harder." Max looked out the window. "Tell me. Why, Aldridge?"

"Me? You have it all wrong. I'm just a cog in the wheel of a larger machine. A machine of control, power, and war. In war, there will always be the disposable ones. Front-line men who have to bite down on a bullet for the greater good. Like you."

"And the innocent people of Chicago?"

"No one is innocent. You should know that by now."

"You better hope your team finds me before I find you."

With that, Max hung up and tossed the phone out the window. It was of no use to him now. It wouldn't prove his innocence. The number would lead to a "not in service" like his work number. His jaw clenched as he gripped the steering wheel tighter. Another piece of the puzzle had fallen into place, but it only raised more questions. What role did Aldridge play in all of this? What was the end game?

As Max drove, his thoughts raced ahead of him. The weight of the gun at his back, the memory of the phone call, and the countdown on his watch all served as constant reminders of the danger he was in and the mysteries he still had to unravel.

Behind him, sirens wailed as the small town was thrown into chaos. Ahead lay uncertainty, danger, and perhaps answers if he was lucky. Max Ryker, or whoever he was, pressed down on the accelerator. There was no turning back now.

27

Jansen pushed out of the black SUV, her eyes immediately drawn to the chaos before her. The once-quiet suburban street, had been transformed into a scene of carnage. Police cruisers were parked haphazardly across the property, their lights still flashing silently. Yellow crime scene tape fluttered in the breeze, cordoning off the area from the growing crowd of onlookers and media personnel.

Her gaze swept over the scene, taking in the EMTs and the somber faces of the local officers. The sight of dead police officers, their bodies still on the ground, sent a shiver of dread through her. She had seen her fair share of crime scenes, but this level of violence in such a peaceful setting was jarring.

As she and Doug approached the house, a Sewickley Borough PD officer intercepted them. "What have we got?" Jansen asked, her voice steady.

The officer's expression was grim, "Besides some of our best guys dead, we've got two deceased unknown males inside. Fake IDs. The owners of the property are Emily and

Noah Sutton. They have one daughter, Mia Sutton. Mrs. Sutton was tight-lipped until her husband spoke up, claiming Max Ryker killed the two men."

"And the cops?" Jansen pressed, her brow furrowing.

"No. They both said those two men inside were responsible," the officer continued. "Strangely enough, she also said Max Ryker is her ex-fiancé. And get this, according to her, the military told her Ryker was killed in action eight years ago. There was a closed-casket funeral. He even has a grave in New York."

Jansen exchanged a glance with Doug. "There was no mention of that in his record when I pulled his file."

The officer nodded. "That's because, according to her, his real name is Andrew McCallister, not Max Ryker. His original name was on the headstone."

Intrigued by this new information, Jansen approached Emily Sutton, who stood near the front porch, her arms wrapped tightly around herself. "Mrs. Sutton. I'm Special Agent Meredith Jansen of the FBI Terrorism Task Force. The officer tells me you think Max Ryker was your ex-fiancé?"

Emily's eyes met Jansen's, a mix of fear and determination in her gaze. "I don't think. He is."

"Can you prove it?"

Without a word, Emily led them into the house and down to the basement. She dug out an old box, rifling through it until she found an envelope. From it, she produced several photographs, handing them to Jansen.

"That was taken in New York twelve years ago," Emily explained, pointing to one photo. "The others were taken here at the house two years later."

Jansen studied the images carefully. There was no

denying the man in the photos looked like Ryker, albeit younger. It was unmistakably him.

"And the military said he was dead?" Jansen asked, her thoughts tumbling over one another.

Emily nodded solemnly.

"Where did he go?"

"I don't know," Emily replied, her voice barely above a whisper.

Jansen's eyes narrowed. "You know it's an offense to lie to law enforcement. Are you lying to me?"

"No," Emily insisted. "He said it was better that I didn't know."

Jansen sighed, handing the photos back. "Well, Mrs. Sutton. Either we are dealing with a chameleon who can change his colors on the fly, or someone has it in for your ex."

As they headed back upstairs, Emily's reply stopped her. "He never bombed that building. The man I knew wouldn't have done that."

Jansen turned, her expression softening slightly. "You're the second person that has told me that. That's for a court to decide."

Outside, Doug approached with new information. "A truck with Chicago license plates matching one stolen was found down the road from here."

Jansen turned to the Sutton family. "Which vehicle did Ryker leave in?"

Before Emily could respond, Noah spoke up. "A black Cadillac. He went that way." He pointed down the street. "I hope you catch him."

"Oh, believe me, Mr. Sutton. I will. I always do," Jansen replied, her determination evident.

As they returned to their vehicle, Jansen felt the familiar

rush of adrenaline that came with closing in on a suspect. “All right, Ryker has been awake for hours. He’s going to be tired. He’s going to make mistakes. When he does, we’ll be there to catch him.”

Doug nodded, matching her pace. “What do you make of all this, Meredith? The ex-fiancée, the supposed death, the different name?”

Jansen shook her head, her mind working overtime to process the new information. “I don’t know. But something doesn’t add up. Ryker’s file was thorough — or so we thought. How does a man with a military funeral and a grave suddenly reappear eight years later as a different person?”

As they climbed into their SUV, Jansen wondered if they were scratching the surface of a much larger conspiracy. The bombing, Ryker’s apparent resurrection, the attack on this quiet suburban home — it all pointed to something far more complex.

“Put out an APB on that Cadillac,” Jansen instructed as Doug started the engine. “And get me everything you can on Andrew McCallister. Birth records, military service, death certificate — everything. If Ryker and McCallister are the same person, I want to know how and why."

As they pulled away from the Sutton residence, leaving behind the flashing lights and yellow tape, Jansen’s mind was already ahead. Ryker — or McCallister — was somewhere, and she was determined to find him. But now, more than ever, she wasn’t sure if she was chasing a terrorist or a victim of something far more sinister.

28

The bustling streets of Chicago held a quiet tension that gripped Charlie Prescott as he stood outside the police precinct. Snowflakes drifted lazily from the gray sky, accumulating on his shoulders and melting into his coffee cup. His eyes darted between his phone and the precinct entrance. He feigned casual interest while his heart raced with anticipation.

The news updates from Sewickley, Pennsylvania, scrolled endlessly on his phone screen. Reports of gunned-down officers and shaky amateur videos of gunfire filled social media feeds. Max Ryker's name was on everyone's lips, now inextricably linked to the carnage. Charlie watched a clip of Special Agent Meredith Jansen, her determined face becoming the symbol of the nationwide manhunt.

As he scrolled, Charlie couldn't help but notice the diverging narratives forming online. Some called for Ryker's head, while others spun elaborate conspiracy theories, painting him as a patsy in a grand cover-up. The conflicting information only fueled Charlie's determination to uncover the truth.

His musings were interrupted by the sight of Shelly emerging from the precinct. Her tight curls bounced as she shivered in the cold, her thin blouse and pencil skirt offering little protection against the winter chill. God, she was gorgeous.

"This is the last time I do this for you, Charlie. I would lose my job if anyone found out," she said.

Charlie grinned, handing her a steaming cup of coffee. "Shelly, you said that last time. Here's your coffee, just the way you like it."

As they exchanged the coffee for a yellow envelope, Shelly's lips curved into a smile. "Why do I continue to do this?"

"For love," Charlie quipped.

"In your dreams," Shelly retorted, turning back towards the warmth of the precinct.

Charlie hurried away into the crowd. He made it around the corner of the next building before he had to look. He pulled out a single sheet of paper with a photo at the top and a full run-down from Clearview, a company that worked with law enforcement using facial recognition.

The cutting-edge technology had been responsible for arrests, investigations, and bringing justice in numerous crimes.

Providing the company with a photo allowed them to quickly and easily conduct identity searches for local persons of interest by matching an image to those found online.

Charlie had given Shelly an enhanced, cleaned-up version of the photo he'd taken of a woman at the bomb site, a person wearing the same overalls as Ryker, a woman who appeared to be watching him from afar. As he couldn't access the full scope of the service provided by Clearview, he'd leveraged Shelly's position within the department.

It had worked, but not in the way he thought.

"What?" he muttered, reading the sheet. He quickly searched online, scrolled a couple of times, then tapped on another website. "No way. That's impossible." He dialed Victoria's number with trembling fingers, pushing aside his guilt over dodging her calls since the article fiasco.

"You son of a bitch, Charlie!" Victoria's voice crackled through the speaker.

"It was an honest mistake," he defended weakly.

"Honest? Don't bullshit a bullshitter."

Charlie stifled a laugh, then quickly sobered. "You're never going to believe this. Remember those photos I took at ground zero?"

"Yes, yes, you managed to snap the suspect," Victoria replied, her voice thick with a cold.

"I got more than that," Charlie pressed on, excitement building in his voice. He explained about the woman in the matching overalls, watching Ryker from afar. "I had my contact run her image through Clearview. There was only one photo of her found online. One. She's younger in the photo, but it's definitely her."

"And?" Victoria prodded, her interest piqued despite her irritation.

"It was found on an obituaries website. According to the site, the woman died over thirty-six years ago in a car accident with her husband. It says she is survived by her two-year-old son, Andrew McCallister."

"And her name?"

"Julie McCallister."

"Okay, that's odd, but—"

Charlie cut her off, his words tumbling out in a rush. "I'm not done. I looked up Andrew McCallister. Turns out he's dead too. Passed away eight years ago while in military service and was buried in upstate New York. But here's the kicker — the photo I'm looking at of him on a funeral website is the spitting image of Max Ryker. Unless he has a twin, this incident just became a lot more interesting."

The line went silent momentarily before Victoria's voice returned, tight with barely contained excitement. "Who else knows about this?"

"Besides me and you? My contact."

"Charlie, if I was there right now, I don't know whether I would punch or kiss you."

He couldn't help but smile at that.

"Find out everything you can about the McCallisters. This is going to be the story of the century," she said.

As the call ended, Charlie stared at the photo of Andrew McCallister, his mind reeling with possibilities. "Who are you?" he muttered before rejoining the flow of pedestrians on the busy Chicago street.

As he walked, the puzzle pieces began to shift in Charlie's mind. The woman at the bombing site — Julie McCallister — supposedly dead for over three decades. Her son Andrew bears an uncanny resemblance to Max Ryker, who is also reportedly deceased. A web of contradictions and impossibilities made his journalistic instincts tingle.

Charlie ducked into a nearby coffee shop, seeking warmth and a quiet place to think. As he settled into a corner booth, he spread the documents from Shelly and pulled out his laptop. The café's ambient noise faded as he dove deeper into his research.

He started with Julie McCallister's obituary, cross-referencing details with public records. The car accident that supposedly claimed her life was documented, but something felt off. Charlie dug deeper, looking for any inconsistencies or loose threads.

Next, he turned his attention to Andrew McCallister. Military records were more challenging to access, but Charlie had his ways. He scoured news articles, social media posts, and public databases for any other mentions of Andrew's service or death.

As he worked, a pattern began to emerge. There were gaps in the records, moments where the official narrative didn't quite align with reality. It was as if someone had carefully constructed a false history but hadn't made it airtight.

Charlie stared at the photo of Andrew McCallister, his mind reeling from what he'd uncovered. The connection between the supposedly dead Julie McCallister and Max Ryker was tenuous but intriguing. And the fact that Andrew McCallister—who should be around Ryker's age—was also reportedly deceased yet bore a striking resemblance to the bombing suspect... it was almost too coincidental.

He glanced at his watch, realizing hours had passed since he'd entered the café. The story was far from complete, but he knew he was onto something potentially big. There were too many questions and inconsistencies in the official narratives left unanswered.

Stepping back into the snowy Chicago day, Charlie pulled his coat tighter around him. He knew he was treading into dangerous territory, questioning official accounts and potentially uncovering secrets that influential people might want to keep hidden.

29

Max's heart pounded as he approached Pittsburgh Union Station, the imposing twelve-story building loomed over him. Clad in brown brick and terracotta, the structure embodied early twentieth-century architecture, with its central atrium allowing light to penetrate the main area. The crowning parapet, adorned with escutcheons and urns, gave the building a regal air.

Every step felt like it could be his last. Max kept his head down, his weathered coat pulled tight around his ears, and his beanie cap pulled low. The heavy snowfall provided some cover, but he felt a constant unease that every pair of eyes was on him, recognizing his face from the news broadcasts that had been playing non-stop.

Inside the station, Max joined the line at the ticket office, acutely aware of the security camera in the corner of the room. Sweat beaded on his forehead and trickled down his face despite the winter chill. He knew buying a ticket here was risky, putting him out in the open longer, but it was better than presenting I.D. to a conductor on the train.

"What time is the next train to Washington, D.C.?" Max asked, his voice low and gruff.

She glanced at her screen. "That would be the Amtrak Capitol Limited. It usually picks people up at around five, but it's running six hours late."

"Why?"

"A brake line failure in Chicago."

The woman behind the plexiglass snapped gum and returned to looking utterly disinterested before she handed over the ticket without a second glance. Max breathed a small sigh of relief as he headed onto the platform, joining the sea of faces waiting for the train.

As he waited, his nerves kicked into high gear. The train would arrive shortly, but the fifteen-minute boarding delay would feel like an eternity. Every passing second increased the risk of discovery. Time seemed to slow.

FINALLY, the rumble of the approaching train in the distance sent a wave of relief through Max.

The Amtrak Capitol Limited pulled into the station with a screech of metal on metal. The smell of diesel fuel mixed with the crisp winter air as passengers began to board. Max moved with the crowd, his eyes constantly scanning for any sign of law enforcement.

Once on board, Max quickly found his private superliner roomette. He slid the door closed, finally allowing himself to sink into the seat with an exhale. Through the window, he watched more passengers board, his eyes darting between the platform and his watch.

"C'mon, c'mon," he muttered, willing the train to depart.

Ten minutes from Sewickley, Thomas Reeves sat in the helicopter, his mind focused on the task. The radio crackled to life with an update that made his pulse quicken.

"We've got a hit using facial recognition. There's been an identification match on Ryker at Pittsburgh Union Station," Jansen said.

Reeves leaned forward. "What's the next train out of there?"

"The Capitol Limited heading for Washington. The next stop is in Connellsville, the one after that is Cumberland."

"Has the train left yet?"

"Not yet. We're en route to Pittsburgh Union Station. Reeves, how far out are you?" Jansen asked.

"About ten minutes."

"Head to Connellsville. I'll have local P.D. there meet you. Either way, we've got him!"

"Roger that!" he replied.

As the pilot moved to change course, Reeves stopped him. "No. Get me close to Union Station."

"But Jansen said."

"I don't work for Jansen," Reeves cut him off. "Now go."

Back in his roomette, Max leaned his head against the window, exhaustion threatening to overtake him. His rigorous training in the Special Forces had taught him to function on minimal sleep, but even he had his limits. He closed his eyes, allowing himself a moment of rest.

His mind drifted to Emily and Mia, to the life stolen from

him. Questions swirled in his head: Why had the Division done this? What was on the file that was worth killing for? What had really happened in Croatia?

The biometric USB in his pocket felt like a lead weight, so close to providing answers yet still frustratingly out of reach. What was his connection to Carol Kingsley? She was a target they'd been assigned to bring in, a person wanted for espionage and stealing state secrets. And yet, everything he'd learned so far would have indicated he was working with her on some level and that whatever that file contained was too valuable and risky to send or give to a journalist in the States.

Carol didn't trust anyone, especially those on American soil. Max remembered Edward Snowden, the former American intelligence contractor and whistleblower who had leaked classified documents. Snowden could have sent them to someone in the USA, but instead, he fled, arranging to meet with journalists abroad out of fear of immediate arrest and U.S. government interference. He'd wanted international attention, to seek asylum, and to maintain control over the narrative.

"Was that it, Carol?" Max thought. "You didn't trust the Division or anyone in places of power. But why? What had you discovered?"

Right then, Max heard a commotion outside the train. His eyes fluttered open, and his pulse sped up at three local P.D. officers elbowing their way through the final group of passengers boarding. There was purpose and urgency in their movement. They were coming for him, of that, he was sure.

Before he could decide what to do, the train hissed and shifted and pulled away from the station. As it picked up speed, Max saw more officers emerge from the station onto the platform, joined by FBI Agent Jansen. Their frustrated expressions faded into the distance as the train accelerated, carrying Max towards Washington and, hopefully, some answers.

Max's pulse ticked up as he watched the figures on the platform grow smaller. He had narrowly escaped the officers on the platform, but the danger was far from over. He tensed as he remembered the local P.D. officers he'd seen boarding just before departure. They would be searching the train at this very moment.

He shifted into high gear, adrenaline coursing through his veins. He couldn't afford to relax or let his guard down. His eyes darted around the small roomette, thinking of all potential escape routes.

He knew he couldn't stay in one place for too long. The police would likely start a car-by-car search soon. Max began formulating a plan, considering how to move through the train without drawing attention to himself. He'd need to blend in with the other passengers. As the Pennsylvania landscape rushed by outside the window, Max steeled himself for what was sure to be a tense and dangerous journey. The answers he sought in Washington seemed tantalizingly close and frustratingly far away. But first, he had to survive the next few minutes on this train.

30

The Amtrak Capitol Limited surged through the snowy Pennsylvania landscape, its rhythmic clatter providing a soothing backdrop to the tension building inside. Sweat trickled down his temple as Max stepped out of his roomette, his senses on high alert. He moved swiftly through the narrow aisle, passing through two cars before reaching the dining area. Through the glass, he spotted an officer approaching, methodically checking faces. Max's instincts kicked in, and he quickly retreated towards the front of the train.

As he passed his room, his blood ran cold at the sight of two more officers heading his way. "Shit," he muttered under his breath.

Everything he'd done up to now had been to avoid harming innocents. The thought of hiding in his roomette and feigning sleep crossed his mind, but he dismissed it immediately. It was too early in the day; such behavior would only raise suspicion. Despite every muscle in his body crying out for rest, he knew he couldn't afford that luxury.

With the police closing in from both directions, Max realized he had no choice but to confront the situation head-on. He made a split-second decision, heading towards the lone officer making his way from the rear of the train. Spotting a bathroom, Ryker ducked inside and waited, his heart thundering in his ears.

The knock came, as expected. “Pittsburgh PD, open up.”

“In use,” Max called out, trying to keep his voice steady.

“Identify yourself,” the officer demanded.

Max gave a fake name, listening intently as the officer radioed his colleagues. He could hear the cop positioning himself outside the door, waiting for Max to emerge.

Thinking quickly, Max sprang into action. He plugged the toilet with paper towels and flushed, then filled the sink with tissue and let the water overflow onto the floor. As the water began seeping under the door, he unlatched it and stepped out, his back turned to the officer.

“Shit. The damn toilet is overflowing,” Max exclaimed, catching the officer off guard.

THE MOMENT of surprise was all Max needed. In a flurry of motion, he elbowed the cop in the gut, struck him in the face, and shoved him into the flooded bathroom. Before the officer could recover, Max had him in a chokehold, quickly rendering him unconscious.

His hands moved swiftly, snatching the radio from the unconscious officer. He partially latched the bathroom door, ensuring it would lock when fully closed. The radio crackled with chatter as the other two officers continued their search.

With his brain on high alert, Max approached the rear

cars, constantly looking over his shoulder. His focus on not getting caught left him vulnerable, and he didn't notice the woman until it was too late. The cold gun barrel pressed into his side as she stepped out of her seat.

"Unless you want these good people to die, smile and head on back to your room," she said, her voice low and threatening.

Ryker glanced down, noting the silencer on the end of her gun. As he turned his head to face her, a flood of memories rushed back. Somehow, he knew this woman — dark-haired, Asian, her face familiar even if he couldn't immediately place her name.

Reluctantly, Max headed back towards his room.

"Yuki Katsumi," he said, the name suddenly clicking into place.

"And I was told you wouldn't remember," she replied, a hint of surprise in her voice.

"How could I forget a team member?" he responded.

As they walked, the train cars shifted back and forth. Max's training kicked in as he assessed ways to disarm her. But he knew Yuki was just as skilled as he was — any move would be risky.

They entered the roomette, and Yuki closed the door behind them. "Sit," she commanded, keeping the gun trained on him as she took the seat opposite.

"You know, two cops will be coming by in a minute," Max said, trying to buy time.

Yuki's smile was cold. "No. Right about now, they're face to face in a bathroom stall with the blood draining out of them." She paused, letting the implication sink in. "My colleague," she added. "Of course, the evidence will point to you. Which reminds me," she held out her hand. "Your gun. Slowly."

Max tossed over his weapon, his mind working fast to find a way out of the situation. “So you’re one of Aldridge’s lap dogs?” he asked, probing for information.

“Aren’t we all?” Yuki replied cryptically.

“You know how it ended for Virgil.”

“Like I told Aldridge — never send a man to do a woman’s job.”

Max leaned forward slightly. “If they would dispose of me so easily, what do you think they will do to you?”

Yuki’s expression remained impassive. “If they wanted me dead, they would have done it after Croatia. I didn’t make the mistake you did.”

“And that would be?”

“Working with a target.”

A frown crossed his face, confusion evident.

“You really don’t remember, do you?” Yuki said, a hint of pity in her voice.

“What is this about?” Max pressed her, frustration building.

“You should know. Croatia was your baby.”

He shook his head. “I don’t know what you’re talking about.”

“Come on, Ryker. Don’t play dumb. The exchange. The file. Where is it?”

He shrugged, genuinely at a loss.

“Oh well, I guess it doesn’t matter now,” Yuki said, her tone mocking.

“So, you going to shoot me?” Max asked, his voice level despite the danger.

“Eventually, but someone wants to talk to you first.”

Without taking her eyes off him or her finger off the trigger, Yuki pulled out a phone. She dialed a number and tossed it to him.

Max brought the phone to his ear and heard a familiar voice on the other end. Aldridge.

"Ryker. The last time we talked, you were full of so much spit and vinegar. It appears my team found you first. How are things looking now?"

Max's jaw clenched, but he kept his voice steady. "Oh, you know, assessing my options."

A chuckle came from the other end of the line.

THE ROAR of the helicopter's rotors filled Thomas Reeves' ears as he peered down at the Amtrak Capitol Limited, snaking its way through the snowy Pennsylvania landscape. His heart pumping with a mixture of adrenaline and determination.

"Get me closer," Reeves commanded, his eyes never leaving the train below.

The pilot's voice crackled through the headset, disbelief evident in his tone. "You can't be serious."

"I want on that train," Reeves insisted.

"It's too dangerous. The turbulence and updraft could—"

"Get me down there!" Reeves yelled, cutting off the pilot's protests.

Reluctantly, the pilot descended, bringing the helicopter closer to the moving train. Reeves watched intently, assessing the situation. The train had reached what appeared to be its full speed, typically around 80 mph for safety reasons, though Reeves knew it could potentially go faster.

As they drew nearer, the truth of the situation began to sink in. This was far from realistic. There were too many variables at play — the danger of falling, the need to match speed and position, not to mention the technical challenges of avoiding a rotor strike, or the limitations of accessing a moving train car.

Just as they seemed to be in position, the pilot suddenly veered away, pulling the helicopter back to a safer altitude.

"What are you doing?" Reeves demanded, frustration evident in his voice.

The pilot's response was firm. "You might not care about risking your life, but you're not risking mine."

"Get back there," Reeves ordered, his tone leaving no room for argument.

But the pilot ignored him, continuing to veer away from the train. Reeves clenched his fists, watching as the distance between them and the train grew.

31

As Max held the phone to his ear, Aldridge's voice crackled through, dripping with smug satisfaction. "You knew it would end this way. It should have happened much earlier, but what can you do? Due to Virgil's little screw-up, Katsumi has landed the clean-up deal. It has to be clean. Can't have people thinking our terrorist here only had aspirations of killing a few cops."

Max's jaw clenched, as he thought of Aldridge's words. The man continued, his tone almost gleeful. "Oh no. You see, right about now, your old teammate, Declan, has put a bullet in the engineer's skull and taken control of the locomotive. By the time the train derails and they find your body, it will all be chalked up as another act of terrorism. A train out of control, a man suffering from PTSD who ended up taking his own life and the lives of so many Americans. A coward taking the easy way out. Can't get much cleaner than that."

"I think you've forgotten about Virgil and his pal," Ryker countered, trying to keep his voice steady despite the growing dread in his stomach. "Quite the wrench in the works."

Aldridge chuckled. “Not really. Reports are adjusted, and errors are corrected. We’re in the business of making things go away. But you don’t remember that, do you?” There was a pause, heavy with unspoken threats.

“I thought you wanted the file,” Max said.

“You have it?”

“Bring me in, and I’ll give it to you.”

“I don't think so. Goodbye, Ryker.” The line went dead.

As Max went to hand back the cell phone, the train suddenly jerked forward, seeming to pick up speed. The sudden motion caught both him and Katsumi off guard. Max fell forward while Katsumi fell back, her gun hand pivoting up. In that split second, he saw his opening and took it.

Max lunged forward with lightning-fast reflexes honed by years of training, grabbing Katsumi’s wrist. The gun erupted, two rounds punching holes in the ceiling as he struggled to control her wrist. His other hand clamped around her throat, fighting for leverage in the confined space of the roomette.

The train shifted violently this time, causing Katsumi to fall forward. Despite her smaller size, she was nimble and highly trained. She drove her knee into Max’s stomach, knocking the wind out of him. He countered with an elbow to her face, feeling the crunch of cartilage as he connected with her nose.

Their bodies slammed into the window, the impact causing the gun to discharge once more. The bullet shattered the glass, sending a rush of freezing air and snow into the compartment. The howling wind added to the chaos as they grappled for control.

Seizing the moment, Max managed to slam Katsumi’s wrist against the jagged edge of the broken window. She cried out in pain, her grip on the gun loosening. With a final twist, the weapon flew from her grasp, disappearing into the snowy landscape rushing by outside.

But the loss of her gun didn't slow Katsumi down. If anything, it seemed to fuel her fury. What followed was a brutal, close-quarters fight for survival. Despite her size, Katsumi was a formidable opponent, her skills in hand-to-hand combat rivaling Max's.

Flashes of memory surged through his mind — images of Katsumi taking down men twice her size in training exercises, her movements fluid and deadly. She struck at his neck with the edge of her hand, a blow that would have incapacitated a lesser opponent. Max barely deflected it, countering with quick jabs to her midsection.

Katsumi twisted her body like a pretzel as she maneuvered around him. Before Max could react, she was on his back, her arms snaking around his neck in a chokehold. The confined space of the roomette worked against him as he tried to shake her off, slamming back and forth against the walls.

Black spots danced at the edges of Max's vision as Katsumi tightened her grip. Desperation fueling his actions, he threw himself backward, using all his strength to slam Katsumi's head against one of the overhead bins. The impact was enough to loosen her hold, allowing him to break free.

What happened next was a blur of motion, instinct, and training taking over. Max spun around, grasping Katsumi's hand and twisting her arm behind her back. With a powerful thrust, he drove her toward the shattered window.

Katsumi teetered on the edge, the wind whipping her hair wildly. For a moment, it seemed she would fall, but her free hand shot out, grasping the edge of the window frame. Blood streamed from her palm where the sharp glass bit into her flesh, but still, she held on.

With a surge of strength born of desperation, Katsumi thrust herself back. Her head connected with Max's face, sending a burst of pain through his nose. But he held firm, using momentum against her. As he pushed forward, he drove her head toward the jagged glass clinging to the window frame.

There was a sickening sound as the glass sliced across Katsumi's neck. Her body went limp almost instantly, the fight draining out of her along with her lifeblood. Max released his grip, watching as her body slumped to the floor in a rapidly expanding pool of crimson.

For a moment, he stood there, chest heaving, the reality of what had just transpired washing over him. The wind howled through the broken window, carrying flecks of snow that melted in contact with the warm blood coating the floor.

But there was no time to process the horror of the situation. Aldridge's words echoed in his mind — Declan in the locomotive, the impending derailment, hundreds of innocent lives at stake. Max knew he had to move and fast.

Stepping out of Katsumi's blood, he made his way to the roomette's door. He paused, listening intently for any sign of the other officers who had been searching for him earlier. The corridor outside seemed quiet, but he knew that could change at any moment.

His thoughts went into overdrive as he formulated a plan. He needed to get to the locomotive, stop Declan, and prevent the derailment. But how could he do that without being spotted by the remaining law enforcement on board — if there were any others? And what about the passengers? If

Aldridge's plan was to frame this as an act of terrorism, there was no telling what other surprises might be waiting.

Taking a deep breath, Max steeled himself for what was to come. He may not have remembered everything about his past, who he was, or what he had done. But at this moment, he knew with absolute certainty that he was the only thing standing between these innocent passengers and a fiery death.

With one last glance at Katsumi's lifeless form, he stepped out into the corridor. The train continued to pick up speed, the countryside outside becoming a blur of white. Time was running out. Whatever came next, Ryker knew it would define not just his fate but the fate of everyone on board.

32

The scream of metal against metal pierced the air as the Amtrak Capitol Limited careened around a sharp bend, its speed far beyond what the tracks were designed to handle. Max gripped the walls, his knuckles white with tension. His heart pounded, his senses on high alert as he walked through the various cars. The rhythmic clacking of wheels on tracks was punctuated by the occasional lurch and sway of the train, a constant reminder of the danger.

Max could feel the tension as he moved from the sleeper cars to the café car. Passengers chatted nervously, their eyes darting to the windows where the world outside had become nothing more than a white blur. The smell of coffee and pastries from the café car seemed jarringly out of place given the circumstances.

As he entered the coach car, Max's blood ran cold. There, making his way forward with purposeful strides, was Declan Lynch. The sight of his former colleague sent a jolt of recognition through Max. Lynch was American, but his Irish roots were evident in the slight lilt to his voice and the fiery glint in his eyes. They had crossed paths multiple times before, working with different teams. Max knew Lynch was as dangerous as they came.

Instinctively, Max's hand moved to his gun, but Lynch was quicker. In one fluid motion, he grabbed a teenage girl from her seat, his arm snaking around her neck as he pressed a gun to her temple. The girl's eyes widened with terror, a tiny whimper escaping her lips.

Screams erupted throughout the car as panic set in. Some passengers hurried towards Max, their faces contorted with fear, while others remained frozen in their seats, terror etched into every line of their faces.

Lynch's voice carried over the chaos, a hint of amusement in his tone. "How you doing, chief? Been a while." His eyes gleamed with a predatory light while fear radiated from his hostage.

The train jostled violently, nearly throwing Max off balance. His hand twitched on his gun, eyes locked on Lynch and the terrified girl in his grasp. Max felt a rush of thoughts, calculating the odds, looking for any opening that wouldn't put the girl in more danger.

"Steady," Lynch warned, tightening his grip on the girl. She winced as he pressed the gun harder against her temple. "We wouldn't want this girl's brains to end up all over her mother."

Max's gaze flicked between the child and her mother, whose face was streaked with tears. The woman's hands were clasped over her mouth, muffling her sobs as she watched her daughter's life hang in the balance. The weight of the situation pressed down on Max, the lives of everyone on the train hanging by a thread.

"Now, I'm guessing Katsumi's left the building." Lynch smirked. "Always said she couldn't walk the talk." He paused, his eyes never leaving Max's.

Lynch's voice dropped lower, taking on an almost conspiratorial tone. "I must say, it's good to see you again. You know, many said you were the best at what you did. A real team leader. Though you probably can't remember that." His eyes narrowed slightly. "You can imagine my surprise when I heard they put a target on your back." Another pause, heavy with implication. "Damn shame."

Max's jaw clenched as he tried to piece together the fragments of his past. "The Division isn't who they say they are," he growled.

Lynch's laugh was cold, devoid of any real humor. "Is anyone in our line of business?" He shook his head, a mock expression of disappointment on his face. "Guys like us don't have many options. But here's the thing about war, Max. Everyone thinks they're the good guys." He paused, his voice dropping to barely above a whisper. "At the end of the day, none of it matters. Only the stories spun after."

"Keep telling yourself that," Max shot back, his voice tight with anger. He could feel the weight of his remembered and forgotten choices pressing down on him.

"Everyone is telling themselves lies, even you, Max." Lynch's eyes narrowed, a hint of something almost like pity crossing his face. "You and I are hired hands, nothing more. We eliminate threats. You have innocent blood on your hands just as much as I do." He gestured around the car with his free hand, the gun momentarily leaving the girl's head. Max tensed, ready to act, but Lynch was too quick; the weapon was back in place before Max could move.

"You think society cares about what we do in secret?"

Lynch continued, his voice rising slightly. "They don't. They're terrified of people like you and me. And they should be. No oversight. No one pulling in the reins. We are wild cards. Contract killers, paid to make problems go away."

Max's grip on his gun tightened, his knuckles white with the strain. "Yeah, and what problem goes away by killing these people?" He gestured to the terrified passengers around them, his voice thick with disgust.

Lynch's smile was chilling, devoid of any warmth. "You, Max. You." He paused, letting the words sink in. "Besides, what difference does it make how they die? They're all just faces in a sea of faces. Everyone dies eventually."

The world outside continued rushing by, nothing more than a blur of white and gray. The train's speed increased with each passing moment, the vibrations growing more intense. Max could feel the situation spiraling out of control, much like the train itself.

"Looks like you're behind schedule," Max said, noticing Lynch's watch beeping. He sneered at the other man, a surge of defiance rising in his chest.

"You made the wrong choice. The Division gave you a life," Lynch said.

"No, they took it," Max corrected, his hand twitching on his gun.

The girl in Lynch's grasp whimpered again, her eyes pleading with Max.

"Steady, Max." Lynch's voice was calm, almost soothing.

Max searched for a way out of this standoff. "Why? Everyone dies eventually, right? That's what you said."

Lynch's eyes narrowed, a flicker of doubt crossing his face for just a moment. "You can't stop it."

In a sudden move that caught everyone off guard, Lynch

shoved the girl towards Max and ducked through the doorway. Max's reflexes kicked in, his gun coming up as he fired. But Lynch was already gone, the door slamming shut behind him with a resounding bang that echoed through the car.

Max rushed forward. The door was locked, the mechanism jammed. Without hesitation, he fired multiple rounds at the glass. The sound of shattering glass mixed with the screams of terrified passengers. Shards flew everywhere as Max reached through the broken window, fumbling for the lock on the other side.

The train's violent motion nearly threw him off balance as he pushed through into the baggage car. Luggage tumbled from overhead compartments, creating an obstacle course of suitcases and bags. Max navigated through the chaos, his eyes scanning for any sign of Lynch.

As he reached the next door, he saw Lynch's smirking face before the man disappeared to the left. Max unloaded on the window, glass exploding outward as he cleared a path to open the door. The rush of cold air hit him like a physical blow as he stepped out onto the small platform between cars.

They were crossing a bridge, the icy waters of a river churning far below. Just as Max's eyes adjusted to the brightness outside, he saw Lynch dive off the train from above. A base jumper's chute blossomed open, the wind catching it and lifting Lynch away from the speeding train.

For a brief, tempting moment, Max considered following suit.

The idea of diving into the waters below, escaping this nightmare, was almost overwhelming. But the thought of all the passengers facing certain death in a derailment steeled his resolve. He couldn't abandon them, not now.

Pushing forward against the icy wind, Max entered the

locomotive car. His heart sank at the sight of the engineer, slumped over with a single bullet wound to his temple. "Shit," he muttered, his eyes darting to the controls and then to the tracks ahead.

The path wound through the valley to Washington, a snaking route that, at their current speed, would inevitably lead to disaster. Max tried to recall any information about train operations. He engaged the throttle lever, moving it through the notches past neutral to the braking setting, but nothing changed. The train continued to barrel forward, picking up speed with each passing second.

Desperate, he grabbed the radio, hoping to reach dispatch or anyone who could help. But the radio had been torn from its mount, leaving only dead air. They were on their own.

Knowing he needed help, Max sprinted back through the coach cars, his eyes searching for anyone who might know how to stop the train. Passengers cried out to him as he passed, begging for information, help, or any sign that they might survive. At the rear of a car, he spotted a conductor, the man's uniform a beacon of hope in the chaos.

"You! Here!" Max shouted, gesturing urgently for the man to follow him. The conductor hurried up, his face pale with fear, sweat beading on his forehead despite the chill in the air.

"Do you know how to slow or stop this train?" Max asked urgently, his words coming out in a rush.

"The throttle?" the conductor suggested, his voice shaking slightly.

"Doesn't work," Max replied grimly, watching the color drain from the conductor's face.

The man gave a wary look and hurried forward, his movements betraying a mix of training and sheer panic. "They give us limited training for emergency situations if an engineer is incapacitated," he explained as they moved, "but I've never run into a situation where the PTC didn't kick in."

"The what?" Max pressed, grasping at any potential solution.

The conductor launched into an explanation about a dead-switch system, a fail-safe designed to stop the train if the engineer became incapacitated. But as they both looked at the lifeless body of the engineer, slumped over the controls, it was clear that the system had failed spectacularly.

After he tried the throttle again without success, the conductor's face paled further, his eyes wide with growing horror. "It's jammed. Shit. The PTC system should have kicked in by now and applied the emergency brakes."

"PTC?" Max asked, desperate for any information that might help them avert disaster.

"Positive Train Control," the conductor explained, his words coming faster now as the urgency of the situation pressed in on them. "It automatically stops a train before a potential accident without human intervention. The onboard system analyzes data and detects safety threats, excessive speed, etc."

"Yeah, well, it's not doing its job," Max said, frustration evident in his voice. He ran a hand through his hair, his mind flipping through possible solutions.

"Maybe it's delayed," the conductor suggested weakly, but the lack of conviction in his voice was clear.

"Forget it. It's sabotaged," Max said, thinking of Lynch and the meticulous planning that must have gone into this attack. He glanced back at the baggage car as luggage crashed around from the train's violent motion.

Max moved back to the space between the locomotive

and the cars behind, racking his brain for any possible solution. He had to act fast; every second brought them closer to disaster. "Is there a way to disconnect the locomotive from the passenger cars?" he said, more to himself than to the conductor.

The conductor's eyes lit up slightly, a glimmer of hope in the midst of chaos. "There is. The coupling system. It's mechanical. It uses a cut lever. Once the lever is in the up position, it allows the knuckle to open. The trouble is, once one car joins to the other, the knuckle closes."

"So there's no way to open it while in motion?" Max asked, his mind already formulating a dangerous plan.

The conductor hesitated, clearly torn between protocol and the dire circumstances they found themselves in. "Theoretically, using the cut lever while the train is in motion is possible. However, it would be extremely dangerous. It's on the outside of the train, and the force acting on the coupler might make it difficult to operate the lever. Even if it works to separate the cars, it could lead to a potential derailment."

Max looked out at the snowy landscape rushing by, weighing the risks in his mind. "Well, if we do nothing, derailment will happen anyway. So how does it work?"

The conductor swallowed hard before continuing. "The air brake system is designed to be fail-safe, meaning if there is any separation of the train, the automatic emergency brake should be applied. Something to do with air pressure going through the hoses which are linked through all the cars."

"Should?" Max pressed, picking up on the uncertainty in the conductor's voice.

"No guarantee," the man admitted, his face grim.

Max nodded, his decision made. "Well, it's better than nothing. Where's the cut lever?"

"I'll show you," the conductor said, moving towards the rear of the locomotive. "But I wouldn't go out there. It's suicide."

"Neither would I if we had any other options," Max replied.

The conductor showed him an exit point and gave him a rough idea of what to look for. "It's a dark bar. Pull up on it. But please, be careful. This is insane."

Max nodded the weight of what he was about to attempt settling on his shoulders. "Go into the cars and tell the passengers to move to the back of the train."

Max took a deep breath as the conductor hurried off to warn the passengers, steeling himself for what was to come. He moved towards the exit, his hand on the door handle, feeling the vibrations of the speeding train through the metal.

With one last look back at the relative safety of the locomotive's interior, Max pushed the door open. The rush of wind and snow nearly knocked him off his feet as he stepped out onto the small platform. The cold gnawed at his skin, the wind whipping at his clothes as he clung to the train's exterior.

Max's eyes scanned the coupling mechanism, searching for the lever the conductor had described. The world around him was a blur of white and gray, the noise of the train drowning out everything else. He spotted the dark bar of the cut lever, just out of reach.

Gritting his teeth, Max began to lower himself, one hand gripping the train's exterior for dear life as he reached for the lever with the other. "Come on, you son of a bitch!" he growled through clenched teeth, his fingers straining to reach the bar.

Suddenly, the train hit a rough patch of track. Max's grip slipped, and for a heart-stopping moment, he felt himself falling. His stomach lurched as he saw the ground rushing by beneath him, certain that this was the end. At the last second, his hand found purchase on a protruding piece of metal. He hung there, legs dangling precariously over the tracks, the wind threatening to tear him away at any moment.

With a grunt of effort that was lost in the train's roar, Max pulled himself back up. His muscles screamed in protest, the cold numbing his fingers.

Once again, he reached for the lever, his movements more desperate now. His fingers brushed against the cold metal — so close, yet still out of reach. The train took another sharp turn, and Max slammed against the car. Pain exploded in his shoulder, but he held on, refusing to let go.

With one final, herculean effort, Max threw all his weight towards the lever. For a moment, nothing happened. The bar refused to budge, frozen in place by ice and the incredible forces acting on the coupling. Max could feel his strength failing, his grip weakening as the cold and exhaustion took their toll.

Just as he was about to give up, the train hit a bump in the tracks. The jolt provided the extra force needed, and suddenly, the lever gave way. Max felt it move upward, the mechanism releasing with a loud clank that was nearly lost in the roar of the wind and the screech of metal on metal.

The locomotive jerked away from the passenger cars, almost dislodging Max from his precarious position. He looked up to see the passenger cars trailing off into the distance, the conductor's shocked face visible in the open door of the nearest car.

A wave of relief washed over Max as he expected the locomotive to slow due to air pressure release, but to his horror, it was still moving fast, if not quicker, now that it was free of the weight of the passenger cars.

As the locomotive took a sharp corner at breakneck speed, Max felt the wheels leave the track. Time seemed to slow as the locomotive tilted, throwing him from his perch. He was airborne for what felt like an eternity, the world spinning in a blur of white snow.

Then, with a bone-chilling splash, Max plunged into the icy river below. The cold hit him like a physical blow, driving the air from his lungs. As he sank into the murky depths, the world around him faded. Everything went black, the roar of the derailing train fading into an eerie, muffled silence beneath the water's surface.

33

The steady hum of the vending machine echoed in the room as Jansen reached down to retrieve her coffee. The sterile hallways of Johns Hopkins Hospital bustled with activity. Multiple police officers and FBI agents huddled in small groups, their hushed conversations creating a low buzz of tension.

"I don't want to hear it. You disobeyed a direct order," Jansen said, her voice tight with frustration as she turned to face Reeves.

Reeves stood his ground, his posture defiant. "I don't take my orders from you."

"This is a federal investigation; you work with us," she retorted, a flash of anger in her eyes. "You put the life of a helicopter pilot in jeopardy, not to mention those on that train if that helicopter had collided with it."

Reeves snorted dismissively. "We pulled out."

"Yes, because of Mack's common sense." Jansen took a sip of her coffee, grimacing at the bitter taste.

"Look, am I the only one who is not insane? Do I need to

remind you that Ryker killed three police officers onboard that train!?"

"Allegedly," Jansen countered. "We haven't gotten ballistics back on that or security footage from onboard the train."

"You can't be serious. We are dealing with a killer here."

"Not according to passengers. There was someone else onboard that train."

"Yeah, where are they?" Reeves challenged.

"Regardless, he saved lives," another FBI agent chimed in.

Reeves roared with laughter, his voice dripping with sarcasm. "Oh, praise the Lord. From terrorist to hero. Only in America! Well, that just makes everything better. Let's roll out the red carpet, shall we?" He raised a finger in the air, mockingly. "Hey Eric, prepare a hero's welcome when Ryker leaves the hospital. Craig, call the media, as they'll want this for a heart-touching segment." His laughter faded, replaced by a stern look. "The only thing that man did was save his own neck. He had no choice; what was he going to do... Jump from a high-speed moving train!? Wake up, Agent Jansen! Hundreds are dead in Chicago because of him. There is a trail of bloodshed all across this country because of him."

"And yet he never pulled the trigger on me or killed those officers back in Sewickley," Jansen pointed out.

"You still think he's clean."

"We're still waiting on camera footage from before and after the bombing. Innocent until proven guilty, right? Of course, unless you can explain why your deadly killer has gone out of his way to avoid killing innocents, while on the other hand, we have two unidentified dead men who went out of their way to kill officers in Sewickley to get to Ryker."

"Allegedly," Reeves threw back, mimicking her earlier tone.

From the corner of her eye, Jansen spotted Doug entering. "You got the records on Andrew McCallister?"

Doug nodded, falling in step with her as she took the files from him and exited the waiting area. "You won't believe some of the stuff inside this."

Jansen noticed Reeves was following. "Going somewhere, Reeves?"

"Checking in on our suspect."

"Don't bother, he's out cold. If you're so determined to nail him, maybe you should busy yourself with following up with our team on the security camera footage from both the train and bomb site."

She walked on, leaving him behind. "Keep an eye on him," she muttered to Doug.

"You don't trust him?"

"Do you trust a baby to stay home alone?"

"Oh, c'mon, I'm no babysitter."

She grinned as she headed down the hall to a room guarded by two Maryland police officers. Entering the room, Jansen was greeted by the steady beep of the ECG machine. Ryker lay motionless on the hospital bed, tubes snaking from his nose and arm. The sterile smell of disinfectant dominated, mingling with the faint scent of flowers from a small vase on the bedside table.

Jansen sat in an armchair on the far side of the room, close to the end of the bed. She glanced at Ryker before thumbing her way through the newly pulled records. "Hmm," she muttered, looking up at him. "McCallister, Ryker, who the hell are you, and how did you get yourself in this mess?"

Tiredness kicked in, her eyes finally giving way after the longest night. At some point, Jansen fell asleep. She awoke to the sound of someone coughing. Looking up, she saw Ryker leaning over to his side table to get a drink of water. He caught her looking at him.

"Where am I?" he asked, his voice hoarse.

"Johns Hopkins Hospital in Maryland. You're in the Critical Care Tower." She paused. "But of course, you're familiar with this place, as you were born here. At least, Max Ryker was." She opened the folder in front of her. "Andrew McCallister is another story entirely, right? He was born to Julia and Michael McCallister in a hospital in Saratoga Springs in upstate New York. Your mother was a language teacher, your father a politician. Unfortunately, both were killed in a collision on a snowy day thirty-six years ago. Of course, you were too young to remember any of this. You were placed into the foster system. Lived some of your young years in a group home. Eventually, you were adopted by Harry Redding and his wife, a man whose ties to the political world eventually brought him to Washington, D.C. You joined the military straight out of high school. You were a helicopter pilot before you went on to the Special Forces. You entered into a relationship with Emily years later, before your eventual death overseas in combat. From there things go a little blurry. Should I go on or would you like to fill in the blanks?"

"I don't remember," Ryker replied, his face a mask of confusion.

"Like you don't remember Croatia?"

"Look, how long have I been out?" he said, looking at his arm to see his watch was gone.

"Almost six hours. If you're looking for your watch it's on the side table. There is a countdown on it. What is that for?"

"I wish I could tell you. Um, where are my clothes?"

"They were trashed. Tossed out. Why, was there something in them that you needed?"

He groaned, pawing at his eyes as tubes pulled at his skin.

Jansen continued, her voice steady. "You were lucky to survive. A man pulled you from the river." She took a deep breath. "Help me out here, Max, or should I call you Andrew?"

"Call me whatever you want."

"Really, who are you?"

"I already told you."

"Of course, Max Ryker. You work for a division of the CIA, a division no one in the CIA acknowledges. I don't know what to believe anymore. The last time we spoke, I was unsure if you were playing a game or if your memory had been affected. So, I had the doctors run some tests on you. It appears you have several things in your system, but one of those is what is known as propranolol. Do you know what this is?"

He shrugged.

"According to a doctor here, it was meant to be a pill that could wipe out the memory of traumatic events." She paused. "Now according to your military discharge, at least the one related to Max Ryker, you were noted as having suffered from PTSD. Yet there is no mention in your doctors' records of propranolol being prescribed. So... care to fill in the blanks?"

"If I could, the blanks wouldn't be there."

"You must see how convenient that is?" Again, she paused. "Well then, let me ask you this. What happened at Emily Sutton's home with those two men? And what happened on that train? Why did you go out of your way to help those people but yet bomb a federal building?"

"I told you, I didn't bomb that building."

"Well, you can't remember. So how can you be sure?"

He groaned.

"Max, place yourself in my shoes. Innocent people don't run."

"They do if someone is trying to kill them and they've been set up."

She regarded him, chewing over his words. "And those two men at Emily's home?"

"They were there for me. They work for the Division."

"The black-bag organization that doesn't exist."

Ryker stared back at her. "Tell me, Agent Jansen, have you had any luck finding records on the two dead men at Emily's house? No, of course you haven't. And you won't. These people operate in the shadows of society. They are in the business of secrecy, misdirection, and cover-ups."

She leaned forward in her chair. "Okay, let me get this straight. You expect me to not only believe you worked for some shadowy arm of the government that doesn't acknowledge you but that same organization has sent their own to kill you?"

"Silence me."

"From saying what? You don't remember anything."

"Tell that to them."

She took a deep breath and exhaled. "So what are they trying to stop you from exposing?"

"Your guess is as good as mine."

"You're holding back."

"I've told you everything I know."

There was a long pause.

"Okay, what about Croatia?"

"What about it?" Max asked.

"Well, you told me the last time we talked that you were in Croatia before the bombing."

"Did I?"

"Ryker. Don't play games with me."

"Agent Jansen. I am groping around in the dark as much as you are."

"Then work with me. I can't help you unless you tell me what you know."

He blew out his cheeks. "I wish I knew more."

"That's not good enough." She studied him for a moment before rising. "The window of opportunity is closing for you, Ryker, or McAllister, or whatever the hell your name is." She paused. "I'm trying to help you."

"If you were, I wouldn't be cuffed to this bed," he said.

With that, she exited the room, leaving him alone. After the door closed behind her, Jansen leaned against the wall. The puzzle pieces were there, but they refused to fit together.

34

The winter night had settled over Baltimore, a thick blanket of snow muffling the city's usual bustle. Agent Jansen stepped out of her vehicle, her breath forming small clouds in the cold as she hurried towards the imposing structure of the Federal Bureau of Investigation building. The wind whipped around her, carrying flurries of snow that stung her face.

As she entered the building, shaking off the snow from her coat, Jansen couldn't help but feel a sense of urgency. She had been called away from the hospital, where Ryker was being held, to view crucial video surveillance from both the Chicago bombing and the train incident. The thirty-minute drive had felt interminable as she circled through possibilities and theories.

Jansen made her way through the building's security checkpoints, her badge granting her swift access. The elevator ride to the designated floor seemed to stretch forever, each floor passing by in a blur of numbers. Finally, the doors opened, and she stepped into a corridor that hummed with activity.

At the end of the hallway, Jansen pushed open a set of heavy doors and entered what could only be described as a high-tech command center. The room was notably different from the building's austere exterior, filled with cutting-edge technology that rivaled anything seen in movies or at NASA's mission control.

The space was dominated by a massive curved screen that covered most of the wall. It displayed a complex array of video feeds, data streams, and analytical graphs. Rows of workstations faced the main screen, each equipped with multiple monitors and specialized equipment. The soft glow of computer screens and the low hum of powerful processors filled the room with focused intensity.

Technicians in FBI jackets moved between stations, their fingers flying over keyboards as they analyzed data and cross-referenced information. The walls were lined with smaller screens displaying various security camera feeds, news channels, and what appeared to be real-time satellite imagery.

In the center of the room stood a large, circular holographic display table, currently projecting a 3D model of what Jansen recognized as the Chicago bombing site. The level of detail was astounding, allowing viewers to examine the scene from any angle with a simple gesture.

As Jansen took in the impressive setup, she spotted Thomas Reeves, Doug Erikson, and a couple of techies gathered around one of the larger workstations. Their faces were illuminated by the blue glow of the screens, expressions tense with concentration.

"All right, tell me you've got something," Jansen said as

she approached the group, her voice cutting through the ambient noise.

A tech turned to face her, gesturing towards the main screen. "So this is taken from multiple security cameras throughout Chicago in the days leading up to the bombing," she began, her voice crisp and professional. "A white van with the logo for Jan Pros - Chicago Cleaning Professionals is spotted doing several rounds of the area close to the building. Hard to make out who is inside due to the tinted windows."

The tech's fingers danced across her keyboard, and the footage on the main screen fast-forwarded. "Cut forward to the morning of the bombing. The same truck with the same plates, pulls up in front of the building. Four individuals get out wearing what appears to be N95 masks, goggles, hard hats, and ear protection. Only two of them were seen on camera removing their mask and goggles for a brief moment. Maybe they couldn't breathe or were adjusting it. It was hard to see the features, but we enhanced it."

Jansen leaned in, her eyes narrowing as she studied the grainy but enhanced images. "Who are they?"

"We'll get to that in a minute," Doug interjected, his voice tight with anticipation. "Just remember their faces."

The footage continued to play, showing the individuals collecting equipment from the back of the truck and heading into the federal building. Jansen watched intently as ten minutes passed, and then a second camera caught one of them exiting the building through a side door and approaching the van's rear.

"Is that Ryker?" Jansen asked, her voice sharp and focused.

The tech shook her head. "Hard to tell without removing the goggles, hat, and mask."

Frustration crept into Jansen's voice. "Do we have another camera angle to see what that person is doing?"

"Unfortunately not," the tech replied. However," she continued, speeding up the footage, "they get into the driver's seat, pull over to an area a block away, back up, get out, go to the rear, and open..."

"And... we can't see a damn thing," Jansen said, her disappointment palpable.

The tech nodded sympathetically before continuing. "The person gets back in and returns to the location in front of the federal building, gets out, and heads back inside. Less than five minutes after..."

The screen erupted in a blinding flash as the explosion ripped through the federal building, obliterating windows in many of the surrounding structures. The violence of the blast, even on video, was shocking.

"What the hell did that person take out of the van in that area?" Jansen asked.

The tech's response was tinged with frustration. "Not sure. After the explosion, the only working surveillance camera was facing in a slightly different direction. It caught Ryker coming through the smoke. That's the shot we have of him. However, he wasn't heading away from the federal building but from the van's location before it returned."

Jansen's brow furrowed. "What are you saying... that he was in the back of the van and someone let him out? Why?"

"That's what we don't know," Doug added, his voice grave. "But it appears the explosive material was also inside that van. Now, bring up the footage from the train station."

As the tech worked to bring up the new footage, Doug continued his explanation. "So the Capitol Limited arrived late at Union Station. Cameras on the platforms caught these two individuals getting on the train."

"Pause that and go back," Jansen said, leaning forward to get a better look. Her eyes widened in recognition. "Is that one of the men from the federal building?"

Doug nodded grimly. "Yep. And here's the interesting part. Now, the train doesn't have cameras throughout, probably for privacy reasons, so we don't know who shot the officers onboard. But it does have one up front in the locomotive where the engineer is. Watch," he said as the video played out.

Jansen watched in horror as one of the two who had boarded earlier entered the locomotive and shot the engineer before beginning to work on the control panel. "It's believed he sabotaged the train," Doug explained.

As the man on screen turned, his head was down momentarily before he lifted his eyes to the camera. Jansen's breath caught in her throat. "Pause. Enlarge that. That's not Ryker."

"No," Doug confirmed. "Our facial recognition provided hits on both of these two. They worked at one time for the U.S. military. Declan Lynch. He served in the Special Forces for six years before being discharged for misconduct. The Asian female, Yuki Katsumi, has a similar story. Multiple years of service before being discharged for a different infraction."

Jansen's thoughts spun, trying to piece together the puzzle. "And I bet, like Ryker, that's not even their names. Did any of these people serve with Ryker?"

Doug shook his head. "That's unknown. Like Ryker, they fell off the map after getting out."

Jansen nodded, her expression thoughtful. "And yet they

are all seen entering the federal building minutes before it explodes. Anyone else find it strange that we have people alive who are either believed to be dead or should be dead?" She frowned, looking back at the screen. "Were these two people accounted for as passengers on the train?"

"No," Doug replied.

"So they got off?"

"It appears so. Where? Who knows. Though I'm sure Ryker could tell us, if he can remember, of course," Reeves said, shaking his head with a smirk.

Jansen ignored Reeves' sarcasm. "You know, there's something that bothers me about this. How did they know he was on that train?"

"Pretty obvious to me. They're working with him," Reeves said, his tone dismissive.

"Or someone told them," Jansen added. She turned to face him, her expression challenging.

"They could be tracking him," Doug said.

"Interesting that Lynch and three others were seen in Chicago going into that federal building, and yet it was only Ryker's DNA that was found in a separate Jan Pros - Chicago Cleaning Professionals van nearby."

"That's right," Doug confirmed. "Traces of explosive material found inside were a match to those found in his home."

Jansen's brow furrowed in concentration. "So they transferred whatever explosive material was in there into another van. Why? Why not just use that van?"

"To screw with us," Reeves said, his frustration evident.

"It was a rhetorical question." Jansen continued her train of thought. "You can't point a finger if there's nothing left behind to connect him."

"And the cameras would make us think those that went inside died in the federal building," Doug added.

"Exactly. That leaves only Ryker to blame. But why him?" Jansen mused.

Suddenly, a voice called out from behind her. "Jansen?!" She turned to see a junior agent approaching. "Assistant Director Carlson is here to speak to you."

"Carlson?" Jansen exchanged a surprised glance with Doug. This wasn't Carlson's usual method of communication; he typically opted for phone calls over in-person visits.

She patted Doug on the back, her voice low and urgent. "Great work. See what you can dig up on those two individuals. Better still, find them if you can."

35

The hallway seemed to stretch endlessly before her as she made her way to meet Carlson. Each step echoed in the quiet corridor. The weight of the investigation pressed down on her shoulders, and she knew that whatever Carlson had to say, it would only add to the case's complexity.

She entered the elevator, pressing the button for the top floor.

The doors opened, and Jansen stepped out into a plush corridor lined with framed commendations and photographs of past directors. She made her way to an office where she was told to wait. Sitting in a leather chair, she blew out her cheeks, trying to steady her nerves. The room was tastefully decorated, with dark wood paneling and a large window.

A moment later, the door opened, and Assistant Director Carlson walked in. He was a tall man in his late fifties, with graying hair and a stern expression that rarely softened. His sharp blue eyes missed nothing, and his presence commanded respect.

"Director. What brings you out here?" Jansen asked, trying to keep her voice steady.

"I can assure you it's not to give you a pat on the back for bringing in Ryker," Carlson replied, his tone grim.

Jansen swallowed hard. Carlson walked behind the desk, his movements deliberate and controlled. "Close the door," he instructed.

Jansen complied, the click of the latch sounded unnaturally loud in the quiet room.

"It seems this shitstorm just got worse," Carlson began, leaning forward on the desk. "The day of the bombing, 25 kilotons of Russian plutonium went missing from a secure location a few blocks from the building that was destroyed. Our investigation revealed that the blast radius prompted immediate safety measures. Among those, authorities evacuated staff from a nearby federal building. While this evacuation was necessary for personnel safety, it inadvertently left the building less secure than usual."

"Hold on a second, you said 25 kilotons?" Jansen echoed, her mind struggling to process the information.

"Back in 1997, a Russian national security advisor claimed that the Soviet Union created 250 suitcase-sized portable nuclear weapons during the height of the Cold War," Carlson explained.

"Right, claimed," Jansen said with almost a chuckle. Carlson wasn't smiling.

"That claim was supported by a former environmental advisor to Russian President Yeltsin. Each of these suitcase nukes is meant to have an explosive yield of 1 kiloton. To put that into perspective, one of these is capable of killing fifty thousand to a hundred thousand people if detonated in a large city. Twenty-five went missing. Each can be transported and detonated by a single person, and they aren't protected by launch codes and can be prepared in thirty minutes."

"Why was it there?" Jansen asked, her voice tinged with disbelief.

"What?" Carlson replied.

"If these suitcases existed, shouldn't the military have had them?" Jansen pressed.

"Jansen, the military didn't know they existed until a day before the explosion. I don't know who found them, how they wound up in Chicago, or why they were held temporarily at that federal building. All I know is that they are gone."

Jansen took it all in, and thinking back to what Ryker had said about the Division. His words replayed in her mind: *"These people operate in the shadows of society. They are in the business of secrecy, misdirection, and cover-ups."*

"So you think the blast was to cover up the theft of these suitcase nukes?" Jansen asked, her eyes narrowing.

"That's where it's pointing," Carlson confirmed, his expression grim.

"But even if that was true, that means someone in a high position had to have known those nukes were being stored there," Jansen said.

Carlson nodded.

"Erikson said that the explosive material found at Ryker's home was dated to the Cold War. You think the Russians have something to do with this?"

"Your guess is as good as mine," Carlson replied. "Listen, if there are plans for those nukes to be used, it will make the explosion in Chicago look like child's play. Get back to Ryker. Dig deeper. Find out what he knows and fast."

"Don't you think I've tried? He claims to not remember. And I'm starting to think he might be right. Doctors found a drug in his system that is known to cause memory loss. It's used in the treatment of PTSD."

"Look, all I care about is that we find those nukes before more people die," Carlson said, his voice hardening.

Jansen nodded, her mind already working on her next steps.

As she exited Carlson's office, Jansen's thoughts were a whirlwind. She returned to the elevator, her steps quick and purposeful. The ride down felt endless, each floor passing by in a blur of numbers.

When the doors opened, Jansen entered the corridor and returned to the high-tech command center.

Doug Erikson looked up as she approached, his expression full of concern. "What did Carlson want?" he asked.

"You ever heard the phrase shit rolls downhill?" Jansen replied, her voice tight. "Twenty-five kilotons of Russian plutonium went missing the day of the bombing. They think the explosion was a cover-up for the theft."

Doug's eyes widened. "They think Ryker is connected?"

"Connected. Yes. Responsible? That's what we need to find out. Carlson wants us to dig deeper into Ryker's background and see if we can find any connections. I'll head back to the hospital soon and see what else I can get out of him."

Doug nodded. "I'll get on it. What about the footage from the train and the bombing?"

"Keep analyzing it. We need to find anything we can use," Jansen said.

As Doug returned to his workstation, Jansen took a deep breath and went to a nearby desk. She pulled up a chair and logged into the system, her fingers flying over the keyboard as she accessed Ryker's files.

Hours passed in a blur of data and analysis.

Jansen's eyes burned from staring at the screen, but she pushed through the fatigue, her mind focused on the task at hand. She cross-referenced Ryker's military records with the new information they had uncovered, looking for any connections.

After hours of painstaking analysis, Jansen decided to take a different approach. She picked up the phone and dialed the Suttons' number. The line rang twice before Emily Sutton answered.

"Hello," Emily's voice came through, a mix of caution and hope.

"Mrs. Sutton, this is Special Agent Jansen of the FBI."

"Is Andrew okay?" she asked.

Jansen paused for a second, the name "Andrew" still felt foreign when referring to Ryker. It was obvious why his ex called him that; it was all she'd ever known. "He's alive," Jansen confirmed, then pressed on. "Mrs. Sutton, I need to know something. When you were informed by the military of Andrew's death, how was it conveyed to you?"

Emily's voice wavered slightly as she recounted the memory. "A man and woman in uniform showed up here. They informed me that he was on a mission overseas. His team got into a firefight and were killed. One of the officers told me it would be a closed casket funeral and said that everything would be taken care of, and there would be no expense."

Jansen's brow furrowed as she listened, jotting down notes. "And he was buried where?"

"They said there was the option to be buried in Arlington

National Cemetery, but perhaps I would appreciate a private cemetery. I chose upstate New York because that's where his parents were buried."

"And these men, did they attend the funeral?"

"Yes, them and several others."

"Did you know them? Had you seen any of them before?"

"No."

"Did you see them after?"

"No."

Jansen paused, considering her next question carefully. "Did Andrew ever show signs of PTSD?"

"Yes. Why?" Emily asked.

"Did he ever end up in a bar fight by any chance?"

There was a moment of silence before Emily responded. "He did, roughly four months before his death. The court ordered him to attend a Stand Down event. It was an event for veterans. He was given a card by someone there for a 120-day residential treatment program for combat-related PTSD. Andrew showed me the card. I think I might even have it around here. Can you hold while I take a look?"

"Sure, go ahead," Jansen replied, her interest piqued.

As Emily set the phone down, Jansen turned to Doug. "Doug, isn't there an organization for military personnel to assist them with PTSD?"

"Yeah, it's called OASIS," Doug replied, looking up from his computer.

"Huh," Jansen mused, her mind working overtime to connect the dots.

Nearly five minutes passed, and Jansen was about to hang up when Emily returned to the line. "Sorry. I had to dig through a box. Yeah, here it is. Um. It's called SHIELD. It stands for Soldiers Healing through Integrated Emotional and Life Development. It says here at the bottom of the card, it's a residential treatment program for post-traumatic stress disorder."

"So he stayed there for the full 120 days?" Jansen asked, her pen poised over her notepad.

"Yes."

"Is there an address on that card?"

"No, just a number. Do you want it?"

"Go ahead," Jansen said, quickly scribbling down the number Emily recited.

Once she was done, Emily spoke up again, her voice tinged with emotion. "I know he's accused of many things, but the man I was planning to marry would have never been capable of harming anyone who was American. He loved this country. It's what led him into service."

Jansen's voice softened slightly. "Between you and me, Mrs. Sutton, I'm starting to think that may be the case. Thank you. If I think of anything else, I'll be in touch."

After hanging up, Jansen sat there momentarily, pondering the new information. She then dialed the number Emily had given her, only to hear the expected "Not in service" message.

"Any luck?" Doug asked, looking over at her.

"Would you agree in a conspiracy, loose ends are tied up?" Jansen asked.

"I'd say so."

Jansen's eyes narrowed as she pieced together the puzzle. "You know, I think the reason why there's no record of a bar fight, an arrest, or a court order for Andrew McCallister is because it was all a setup. Max Ryker's record is the only one listed as having been in a bar fight, attended court, and court-ordered to go to a stand-down event. Everything about who he is isn't true. It was all fabricated."

Doug's eyebrows shot up. "But to pull that off, you would need either a slew of actors or..."

"People integrated into many areas of society," Jansen finished.

She rose from her seat, determination etched on her face. "I need to speak with Ryker."

As Jansen gathered her things and headed for the door, she noticed Reeves shadowing her movements.

"Is there something you need, Reeves?" she asked, her tone clipped.

Reeves matched her stride as they exited the room. "I'm coming with you. Someone needs to keep an eye on things, make sure we're not being led down further rabbit holes."

Jansen bit back a retort, knowing that arguing would only waste precious time. Instead, she focused on the task ahead.

As they made their way through the building, the bustling activity of the FBI headquarters seemed to fade into the background. Jansen's thoughts were consumed by the web of lies and misdirection they were uncovering. The more they dug, the more complex the situation became.

They reached the parking garage, the cold air hitting them as they exited the elevator. Jansen's breath formed small clouds in front of her as she spoke. "We're taking my car. I'll drive."

Reeves nodded, falling into step beside her as they approached her vehicle. The drive to the hospital would take about thirty minutes, giving Jansen time to organize her thoughts and plan her approach.

As they pulled out of the garage and into the snowy Baltimore night, Jansen knew they were on the verge of uncovering something more significant than they had initially thought. The pieces were scattered and jumbled but slowly came together to form a picture that was as terrifying as unbelievable. She glanced at Reeves, who sat silently in the passenger seat, his eyes fixed on the road ahead. Jansen knew he had his own agenda and theories about Ryker. But right now, she needed to focus on getting to the truth, no matter where it led them.

36

The steady beep of medical equipment resonated through the room as Max lay in his hospital bed, his mind churning with unanswered questions. The sterile smell of disinfectant permeated everything, a constant reminder of his confinement. Outside, the winter night had settled in, snow falling heavily against the window panes.

As Max's eyelids grew heavy, his consciousness began to drift.

Suddenly, he was no longer in the hospital room but somewhere else entirely...

The harsh Croatian sun beat down on Max as he lay drenched in the back of a small boat. The azure sky above seemed at odds with the darkness that threatened to engulf him. Two men stood over him, their shadows providing momentary relief from the relentless heat. Through slitted eyes, Max could make out their familiar silhouettes — members of his old team.

Consciousness wavered, threatening to drag him back into the depths of blackness. The boat bounced over the waves, each move-

ment sending a jolt of pain through his battered body. Salt spray misted his face, the tang of the sea filling his nostrils.

Above him, the men's voices drifted in and out of focus.

"He's one tough sonofabitch. I figured if the rubber round didn't injure him, he'd be dead from that fall," one man said, his tone grim. "I can't believe he went rogue."

"Let it be a lesson. That's what comes from asking too many questions," the second man replied, his voice tinged with bitterness.

"Now what?" the first man asked.

"I spoke with Aldridge. They want him back in the USA alive."

"Alive?" the second man questioned, surprise evident in his voice.

"For now," the first replied ominously.

There was a pause, filled only by the sound of lapping waves and the distant cry of seagulls.

"What will they do with him?" the second man asked, a hint of concern in his voice.

"Debrief."

Another pause. Max fought against the encroaching darkness, straining to hear their words.

"He won't remember the mission, will he?"

The first man turned to his companion, his face a mask of resignation. "Do we ever?"

One of the men crouched. Max felt a sting as a needle pierced his arm.

The scene began to fade, the bright Croatian sun dimming...

Suddenly, the door swung open, and a woman in nurse's scrubs entered, her hair pulled back in a tight bun. She rolled in a cart, her movements quick and purposeful. Max's instincts, honed by years of training, immediately sensed something was off.

"Hello, Max," she said, her voice low and urgent. Her eyes

darted to the door, then back to him. "You have thirty seconds before they come back. Take the elevator up. Get to the roof. There's a medical helicopter waiting. Take it and head to this address in upstate New York." She thrust a scrap of paper into his hand. "Red will be waiting."

Max's mind reeled. "You know, Red?"

She nodded curtly as he began tearing away his tubes with one hand, wincing at the sharp pain.

"But he's in Washington, D.C.," Ryker protested, confusion evident in his voice as the woman uncuffed his restrained wrist.

"Not anymore," she replied, already turning towards the door.

"Wait. Hold on. Why should I trust you?" Max called after her.

The woman paused at the threshold, her hand on the doorknob. She turned back, her eyes meeting his with an intensity that made him catch his breath. "Because I'm your mother."

She was gone before Max could process her words, leaving him stunned.

The revelation hit him like a physical blow, sending his mind spinning.

Shaking off his shock, Max sprang into action. He swung his legs over the side of the bed, nearly losing his balance as he stood. His hand caught the back of a chair, sending it clattering to the floor. Ignoring the pain that shot through his body, he stumbled to the door and peered out into the hallway.

The corridor stretched empty before him, with no sign of the cops who were supposed to guard his room. In the distance, he saw a stairwell door swinging shut. Max rushed back to the bedside table, snatching up his watch. The cold floor bit at his bare feet as he ran out into the hallway, the thin fabric of his hospital gown offering little protection against the chill.

Heart pounding, Max made a run for the elevator.

As he stepped inside and jabbed the button for the top floor, movement at the end of the corridor caught his eye. Agent Jansen and two cops rounded the corner, their faces flushed with exertion. Jansen's eyes widened as she caught sight of him.

"Ryker!" she shouted, her voice echoing down the hallway as the elevator doors slid shut.

The elevator jerked upward, and Max watched the floor numbers climb, each ding of a passing floor ratcheting up his tension. His brain buzzed, trying to make sense of what was happening. Who was that woman? Could she really be his mother? And what did Red have to do with all of this?

As the doors opened on the top floor, Max stumbled out, his legs still weak from his time in the hospital bed. He pushed through the door to the stairwell, the sound of radio chatter and pounding footsteps echoing from below.

Law enforcement was closing in fast.

Gritting his teeth against the pain and exhaustion, Max climbed the final flight of stairs. He burst through the roof access door, the cold of the winter night hitting him like a physical blow. Snow whipped around him, stinging his face and exposed skin. Icicles hung from the edges of nearby structures, glinting in the dim light.

Through the swirling snow, Max spotted the red medical helicopter on the helipad. Without hesitation, he sprinted towards it, his bare feet numb against the icy surface of the roof. He yanked open the door and hauled himself inside, muscle memory from his days as a helicopter pilot taking over.

Max's hands flew over the control panel, flipping switches and pressing buttons in a well-practiced sequence. The cockpit came to life around him, displays lighting up and systems humming. He ran through the startup checklist with lightning speed, each action automatic and precise.

The rotors began to turn, their rhythmic thumping growing louder as they picked up speed. Max's heart raced in time with the accelerating blades, knowing that every second counted.

Just as the helicopter began to lift off the helipad, the roof access door burst open. Agent Jansen and a group of cops spilled out onto the roof, their shouts barely audible over the engine's roar and the howling wind.

Max pitched the helicopter away from the Johns Hopkins Critical Care Tower, his hands steady on the controls despite the adrenaline coursing through his veins. The sound of gunfire erupted behind him, bullets pinging off the helicopter's frame. But within moments, the noise faded, replaced by the steady thrum of the rotors as Max guided the aircraft into the night sky.

The lights of Baltimore spread out below him, a glittering tapestry against the darkness.

As he flew further from the hospital, Max had even more questions. What awaited him in upstate New York? And most importantly, how would Red help?

With the city falling away behind him and an uncertain future ahead, Max set his course, disappearing into the night sky.

PART III

37

The historic mansion in Kalorama, an exclusive section of Washington, D.C., was a symbol of power and wealth. Its stately facade was illuminated by soft exterior lighting that cut through the snowy evening. Inside, the opulence was even more apparent, particularly in the library where Aldridge stood, his phone pressed to his ear.

The room exuded old-world charm and luxury. Floor-to-ceiling bookshelves lined the walls, filled with leather-bound volumes and first editions. A massive mahogany desk dominated one end of the room, its surface adorned with an antique brass lamp. A state-of-the-art computer was incongruously nestled among vintage writing implements. The ceiling, adorned with intricate crown molding, soared high above, from which a crystal chandelier cast a warm glow over the space.

"No, sir. Yes sir. You have my word," Aldridge said before hanging up, his voice tight with frustration. He looked exasperated as he crossed the plush Oriental rug to a side table where a crystal decanter stood. With practiced ease, he poured himself two fingers of expensive bourbon into a heavy-bottomed tumbler.

Declan Lynch lounged in a high-backed leather armchair near the fireplace, where flames danced and crackled, casting flickering shadows across the room. He casually picked at his teeth with a toothpick.

“Trouble in paradise?” Lynch asked.

Aldridge turned his face, a mask of controlled anger. “You told me you eliminated Ryker.”

“I did,” Lynch replied, unfazed.

“Yeah, well, that’s interesting because not only did Ryker survive that train derailing, but according to one of our insiders, he just escaped from Johns Hopkins Hospital!” Aldridge’s voice steadily rose, echoing off the wood-paneled walls.

Lynch smiled, a predatory gleam in his eyes. “Steady, Aldridge, you don’t want that pacemaker of yours to suffer a glitch.”

“This is on you!” Aldridge snapped, his knuckles white around the glass.

“Is it? Or is it on the Division?” Lynch countered, leaning forward slightly.

“You were given strict orders—”

“As was Katsumi,” Lynch interrupted. “And look where she is now. If you’d allowed us to neutralize him in Croatia, we wouldn’t have had this problem, but if I recall, you wanted him back in the USA.”

Aldridge downed his bourbon in one gulp, grimacing at the burn. “I never made that call.”

“So your voice was deep-faked by someone?” Lynch’s sarcasm was palpable.

“How the hell would I know?” Aldridge snarled, slamming the empty glass down on the desk. He took a step back, visibly trying to regain his composure. "I was told, after the fact, that someone higher up wanted him back. He should have been dead by now. There have been multiple opportunities. Someone is helping him."

"You think?" Lynch said in a way that made it sound like he was bored with the conversation. He rose from his seat and moved to the window. Outside, the exclusive Kalorama neighborhood was blanketed in snow, the elegant homes of diplomats and political elites barely visible through the swirling flakes. The streetlights cast a soft, diffuse glow, creating an almost ethereal scene that belied the tension within the room. "If someone is helping him, perhaps Ryker knows now about Operation New Year."

"Damn you! He could compromise this operation. Everything we have been working towards."

"Oh, relax," Lynch said. "Your hissy fit is embarrassing," Lynch continued, his breath fogging the cold glass.

Aldridge's reflection appeared beside Lynch's in the window, his face a study in contained fury. "We have just over thirty hours remaining. I want him found and eliminated. And this time, Lynch, make sure he's dead. You wanted Ryker's position. Show me you can handle it. And remember, if I go down, everyone in the Division will."

Lynch turned from the window, his eyes meeting Aldridge's. "Is that a threat?"

"No, it's a promise," Aldridge growled. "We're too close to let one rogue agent derail everything we've worked for."

Lynch moved away from the window, his steps measured as he circled the room. His fingers trailed along the spines of books, pausing occasionally as if considering their titles.

"And what exactly have we worked for, Aldridge? Remind me."

Aldridge's eyes narrowed. "You know damn well what's at stake. The culmination of decades of planning, the reshaping of global power structures. We're on the cusp of changing the world order, and you're acting like this is all a game."

"Isn't it, though?" Lynch mused, plucking a book from the shelf and flipping through it absently. "We move pieces around the board, sacrifice pawns when necessary. But sometimes, a pawn will surprise you and become more than it was meant to be."

"Ryker is no pawn," Aldridge spat. "He's dangerous. He's a liability. One that needs to be eliminated before he can do more damage."

Lynch snapped the book shut, the sound echoing in the quiet room. "And what damage has he done so far, exactly? Besides refusing to die when we tell him to?"

Aldridge moved back to the decanter, pouring another drink. His hand shook slightly as he raised the glass to his mouth. "He knows too much. Or he will if we don't stop him. The things he saw in Croatia, the connections he could make... If he remembers, if he puts the pieces together..."

"Then what?" Lynch pressed. "What's the worst that could happen?"

Aldridge drained his glass, setting it down with a heavy thud. "The worst? The entire operation falls apart. Years of careful manipulation and moving assets into place all undone because one agent couldn't follow orders." He paused.

Lynch returned to his seat by the fire, stretching his legs and crossing them at the ankle. "So we find him again. We end him. Problem solved."

"It's not that simple," Aldridge muttered, pacing the room. "He's proven remarkably difficult to kill. And now, with him in the wind, we don't even know where to start looking."

"Oh, I wouldn't say that," Lynch said, a slow smile spread on his face. "I have a few ideas."

Aldridge stopped pacing, turning to face Lynch. "What aren't you telling me?"

Lynch's smile widened. "Let's just say I gained some intel on him that will act as an insurance policy. A way to draw out our wayward agent."

"And you're just mentioning this now?" Aldridge's voice was dangerously low.

Lynch shrugged. "You didn't ask, and I thought he was dead."

Aldridge's fist fell hard on the desk, rattling the items. "Damn it, Lynch! This isn't a game. The stakes are too high for your petty power plays."

"Are they?" Lynch asked, his tone suddenly serious. "Or is that just what you've been told? Have you ever considered what we're doing here, Aldridge? What the endgame truly is?"

Aldridge's face paled slightly. "What are you implying?"

Lynch stood, moving across the room to stand directly in front of Aldridge. "I'm implying that perhaps it's time we both took a step back and looked at the bigger picture. Who's really calling the shots? And to what end?"

For a moment, the only sound in the room was the crackling of the fire and the ticking of an antique clock on the mantel. Aldridge's eyes darted around the room as if searching for hidden listeners.

"I don't have time for this," he finally said, his voice barely above a whisper. "New Year's is approaching fast. Whatever doubts or questions you have, they can wait. Right now, we must focus on finding Ryker and neutralizing him before he can interfere."

Lynch held Aldridge's gaze for a long moment before nodding. "I'll make the necessary arrangements."

As Lynch approached the door, Aldridge called, "And Lynch? Remember, failure is not an option. Not this time."

Lynch paused his hand on the doorknob. Without turning, he replied, "It never is." Then he was gone, leaving Aldridge alone in the opulent library.

Aldridge sank into the chair behind his desk, suddenly feeling every one of his years. He glanced at the computer screen, where a countdown timer ticked away the seconds until New Year's Day. Less than thirty-two hours remained until the plan was set in motion. Less than thirty-two hours to eliminate Max Ryker.

38

Max's hands gripped the controls of the medical helicopter as he navigated through the night. The rotor blades cut through the air, their rhythmic thumping a steady reminder of the urgency of his escape. The lights of Baltimore had long since faded, replaced by the dense, snow-tinged forests of upstate New York.

It had taken roughly two hours of flying.

As he approached the Adirondack Mountains, Max scanned the landscape below for a suitable landing spot. The dense trees and rugged terrain made it difficult to find a clearing large enough to safely set down the helicopter without risking a crash.

After several tense minutes, Max spotted a small clearing near a frozen stream about 10 miles from Bolton Landing. It wasn't ideal, but it would have to do. He brought the helicopter down carefully, the skids touching the ground with a gentle thud. The clearing was surrounded by tall pines, their branches heavy with snow, offering some natural camouflage.

Max shut down the helicopter, the rotor blades slowing to a stop. He had to move fast. His thin hospital gown offered little protection against the numbing cold. He needed to find warmth and shelter. He grabbed the emergency survival kit from the medical helicopter, which included a thermal blanket, a small first aid kit, and a flashlight.

He looked around, assessing his options.

Max remembered passing a small cabin on his way to the clearing.

It was about half a mile back, nestled among the trees. Max set off in that direction, his breath forming clouds. The snow crunched under his feet, each step a painful reminder of his vulnerability.

After what felt like an eternity, Max reached the cabin. It was a simple wooden structure, likely used by hunters during the fall season. He shivered hard as he tried the door, but it was locked. Without hesitation, he wrapped his hand in the thermal blanket from the survival kit and smashed the small window on the door. The sound of breaking glass seemed deafening in the quiet forest. Max reached through, unlocked the door, and slipped inside.

The cabin was cold and musty, but it offered shelter from Mother Nature.

Max's eyes adjusted to the darkness and searched for anything useful. In a trunk near the bed, he found some old but serviceable clothes: a thick flannel shirt, a jacket, pants, and wool socks. He changed quickly, relishing the warmth of the layers. Near the door were multiple pairs of sturdy boots. He slipped on a pair that was a little too tight but would suffice.

As he continued exploring the cabin, Max found a few cans of food and a water bottle. He wolfed down some cold beans, his stomach growling in appreciation of its first meal in hours. But even as he ate, Max knew he couldn't linger. He had to keep moving.

He gathered what supplies he could into a small backpack he found hanging on a hook. Then, stepping back out into the night, Max noticed the snow falling even heavier now. He pulled the collar of his newly acquired jacket up around his face for extra warmth.

Trudging through the snow, Max consulted the map he had found in the cabin.

Bolton Landing was still a good distance away, and in this weather, it could take him hours to reach it on foot. He needed a faster way to travel.

As if in answer to his unspoken prayer, Max heard the distant hum of vehicles passing on a road. He pressed on until he saw headlights. Moments later, he heard the rumble of an engine. He carefully went through the trees until he came to a minor road.

In the distance, he could see the lights of a gas station.

Moving stealthily, Max approached the station. An eighteen-wheeler was parked at the pumps, its driver inside paying for fuel. As he crept closer, Max overheard snippets of conversation.

"... heading over to Lake George. Should be there shortly if this snow lets up," the driver was saying. "Been one hell of a night."

Max's heart raced. This was his chance. Before the driver climbed back into the cab, Max made his move. He slipped around to the rear of the truck and, with a grunt of effort, unlocked it and pulled himself up and into the trailer. He wedged himself between pallets of boxes, pulling a tarp over himself for good measure.

The truck rumbled to life, and soon, they were on the move.

Max felt every bump and turn, his body tense with the fear of discovery. But as the miles rolled by, he allowed himself to relax slightly. The enclosed space's warmth and the truck's rhythmic motion lulled him into a light doze.

Max jerked awake as the truck came to a stop.

He heard voices outside and realized they must have reached their destination. Holding his breath, he waited as the trailer doors were unlocked and opened.

"Let's get this unloaded quick," a gruff voice said. "I want to get home before this storm gets worse."

As the men began to move boxes, Max saw his opportunity.

He slipped out under the tarp and, in one fluid motion, dropped to the ground and rolled under the truck. He lay there, heart pounding, as feet moved around him.

Once the activity died down, Max crawled out from his hiding spot. He found himself in a small industrial area on the outskirts of what he assumed was Bolton Landing.

Max oriented himself using the map he had taken from the cabin. The cottage by Lake George wasn't far now. He set off on foot, sticking to the less traveled roads.

The snowy road wound through the dense forest, the bare branches of the trees reaching out like skeletal fingers. Max trudged along the shoulder, his borrowed clothes offering meager protection against the cold. The lights of Bolton glimmered in the distance, a beacon of hope after his arduous journey.

As he approached the town's outskirts, the forest gave way to scattered houses and cottages, their windows glowing warmly against the encroaching darkness. Max consulted the scrap of paper in his pocket, double-checking the address before continuing down a narrow lane toward Lake George.

The lane curved gently, revealing a stunning vista of a frozen lake stretching out before him. Nestled among the trees on the shoreline stood a luxurious cottage, its cedar shingles and stone chimney blending seamlessly with the natural surroundings. Large windows reflected the moon, giving the impression that the property was aglow.

Max paused at the foot of the driveway, taking in the scene.

The cottage was a masterpiece of rustic elegance, with a wraparound porch and a boat dock extending into the icy waters of Lake George. A wisp of smoke curled out of the chimney, promising warmth within.

He made his way up the path to the front door, his footsteps crunching softly in the stillness of the evening. The porch creaked slightly under his weight as he approached a heavy oak door adorned with intricate iron hardware.

He took a deep breath, steeling himself for whatever lay beyond, and knocked firmly on the door.

Silence.

He waited a moment, then knocked again, louder this time. Still no response.

"Hello?" he called out, sounding unnaturally loud in the quiet evening. "Red?"

Only the whisper of the wind through the trees answered him.

Max reached for the doorknob, half expecting it to be locked. To his surprise, it turned easily in his hand. The door swung open with a soft creak, revealing a warm and inviting interior.

He stepped inside, immediately enveloped by the

cottage's comforting warmth. The entryway opened into a spacious great room dominated by a massive stone fireplace, where a fire crackled merrily. The aroma of wood smoke mingled with the lingering aroma of a recently cooked meal —perhaps a hearty stew or roast.

Max paused to shake the snow from his jacket, the melting flakes forming small puddles on the polished hardwood floor. He stomped his boots on the thick welcome mat, dislodging clumps of snow and ice.

The great room was both luxurious and comfortable. A plush sectional sofa faced the fireplace, piled high with soft throws and pillows. Above the mantle hung a large flatscreen TV, currently dark and silent. To one side, a modern kitchen gleamed with stainless steel appliances and granite countertops. A half-empty wine glass sat on the kitchen island, suggesting someone had recently been there.

Max moved further into the room, his eyes scanning for any sign of movement or life.

The walls were adorned with a mix of local artwork and framed photographs, many featuring scenes of Lake George in different seasons. A spiral staircase in one corner led to an upper level, while a hallway to the right led to other rooms.

He went down the hallway, passing a bathroom with a spa-like shower and a guest bedroom decorated in soothing blues and greens. At the end of the hall, a door stood slightly ajar. Max pushed it open, revealing a well-appointed study.

The room was lined with built-in bookshelves, filled with diverse titles ranging from classic literature to modern thrillers. A large desk dominated one corner, its surface neat and organized. A sleek laptop sat closed in the center, a single pen placed precisely beside it.

What caught Max's attention, however, was the collection

of framed photos on a side table. He moved closer, drawn to one in particular. Picking it up, he studied the image intently.

The photograph showed a younger version of the woman he had seen at the hospital. Her long brunette hair cascaded over her shoulders, framing a face full of joy and laughter. She stood on the deck of a boat, the sparkling waters of what he assumed was Lake George stretching out behind her. She proudly displayed a large fish in her hands, its scales glinting in the sunlight.

Next to her stood a bearded man, his arm wrapped protectively around her waist. His weathered face bore a proud smile as he gazed at the woman. What struck Max most, however, was the slight swell of the woman's belly, visible even in her casual clothes. She was pregnant.

A third figure in the photo drew Max's attention.

A younger man stood on the woman's other side, his arm around her waist. The scene radiated happiness and pride, a moment of pure joy captured in time.

As Max studied the photo, trying to make sense of the connection between these people and his fragmented past, a sound behind him made him freeze.

He turned slowly, the photograph still clutched in his hand.

An older man stood in the study doorway, his arms full of firewood. His weathered face resembled the bearded man in the photo, though the passage of time had etched deep lines around his eyes and mouth. His salt-and-pepper hair was cut short, and he wore comfortable, well-worn clothes that spoke of a life close to nature.

The man's eyes flicked from Max's face to the photograph in his hand, a complex mix of emotions playing across his features. Recognition, surprise, and something that might have been regret flashed in his eyes before his expression settled into a mask of calm resolve.

"I see you've found the photo," Red said, causing Max to flinch slightly. "I suppose that's as good a place as any to begin."

"Are you Red?" Max asked, his voice hoarse from the cold and lack of use.

The man nodded. "I am. Don't worry, I knew you wouldn't remember."

"Who are these other people? And why do I feel like I should know them?"

Red sighed heavily, gesturing for Max to sit by the fire in one of the armchairs. "It's a long story, Max. One that goes back much further than you might imagine. But I promise you this — by the time we're done, you'll have the answers you've sought. Whether you'll like those answers remains to be seen." Red motioned to a chair as he carried the logs to the fire. "Take a seat."

As Max sank into the chair, the warmth of the fire seeping into his tired bones, he knew he was on the verge of uncovering truths that would change everything.

39

The aroma of coffee lingered along with the warmth of the crackling fire. Red poured a cup and handed it to Max Ryker, who accepted it with thanks. Red sat across from him, the weight of years and secrets evident in his every movement.

"Whose place is this?" Max asked.

"No one can find you here if that's what you're asking. It's a former safe house slash summer cottage."

Red held the photo that Max had been examining earlier. "This photo was taken in 1984, four years before all our lives were changed. That's your mother and father." He turned the photo toward Max. "You look more like your father every day."

Max studied the faces in the photograph, searching for any flicker of recognition. Although he could see some form of resemblance, he held no memory. He shook his head. "You know — I saw her at the hospital. I don't remember any of you."

"You wouldn't. She made sure of that," Red replied, his voice tinged with regret.

Max frowned. "Is my father alive?"

"No. Unfortunately," Red said, his eyes clouding with sorrow.

"So, what's your connection to them?" Max asked, his curiosity piqued.

Red nodded. "Your parents and I go way back. I was an old friend. A relic from the Cold War, your mother would say." He smiled wistfully. "I was someone she trusted."

"Before she walked out on me?"

"You don't understand," Red said, shaking his head.

"No, I don't. I don't understand what the hell is going on. Not only have I been accused of terrorism and murdering my girlfriend and a taxi driver, but the CIA have turned their back on me. Oh, and apparently, I was going to be married to a woman living outside Pittsburgh," Max said, holding up his ring finger. "And I have a child that I only just met. So yeah, I don't understand. Hell, I don't even remember."

"And there is a reason for that. Allow me to explain." Red took a deep breath, steeling himself for the revelations to come.

"How about you start with why you are here and not in Washington, D.C.?" Max asked. He felt nothing for the man in front of him. Not even a single memory stirred.

"I'll answer that. But first, what do you remember?" Red asked.

Max stared at him. "One of the last memories I had before I woke up outside a federal building in Chicago was being in Dubrovnik, Croatia. I sent a video to myself telling me to head to you in Washington. So, why are you here?"

"For the same reason you are on the run," Red replied.

"The Division?" Max asked, his voice edged with suspicion.

Red nodded. "Yes."

"I don't understand. Why is the CIA doing this?" Max demanded.

"The CIA isn't. The Division is not the CIA," Red corrected.

"That's not what I was told."

"No, that's what you were programmed to believe. It allows them to operate within the gray."

"What are you talking about?" Max asked, frustration creeping into his voice.

Red took a sip of his coffee, his expression grave. "I'm getting ahead of myself. Look, what I am about to tell you is the truth, no matter how hard it is to hear. Your mother's real name was not Julia McCallister. It was Oksana Nemcova. She was born in 1950 in East Germany, not long after the country's partition. Her mother was Russian, and her father was German. The Soviet Union's influence over East Germany at that time was strong, allowing the development of the Soviet-controlled German Democratic Republic. Having a Russian mother, many of her political views growing up were heavily influenced by Marxism-Leninism. Julia's parents divorced by her mid-teens, and her mother — your grandmother — moved back to Russia. Julia chose to stay with her father, studying in East Germany and earning a degree there. It was in those impressionable years that your mother became interested in communism. She joined a Communist Party that had close ties to the Soviet Union. Her involvement with that party, her academic achievements, and her Russian mother garnered the attention of the KGB, who at that time were actively recruiting individuals from Soviet-aligned countries. On one of Julia's many visits to see your grandmother in Moscow, the KGB approached her and recruited your mother. It was an easy sell. Your grandmother was poor. The KGB said if she agreed, her mother wouldn't want for anything. Add to that Julia's age and the influence of the Communist Party, and an agreement was made. After recruitment, she underwent extensive training by the KGB, including language skills, self-defense, and spy craft, preparing her for a role as a sleeper agent in the United States."

"Hold on a minute. What?"

"It's the truth, Max."

Sleeper agent? Max couldn't believe what he was hearing. He sipped his coffee, never taking his eyes off Red for even a second.

"The KGB never told your mother the full extent of the program she was involved in, only that she would need to rub shoulders with policymakers and others in powerful positions in the USA. Unable to obtain an American passport, the KGB resorted to a common tactic used back then. The KGB found a gravestone of a girl who had died at birth in 1950 in upstate New York. 1950 was when your mother was born in Germany. That American girl's name was Julia Green. Moscow managed to obtain a birth certificate and identification papers so that your mother could assume the identity of Julia Green. In 1977, at 27, she left Moscow, traveling through various European countries until she could obtain a Canadian passport under the name of Valerie Colden. She then bought a ticket to South America and, from there, headed to Vancouver via Montana. That two-day stopover was key. The U.S. believed she was sightseeing before she headed back to Canada. She never went to Canada. Once in Montana, she burned her passport and disappeared, later winding up in New York with Julia Green's new birth certificate. Through a series of ways, she obtained different I.D.s and then a Social Security card. Eventually, she met your father, Michael McCallister, married him, and took his last name."

Max stared back, chewing it all over. "You're telling me my mother was a sleeper agent for the Soviet Union?" Max asked, incredulous.

"For almost ten years," Red confirmed.

"And my father?"

"American. Michael didn't know. Not at first. No one knew. Julia would feed Moscow sensitive information through letters sent to Europe, where a handler would transfer it to the KGB. The encoded message would be hidden within the letter and require chemicals to develop it."

Max ran a hand over his forehead, trying to grasp what he was hearing.

"Two years after she married Michael, you were born. Life was good. At least, your mother would say so. Eventually, the KGB believed the FBI was on to Julia. They wanted her to return to Moscow, but she didn't want to leave. She had created a family, a life that had now become disillusioned with communism. But she was in too deep to defect. It would have cost her your lives. She loved you and Michael more than anything. For a time, she lied to the KGB and told them all manner of stories to delay the inevitable, hoping that they would have better things to do than to chase down a rogue agent. She believed if she held out long enough, things would change. And things in the world were changing. The situation in the USSR began to deteriorate by 1987 as Mikhail Gorbachev sought to restructure and create more openness. By 1988, Julia was no longer sending messages to Moscow, but they wouldn't let it go. They saw her as a valuable asset. They wanted her back until they could be sure that the FBI wasn't on to her. Your mother knew she had to return, at least for a time. The KGB didn't know about you. So, that is when she told your father the truth. Of course, Michael was outraged that she would lie to him and endanger his life and yours. He felt betrayed. He felt like a pawn in a game he never asked to play."

Max snorted, thinking how much he and his father were alike. "Tell me about it."

Red sighed. "That evening, they had a huge fight, and Michael took you and left in a car, vowing that Julia would never see you or him again and that he would expose her. Julia followed him. He didn't get far. The weather was bad, and speed also played a big factor — he crashed into another vehicle. Michael, along with the occupants of the other car, died instantly. You were in a kiddie safety seat and the only one that survived. That night, your mother placed you in my care. Arrangements were made to cover up the accident and make it look like both of your parents had died. You were then entered into the foster system, and I later adopted you, raised you, even trained you."

"Trained?" Max's voice was tinged with disbelief.

"Perhaps that's not the right word. *Prepared* you for what I knew was to come."

"Which was?"

"Your mother's return. Scrutiny by the Division. The next wave of sleeper agents integrated into American society. The next operation was to be guided by your mother within a larger network, far beyond what even she was privy to."

"Why her?"

"She was one of the first. Someone who had laid the

groundwork. Julia intricately knew the ins and outs of American life. How to make contacts. How to infiltrate. She would no longer be a field agent but a senior officer for Russia overseeing recruitment and training for a new program. A black bag operation."

Max slowly turned over his hand. The fading ink was gone, but he could still see it in his mind. "Black Raven. That was scrawled on my hand."

He nodded. "Julia wanted you to know the truth. Your mother was involved in creating Russian assets. Those who would not only spy on America but would influence political policy and gather classified information that could be used to damage U.S. national security. It would go far beyond inserting sleeper agents in the U.S. — though that was a large part of developing the network. The arrest of ten of them in 2010 only skimmed the surface."

"And this program?"

"Black Raven was to be touted as a clandestine division of the CIA using disposable assets."

"Disposable?"

"Disillusioned, PTSD suffering, dishonorably discharged and homeless American veterans found through the Stand Down event. This was to ensure that what happened in 2010 would never happen again. They would always be one step ahead."

"Was the Stand Down event a part of it?"

"No. That is a legitimate event aimed at helping veterans. No, the Division leveraged contacts made through the Stand Down event to recruit those without jobs, food, clothing, medical, legal or mental health assistance."

"By making them believe they were recruited for a secretive branch of the CIA?"

"Yes. Well, not immediately. That's where the 120-day rehabilitation program came into play. It allowed them to weed out those of no use and find those of value. It allowed them to manipulate and program them. If any recruit became a liability or a threat, they could dispose of them, and the American public would see their deaths as either accidents or the result of combat PTSD. An ex-military guy kills his wife and children and then himself. You hear it happening all the time. It was a perfect cover. It worked for a long time until it didn't."

"How so?"

Red brushed off dust from his pant leg. "Carol Kingsley. Another operative within the Division. She was flipped by the CIA and became a double agent working to gather intelligence."

"So the CIA found out about the Division?"

"They were closing the net. Your mother knows because she was the one who exposed them through Carol. A woman she trusted, a woman who had been asking questions."

"But why would she do that after all these years of loyalty?"

"You." He took a deep breath. "And... she was tired. Getting older. Guilt was weighing her down."

"Guilt? That's a good one." Max exhaled. "I don't understand. If my mother had told the CIA the truth about the Division, why didn't they react sooner? Shut them down? Why didn't they come to my aid when I was arrested by the FBI?"

"Too much at stake. The CIA is after a larger network that controls the Division — a global criminal organization known for elaborate schemes aimed at achieving global domination through terrorism, extortion, and intelligence manipulation."

"Who are they?"

"I don't know."

Max struggled to wrap his mind around it all. "The CIA did nothing but just looked on?"

"Put yourself in their shoes. If the general public really knew what went on behind the scenes and what was done in the name of counterintelligence, there might be riots. What I'm saying is that it wouldn't have looked good on them if the public had found out that they had been gathering evidence for years while Americans were dying. Add to that the hundreds killed in that federal bombing, and they would never save face. Think about it, Max. The FBI knew ten years in advance about ten sleeper agents operating in the USA before they were arrested. Why wait? Why keep it under wraps? The FBI needed to build a case, gather evidence, and determine who ran the larger network. It's no different than the work that cops do with drug dealers. They don't want the dealer. They want the organization behind the drugs. This is no different. As a field agent, Carol was perfectly suited to that role. Your mother, even more so as a senior officer. Two individuals working together. The CIA didn't just want ten Russian sleeper agents this time, Max, they wanted them all. And they would have had it if that mission in Croatia wasn't compromised."

"Carol was supposed to give a drive to a journalist with information about the Division, wasn't she?"

"That's right. You are remembering."

"Very little." Memories formed again in his mind. "I was told Carol was wanted for espionage. They said she was planning on exposing sensitive information that could harm the

American people, but instead, she was trying to bring down the Division."

"Yeah, with your mother's help and yours."

Max closed his eyes. Flashes of memory—conversations, revelations, Croatia—came rushing back, forming in his mind.

"Max, your mother wanted out; she wanted you out, and this was the only way."

"The watch, the ring, the phrase on my hand," Max said, his voice trailing off as he tried to piece together the fragments of his past.

Red nodded. "Last-minute choices."

"So she was there at the bomb site?"

"Briefly. If it wasn't for her, Max, you would already be dead. Once she learned that the mission was compromised and the Division had found out about Carol and you, she prevented them from killing you in Croatia using deep-fake technology. Once you were back on U.S. soil, she had plans to get you to safety, but things moved too fast. Her higher-ups wanted you to take the fall for the bombing. She couldn't control every decision made. However, she intervened. Saved your life. She figured the least she could do was point you in the right direction — to the life you had before the Division."

"Why not just tell me?"

"Time. Risk. But don't misunderstand. She did tell you. That's why you went to Croatia to stop an agent from killing Carol and to ensure that the file wasn't lost."

Max brought a hand to the bridge of his nose, feeling a tension headache.

"You have to understand that since your mother returned to the United States, she has watched your life from afar. No mother should have to do that."

"She chose that life," he said in anger.

"Partly. She was young and naïve, and the Russian SVR was heavily involved. She wanted the best for you, Max, which meant making choices that kept you alive, even if that included not being in your life. She was careful. She never contacted me other than to check in and see how you were doing. Believe me, Max, when I say she would have laid down her life for you, she would have. She didn't want you to be put under the microscope like her. She wanted you to have a life away from the intelligence community."

"A life? Everything in my life was taken from me because of her," Max said, his voice rising with anger.

"No. It was because of the Division. You were never meant to become part of the Division. That was the last thing she wanted. Someone in the Division intercepted a communication between her and me. My guess is your mother wasn't as careful as she used to be, and SVR believed they had a mole in the Division after the recent string of arrests. They did. Her. When your mother found out that Emily was pregnant and that SVR was monitoring her movements, she knew it would only be a matter of time before you, Emily, and your child would be taken out. Instead of allowing that, she convinced them that her interest in you was for the purpose of recruiting. Nothing more. She had to orchestrate everything to wipe the slate clean on your life. The fight at the bar, your court case, the man you met at the Stand Down event who directed you to the rehabilitation program, that was all her doing."

"To bring me into the Division?" Max's voice was filled with disbelief.

Red nodded. "To keep you close. To keep you alive."

Max felt like his brain was malfunctioning. It was just all

too much, coming at him all too fast. “No, I worked for the CIA. We were going after terrorists.”

“They weren’t terrorists. Max. They were enemies of Russia. You were going after American assets, double agents, snooping journalists, and American political figures. Everyone eliminated, either foreign or domestic, was done to neutralize threats to the Division, damage U.S. national security, and influence policy and war.”

“Are you saying the Division killed innocent Americans? No, I can’t believe that.”

“Wait here,” Red said, getting up and heading out of the room, only to return a few moments later with a stack of newspapers. He dumped them on Max’s lap. They were dated June 2010 and detailed how the FBI arrested ten Russian sleeper agents that had been planted in the U.S. by the SVR, the Russian Foreign Intelligence Service. They had posed as ordinary American citizens, developing contacts with politicians, industrialists, academics, and policymakers to gain intelligence and damage national security. The investigation had been ongoing for almost a decade before any arrests were made. Homes had been bugged, agents had followed them on their travels, and they even managed to crack their secret communications network. In the early part of July 2010, arrests were made before they were exchanged for four Russian nationals convicted of espionage on behalf of the USA and U.K.

“The SVR have been inserting them into every facet of American life for decades,” Red said.

40

Jansen stood in the FBI's high-tech command center, her eyes fixed on the large screen displaying the stolen medical helicopter's real-time tracking data. The room buzzed with activity, agents, and technicians moving with purpose as they monitored various feeds and data streams. The tension in the air was palpable, amplified by the soft hum of powerful computers and the muted conversations of the team.

She'd spoken with a medical helicopter pilot immediately after Ryker's escape. The pilot had explained that the ground operations center would have been alerted to the theft through an automated alert from the Sky Connect Tracker III system inside the helicopter. The system was designed to detect unusual activity or if a report was made from personnel.

The pilot had already phoned it in minutes earlier.

Jansen contacted the Ground Operation Center. "This is Special Agent Jansen with the FBI. I need real-time tracking data on a stolen medical helicopter."

The voice on the other end was calm and professional. "We've been monitoring the helicopter since the alert came through. Based on the tracking system's flight path, it's heading for upstate New York. We can provide you with access to the real-time tracking data."

"Appreciate it," Jansen replied. "Send the data to my team immediately."

Ten minutes later, the large screen in the command center updated to show the helicopter's flight path. The red line traced a path from Baltimore to a remote area near Lake George in upstate New York. The aircraft had landed, and its coordinates were displayed on the screen.

Jansen turned to Reeves and Doug Erikson, who stood nearby, their expressions tense.

"Looks like our boy is heading back to his old stomping ground," Reeves said.

Jansen grabbed her jacket. "It's near Lake George. Let's go."

Reeves nodded, his jaw set with determination. "I'll coordinate with local law enforcement."

Jansen quickly arranged for a private aircraft, a Cessna Citation Jet, to take them to the nearest airstrip. "We're leaving immediately," she said, her voice brooking no argument.

The team moved with practiced efficiency, gathering their gear and heading to the waiting jet. The snow fell heavily as they boarded, the cold nipping their faces. Jansen settled into a brown leather seat, focusing on the task ahead.

As the jet taxied down the runway and lifted, Jansen turned to Reeves and Doug. "So what do we have so far?"

Reeves wiggled a pen between his fingers. "Beyond the obvious? A lunatic on the run."

"I meant evidence."

"Take your pick. Security footage and DNA point to Ryker's involvement in the bombing that killed hundreds. We have eyewitnesses that place him running from the scene of one dead taxi driver, millions in an offshore account, a gun that can be linked to the murder of the taxi driver, and a knife used in the brutal murder of his girlfriend. Not to mention, both of his parents are dead."

"Allegedly," Doug added, his tone cautious.

"The evidence is undeniable," Reeves retorted, frustration evident in his voice.

"So where do the two dead men responsible for the death of multiple officers in Sewickley fit into this?" Jansen asked.

Reeves was quick to answer that. "Mrs. Sutton has a reason to lie."

"Do her neighbors? Or the conductor who said he saved people on that train?" Doug countered, his eyes narrowing.

Reeves ran a hand over his tired face. "Really? How many times are we going to entertain this? Do you know the number of variables that would have to be working against this man for him to be innocent? C'mon, you can't be that naïve."

"I admit, it's a lot, but not any more than any other terrorist group looking for a patsy to take the fall," Jansen added.

"Right. And next, you're going to be waffling about how Lee Harvey Oswald and Timothy McVeigh were innocent," Reeves said sarcastically.

"I'm just considering all options," Jansen said. "Don't you think that's wise?"

Reeves' eyes darted between them. "Not really. Unlike the FBI, who seem so intent on making him the poster child for the next Manchurian candidate, I can see him for what he is."

"And that would be?"

"A dangerous man."

"But what if he is telling the truth? Who could pull strings to make it happen, and how would they benefit?" Jansen asked.

"No one benefits. Again, that's the problem with you two. You are on a witch hunt. You keep using the word 'truth,' but this man can barely tell you the truth about himself, let alone anything else. And since his capture, somehow his memory seems to be getting worse," Reeves said, shaking his head.

"I know," Jansen said, leaning forward. "But have you stopped to ask why? You see, according to doctors at the hospital, his body was full of drugs known to dampen or even block memory. Now, we've all seen that video. Besides a couple of faces of other people that we were able to identify at the train station, there is little that is concrete, other than the overalls he was wearing, that indicates Ryker was directly involved with that bombing."

Reeves laughed. "Are you joking? Is this really where my tax dollars are being spent? Geesh. I thought they trained the FBI better than this. You're not seeing the evidence. Wake up! Have you forgotten his DNA is all over that van, that knife, that gun, and explosive material found at his home," Reeves shot back?

"Yeah, DNA that conveniently was found in another van left behind by the same people who bombed that building," Jansen replied. "DNA that was conveniently left behind on a knife found at his home. DNA that was conveniently left behind on a gun found in the taxi. Are we supposed to believe that this man conspired, planned, and implemented a bombing of a federal building without triggering one red flag? No warning signs. No trail as to how this explosive material from the Cold War ends up in his home. Not a single person in his life said a damn thing. But, yet, according to you, he's dumb enough to leave his DNA behind — not once but three times?" She paused. "Reeves, there's a saying if something happens once, it's chance. If it happens twice, it could be explained as a coincidence. If it happens three times, it's enemy action."

"That's right. He's the enemy. Criminals make mistakes under duress, Jansen. That's interrogation 101. And I didn't say he acted alone. You saw the others that entered that building," Reeves corrected.

"Yeah, Lynch and Katsumi, and two other individuals. Bogus IDs, by the way. Bogus military history. Much like our man. And much like our man, still alive," Jansen said, her voice rising. "At least that we know."

Reeves drummed his fingers on his chair, looking exasperated by it all. "What can I say? They executed it with precision."

"See, that's the thing, I didn't see precision. I saw a few people who didn't care if their faces were seen on surveillance cameras. Now, either they were sloppy or suicidal, which clearly, they weren't because they're alive. Or is it possible they were unaware of what they were doing?"

"Oh, back to the Manchurian candidate theory."

"Reeves, we have 25 kilotons of plutonium in portable suitcases stolen from a federal building close to ground zero. Now, I'm no conspiracy theorist, but I'm always willing to admit when I can't see the forest for the trees because I am so focused on only one aspect of a situation; the question is, are you?"

Reeves rubbed his stubble. "Look, I know he didn't shoot you, Jansen, and somewhere deep down, you're struggling to make sense of that, but wake up and smell the coffee. That doesn't make him innocent."

"I never said he was. But for someone who was supposed to be heartless enough to kill hundreds in a building and walk away, he sure went out of his way to keep people alive on that train," Jansen argued.

"You are overlooking the evidence. Listen, you're going to see really fast that this man is a cold, calculated terrorist. I just hope we catch him before he strikes again because the next time, that will be on us."

"He won't."

"You don't know that. An innocent man doesn't run," Reeves said. "You said it yourself."

She couldn't argue with that except to echo Ryker's own words. "They do if someone is trying to kill them and set them up," Jansen replied.

Silence stretched between them for a few minutes before Jansen piped up one last time. "You know, there a few things that have troubled me about this case."

"Yeah, what?" Reeves asked.

"How did they know he was in that taxi? How did they know he was at Emily Sutton's house? How did they know he got on that train?" She paused for a second. "Makes you wonder, right?"

Reeves said nothing. Doug glanced at her, his eyes darting between them. He understood what she was implying. Either Ryker was set up, or someone in-house tipped them off.

Silence followed as the jet began making its descent.

They touched down at Floyd Bennett Memorial Airport in upstate New York, minutes away from Lake George. A snowstorm was raging outside. The team quickly disembarked and was met by a black sedan waiting to take them to the helicopter's last location.

The drive was treacherous, with heavy snow falling in thick flakes that obscured the road. As the sedan's headlights cut through the darkness, illuminating the swirling snow, Jansen sat in the back, wondering what would happen if Reeves was right.

They arrived at a farmer's field. The lights of police vehicles flashed blue and red, pulsating in the night, slashed by falling snow. Jansen pulled up her coat collar as she stepped out of the sedan.

A police officer approached, squinting into the snow. "A neighbor saw it come down. The field is owned by a farmer. We've got the dogs out, eyes in the sky, but there are no footprints because of the storm. It will be hard to track him in this," the cop said.

Jansen hurried toward the abandoned helicopter, hoping to find something, anything that could give them a lead. The helicopter's rotor blades were covered in thick snow. Jansen peered inside, her flashlight cutting through the darkness. The cabin was empty.

Jansen's breath was visible. "All right, folks, he couldn't have gotten far. All he was wearing was a hospital gown."

Frustration gnawed at her as she stepped back from the helicopter. The officer was right — the storm would make it nearly impossible to track him, and time was running out. She turned to Reeves and Doug, who were speaking with local law enforcement officers.

"Widen the search area," Jansen said, her voice firm. "I don't expect he has made it far in this weather. Check any nearby buildings, cabins, anything that could provide shelter."

Reeves nodded, relaying the orders to the officers. Doug approached Jansen, his expression serious. "The weather is getting bad, Meredith. Maybe we should hold off until the morning?"

Jansen shook her head. "We can't afford to wait."

"What do you think his next move is?" Doug asked.

Reeves walked over and answered that. "If he's smart, he'll find somewhere to lay low until the storm passes and then try to get out of the country in the morning."

The team fanned out, searching the surrounding area with flashlights and dogs. The snow continued to fall heavy, making visibility difficult. Jansen's mind was a whirlwind of thoughts and theories as she trudged through the snow, her flashlight cutting through the darkness.

As they searched, Jansen knew that if Ryker was a trained operative, he wouldn't make it easy for them to find him, nor would he make reckless decisions.

She paused, looking around the field.

The helicopter had landed here for a reason. Ryker must have known someone nearby who could help. She turned to Doug. "Talk to local PD and get their thoughts. They know this area better than anyone else."

Doug pulled out a map, his flashlight illuminating the paper as he went and talked with several officers. A few moments later, he returned, tracing a path on the map with his finger. "According to one of the officers, there's a hunting cabin about half a mile from here. It's not much, but it would provide shelter. However, we can't get to it by vehicle."

"Lead the way," Jansen said, her resolve firm.

They set off through the snow, the wind howling around

them. The journey was arduous, each step through the deep snow sapping their strength.

After what felt like an eternity, they saw it. It was a small, weathered structure, its windows dark. Jansen approached the cabin cautiously, her flashlight beam cutting through the darkness. As they neared, she noticed the door was slightly ajar, with shards of broken glass scattered on the floor just inside.

"Keep your eyes peeled," she said, her voice low before she shouted. "Ryker! FBI."

Jansen pushed the door wide, the creak of rusty hinges breaking the silence of the night. The cabin was cold and musty but offered shelter from the wind and snow. She stepped inside, her flashlight illuminating the interior. The cabin was sparsely furnished, with a small wood-burning stove, cot, and shelves stocked with canned goods and basic supplies.

They searched the cabin for any clues that Ryker had been there. Jansen moved to the cot, her flashlight revealing a set of old but serviceable clothes. She picked up a thick flannel shirt. Then, her light caught something on the floor — droplets of water. The melted snow led to a crumpled hospital gown.

"He was here," she said. Her voice filled with certainty as she held up the discarded garment. "Okay, folks, our guy has changed and is on the move."

CHAPTER 41

The fire crackled, its warmth spreading throughout the room. Max scanned multiple headlines, the weight of the revelations pressing down on him.

"FBI: 10 Russian Spies Arrested in U.S." – CBS News

"FBI breaks up alleged Russian spy ring in deep cover." – The Guardian

"The Russian spies living next door." – CNN

His entire life had been a lie, a carefully constructed facade designed to manipulate and control him. The anger and betrayal he felt were almost overwhelming.

"You have to understand, Max," Red said softly. "Your mother did everything she could to protect you. She made mistakes and told lies, but her love for you has never been in question. Julia wanted you to have a chance at a normal life, free from the shadows that haunted her."

"Then maybe she should have left me alone."

"She couldn't. You would have been killed."

"Better that than to strip me of my family and force me into living a lie."

Max looked up from the newspapers, his eyes full of anger. "How is it possible that I can't remember?"

Red sighed his expression one of deep regret. "You wouldn't."

As the fire crackled in the hearth and the snow continued to fall outside, Red began to tell Max more about his past and the development of the Black Raven program.

"As far back as the 1950s, the CIA was trying to discover how a doctor could erase a person's mind and instill new memories, new patterns of behavior," Red began, his voice low and serious. "Hundreds of unwitting subjects in psychiatric hospitals became part of these experiments. Sometime in the 1970s, the CIA began funding experiments into mind control and brainwashing at a psychiatric hospital in Montreal, Canada. That project became known as MK Ultra."

Max leaned forward, his brow furrowed in concentration. "MK Ultra? I heard rumors about that but always thought it was a conspiracy theory."

Red shook his head grimly. "It was very real. It was born out of fear that Soviet, Chinese, and North Korean forces had developed mind control techniques that could be used on U.S. prisoners during the Korean War. So the CIA began their own experiments, messing with LSD, drug-induced comas, and reprogramming to create a Manchurian candidate who could perform actions without conscious awareness."

Max ran a hand around the back of his neck.

"The experiments went beyond that," Red continued. "They looked at how they could enhance interrogation and get the truth out of people by erasing memories and manipulating behavior to make subjects compliant. Back then, the CIA wanted to use these techniques for covert operations. It didn't take them long to realize that even their most trusted agents could be seen as a liability if they were captured or if agents returned and decided to sell what information they knew. But if they could block or erase areas of memory, now that would be control."

"The Russians used this research?"

Red nodded. "They stole the research, adapted, and improved it."

"In what ways?"

"Are you familiar with drugs that can alter cognition, mood, and memory?"

"Somewhat."

"For instance, Ritalin and Modafinil are used today to enhance cognition, then there's Prozac to enhance mood. SVR worked on the reverse. What was discovered through those suffering from PTSD was that a drug called propranolol, which is a beta blocker, had the ability to dampen memory so that short-term memory wouldn't become long-term. In essence, administering before or after a memory could interfere with the reconsolidation process and weaken the memory. Meaning they could use it to wipe out the memory of a traumatic event. What SVR did was simply find a way to alter and enhance that drug."

Max's mind was reeling. "That's why doctors found propranolol in my system?"

Red nodded solemnly. "A modified version. You see, there's an even more powerful drug known as ZIP, which can control the reconsolidation of memory. The way it works is every time we try to remember something, certain proteins must come together inside the brain to put that memory together again."

"And?" Max said, shaking his head in confusion.

Red leaned forward, his eyes intense. "Well, imagine a

JOYE

Beck Lake Rim
Age 3, Mixed

This sweet rescue pup loves all the attention and being close to her humans. Her favourite things are food, belly rubs, and hikes. She's a sweet girl and very loved by her new mom.

BILLIE

Buffalo Bill Reservoir
Age 5, Labrador Retriever

This dog is a total people-lover! Whenever visitors come by, he greets them with a stuffed animal, making everyone feel welcome. He's officially earned the title of Canine Good Citizen, showing off his great manners and friendly personality.

TEEMU AND KYIA

Red Lakes
Ages 7 and 4, Siberian Husky and Black Mouth Cur

Teemu is a social pup who adores all humans, car rides, and swimming. Kyia, the shy rescue dog, warms up to her family and loves hanging out with other dogs. They are always excited for an outing together!

SLOAN AND BUCKY

Manitou Springs
Ages 6 months and 3, Boston Terrier and Shepherd/ Ridgeback mix

Sloan is a cute pup with a crooked tail who was recently adopted from Mid America Boston Terrier Rescue. She adores Bucky, who was a beloved foster failure. Bucky loves playing fetch and truly believes he's a lap dog!

TAILS FROM . . .

Colorado Springs, Colorado USA

Known for stunning natural landmarks like Pikes Peak and the Garden of the Gods, as well as the prestigious US Air Force Academy.

A DOG'S GUIDE:

1. Enjoy a meal at Pub Dog Colorado, where you can relax with your pup in a huge 9,000 square feet of off-leash space to play.
2. Hit the trails for a hike with your dog at stunning spots like Garden of the Gods, Red Rock Canyon Open Space, or Seven Bridges.
3. Splash around in the creek at Bear Creek Off Leash Dog Park, which boasts 25 acres of open prairie and trails.
4. Dive into fun at the dog-friendly Stratton Reservoir.
5. Soak in the amazing views of Colorado Springs from the top of Pikes Peak.

NATIONAL MILL DOG RESCUE

These photoshoots raised funds for National Mill Dog Rescue, which advocates for discarded breeding dogs and honors the rescue of a little Italian Greyhound named Lily. Visit nmdr.org to learn more

ALICIA ROHLFING
WILLOW CREEK PORTRAITS

Throughout my life, having pets has been a constant, and I can't imagine being without them. The fleeting nature of their presence is, however, an unpleasant reality. This awareness has instilled in me the importance of preserving memories through images that encapsulate the unique bond we share with these special creatures. While it's heartbreaking to know that our fur babies are only with us for a limited time, it underscores the significance of capturing moments with them.

My favourite thing about being a pet photographer is experiencing first-hand that special bond between pets and their people and the joy they bring to each other!

WILLOWCREEKPORTRAITS.COM

SUSIE, AUGUST, RUBY AND CONNER

Rock Ledge Ranch
Ages 8, 9, 12 and 10

Susie, a puppy mill survivor, transformed from full of fear to a crazy little spitfire! August is another puppy mill rescue and as sweet as he is shy. Independent Ruby is full of charm. Finally, little Conner is a lover of booty scritches - though unfortunately he does carry some PTSD from his time at the puppy mill. All four of these gorgeous dogs are now thriving in their forever home!

GYPSY

Downtown Colorado Springs
Age 8, Mini Australian Shepherd

She's a rescue from the National Mill Dog Rescue who adores toys and can't get enough of car rides. Whether she's playing or cruising around, Gypsy's joyful spirit shines through!

KOJI, AKEMI AND MAKANA

US Olympic and Paralympic Museum
Ages 5, 6 and 7, Shiba Inu

Koji has various AKC CGC, Therapy Dog, and Trick Dog titles. Meanwhile, Akemi's on a journey to be brave and see the world isn't so scary. And let's not forget Makana, who has her own AKC CGC titles and has been a therapy dog for a year now!

GEMMA AND MAVERICK

United States Air Force Academy
Ages 15 and 2, Maltese Dogs
Gemma still has a lot of spunk for 15 years old and is a roly poly pup at heart. Maverick, adopted from NMDR, is a curious adventurer who loves to leap off furniture and chase balls.

JODY, BLACKJACK, IRIS AND SHEP

Garden of the Gods
Ages 5, passed, 10 and 7, Alaskan Huskies and German Shepherds

Jody is still learning to trust, but loves being around people. Blackjack was the first dog the family adopted from the National Mill Dog Rescue, and passed away before this photoshoot. Iris brings the sass and humour, while energetic Shep is a total goofball who adores his family.

WILLA AND GEORGY GIRL

The Club at Flying Horse
Ages 10 and 6, English Setter and Cocker Spaniel

Willa and Georgy Girl are two adorable rescue pups from the National Mill Dog Rescue. Willa, who snores loudly, was too small to breed. Georgy has just two teeth due to the poor conditions in the puppy mill, but she's a super happy girl who loves to learn.

MARJORIE

Cheyenne Canyon
Age 8, Long Haired Dachshund

The little dog of many nicknames, Marjorie also goes by Miss Margarita, Little Marzipan, and Mama Marjorie. She celebrates potty breaks with zoomies, delights in belly rubs, and loves jumping on her person. She prefers to be carried like royalty and who could deny her?

COCO

Colorado College
Age 2, Irish Wolf Hound/Standard Poodle mix

Coco is a super loving dog with beautiful eyes and a unique blend of both breeds. She's not just adorable; she's also really smart!

RILEY

Whetstone Park of Roses
Age 1, Australian Shepherd

Riley boasts piercing blue eyes and a heart full of love for cuddling everyone he meets. He enjoys sneaking out of the house to play with the neighbour dogs.

TAILS FROM . . .

Columbus, Ohio USA

Known as Ohio's capital and cultural hub, home of OSU Buckeyes stadium and host of Arnold Schwarzenegger's annual Arnold Sports Festival.

A DOG'S GUIDE:

1. Dive into fun at Alum Creek State Park Dog Beach.
2. Chill out with your pup at Nocterra Brewing Company's dog-friendly beer garden.
3. Delight your furry friend with tasty treats from The Cakehound in German Village and capture a memory at their photo station.
4. Spoil your dog with gourmet meals from Boujee Dog Bites self-serve fridges at various locations.
5. Savor a giant pretzel and German beer at Hoffbrauhaus, while your pup enjoys a special treat from the restaurant.

SPEAK! FOR THE UNSPOKEN

These photoshoots raised funds for Speak! for the Unspoken, a foster-based rescue dedicated to finding homes for special needs dogs and educating the public.
Visit speakfortheunspoken.com to learn more

ERICA SCHOMAKER

ASH AND ALDER PHOTOGRAPHY

I'm Erica, I grew up in Columbus, however in 2016, my husband and I moved just outside of the city to enjoy a quieter life with our pets, which now include 3 dogs, 10 chickens and 6 pigs. With a deep passion for animals and a dedication to honing my craft, I specialize in capturing the unique beauty and essence of our furry companions.

Drawing inspiration from my own dogs and my experience in dog training, including trick training, I strive to create images that truly reflect the personality and character of each pet. Through a personalized and tailored approach, I aim to deliver a stress-free and memorable experience, ensuring that every moment with your pet is beautifully immortalized.

ASHANDALDERPHOTO.COM

BOSCO

Gantz Park
Age 5, Cavachon

This dog is totally obsessed with Chuck-it balls - he can't get enough of them! He adores cats and is always down for a fun game of dress-up. Whether it's fetching or playing fashionista, he's ready for a good time!

GIDGET

Ariel Foundation Park
Age 8, Border Collie mix

This dog is all about the outdoors! She adores playing with balls, munching on treats, and hanging out with kids. When she goes for walks, you can bet she'll be proudly carrying her favourite tennis ball along for the ride!

NORA

Whetstone Park of Roses
Age 3, Husky/Malamute mix

Nora has special needs due to entropion in one eye and a liver shunt that requires surgery, but that doesn't stop her from tagging along on any adventure. Her adorable bat ears jiggle when she jogs and she loves to explore the world.

BUG

ML "Red" Trabue Nature Preserve
Age 1, Staffordshire Terrier

Meet Bug, the adorable rescue dog from Texas! She's a total love/cuddle bug, but after a recent skunk encounter, she's been hilariously dubbed the stink bug. She loves a good splash around in the water.

ELLE

Highbanks Metro Park
Age 3, Australian Shepherd

As the friendly store greeter at Equus Now, Elle loves to show off her many tricks, making her a delightful companion for both customers and staff alike! She also enjoys swimming and playing fetch.

TUCKER

Schiller Park
Age 8, Catahoula

Tucker is a remarkable blind and deaf therapy dog who loves agility. He delights in showing off his favourite trick: playing dead. His spirit shines brightly, proving that he's a true inspiration to everyone he meets!

LOLA

Quarry Trails Metro Park
Age 2, Aussie Poodle

Lola is pure joy, always gravitating toward children, especially her human's grandchild. She carries her beloved stuffed white dog, "Lola's baby," everywhere and loves to hide her bones all over the house, under the pillow, cushions and behind furniture.

CHARMIN AND LEXI

Whetstone Park of Roses
Ages 4 and 8, Great Pyrenees/Husky and Great Pyrenees/Collie

Charmin and Lexi are adorable pups rescued from a high-kill shelter. Charmin's a certified therapy dog, earning her credentials at just one year old. Lexi likes to get close to your face so she can smell it (but she won't lick you).

COOPER AND DELILAH

Darby Bend Lakes
Ages 5 and 8, Cocker Spaniel and Mini Dachshund

Delilah rocks her pink bikini at the beach, while Cooper is happiest when he is chasing his favourite ball. Delilah has participated in her hometown wiener dog race for the past 4 years and has yet to cross the finish line.

LLOYD

Nymph Falls
Age 2, Golden Retriever/Aussie Shepherd

With a name guaranteed to make Jim Carrey fans grin, Lloyd loves to make friends!

He leaps and jumps like a horse when he wants to be chased and has an adorable obsession with selecting the perfect greeting gift for people at his front door.

TAILS FROM . . .

Comox Valley, BC Canada

Known for its diverse natural landscapes, extensive mountain biking trails, and vibrant breweries and wineries.

A DOG'S GUIDE:

1. Explore the North East wood and Nymph Falls Trails for off-leash forest walks and stunning waterfalls along a beautiful river.
2. After a fun hike, enjoy lunch at one of the many pup-friendly patios.
3. Visit Comox Lake to hike along the forest trail leading to a scenic bluff overlooking the glacier-fed water.
4. Take a leashed stroll on the Paradise Meadow walk at Mt Washington for mountain views and alpine plants.
5. Discover Kye Bay beach, where low tide reveals a wonderland of tidal pools and miles of sandy shore.

NORTH AMITY DOG RESCUE SOCIETY

These photoshoots raised funds for North Amity Dog Rescue Society, dedicated to saving dogs from shelters at risk of euthanasia and assisting local surrenders. Visit nadrs.org to learn more

KRISTEN NICHOLSON
FIT FIDO FURTOGRAPHY

I am a dog trainer and photographer from Courtenay, BC in the Comox Valley situated on the gorgeous west coast of Canada. I am drawn to the amazing connection and bond you can grow with your dog and this lead me to dog training.
I have had a camera in my hand since my teen years but within the last few years I have focused on photographing animals and this has quickly become my passion.
Capturing dogs surrounded by the stunning beauty of my local environment makes my heart happy and the joy on their human's face when they see them is so special to me. You will never get this moment back so make the most of it.

FITFIDO.CA/FURTOGRAPHY

COPPER

Croteau Beach
Age 3, King Charles Cavalier

Copper is a great emotional support pup at the dental office, spreading love with his kisses. He has endless energy for playtime and can fetch his toys from anywhere. When he's not busy at the office, you'll find him cuddled up under blankets, snoring away!

KAZOO

Mt. Washington
Age 4, Irish Wolfhound/ Pyrenees mix

This gentle giant is a total people lover who thrives on human interaction. He has a soft spot for baby toys and will happily play with them like they're his prized possessions.

BOESER

Croteau Beach
Age 6, Golden Retriever

Boeser is a cucumber loving pup who enjoys hiking with his ladies and rubbing against his favourite tree.

GUS

Fairy trail forest walk
Age 1, Pyrenees/Husky

This dog is a giant teddy bear with the most loving nature. His two best friends are miniature rescue donkeys, and if you look closely into his unique eyes, you can almost see the universe.

RUPERT

Croteau Beach
Age 1, Golden Retriever

This dog is such a friendly little helper! He loves to carry groceries upstairs and always manages to do it with a wagging tail. He has a habit of sleeping in the weirdest positions that never fail to make everyone smile.

KOBE

Browns River Falls
Age 7, Border Collie/Akita

This dog is a gentle soul who's super loveable and never leaves his humans' side. He's smart, too - he pushes the door open to the backyard and barks once when he wants back in. With his tall legs and unique features, Kobe is always getting compliments on his handsome looks!

MAUI

Tsolum River
Age 2, German Shepherd

Maui is a food enthusiast who adores cheese, tortilla chips, and cooked yams. Her favourite morning routine involves relaxing on her back while her parents hold her paw during coffee time. No matter the destination, she eagerly hops into the car, ready for an adventure!

NIGEL

Kye Bay beach
Age 1, Miniature Dachsund

This little guy doesn't realize he's miniature - as far as Nigel is concerned, he is a Big Dog. He loves to snuggle under the covers, making him the perfect cuddle buddy and he's surprisingly fast, zooming around like he owns the place!

GINGER

Home
Age 13, Corgi/Papillon

Ginger is a spirited 13-year-old who still bounces around with the enthusiasm of a puppy. She doesn't walk or run; she levitates! She adores lounging on her back with her four little paws in the air and racing her best buddy, Jasper the cat.

HENRY WADDLESWORTH LONGFELLOW

Morehead City
Age 1, Pembroke Welsh Corgi

Henry Waddlesworth Longfellow (or Brigsby, to his friends) comes from a family of fancy names. He's an adventurous pup who made a splash at the first-ever Wolfpack Corgi race and enjoys water sports like kayaking and paddleboarding!

TAILS FROM . . .

Crystal Coast, N Carolina USA

Known for its 85 miles of pristine coastline, the Crystal Coast is home to diverse marine life and popular fishing tournaments.

A DOG'S GUIDE:

1. Take a ferry to Cape Lookout National Seashore to see the lighthouse and wild horses.
2. Visit Carolina Home and Garden for beautiful gardens, live music, and fun with alpacas and goats.
3. Enjoy the Morehead City waterfront, have lunch at Yellowfin Pub, and grab a treat for your pup at Sea Paws.
4. Head to The Point at Emerald Isle for stunning sunset views with dinner and chairs.
5. Explore dog-friendly trails like Boathouse Walking Trails, Emerald Isle Woods Park, and Fort Macon State Park!

MISPLACED MUTTS

These photoshoots raised funds for Misplaced Mutts, a non-profit organization rescuing dogs and cats from shelters and neglectful situations in North Carolina.
Visit misplacedmutts.com to learn more

JENNIFER WAKEFIELD
CRYSTAL COAST DOG

Jennifer has worked in photography for many years prior, both studio and on-location. However, it wasn't until she brought home a Great Dane puppy that she even thought about photographing dogs. That puppy is almost 13 years old and he is still her muse.
She started Crystal Coast Dog after relocated to the coast of North Carolina to not only photograph dogs but to highlight all the amazing dog-friendly things to see and do in this tiny beach town.
Jennifer's goal is capturing the special connection between people and their dogs to be displayed as art work in their homes; as these important moments shouldn't be hidden away on tech devices to be forgotten.

CRYSTALCOASTDOG.COM

SNICKERS

Cape Lookout
Age 6, Pit Bull/Boxer

Snickers is a sweet pup who loves giving kisses - she'll even dole them out on demand. She's a natural herder, always chasing her ball, and she loves riding in the boat.

XERXES

Boathouse Creek
Age 9, Boston Terrier

Xerxes was the runt of the litter, but that hasn't slowed him down - he's the self-appointed fearless protector of the yard, chasing off scary birds! With a legendary sense of smell, he can sniff out hidden toys effortlessly. Every birthday, he gets a lobster treat - because what else do you give a dog this fancy?

WEST
TOWER

EGYPT

Emerald Isle
Age 13, Doberman

Egypt is an adorable Misplaced Mutts rescue who is now loving the coastal life. Whether it's running on the beach, rolling in the grass, or enjoying a lazy ride in the golf cart - every day brings laughter and joy!

KNOX

Fort Macon
Age 1, Great Dane

Knox is a lovable bulldozer who is completely unaware of his own size and strength. He has earned both his CGC (Canine Good Citizen) and Novice Trick Dog Title - he's got the brains and the charm! Knox loves to sling his jolly rope ball or any toy attached to a long sock.

BUDDY

Radio Island
Age 8, Cattle Dog

Buddy is a beloved foster fail who inspired Wagon Tails Farm Rescue. He's a master of the "Booty Trap," to get other dogs to play. He'll feign sleep by lying upside down, but his cute wiggling tail stump gives him away.

EAMES

Emerald Isle
Age 3, Great Dane

Eames insists on a daily adventure, usually a trip to the local trails or beach. He's the boss! His obsession with rabbits in the backyard occasionally leads to unexpected "yardwork" (a.k.a. holes). He loves chasing water so much that his people have to spell the word H-O-S-E.

INDIANA JONES

Emerald Isle
Age 3, Indian Street Dog

Meet this charming street dog from India, now enjoying a cosy life filled with stolen socks! Every morning, he strikes a prairie dog pose, eagerly waiting for belly rubs. His ears stand tall, but when he snoozes, they transform into adorable "Yoda mode."

SNICKERS

Atlantic Beach
Age 9, Lemon Dalmatian

Snickers is a lovable, grumpy old man who loves to groan and sigh dramatically. A true velcro dog, he warms up to his favorites and sticks by them for life. His ultimate joy? Burrowing under the covers and being cradled like a baby during cuddle time!

MARIBEL, MATEO AND MELODY

Home
Ages 2, 3 and 3, Rat Terrier/Chihuahua, Pomeranian/Chihuahua and Cocker Spaniel/Chihuahua

Maribel is a total mommy's girl who loves rolling in anything from dead fish to horse poop! Mateo is the protector of his girls and is always ready to shower you with kisses! Melody is a total foodie who never quite outgrew the puppy phase - she's forever young at heart.

KUZO

Lodhi Art District
Age 4, Indie

Kuzo loves to run! He's absolutely a "catch me if you can" kind of dog & wants to make it into a game every time. Cuddles sessions are his favourite, especially when they involve a good gossip. He loves snuggle in between his hooman and her mom when they're chatting so he can listen in on the conversation!

TAILS FROM . . .

Delhi, India

Known for delicious food, vibrant street shopping, and rich historical sites.

A DOG'S GUIDE:

1. Take a stroll through UNESCO-awarded Sunder Nursery, where sunlight dances through tall trees.
2. India Gate is a must-visit, especially at sunrise. Walk the 2.5 km path from Rashtrapathi Bhavan to India Gate and feel the history beneath your paws.
3. Picnic on the grass at Nehru Park in Chanakyapuri.
4. Discover the tranquillity of Lodhi Garden, filled with tree-lined walkways, duck ponds, and historical tombs.
5. Head to Tail Club, the ultimate dog playground! Let your pup run free on the grassy lawn, splash in the dog pool, and enjoy treats from the café.

TAILS OF COMPASSION TRUST

These photoshoots raised funds for Tails of Compassion Trust, which rescues and provides care for senior and special-needs animals, promoting compassion and education.

PRATHIMA PINGALI

PAWPARAZZI BY PRATHIMA

I'm India's first & leading pet photographer. I started Pawparazzi after my dog Pax passed away in 2018. Over the last 5 years I have photographed more than 430+ dogs & helped 375 + families capture beautiful memories with their furry ones.

My specialty lies in capturing a pet's true personality and relationship with their hoomans. I'm based out of Mumbai, but all across India for shoots.

Pawparazzi has been featured in publications such as Vogue India, New Indian Express, Hindustan Times, The Sunday Times, Mumbai Live, Dogs & Pups Magazine, Creature Companion & more!

PAWPARAZZI.IN

WIGGY

DLF MAGNOLIAS
Age 17, Indie

Wiggy, the little survivor born in a drain, earned her name by wiggling with joy whenever she saw her hooman. This treat-loving pup will do anything for a snack - dancing, hopping, rolling over - you name it, and she's still at it today!

CHAMCHAM

Qutub Minar
Age 3, Indie

Chamcham is a small, shy pup who takes her time to warm up to new people. She was found near a tree, almost lifeless at just 3 months old. While her brother is the brains of the operation, Chamcham is all about beauty and just wants love and cuddles!

DATA

Sundar Nursery
Age 4, Indie

When Data was first adopted, he had no idea how to walk on slippery indoor floors (having spent his entire life outside). He learnt to walk on Persian carpets. His obsession with butter chicken taught Data how to "speak" and he is known for zoomie sessions that last precisely 3 minutes.

SKY

India Gate
Age 3, Indie

Sky was adopted when she was only 45 days old. She a nervous gal, easily spooked by big objects and large hoomans, but she quickly warms up to women. Her favourite distraction is squirrels, which send her zooming off like a rocket. This goofball loves playing tug and fetch all day long!

JACKIE
Lodhi Gardens
Age 4, Indie

Jackie is happiest when she's enjoying her time lounging in the grass and watching the world go by. She springs into action if a fly comes close though - suddenly as focused as a soldier on a war front, brave & determined to protect everyone from those dastardly flies!

OLIVE

Kartavya Path
Age 4, Indie

Olive loves to sing along to Vivaldi, putting on opera shows for guests. She's famous in her condo for making friends with the monkeys and she thoroughly enjoys a good "sniffari" session when she can chase squirrels and pigeons.

MISHTI

Yamuna Ghat
Age 2, Indie

Mishti is one of the three lucky puppies who survived a traumatic start to life. She has a serious love for treatos and car rides. This adventurous pup has travelled everywhere with her hoomans, even enjoying thrilling speedboat and paddle boat rides!

SIMBA

Mehrauli Archeological Park
Age 5, Indie

Watching Simba run is a treat to the eyes - she's so fast that she looks like a cheetah running in the wild! She's totally spoilt and still insists on sitting on her hooman's lap - although now that she's older, she also craves her own space (typical teenager).

GOLDY

George George Memorial Park
Age 11, Labrador Retriever

Goldy is an Honour Scout with Dog Scouts of America, always ready to help out without being asked. She adores water, especially swimming with her bumper, and spreads unconditional love to everyone around her.

TAILS FROM . . .

Detroit, Michigan USA

Known for its auto industry, expansive geographical area, and passionate sports fans.

A DOG'S GUIDE:

1. Swim with your pup at Belle Isle, Orion Oaks Dog Park, Mill Race in Saline, or Island Lake Recreation Area.
2. Cheer on the Detroit Tigers! Enjoy dog-friendly baseball games throughout the season.
3. Discover dog-friendly patios in Royal Oak and Ferndale for a local beverage with your furry friend.
4. Explore the outdoors! Take walks in 13 Metroparks, along the Detroit Riverwalk, the Dequindre Cut, or at various state parks.
5. Experience fall delights! Visit apple orchards or cider mills with your dog, enjoying many pet-friendly options.

I HEART DOGS RESCUE AND ANIMAL HAVEN

These photoshoots raised funds for I Heart Dogs Rescue and Animal Haven, supporting no-kill initiatives and aiding homeless dogs and domestic violence survivors' pets. Visit iheartdogs.org to learn more

JENNIFER MCCALLUM
FIREFLY PET PHOTOGRAPHY

Jennifer's work with animal rescue led her to starting Firefly Pet Photography. She is committed to improving the lives of animals and knew that she would be able to help more as a business than as an individual.

Jennifer believes that pets are members of the family and the Firefly experience is designed for both ends of the leash. With an eye for detail and a passion for storytelling, Jennifer specializes in capturing the wonder and whimsy of life's simple joys, creating one-of-a-kind images that capture the essence of the entire family.

Jennifer is the chief butler to two dogs and two cats, though she is always trying to sneak in a foster pet or three.

FIREFLYPETPHOTOGRAPHY.COM

JAZZY AND VINNIE

Carpenter Lake Nature Preserve
Ages 7 and 11, Staffordshire Terrier/ Beagle and Labrador Retriever

Jazzy, a joyful rescue from Happy Days Dog and Cat Rescue, adores her family and loves snuggling. She enjoys playing ball and chasing squirrels with her cousin Vinnie, an old soul with a puppy heart who delights in peanut butter and lounging in the grass or on the beach!

RILEY

George George Memorial Park
Age 12, Border Collie

Riley, affectionately nicknamed "Peanut" for her tiny size, is a proud Dog Scout who hits up camp every summer.

She loves hiking the trails at the Ford House, the former estate of Eleanor and Edsel Ford, enjoying the beautiful views by Lake St. Clair.

KENNA, DOUGAL AND CILLA BEAN

Sandra Richardson Park
Ages 3, 8 and 5, Malinois/Bully, Malinois/Bully and German Shepherd

These three dogs play well together, enjoy each other's company, and socialize beautifully with others. Their human is a dog trainer who proudly shares that each dog has been a beautiful learning journey.

KAREN

Carpenter Lake Nature Preserve
Age 4, American Pitbull Terrier

Karen loves to sprawl out when she sleeps and changes position by pushing off her human. Super athletic, she enjoys learning new tricks and skills to show off her muscles. Her favourite snacks are anything but Tostitos, including broccoli, carrots, strawberries and popcorn.

PJ

Douglas Evans Nature Preserve
Age 5, Pomsky

PJ is a total attention seeker and a ladies' man! He enjoys the outdoors, splashing in the pool during summer and playing in snowbanks come winter. He's an awesome fur sibling, always looking out for the special needs and senior foster pups and kitties in his home.

MOCHI

Stony Creek Metropark
Age 5, Chihuahua mix

Meet Mochi the Shoe Thief! He will empty the closet if given the chance, so his family has to keep the closet doors locked. He loves licking the kitchen floor at his grandmom's house, always hunting for tasty leftovers.

DRIZZLE AND GHILLIE DHU

Greenmead Historical Park,
Ages 14 and 5, Siberian Husky

Drizzle's main claim to fame is being the official poster dog for the Michigan Winter Dog Classic show! He and his brother Ghillie Dhu (who was diagnosed with epilepsy at the age of 2) have both earned an array of titles. They are proud members of Dog Scouts of America.

MOLLY

Dog Scouts of America camp
Age 6, Labrador Retriever

Molly is a spirited dog with a passion for trying new things. She particularly loves agility and dock diving, showcasing her energetic personality. As a proud member of Dog Scouts of America, she embraces every adventure with enthusiasm and joy!

LARRY

Home
Age 11, St. Bernard/Labrador

Larry was (believe it or not) the smallest pup in the litter. All grown up now, he struts around his kingdom like royalty, proudly patrolling the property line. This spoiled prince insists on having his water freshly filled, refusing to drink anything that's been left for even a few hours!

TAILS FROM . . .

Douai, France

Known for old coal heaps, numerous bell towers, and Les Fêtes de Gayant (the Festival of Giants).

A DOG'S GUIDE:

1. Take a hike in Marchiennes Forest, where you can explore beautiful trails and enjoy nature.
2. Stop by the Waf Café in Lille, a cosy spot that welcomes dogs and helps those in need of a home.
3. Visit Souchez Waterfall, where lovely trails let you discover local plants.
4. Walk to the Rieulay slag heap, where a trail circles a serene lake surrounded by greenery.
5. Visit Vaucelles Abbey, a beautiful 12th-century monument rich in history. It's a great place to explore and appreciate the architecture of the region.

BEAGLES EN NORD

These photoshoots raised funds for Beagles en Nord, supporting rescue, fostering, and adoption of distressed beagles and fighting against animal mistreatment and abandonment. Visit beaglesennord.com to learn more

HELENE CARAUX

DIGRESSION PHOTO

Hello ! I'm Hélène, dog and horse photographer for... a long time! Like many of my colleagues, I've had a passion for animals ever since I was a little girl, and I'd run out of disposable cameras to take pictures of every animal I came across.

I love capturing the unique and often very funny expressions of dogs. Nothing amuses me more than photographing a dog running with its ears to the wind, making a face at certain noises, or catching a treat in mid-air!

I'm very active in animal protection, so I'm delighted to be part of this Tails of the World adventure.

ANIMALIER.DIGRESSION.PHOTO

OONA

Home
Age 6, Alaskan Malamute

Oona, the long-haired malamute, has been nicknamed "The Hairy One". She is a rescue dog and was adopted with some intense fears to overcome, but her playful spirit shines through. She is an excellent mole hunter!

NDY

Cascade de Souchez
Age 8, Beagle

Ndy, a cheerful rescue dog, joined her family a few months ago. She loves accompanying her human to work at the school and enjoys life alongside her furry friend, Poupette, another rescue dog.

HOOPER

Rieulay
Age 12, Beagle

Hooper is a quirky pup who thinks he's a cat, so he's way more excited to meet felines than other dogs. Despite having four cosy doggy baskets, he prefers crashing on the floor. Out in the street, folks often confuse him for a baby labrador because of his striking white fur!

NJALA

Douai
Age 1, Alaskan Malamute

Njala is a rescue dog who enjoys lounging in the garden and keeping an eye on the pigeons. She used to be terrified of other dogs but now loves playing with them at the park. Njala is very sensitive and has been deeply affected by the loss of his two playmates in one month.

MAJI

Stoney Point
Age 6, Mixed

This dog is all about that tennis ball life and can't resist a crunchy carrot snack. When he's feeling happy, he trots around like a horse, making everyone smile with his playful spirit.

TAILS FROM . . .

Duluth, Minnesota USA

Known for its scenic views and outdoor activities, Duluth is a popular port city and tourist destination on Lake Superior.

A DOG'S GUIDE:

1. Pack your favourite toys and head to Park Point Beach for a sandy picnic where you can dig, run, and splash in Lake Superior.
2. Visit Canal Bark doggie daycare or enjoy a doggie vacation while your humans are busy.
3. Enjoy the dog-friendly patio at Canal Park Brewing Company with great views of Lake Superior.
4. Explore over 200 scenic miles of hiking trails.
5. Treat yourself to a gourmet pup cup from Love Creamery and stroll around the Lincoln Park Craft District.

RABBIT RESCUE OF MN

These photoshoots raised funds for Rabbit Rescue of MN, a volunteer-driven nonprofit dedicated to helping unwanted and abused domesticated rabbits in need. Visit rabbitrescueofmn.com to learn more

ALYSSA LOVDAHL
SHINE PET PHOTOGRAPHY

I've always been a dog mom but this chapter of my life has been lovingly stolen by 3 rescue bunnies & now I'm that bunny mom. Ya know, the one taking them exploring, giving them a spoiled free-roam life & letting them fill up my heart & camera roll.
I've worked with animals in every chapter of my life. To my core I've always been a creative & animal lover so it only made sense and felt right when Shine Pet Photography came to life. I absolutely love helping animal lovers freeze time, celebrate the soul pets in their lives, while giving them a moment to shine because they're so much more than pets.

SHINEPETPHOTOGRAPHY.COM

EMBER

Duluth Rose Garden
Age 3, Golden Retriever

Ember makes dinosaur noises when she's happy and loves lounging on her back while holding a tennis ball up in the air.

JACK

Park Point Beach
Age 2, Border Collie

Jack is a playful dog who herds everything in sight! He's always on the lookout to steal sticks from his brother and enjoys chasing squirrels with boundless energy.

LILY

Enger Park
Age 4, Shepherd mix

Lily's best buddy is a tortoise, and she's got two AKC Trick Dog Titles to her name. When she's eager to head outside, she'll sneak up and give her human a gentle paw on the face. What a clever pup!

JUNIPER

Hartley Park
Age 6, Dutch

Juniper is a delightful rabbit who believes the fridge is magical, hoping it opens with his gaze. He thinks he's a dog, he will beg for food, greet you at the door and has the tricks to prove it. He's also fully aware that he's the spoiled golden child.

MIRA

Lester Park
Age 5, Jersey Wooly

Mira is the loafing queen, lounging around all day to remind everyone of her royal status. She is the bunny with a princess face, werewolf feet and heart of gold.

REME

Brewer Park Loop
Age 6, Jersey Wooly

Reme might only weigh 2.5 pounds, but he struts around like he's 50 pounds and has the attitude to go with it. His mustache sits above his nose, so it's technically not legit (but don't tell him that). He's a prickly pear: thorny outside, but oh so sweet inside!

BALOU

Brighton Beach
Age 14, Mixed

For Balou, balls are life. She won't leave the house without a stuffed animal in tow, and she's got grandma totally convinced that sharing meals is a must.

RUBY

Chester Creek Trail
Age 1, Siberian Husky

Ruby is a fabulously sassy show dog who adores strawberries. She enjoys running with her friends, exploring new places, and snuggling with her beloved family.

BOOTS

Park Point Beach
Age 8, Collie mix

Boots is a chatty pup who loves to howl. He enjoys hopping on the boat for some swimming fun and can't resist a good game of catch.

MARLI

Downtown Edmond
Age 3, Pitty/Labrador

Marli is a total water lover, always diving into the pool for a swim. She also enjoys going for car rides and feels the wind in her fur. Back home, you can find her happily chasing squirrels around the backyard!

TAILS FROM . . .
Edmond, Oklahoma USA

Known for its numerous statues, the lively Heard on Hurd street festival, and one of the country's best 4th of July fireworks shows.

A DOG'S GUIDE:

1. Splash around at Lake Arcadia – swimming and boating fun!
2. Explore Mitch Park's new walking trails for a great hike.
3. Enjoy tasty treats at restaurants near Stephenson Park, and munch at the picnic tables.
4. Chill out with a drink at Frenzy Brewing, bringing your human and hanging out together.
5. Visit Hafer Park to feed the ducks, stroll the trails, play at the playgrounds, and check out special events.

SUZY MCCRACKEN
SUZY MCCRACKEN PHOTOGRAPHY

Suzy is a highly skilled and experienced pet photographer who specializes in capturing beautiful pictures of dogs, their unique characteristics, and the bond they share with their owner.

Her knowledge in handling and training dogs helps foster a comfortable environment that makes animals feel at ease. Her clients often remark on how quickly their pets warm up to Suzy and how much they enjoy the experience.

SUZYMCCRACKENPHOTOGRAPHY.COM

BORDER COLLIE SAVE & RESCUE

These photoshoots raised funds for Border Collie Save & Rescue, supporting the rescue, rehabilitation, and rehoming of Border Collies in Texas, Oklahoma, and Louisiana.
Visit bcsave.org to learn more

MILEY

Hafer Park
Age 4, Cockapoo

This dog is a bubbly enthusiast who loves popping and chasing bubbles. She's a bit of a scaredy-cat when it comes to actual cats and adores her dad, the family cook, more than anyone else.

IBAKA

Fink Park
Age 13, Shitzu/Schnauzer

Meet Serge, the dog named after basketball star Serge Ibaka! Just like his namesake, he can jump and block with ease. He's a friendly pup who loves hanging out with both kids and adults.

NOVA AND BENTLEY

Home
Ages 1 and 6, Boston Terriers

Nova and Bentley are total Velcro dogs, following their owner everywhere. They absolutely love going on walks and can't get enough of car rides. It's all about those adventures together!

OZZY

Hafer Park
Age 1, Berndoodle

Ozzy watches animals on TV, eagerly following them off-screen and peeking behind the TV in curiosity. Truly like having a live stuffed animal, he's incredibly cuddly and loving.

PIPER, SHERLOCK, WATSON, GROOT AND SOPHIE

Hafer Park
Ages 11, 7, 7, 6 and 16, Border Collies

These dogs are all incredibly affectionate and loyal, with a bit of a crazy side that's true to the breed. While mostly well-trained, there's definitely some naughtiness that pops up now and then, adding to their collective charm!

TALLI

Mitch Park
Age 4, Red Heeler/ Pit Bull

Meet the sweetest pit bull mix in the world (according to her totally unbiased mom and dad!) Grateful for her second chance at life, she showers them both with affection. She's slightly ditzy, but is generally on top of things - both literally and figuratively!

SHADOW, JOJO AND CRICKET

Lake Arcadia
Age 7, 9 and 12, Aussie, Min Pin and Pomeranian mix

They comfort overnight guests that their Dad (a vet) brings home by lying beside the crate, providing company all night. Cricket takes caregiving to a new level - she alerts her human before neurological episodes, stays until she's recovered and retrieves dropped items.

BOOMER

Mitch Park
Age 7, Goldendoodle

This sweet dog is a bit nervous at first, but once you get to know him, his loyalty and intelligence shine through. He adores kids, enjoys playing catch, and loves chasing after squirrels and rabbits.

EGGSY

Stephenson Park
Age 12 weeks, Goldendoodle

This dog has an adorable underbite that gives him a permanent smile. Super smart, he's already potty trained and full of life. He has got zero fear, making him quite the adventurous little buddy!

TAILS FROM . . .

Emerald Coast, Florida USA

Known for its beautiful beaches, vibrant marine life, and numerous hiking trails.

A DOG'S GUIDE:

1. Hit the trails at Tarkiln Bayou Preserve State Park in Pensacola for a pawsome hiking adventure.
2. Unwind with your dog at dog-friendly breweries, enjoying a cold beer or wine on the patio together.
3. Splash around at Pensacola Beach's East and West Dog Beaches for a day of sand and surf.
4. Join the fun at Paw Di Gras by Wolfgang Pensacola, where pups can parade and show off their style.
5. Enjoy a sunny day at Crab Island with a dog-friendly pontoon rental from Crab Island Cruises in Destin.

GULF COAST ROTTWEILER RESCUE

These photoshoots raised funds for Gulf Coast Rottweiler Rescue, a foster-based organization dedicated to helping Rottweilers find loving families across the Gulf Coast. Visit gulfcoastrottweilerrescue.org to learn more

SHARMAYNE KAY

WOOFTOGRAFIE

Kay is a Pensacola pet photographer who specializes in fine-art pet portraits. A tea enthusiast & introvert by nature, she finds her extroverted side emerges when she's with her two affectionate Rottweilers or in the company of fellow dog enthusiasts.

Her passion for animals ignited during her time in Spain, where she & her husband welcomed their first puppy. This experience fuelled her love for pet photography, which she seamlessly merged with her background in graphic design upon settling on the Emerald Coast.

When not behind the lens, Kay can be found exploring the outdoors with her beloved pups. The adventures fuel her creativity and provide moments of tranquillity.

WOOFTOGRAFIE.COM

MAGPIE

Bayview Park
Age 6, Pittie mix

This sweet, loyal dog always wants to snuggle up like a lapdog. She's not a fan of walking on hardwood or tile floors, so her family have filled the house with rugs around the house to help her get around. She and Echo, the cat, are total pals and are often spotted playing and snuggling together.

AMBER

Fort Pickens
Age 2, German Shepherd/Kelpie

When she's excited to see you, Amber proudly offers her favourite toy - a gesture that's truly an honour. She loves swimming, whether it's at the beach or in a pool, but mention the word "bath," and she'll bolt to hide. She's a curious explorer, but also cautious with new things. Amber has mastered a little dance, inching closer to investigate without getting too close.

VENTURE

Village of Baytowne Wharf
Age 6 months, Beauceron

Often mistaken for a Doberman/Shepherd mix, the Beauceron is actually an ancient French herding breed recognized by the AKC. Venture is a playful goofball, and his favourite pastime is body-slamming his mom. He is a promising prospect for future sports, shows, and demos!

CUPCAKE AND YOSHII

Downtown Pensacola
Age 9 and 4, Rottweiler

Cupcake's world revolves around her blue frisbee and whistle ball, while Yoshii is all about his kick-ball and ultra ball. If they snag the wrong toy, they hilariously spit it out, like, "No thanks, this one's yours!" These goofy pups also moonlight as doggy models and even lend a paw with dog training.

FRANK

Tudor Street
Age 2, Cavalier King Charles Spaniel

Frank is all about Frankfurters and will do anything for his favourite snack. He is a butterfly hunter - albeit not a very good one. This little lap dog gets hot quickly, so tends to sprawl out on the cool stone floor after a cuddle.

TAILS FROM . . .

Exeter, England UK

Known for its Roman origins, unique medieval underground passages and being home to Parliament Street, the narrowest street in Britain.

A DOG'S GUIDE:

1. Start your day at one of the cafés on the Quay, sipping coffee while you and your pup soak up the atmosphere.
2. Take a train from St David's to Okehampton, or head to dog-friendly beaches like Exmouth or Dawlish Warren.
3. Paddle down the Ship Canal in a canoe from Saddles and Paddles, stopping by pubs like Double Locks or The Turf.
4. Explore Exeter's green spaces, including the historic Northernhay Gardens and the University of Exeter.
5. End your day with a pint at The Prospect, a dog-friendly pub with a rich history and a menu full of treats for both you and your dog.

K9 FOCUS

These photoshoots raised funds for K9 Focus, a volunteer-run dog rescue in Devon dedicated to rehoming dogs from challenging situations across the South West.
Visit k9focus.co.uk to learn more

FIONA CRAWFORD

FIONA CRAWFORD HORSE AND DOG PHOTOGRAPHER

Hi, I'm Fiona and the first thing you need to know about me is that my pets are my therapy, without them I would be a lost soul.

My horses and dogs are exercised, fed and watered every morning before my husband or I even get a look in at breakfast. Animals have always come first: their comfort, their wellbeing and their enjoyment. I have spent the last 20 plus years photographing dogs and horses across the south west of England. From major events to local parks. It was my passion at school and I just wouldn't let go of the dream.
I have limitless patience and a great sense of humour which helps with my job choice, I suppose.

FIONACRAWFORD.CO.UK

EMBER

Gandy Street
Age 4, Sprocker Spaniel

Ember is an eager pleaser who thrives on learning new activities. A beautiful poser, she's gaining a following on social media. Always ready for a challenge, Ember is currently training in gun dog skills, agility, and scent work, showcasing her love for using her brain!

OSKAR

Northernhay Gardens
Age 4, Boxer

Oskar is an eccentric and excitable white boxer with a coloured eye patch. He also has black spots and thinks he is part Dalmatian. He has a proud Icelandic heritage that makes him even more unique!

HOLLY AND MAISIE

Cathedral Steps
Age 3, Beagles

Holly and Maisie are sisters who love hanging out with their mummy beagle, Delilah, and their litter mates. Born on Halloween, their registered names are inspired by spooky movies - Holly's name is Halloween Mary and Maisie is Sarah Sanderson from Hocus Pocus.

LUCY AND RUFUS

University Gardens
Age 3, Miniature Labradoodle

Rufus loves to bury biscuits in the garden, waiting a few days for a soggy snack. He loyally sat by his human's feet while she studied and he squeals with excitement every time she returns home from work, rushing to greet her with a toy in his mouth.

JOE COCKER

Parliament Street
Age 9, Red Setter/Cocker Spaniel

Joe is a watcher. He likes to sit or lie, with his back against something solid for safety and then he is happy to watch the world go by for hours. He's totally obsessed with his flying squirrel frisbee and won't let any pigeon fly by his garden unchallenged!

REGGIE

Cathedral Green
Age 6, Boxer

Reggie, the rescued pup from Poland, loves nothing more than chasing his ball. This clever boy even topped his class in dog obedience training, proving he's not just cute but also super smart!

GHOST

Exeter Library
Age 7, Chihuahua

Ghost is a charming dog with stunning blue eyes who loves to chase seagulls. His name is inspired by Jon Smith's dire wolf from Game of Thrones.

GRIZZLY AND SEVEN

Best Farm on Monocacy National Battlefield
Ages 3 and 2, Siberian Husky and Husky mix

"Grizzly saved me," his mom says. After a devastating divorce, Grizz became her reason to get out of bed every day. His unmatched energy required hours of training and long walks. Grizzly gave her the confidence to re-enter the world and rebuild her life. Seven was found abandoned behind the local hospital on Seventh Street, so the name Seven was a perfect fit. His appetite is endless as is his love for his big brother.

TAILS FROM . . .

Frederick, Maryland USA

Known as the "City of Clustered Spires" due to their many churches, the highrise ban that ensures they remain at the top of the skyline and the Clustered Spires High Wheel (Penny Farthing Bike) Race.

A DOG'S GUIDE:

1. Join the fun at the Canines on the Creek costume contest and parade along Carroll Creek, helping great causes while showing off your stylish look!
2. Treat yourself at Anchor Bar, where you can choose your favourite meal from the Pup Menu.
3. Relax at Dublin Roasters Coffee shop with a coffee for you and a tasty pup cup for your furry friend.
4. Stay cool by kayaking down the Monocacy River.
5. Stroll along Carroll Creek, admiring the blooming water garden and beautifully lit boats. Don't forget to explore the dog-friendly boutiques in Downtown Frederick!

CANINES & KITTIES RESCUE

These photoshoots raised funds for Canines & Kitties Rescue, a volunteer-based organization dedicated to fostering and supporting pregnant, unwanted animals in the region. Visit caninesandkittiesrescue.org to learn more

MEGAN PURTELL

MEGAN PURTELL PHOTOGRAPHY

Megan Purtell has always been passionate about working with animals. She has fostered close to 400 rescue dogs, owned a kennel-free dog daycare & boarding business, and works tirelessly to support the pet rescue community.

Since starting her award-winning professional pet photography career in 2021, her images have elicited strong emotions from her viewers with the deep connections between pets and their people.

Megan has an ability to adapt to a variety of photography styles, from tranquil portraits to fast action, which produces beautiful work for clients. She regularly participates in educational programs to expand her critical skills in photography in the U.S. and internationally.

MEGANPURTELL.COM

CHARLIE

Weinberg Centre for the Arts
Age 15, Shichon

Charlie is a special dog who wears UV-protective glasses for his aging eyes. This super friendly (and sometimes grumpy), old man spreads joy and love while teaching kids that glasses are cool.

Together with his mom, they've written a children's book celebrating differences. In his spare time, he is an ambassador for dog-friendly places around the area.

STARBUCK AND ACE

Joseph Dill Baker Memorial Carillon
Ages 18 and 14, Malamute/ Curly Coated Retriever and Boxer/Bulldog

Everyone loves Starbuck and he loves the attention. He has a warm personality and loves to talk with gurgles, howls, coos, trills and barks. Ace is the smartest and most obedient dog his family has ever had. When their family first started fostering Starbuck, they noticed that he was like a therapy dog for Ace, who was shy and timid. Starbuck gave Ace support and confidence. Their family adopted them within two months of each other in 2013.

DUBLIN

Carroll Creek Linear Park
Age 8, Cavalier King Charles Spaniel

Dublin is a cuddly pup who loves giving kisses and hitting the road for adventures with his mom. He enjoys visiting family and friends and has a taste for gourmet food, although he surprisingly turns his nose up at mac and cheese!

COLLINS

Gambrill State Park
Age 8, Miniature Schnauzer

Collins is the sweetest little pup around, adored by everyone! This 10-pound bundle of joy loves to travel, whether it's road trips or plane rides. She tags along to work daily, where she's a great supervisor, although you'll often find her snoozing on the job!

SHEPARD

National Clustered Spires High Wheel Race
Age 18 months, Silken Windhound

Shepard is named after American Astronaut Alan Shepard due to his tendency to explore. He loves chewing on sticks, snacks, and is incredibly fast. Someday he may pursue agility or lure coursing, but right now he's loving being a companion dog and ruling the household.

LUCAS

South Mountain Creamery Dairy Farm
Age 3, Golden Retriever

Lucas is a chill dog with a big personality who makes his family laugh daily. Most of the time you'll find Lucas lying beside, behind or under Corey's wheelchair, always within arms reach. Lucas loves lounging on the couch like a human, even burping like a guy watching football.

JOEY AND LILY

Roddy Road Covered Bridge
Ages 4 and 15, Golden Retriever and Beagle/Pitbull

Lily was a timid dog until her family showered her with love, helping her blossom into a friendly companion. With her mom in college and the pandemic going on, she brought home Joey, a golden retriever puppy. Now, they're best buds, with Joey training as a search and rescue dog!

PRETZEL

Cunningham Falls State Park
Age 1, Standard Poodle

Pretzel is a friendly and silly pup who's the ultimate mentor for new foster puppies. He teaches them to potty outside, shares toys and bones, and plays until they're worn out. He often gets to hang out with his doggie brother, thanks to his grandparents adopting him!

FOXY

Schifferstadt Heritage Garden
Age 11, Pomeranian/Maltese

After running away from people who didn't care for her, Foxy ended up right where she belonged: in the arms of a new family who treated her like a princess. She was loyal, sweet, and loved watching over foster kittens. Her journey ended June 22, 2024 but is forever loved.

VALOR'S ZHAZOU LEGACY OF ZOLA

City Dock with FXBG Bridge
Age 18 months, Doberman

This dog is a total adventure lover who speaks German and adores little people. She's always ready for fun and brings a unique charm to every outing.

TAILS FROM . . .
Fredericksburg, Virginia USA

Known for its rich Civil War history and outdoor adventures along the Rappahannock River.

A DOG'S GUIDE:

1. First stop, Dog Krazy – a paradise for pups with everything to make you wag your tail!
2. Explore awesome local parks like Alum Spring Park, Lake Mooney, and Chancellorsville Battlefield.
3. Stroll the canal path by the Rappahannock River and treat yourself to a pup cup at the Italian Station.
4. Check out Needful Things Thrift Store, where you get a treat and a toy whilst supporting The Hero Academy for service and therapy dogs.
5. After a fun day, unwind at the Barking Barley for "Suds, Buds, and Belly Rubs!"

ANIMAL AWARENESS AND ASSISTANCE

These photoshoots raised funds for Animal Awareness and Assistance, providing education and resources to help people care for their animals better.
Visit animalaa.org to learn more

CYNTHIA PIXLEY

PIXELS BY PIXLEY PHOTOGRAPHY

Their eyes light up and widen at the sight of their special person. The facial lines of both "owner" and "animal" soften. Collectively, they both breathe slower, closing their eyes. It is a moment where the two come together and the world falls away. This is when I know they have a bond - a special relationship that is just between them. And that's the moment I capture in my work - the moment when the hearts meet and speak as one.

Hi, my name is Cynthia Pixley, of Pixels by Pixley Photography. I am just a horse crazy, poodle loving photographer, in the heart of Virginia. I love bearing witness to the bonds shared between animals and their people so that this moment leaves a legacy of love.

PIXELSBYPIXLEYPHOTOGRAPHY.COM

SPARROW

Alum Springs Park
Age 4, Border Collie

Sparrow is an incredibly smart dog with a goofy streak that keeps everyone entertained. With springs for her back legs, she bounces around joyfully, showcasing her playful personality and infectious energy!

CASPIAN

Alum Spring Park
Age 6, Alaskan Malamute

Caspian is the friendliest boy around - super chill and always ready to hang out. As Sparrow's older "sibling", he brings a laid-back vibe to their adventures, making every day a fun one!

GOLDIE

Home
Age 6 months, Labrador Retriever

Goldie is a laid-back pup who enjoys hanging out at the barn, eagerly watching the neighborhood kids hop on the school bus every morning. She also has a tasty morning routine of sipping on apple juice for breakfast!

PADRE

Home
Age 13, Border Collie

Padre was a guardian of the family farm, fiercely protecting everyone against the "bad" pitchfork. One of his favourite places to visit was the state fair but sadly, he passed before his fairground photoshoot.

JACKSON

Hazelwild Farm Equestrian Centre
Age 1, Jack Russell

This charming dog has no fear of people or animals, loving them all equally. With a charismatic and sarcastic personality, he brings joy to everyone around him. Each day, he happily commutes to work on the horse farm alongside his humans.

AUGGIE

Hazelwild Farm - Hazel Run
Age 11 months, Labrador Retriever

This dog totally loves water and sticks, making him the ultimate adventure buddy. He's super talkative, always ready to chat, and is the best shotgun rider around. Adventures just wouldn't be the same without him!

HUGO

Geelong Bollards
Age 7, American Akita/Siberian Husky

Hugo was adopted from the pound at 11 months old. He's the most confident dog ever, fully aware of his handsome looks. With an independent spirit, he will happily sit, drop, and stay - as long as there's a treat involved!

TAILS FROM . . .

Geelong, VIC Australia

Known as the region where the coastline meets the countryside and recognised by the iconic Geelong Bollard statues along the Waterfront Esplanade.

A DOG'S GUIDE:

1. Wander through one of Australia's oldest Botanic Gardens, established in 1850. Grab a puppacino at Where You Meet cafe and enjoy the lush scenery.
2. Grab a pint and a pizza in Little Creature's colourful, dog-friendly beer gardens.
3. Hit the surf at Fisherman's beach in Torquay and be sure to drop into the Salty Dog Cafe - known for their dog-friendly atmosphere.
4. Take in spectacular views with a hike up the You Yangs.
5. Hop aboard the dog-friendly Swan Bay Express for a historic train ride that departs from Queenscliff Station.

GEELONG ANIMAL WELFARE SOCIETY

These photoshoots raised funds for Geelong Animal Welfare Society, supporting their care, education, and re-homing programs for animals in need.
Visit gaws.org.au to learn more

CAITLIN J. MCCOLL

RAGAMUFFIN PET PHOTOGRAPHY

I've been creating personality-filled portraits of happy dogs for 14 years with my business, Ragamuffin Pet Photography.

I'm also the author of eight dog-filled books and founder of the Tails of the World Collective. I love teaching other photographers how to build their business whilst making a difference!

When I'm not behind the lens or computer, you can find me pottering around our sunny garden - usually with my two toddlers and their furry sister Maple by my side.

RAGAMUFFINPETPHOTOGRAPHY.COM.AU

CHINO

Geelong Botanic Gardens
Age 2, Greyhound mix

Chino is a total champ, competing in tricks, agility, scent work, and sprinting. His latest obsession? Crocodile treats! He's also famous for his epic zoomies with friends and family.

HENRY

Geelong Botanic Gardens
Age 5, Toy Poodle

Henry is a playful pup who loves hide and seek and being chased for toys. At bedtime, he scratches at the covers to snuggle under them, popping his head out next to his humans.

He has a flawless memory, particularly for treats received in obscure locations! He loves the local Bean Squeeze because he gets a treat there every time.

RAF AND SONNY

Geelong Botanic Gardens
Ages 1 and 5, Whippets

Sonny loves to gaze into your eyes while you cuddle. Raf can sniff food out from anywhere, even if it's an old dog treat crumb in the pocket of your shorts, and those shorts are in the bottom of a drawer! They're both speedy boys and love to race eachother at the beach.

ARLO

Geelong Botanic Gardens
Age 3, Schnauzer/Poodle

Adorably mischievous Arlo will wait until he thinks you can't see him, gently grab a scrunchy or sock and slowly, stealthily walk away. He doesn't actually know what to do with the socks or scrunchies once he's got them, but boy does he enjoy the hunt!

JESSIE

Geelong Botanic Gardens
Australian Terrier

Meet Jessie, the adorable little lady with a long, messy coat that adds to her charm! She loves nothing more than lounging on her back with her legs up in the air, soaking up the good vibes. Before she settles in for a nap, she has this cute little ritual of preparing her space, making sure everything is just right.

BARNEY

Geelong Botanic Gardens
Age 7, Beaglier

Food obsessed Barney has a bad habit of sneaking into neighbours' homes and tracking down their dog food! He's spoilt with sleepovers at the grandparents house and also comes home happy (and a little bit chubby). He's a clever boy who never forgets a trick!

AXEL

Geelong Botanic Gardens
Age 5, Rottweiller/Kelpie

Axel can drop on command with a "bang bang!" and is rarely seen without his blue and yellow squeaky ball. He insists on being in physical contact at all times, preferably on a couch or bed, with all 47kg of his weight on top of you!

EVIE

Geelong Waterfront
Staffy/Stumpy Tailed Heeler

This playful pup adores cheese as her favourite snack, enjoys delightful days at doggie daycare, and shares a special bond with her best friend, Ruby the cat.

KIKO

Ocean Grove
Age 2, Griffon Bruxellois

Kiko is a sweet, cuddly little girl who has the cutest underbite! She will do anything for food and loves going on beach walks with her family.

TAILS FROM . . .

Gent, Belgium

Known for its historical medieval architecture, vibrant arts scene, and iconic landmarks like the Ghent Altarpiece and Castle of the Counts

A DOG'S GUIDE:

1. In summer, head to Yachtdreef by the Watersportbaan for a refreshing swim or book a stand up paddling session (SUP) with your dog.
2. Looking for space to roam? There are over 20 off-leash areas in Ghent where your dog can play.
3. Enjoy the best Belgian beer at Bier Central, where your dog gets his own bowl (non-alcoholic, of course).
4. For a great view of Sint-Jacobskerk and tasty Belgian cuisine, visit ChopinChopin.
5. Explore the waters of Ghent with Rederij Dewaele for a unique perspective of the city with your dog.

HACHIKO VZW

These photoshoots raised funds for Hachiko Vzw to provide professionally trained assistance dogs, enhancing the quality of life for individuals with care needs.
Visit hachiko.org to learn more

ELKE BRAET

ALL NATURE PHOTOGRAPHY

Starting in 2017 as a professional photographer, the main focus lies on the contrast between light and dark, putting more emotions and meaning in the photo. Due to the loss of my own mother at an early age, the subject of 'past - present - future' is a main theme in my photos.

The favourite scènes are Urbex and Urban photographs.

Having won several international awards All Nature Photography tries to create new insights in the dog photography world.

ALLNATUREPHOTOGRAPHY.BE

STRIX

Gent Zuid and Cadzand
Age 13, Canis Vulgaris

Suzy stole her owner's heart the moment she arrived at the dog shelter in Ghent. This small but fierce pup has a loving nature and truly is one of a kind. Despite being tiny, she confidently manages her five big dog siblings at home!

BEAU

'De Krook'
Age 2, Hungarian Vizsla Shorthair

Beau was adopted at 6 months and quickly stole his family's hearts. He's a Velcro dog who craves attention, sometimes getting jealous of his little sister Lilo. His best bud Bo the Doberman keeps him company, and he's aced level C in obedience training!

P'DADDY VOM HAUSE SULTAN

Poeljemarkt
Age 8, Rottweiler

This gentle giant weighs nearly 60 kg of pure muscle but is as cuddly as a teddy bear! Déspite his size, he's a playful puppy at heart, always ready for fun. With a tough exterior, he fiercely protects his loved ones while having a heart of gold.

IZA

De Krook, Universiteitsstraat
Age 2, Labradoodle

This dog is in training to be a guide dog at the Belgian Centre for Guide dogs. He absolutely loves walks on the beach and has a super high cuddle factor, always in great need of hugs from everyone around!

NIELSSON

Circa
Age 7, Dogo Argentino mix

Niel is the friendliest dog ever, eager to make friends with everyone he meets. He loves splashing around in the water but absolutely hates bath time. He's a fussy eater, but loves croissants and pizza!

TAILS FROM . . .
Gers, France

Known for its rural charm, Gers features sweeping panoramas of undulating fields of sunflowers, corn, and rapeseed, along with pastures of extensively kept cattle.

A DOG'S GUIDE:

1. Woods of Berdoues: Discover the shady pathways where you can enjoy green strolls and cool off in the creeks.
2. Lake of Astarac: Have a picnic with your human, then walk the trail and let your paws splash in the lake.
3. Sansan Paleosite: Sniff around the Gascony countryside and check out cool fossil replicas, like ancient elephant relatives and bear-dogs.
4. Île d'Ager Park: Find a tree-filled spot with a waterfall and a small island where you can swim and play safely.
5. Cafés in Gers: Relax at outdoor cafés where you can grab a drink or snack with your human by your side.

LES POTES À POUF

These photoshoots raised funds for Les Potes à Pouf, which shelters abandoned dogs and relies on volunteers for care and financial support. Visit potesapouf.com to learn more

FRANÇOISE SACHDÉ

VETOPHOTO FRANÇOISE SACHDÉ

I work as a veterinarian in the south of France and turned my passion for photography into a part-time business alongside my veterinary practice since 2021. Animals are at the centre of my interests. I live with two dogs, a cat and several horses and it is therefore natural that they attract me as models. Although I explored different genres of photography, I found pet photography the most captivating. I appreciate their naturalness and spontaneity in front of my lens, without worrying about the camera. I really like to capture the soul and character of the animal, but also the bond and the relationship they have with their humans. This really melts my heart.

VETOPHOTO.COM

RIO
Auch
Age 4, Saarloos Wolfldog/Malinois

This dog is super shy around strangers and takes her time warming up to new people. She's also super obedient and loves showing off her tricks for treats.

ROSKO KUTAMBA DES SABLES DU NORD
Sarrant
Age 4, Rhodesian Ridgeback

Rosko is a woods-loving dog who's mad about hunting rabbits. He adores his family and is always eager to please them. He enjoys his cosy comforts and sticking to his daily routine.

MATISSE
Bellegarde
Age 5, Cavapoo

This clever dog knows a lot of words and loves to show off his smarts! Though he's a bit shy with strangers, he shares a special bond with his Mum and enjoys playful moments together.

CAMILLE

Bellegarde
Age 5, Cavapoo

This friendly and joyful little dog loves to greet everyone by bringing them her toy, although she never actually wants to play. She's like a therapy dog too, staying close to her mum when she's upset and helping her feel better until she calms down.

LOUMI

Former Cordeliers convent
Age 8, Pinscher

When he's happy, Loumi flashes a big smile with his front teeth and bounces around like he's floating. Despite his small size, he's packed with attitude, energy, hunger, and courage. He's definitely a spirited little powerhouse!

DIEGO

Sainte-Arailles
Age 20, Spanish Horse

Diego is a bundle of energy, often tricky to catch when he knows a hike is on the agenda. His friends affectionately call him "the moped" because he zooms around like a small horse. He's also super playful and loves to put on a show for an audience!

GAME AND ULYA DE NIBÈLE

Berdous abbey
Age 1, Eurasier

Ulya, a home bred Eurasier, is a friendly and calm companion who adores cuddles. She loves to accompany and support Game and Kylian in their equestrian competitions, making her a cherished part of their team.

GAME OF TERREMER

Sainte-Aurence-Cazaux
Age 8, Welsh Part Bred

Game is a cool riding and breeding stallion who gets to hang out with kids in riding classes. He recently started jumping competitions with his 9-year-old buddy Kylian, and they're learning and growing together, making it an awesome adventure for both of them!

LAVENDER TRUFFLES

Old Town Sacramento
Age 1, French Bulldog

Lavender Truffles, aka Girly, is a quirky mix of the Energizer Bunny and a mischievous dragon. With her endless energy and playful antics, she keeps everyone entertained at home. She is beautiful and brilliant, with zings of spicy!

TAILS FROM . . . Gold Country, California USA

Known for the California Gold Rush from 1849-1855, home to Sacramento (the State Capital) and over 100 wineries.

A DOG'S GUIDE:

1. Sniff out tasty apples and pumpkins at Apple Hill, plus enjoy some wine with your human.
2. Relax with a cold beer at dog-friendly breweries in Sacramento.
3. Explore the great outdoors with hikes along the American River Parkway, Folsom Lake, and Lake Tahoe.
4. Take a leisurely walk through dog-friendly farmer's markets in Sacramento, Folsom, and Placerville.
5. Get a private shopping session for your reactive dog at Paws N' Play in Sacramento.

SIERRA NEVADA GERMAN SHEPHERD RESCUE

These photoshoots raised funds for Sierra Nevada German Shepherd Rescue, which rehabilitates and adopts out neglected German Shepherds while educating the public on animal welfare. Visit edcgsr.com to learn more

KYLEE DOYLE

KYLEE DOYLE PHOTOGRAPHY

Kylee of Kylee Doyle Photography serves pet parents in Northern California, helping them capture memories with their furbabies and turn them into photographic artwork they can proudly display in their homes. She uses outdoor locations in the greater Sacramento and Tahoe areas as stunning backdrops for pups' portraits.

Kylee's own dogs have helped shaped her experience. She works with dogs of all training experience and sociability. Her own highly sensitive dog has led her to specialize in working with reactive pups, helping them shine in front of the camera.

Sessions are customized to the dog's needs in order to create a comfortable environment where their true personality can be captured.

KYLEEDOYLEPHOTOGRAPHY.COM

ANYA

Pleasant Valley
Age 10, German Shepherd/Husky

Anya's family bid her farewell in June 2024. She adored exploring their 5 acres, hunting squirrels, and playfully chasing away geese. With her friendly spirit, she made friends with every human she met, leaving a joyful memory in the hearts of those who knew her.

KOA

Fair Oaks Bridge
Age 1, German Shepherd

This dog is a total goofball who loves playing with her toys and siblings way more than eating. When it comes to treats, the stinkier, the better - she's all about those fish and cod chews! Overall, she's one of the happiest pups around.

DRACO

Fair Oaks Bridge
Age 7 months, Border Collie

Draco is a friendly dog who adores swimming and loves to be hugged by people. Named after the Harry Potter character Draco Malfoy, he brings joy to everyone around him with his playful spirit and affectionate nature.

KIMBER
Folsom Lake
Age 3, Belgian Malinois

Kimber is getting ready for PSA, a dog sport that has really strengthened her bond with her human. She absolutely LOVES all the toys. Sometimes she get a funny expression on her face that looks like she's blowing a raspberry at you!

IROC

Gibson Ranch
Age 10, Belgian Malinois

Iroc is a sweet dog who loves doing PSA with her dad. She's a superstar with her CGC, CGCA, CGCU, and CSAU titles from AKC. Plus, she can't get enough cuddles and loves to "talk" to everyone around her!

GUSTAVO

Cellito Beach
Age 2, English Border Collie

Gussy believes he is an elderly gentleman. He likes to sit in his chair in the sun with his paw in your hand, admiring the cows.

He also enjoys watching TV shows like Muster Dogs and sci-fi flicks with laser sounds. His sleep yoga skills are impressive, his favourite being the backward-hanging bat, off the lounge with paws extended.

TAILS FROM . . .

Great Lakes, NSW Australia

Known for its stunning beaches, serene lakes, and lush forests.

A DOG'S GUIDE:

1. Start your day by watching the sunrise with your human from the top of the giant sand dune at One Mile Beach.
2. Treat yourself to a tasty breakfast at the dog-friendly Beach Bums Cafe with a view of Forster Main Beach.
3. Grab a coffee and a light lunch at Kembali Cafe, and explore the shops at Blueys.
4. Take a fun drive to Seal Rocks and explore the shoreline at the dog-friendly Boat Beach.
5. End your day by watching the sunset over Lake Wallis from the dog-friendly lawn area at The Recky in Elizabeth Beach.

DOG RESCUE NEWCASTLE

These photoshoots raised funds for Dog Rescue Newcastle, supporting their mission to reduce unwanted animals, lower euthanasia rates, and promote long-term animal welfare. Visit dogrescuenewcastle.com.au to learn more

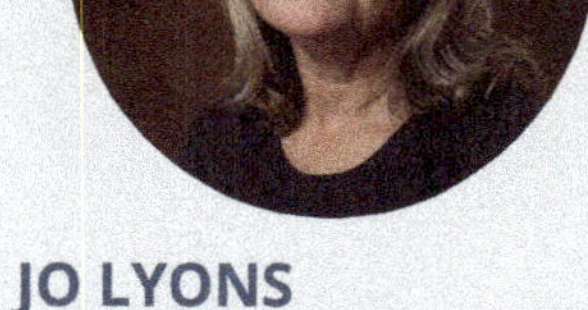

JO LYONS

JO LYONS PHOTOGRAPHY

I'm a specialist dog photographer who creates stunning, heartfelt portraits of dogs and the people who love them. Located in the picturesque Great Lakes NSW, I provide a custom experience with studio or scenic locations from the countryside to the sea - creating beautiful artwork that will last a lifetime.

My engaging portraits have been instrumental in promoting shelter animals and aiding their quest to find the loving homes they deserve. I proudly partner with Dog Rescue Newcastle, providing their dogs with a full countryside and studio experience, where I create captivating imagery that supports their adoption profile and helps attract their perfect forever family.

JOLYONSPHOTOGRAPHY.COM

SPRITE

Wootton
Age 1, Terrier mix

Sprite was rescued from a rural road, abandoned and flea-ridden. These days she happily spends hours wrestling with her big buddy, Henry. Her super-excited "Aroo-roo-roo" bark always cracks everyone up!

SKYE

Smiths Lake
Age 1, Groodle

Skye is a happy pup who enjoys every day and loves her walks. She sees the world through her nose, sniffing everything in sight. She absolutely loves visiting the local pet store, where the friendly staff always love to see her!

TAHI

Boat Beach Seal Rocks
Age 1, Chinese Crested Powder Puff/Chihuahua

Tahi's got a cool mohawk and a goatee beard, and he loves to dance on his hind legs for treats. At night, he snuggles under the doona, often waking up with his head on the pillow. He thinks he's 10 feet tall and bulletproof - classic Chihuahua!

TRIXIE

Boat Beach Seal Rocks
Age 1, Australian Kelpie

Trixie is all about fun! She enjoys playing fetch at the beach, tagging along to work with her dad, and hanging out with her pals at the dog park. Life is one big adventure!

BORIS

Blueys Beach
Age 10 months, Beaglier

Boris is an adventurous dog who is mastering agility and loves to show off at the park. As the team mascot for the local girls' soccer team, he enjoys receiving kisses from his fans. He also delights in visiting the duck pond to feed the ducks and swans!

RIP

Boomerang Beach
Age 3, Alaskan Malamute

Rip is a friendly dog who adores his feline sisters and his brother Max, the cow. His favourite toy squeaks, bringing him joy. Rip dislikes being left alone and feels happiest when surrounded by his family.

MINDY

Blueys Beach
Age 4, Maltese Terrier mix

Mindy is a social pup who adores getting pats from people. She likes to sneakily take socks and hide with them under the dining table. She also enjoys munching on crusts, Cruskit biscuits, cucumber, and even licking empty egg shells and strawberries!

DUDLEY

Blueys Beach
Age 1, Great Dane mix

Dudley is a 50kg lapdog currently in foster care. Don't sit down; he'll find your lap and snuggle in for a cuddle. He is blind in one eye, but doesn't let things like chairs or doors stop him; he runs right into them to get them out of his way!

WILLOW

Hawks Nest
Age 10 months, German Shepherd

Willow is a lovable foster dog with Dog Rescue Newcastle, and her foster family can't imagine her with anyone else. She's full of personality, loves exploring, playing ball, and going for walks - though roast chicken is her ultimate weakness!

MAGGIE AND SAMMY

Harvard University Area
Ages 10 months and 2,
Golden Retrievers

Maggie, aka "Midge", enjoys playfully antagonizing her older sister. Sammy, a delightful surprise wedding gift, is named after the golden retriever from the Parent Trap. She has been affectionately compared to "Weird Barbie".

TAILS FROM . . .

Greater Boston, Mass. USA

Known for its historic neighborhoods featuring charming cobblestone streets and prestigious universities.

A DOG'S GUIDE:

1. Explore the woodlands just outside the city for some great hiking adventures.
2. Check out the coastal towns with stunning beaches and breathtaking sunsets.
3. Stroll through Beacon Hill, home to Acorn Street, the most photographed street in the U.S.
4. Enjoy time at the many dog-friendly cafés and breweries around the city.
5. Wander through the charming area of Cambridge, which includes part of Harvard University.

ELIZABETH BOUDREAU

ELIZABETH BOUDREAU PHOTOGRAPHY

Hi I'm Beth! As a dog owner for most of my life, I know first-hand the immense joy and love that a dog brings into ones life!

As a dog photographer, I have the privilege of capturing the unique personalities and beauty of dogs through my lens. Dogs hold a special place in the hearts of their owners and my work allows me to celebrate and immortalize the bond between humans and their beloved dogs. Through my photography, I am able to create timeless memories for dog owners to cherish.

ELIZABETHBOUDREAUPHOTOGRAPHY.COM

JET WAG ANIMAL RESCUE

These photoshoots raised funds for Jet Wag Animal Rescue, assisting shelters, facilitating adoptions, and promoting spay/neuter efforts for at-risk dogs and cats.
Visit jetwagrescue.org to learn more

MOLLY

Horn Pond
Age 2, Whoodle

She's definitely the fastest dog at the park and just can't resist cheese! She also insists on being part of all family activities, making sure she never misses out on the fun.

CASHEW

Winter Island
Age 5, Golden Retriever

Cashew loves to cosy up in the backyard shrubs. Her family believe that she may be half golden retriever, half chicken because Cashew is afraid of everything (including thunder, trash trucks, and any piece of furniture that moves). She absolutely adores her favourite treat - peanut butter!

CAPTAIN AND JESTER

Horn Pond
Age 2 and 1, Golden Retriever and Golden Pyrenees

Captain, aka Marvelous First Avenger Marks, is a total charmer who loves to smile when excited and was even named "Valedogtorian" in puppy class! Jester Joy is named after a Critical Role character, embodying silliness and love, and snagged the "Most Improved" title in training class.

BEN

Breakheart Reservation
Age 12, Treeing Walker Coonhound

Ben, the adventurous dog, got arrested in New Hampshire for roaming off-leash on a hiking trail. His loud "voice" can be heard for miles! He's even a star in an indie YouTube film called "The Hunt for Ben October."

BESSIE

Beacon Hill
Age 2, English Cream Labrador

Bessie may be almost fully deaf, but that doesn't stop her from living her best life! As the queen of the household, she claims most of her parents' king-sized bed each night and even played a special role as the witness at their marriage in Boston City Hall.

MILLIE

Jones River Salt Marsh
Age 5, Pit/Cattledog mix

Millie is a proud mom who gave birth to 8 puppies and even adopted a 9th while at her nursery foster. Although Millie is mostly white, none of her puppies have her coloring. Whenever someone gets ready for a run, she stands there smiling, excited for the adventure!

STANLEY

Winter Island
Age 4, Bernedoodle

Stanley, named after the Stanley Cup, tags along to work with his owner daily and even made it into the company holiday photo! He's such a lovable pup that sometimes the neighbors pick him to spend time at their own house.

LOLLIE

Breakheart Reservation
Age 1, Mixed Breed

This playful pup loves everyone and everyone loves her. The neighbors even joke that she put a spell on the neighborhood when she moved in! Her breed is a mystery, she's a perfect mix, sometimes looking like a corgi or a collie. She'd happily play fetch and chase rabbits all day!

WILLOW

Pebble Beach
Age 1, German Shepherd mix

Willow, lovingly known as "Queen," adores bedtime, dancing in circles and barking joyfully at the mere mention of it. With a quirky cat-like flair, she often finds her cosy spots on coffee tables or the back of the couch.

SPUD

St Albans
Age 4, Pug Cross

Spud is the cuddliest little guy who just can't get enough lap time. He hails from a planet unknown, and after a DNA test, it turns out he has no hairless breed in him - just a quirky mutant hairless gene!

TAILS FROM . . .

Hertfordshire, England UK

Known for being home to the UK's oldest pub, the birthplace of the doughnut, and the world-famous Harry Potter Studios.

A DOG'S GUIDE:

1. Have a blast at Ross and Friends, the biggest dog park in the UK, where your pup can run free and play all day!
2. Treat yourself to a scrumptious slice of carrot cake at Halsey's Deli & Eatery in Hitchin, a charming Tudor spot.
3. Sniff the amazing scents at Hitchin Lavender and sip on their tasty lavender infused lemonade.
4. Discover the vast beauty of Lee Valley Park, with 10,000 acres of lakes, parkland, and rivers perfect for exploring.
5. Stroll through Ashridge Estates, where you can enjoy ancient trees, rolling chalk downs, and lush meadows with your furry friend.

ANDREW RICHARDSON
RAVEN IMAGERY

Andrew Raven Richardson, an international dog photographer, renowned for capturing the unique and profound bond between people and their beloved pups.

What began as a passion for helping dogs in kennels evolved into an incredible journey - one Andrew still finds hard to believe is real. With a deep passion for dog welfare and a strong advocate for reducing the stray population through sterilisation programs, Andrew brings both dedication and purpose to his photography. Every image holds a timeless memory of the joy, love, and deep connection dogs bring into our lives—an experience that fills him with gratitude every single day.

RAVENIMAGERY.CO.UK

SOI DOG

These photoshoots raised funds for Soi Dog, supporting spaying, neutering, rescuing, vaccinating, and adopting over 70,000 stray animals in Phuket, Thailand. Visit soidog.org to learn more

DAVE AND DOUG

Hitchin
Ages 6 and 4, Cavapoo

Dave and Doug may look identical, but they each bring unique qualities that complete the family. While Dave lives a cautious life, Doug zooms through at 100 miles per hour. Together, they fill every moment with smiles, hugs, and kisses - life wouldn't be the same without them!

LULU

Hitchin
Age 9, Toy Poodle

Lulu had a rough start, used as a breeding dog and found on a dog meat truck near Beijing. Thankfully, a local activist saved her, and she landed at Slaughterhouse Survivors. After her Mum lost her heart dog, Darcy, the universe led her to Lulu.

ZELDA

St Albans
Age 10, Poodle mix

Zelda had a rough start until she was rescued by slaughterhouse survivors in China. Now, she's a hilarious little character who loves stealing things for her stash and snoozing on her human's shoulder - or sometimes their head!

FELIZ

St Albans
Age 7, Toy Poodle

This little dog was rescued by Slaughterhouse Survivors in China. Despite having only three legs, he hops along happily and following his human everywhere. His official name is Feliz because he's always so happy, and his nickname is Greybeard.

ARWEN AND THIBAULT

St Albans
Ages 3 and 4, Ragdoll and Alaskan Klee Kai

Arwen and Thibault absolutely adore eachother. They both have quirky personalities that shine bright, and it's heartwarming to see how closely they look out for each other.

DON PEPE

St Albans
Age 13, Chihuahua

Don Pepe, once confined to a cage, now reigns as the beloved king of his home. He adores vegetables, especially broccoli and peas, and enjoys jet-setting around the globe with his family.

JULES

St Albans
Age 5, Staffordshire Bull Terrier

Jules is a big, cuddly marshmallow with a log obsession; if he can't find any at the park, he'll hang off tree branches for his fix. All the tiny dogs boss him about and he accepts it like a gentleman.

RODGER, RAFA AND ANDY

Hitchin
Ages 2, 3 and 1, Poodles

This curly trio bring daily laughter to their family. As brothers they are all so unique. Rafa is majestic strong and loyal, Roger is kind gentle and soft and Andy is a bundle of energy and pure joy.

NALU AND TALLULAH

Puu Pale Ranch
Ages 2 and 9, Mixed and Rottweiler

Nalu is a silly boy who adores his toys and friends. His pal Tallulah, a rescue rottweiler from Rainbow Friends Animal Sanctuary, resembles a cuddly teddy bear. This lovable couch potato enjoys treats and pets, making her the perfect companion for Nalu's playful spirit!

TAILS FROM . . .

Hilo, Hawaii USA

Known for its rainy weather, stunning landscapes, the Merrie Monarch Festival, and being home to the world's most active volcanoes.

A DOG'S GUIDE:

1. Take a nice stroll at Liliuokalani Gardens and soak in the beautiful views.
2. Sip on a refreshing glass of wine or beer at local spots like Volcano Winery or Hilo Brewing Co.
3. Spend fun times at parks such as Ainaola Park or Gilbert Carvalho Park.
4. Participate in the Hāmākua Mutt Contest at the Hāmākua Sugar Days Festival and dress up for a fun dog pageant.
5. Enjoy a mini drive on Daniel K. Inouye Highway and picnic at Gilbert Kahele Recreation Area.

HAWAI'I ISLAND HUMANE SOCIETY

These photoshoots raised funds for Hawai'i Island Humane Society, supporting lifesaving programs, community outreach, and efforts to prevent animal cruelty and overpopulation. Visit hihs.org to learn more"

CRYSTAL RAMBAYON
CRYSTAL R PHOTOGRAPHY

Crystal Rambayon was born and raised on Hawai'i Island. She developed a love for animals and a passion for photography at an early age.

After nurturing her passion, Crystal made the courageous decision to pursue her dreams as a pet photographer. She specializes in capturing the unique personalities of pets while creating timeless memories for their owners.

Crystal is also committed to giving back to her community. She volunteers her time and skills to a local rescue by using her photography to capture heartwarming images of dogs in the Aloha State who are looking for their "fur"ever home.

CRYSTALRPHOTOGRAPHY.COM

PEARL

Puu Pale Ranch
Age 8, Big Island Mutt

Pearl is a super smart girl who was born blind and deaf, but that doesn't slow her down at all! She absolutely loves meeting new people and explores her world through scent.

TINA

Suisan Fish Market
Age 6, Terrier mix

Tina was adopted from the Hawaii Island Humane Society and now rocks her job as a certified therapy dog at Kea'au High School. She's got some impressive AKC titles under her collar, including Community Canine, Trick Dog Intermediate, and FIT Dog Silver.

SOPHIE AND DOBBY

Moku Ola (Coconut Island)
Age 5, Catahoulas

Sophie has been blind since birth and enjoys playing bling tag by following sounds. Dobby, formerly known as Goose, has THE biggest heart.

MAILE

Lili'uokalani Gardens
Age 8, Pit Bull/Labrador mix

Maile, a delightful rescue from Aloha Ilio, is a talented pup trained in nose work. With her high food drive, she brings enthusiasm and excitement to every training session, making her a joy to be around!

JOEY, WINK AND OLINA
Lili'uokalani Gardens
Ages 4, 7 and 10, Shih Tzu mixes

Olina is a retired agility champ and has fostered 150 dogs in her home. Joey is an aloha ambassador and playmate to the foster dogs. He is an AKC canine good citizen who has done obedience, trick classes, scent work classes and agility training. Wink has one eye and it's a beautiful blue. He must have a toy in his mouth whenever he goes!

FREYJA AND COOPER

Hilo Bayfront Beach Park
Ages 6 and 8, Mixed

Freyja and Cooper, both adopted pups, are a bit weird but totally adorable. Their quirky charm is hard to resist!

HUEY

Lili'uokalani Gardens
Age 1, Great Dane

Huey is a total sweetheart - super loving and loyal, he truly embodies the gentle giant vibe. He's the kind of dog that brings warmth and joy to everyone around him.

KENAI

Lili'uokalani Gardens
Age 1, Great Dane

Kenai is a goofy dog who brings joy wherever he goes! With his endless supply of hugs and kisses, he spreads happiness to everyone around him, making every day a delightful adventure.

SAMMY

Lili'uokalani Gardens
Age 6, Border Collie/Australian Shepherd

Sammy is a cheerful and smart dog who absolutely loves being around people. His friendly personality makes him a joy to be around, and his intelligence shines through in everything he does.

HUMPHREY

Dillingham Ranch
Age 5, Golden Retriever

This playful pup is absolutely obsessed with the ocean and loves to dive for rocks! He's such a good sport that he'll wear anything his owner puts on him, making him the most stylish swimmer at the beach.

TAILS FROM . . .

Honolulu, Hawaii USA

Known for its beautiful beaches, diverse food and culture, and year-round summer weather with daily rainbows.

A DOG'S GUIDE:

1. Start your day with a sunrise hike at the Makapuu Lighthouse trail, an easy, paved path offering stunning 360-degree views of East Oahu at the top.
2. Take a stroll at Kuliouou Beach Park, the most dog-friendly beach on the island. At low tide, enjoy a vast sandbar where your dog can run and play freely.
3. Try a standup paddleboard lesson with SUP Dog Hawaii on the North Shore for a fun water adventure.
4. Relax on a waterfront patio at Island Brew Coffeehouse.
5. Enjoy locally sourced treats and a special dog menu at Kahuku Farms.

KERI PARADO

KERI NAKAHASHI PHOTOGRAPHY

Keri has been a dog photographer since 2015, specializing in beach portraits full of vibrant colors, personality, and beautiful landscapes. What started as a hobby to photograph her dog Kobe, has grown into a dream job that allows her to travel the world, give back to local rescues and capture heartfelt moments for her clients. The artwork she creates is an instant jolt of happiness and a return ticket back in time to their furbaby.

To celebrate the 20th anniversary of Lost, this year Keri recreated some of the iconic moments from the show with dogs!

KERINAKAHASHI.COM

HINA'S LEGACY RESCUE FOUNDATION

These photoshoots raised funds for Hina's Legacy Rescue Foundation, which combats animal cruelty, rehabilitates abused animals, advocates for better legislation, and promotes community support. Visit hinaslegacyrescue.org to learn more

KAIA

Judd Trail
Age 9, Goldendoodle

Kaia is a friendly therapy dog who absolutely loves people. She has a special knack for bringing joy to everyone around her, making her a true delight to be with.

DECAF

Ala Wai Boat Harbor
Age 5, Pocket Bully

This dog lives for ultra chuck-it balls. She goes full gremlin mode, drooling uncontrollably at the sight of a banana.

HARLEY

Papailoa Beach
Age 2, Mini American Shepherd

This dog is very mellow considering his breed, but he still enjoys activities like Fast Cat, Agility, Scentwork, and Obedience trails.

KOA

Allen Davis
Age 6, Corgi

Koa is a lovable dog who is always hungry and enjoys long naps. His favourite toy is a squeaky ball, which brings him endless joy during playtime.

HANA

Papailoa Beach
Age 4, Yellow English Lab

Hana is a super happy and lovable goofball who's always ready for fun. This food-motivated pup adores humans, believing they're way better than other dogs.

KOA

Mokuleia Beach
Age 10, Min Pin mix

When Max was adopted, they thought he was 3, but a DNA test showed he's actually around 10! He does an adorable "Min Pin Spin" when excited.

XION AND BEAR

Kawela Bay
Age 1, Hmong Bobtails

This breed is naturally born without a tail and originally travelled with the Hmong people throughout SE Asia. They settled in villages and were used to guard homes, pull carts, hunt and even detect bomb!

FINLEY

Makua Beach
Age 4, Pit mix

Finley is a local Oahu boy, rescued from the Fur Angel Foundation. He loves to be outdoors, whether that means hiking in the mountains or shredding coconuts at the beach. He rarely barks but will make wookie sounds when he's really excited!

KAILANI

Waimea Falls
Age 4, Pit mix

Kailani is a total water lover who enjoys swimming, paddle boarding, and surfing. This giant cuddle bug is the sweetest, gentlest big fur baby around. She's also a social butterfly, always up for playing with her friends and spreading joy wherever she goes.

STELLA AND BAILEY

Edgewater Park
Ages 7 months and 12, Golden Retriever and Cavachon

Stella, named after Stella beer, enjoys watching the cartoon "Bluey". Bailey was named for the Irish cream and loves long road trips to the mountains.

TAILS FROM . . .

Indian Rocks Beach, Florida USA

Known for its scenic walking tours, wildlife rehabilitation efforts, and vibrant mural art.

A DOG'S GUIDE:

1. Visit Earthwise Pet for top-notch nutrition and wellness
2. Enjoy a meal at The Original Crabby Bill's, a dog-friendly restaurant with delicious seafood, live music, and a patio just for pups.
3. Head to Belleair Causeway Dog Beach to soak up the sun and splash in the water.
4. Stop by Maggie Mae's on the Bluffs for an award-winning southern breakfast, complete with mimosas on Sundays and plenty of outdoor seating for you and your dog.
5. If your pup needs a check-up, Bluffs Animal Hospital offers excellent veterinary care without appointments.

HEALY PACK SENIOR GSD SANCTUARY

These photoshoots raised funds for Healy Pack Senior GSD Sanctuary, dedicated to rescuing senior German Shepherds from kill shelters and providing care until adoption. Visit healypack.org to learn more

YAMILE HAIBI
BLUE MERLE PHOTOGRAPHY

Hi! I'm Yamile, Pet Photographer. My studio, Blue Merle Photography, is dedicated to photographing "pets and their people" and raising awareness to help animals in need. The studio is named in honour of my dog, Rascal, a blue merle Aussie mix.

Believe me, he lives up to his name! At Blue Merle Photography, I believe every pet has a story to tell—a story of loyalty, love, and the unique bond they share with you. I specialize in creating custom pet portraits that perfectly capture the personality, charm, and quirks of your furry companions.

BLUEMERLEPHOTO.COM

CHIEF

Pop Stansell Park
Age 5, German Shepherd

This happy boy is all about fun and adores his jolly ball and frisbees. He is always ready to chase a squirrel or duck - but leaves them alone because he's good boy and always listens to his Mom.

CRUSH

Pop Stansell Park
Age 6, German Shepherd

Crush is named after the orange Crush soda. He loves to play in the water and tries to "bite" the water from the hose.

BLU AND JUDGE

Downtown Dunedin
Ages 3 and 5, Pitbull Rottweiler mix and Chow Rottweiler mix

Judge was adopted from St. Croix and flew to Florida to rescue his mom, Annie. Blu, one of the smartest and gentlest pups around, loves to dance and has an incredible smile.

BUCKY

Chic A Si Park
Age 4, Hound mix

Bucky, the little dog with a big personality, absolutely loves bananas! He likes to hop around like a deer and despite weighing just 30lbs, he confidently acts like the biggest dog at the park.

YULE

Tropical Hills
Age 9, Chinese Crested mix

Yule is a cuddly pup who adores snuggling with her pack mate, Potato. Her favourite toy is her Mr. Bill doll, and she's never far from her mom side.

MAYA

Florida Botanical Gardens
Age 6, Beagle Pitbull mix

Maya, named after the video game character Maya Fey, has a hilarious quirk: when she barks, she bounces up on her hind legs like her bark gives her a little recoil.

STELLA, MILEY AND COCO

North Staub Park
Ages 10, 1 and 4, Boston Terrier, Hound Curr mix and Boston Terrier

Stella is a puppy mill survivor who finally has her "own" puppy to raise - 55 pound rescued Miley who insists that Stella groom her face and ears every night. They're joined by Coco, a playful rescue who loves wrestling and tugging with Miley.

ALBY

Gizella Kopsick Palm Arboretum
Age 7, Boston Terrier

Alby can often be found cuddled up napping with his cat sisters, Juniper and Karma. His favourite adventures include riding in shopping carts at stores and paddling on kayaks.

MIDGE AND DUKE

Whitewater Canal Trail
Ages 9 months and 4, Boxer mix and Great Dane

Duke, a sensitive dog who struggles in new situations, has found a perfect companion in Midge, an adventurous pup who greets everyone with enthusiasm. These two couldn't be more opposite, yet they adore each other and have quickly become the best of friends!

TAILS FROM . . .

Indianapolis, Indiana USA

Known for the annual Indianapolis 500 automobile and proud of their 'Hoosier Hospitality' way of life.

A DOG'S GUIDE:

1. Enjoy a cold beer while your pup has a blast at the puppy park at Metazoa Brewing Company.
2. Treat your furry friend to a custom cake from Three Dog Bakery.
3. Explore Eagle Creek Park, one of the biggest city parks in the country.
4. Shop for dog goodies at City Dogs Grocery, a store just for dogs!
5. Savor a delicious treat for you and your dog at BRICS, with over 40 yummy ice cream flavors.

MARIA SORENSEN

SHORT BUT SWEET LIFE

Three years ago I adopted my dog, Ahsoka. She quickly became my whole world. I have always loved photography and asked if I could "borrow" my mom's Canon Rebel to take some better photos of Ahsoka.

With no formal training or direction of where to go, somehow, three years later, I am still using my mom's camera and am the founder of Short but Sweet Life Photography.
I have tried other types of photography, but pets are by far my favourite. I strive to help pet parents memorialize their pets with captivating photos they can cherish forever. Reactive, skittish, obedient, big or small, any and all pets are welcome. Life is short but sweet, so let's capture it together!

SHORTBUTSWEETLIFE.COM

FRIENDS OF FRANKLIN COUNTY INDIANA ANIMAL SHELTER

These photoshoots raised funds for Friends of Franklin County Indiana Animal Shelter to support animal care, find homes, and assist low-income families in need. Visit friendsfcanimalshelters.com to learn more

EVVY AND BUBBA

Obelisk Square
Ages 8 and 3, American Foxhound mix and Pitbull/Staffy mix

Bubba, the sweetest three-legged pup, loves playing with whatever toy his sister has. Evvy is an awesome car rider, enduring multiple 15 hour road trips when mom was in grad school.

PONGO

Scottish Rite Cathedral
Age 1, Golden Retriever

This dog loves to "torpedo" through grass on walks, snacking on flowers along the way. His owner jokes he must've been a bunny in a past life, thanks to his playful jumps. He's a total "blanket monster," burrowing under blankets to get comfy and play

PERCY JACKSON

Local Farm
Age 7, Long Hair Cat

Percy Jackson is a big cuddly guy who will follow you anywhere. He found his owner when she was just sixteen and they have been besties ever since.

ARES

American Legion Mall
Age 2, European Doberman Pinscher

Ares might seem big and intimidating, but he's actually a goofy, lovable guy who loves playing fetch at the park with his favourite ball. He gets along well with his sister Chanel, the only cat he tolerates.

WINCHESTER AND MOZZIE

Beckenholdt Park
Ages 9 and 10, Mixed

Mozzie is all about comfort, snuggling up with blankets and toys. His brother Winchester has a funny quirk - scratch his back, and he starts "twerking"! These full-blooded siblings bicker like typical brothers but can't stand being apart.

RIO

Indiana War Memorial Museum
Age 2, Border Collie mix

Rio is an adventurous dog who has dabbled in various sports like Agility, Dock Diving, and Scent Work. With 25 AKC titles under his belt, he's especially fond of Scent Work and is aiming for his Master Title. When not competing, he enjoys hiking, frisbee, and swimming!

TAILS FROM . . .
Inland Northwest, Wash. USA

Known for being a paradise for outdoor enthusiasts, hosting the largest 3-on-3 basketball tournament on Earth, and being the home of Bing Crosby.

A DOG'S GUIDE:

1. Explore miles of trails like Post Falls Community Forest and Farragut State Park without bumping into humans.
2. Chill on dog-friendly patios at places like Vantage Point and Trailbreaker while enjoying a tasty drink.
3. Take your leash, coffee, a good book, and a blanket to parks like Manito and McEuen for a cosy day out.
4. Visit farmer's markets from spring to fall for fresh produce and local crafts—most welcome dogs!
5. Cool off in the Spokane River at spots like Boulder Beach or enjoy a picnic at beautiful lakes like Coeur d'Alene.

COMPANIONS ANIMAL CENTER

These photoshoots raised funds for Companions Animal Centre, supporting their mission of humane care, rehabilitation, and adoption for homeless animals in Idaho.
Visit companionsanimalcenter.org to learn more

ANGELA SCHNEIDER
BIG WHITE DOG PHOTOGRAPHY

Angela Schneider takes her clients on adventures throughout the Pacific Northwest, creating kickass images and artwork for their homes.

She is inspired by the rugged, raw landscapes Mother Nature has created and by the rugged, raw love we have for our dogs. Angela believes our dogs are our greatest teachers, guiding us onto our true paths. She has been fortunate to have been led by two Maremma sheepdogs, first Shep then Bella, to find wholeness and fulfillment in dog photography.

BIGWHITEDOGPHOTOGRAPHY.COM

ATHENA

Rocks of Sharon
Age 5, German Shepherd/Great Pyrenees

This dog is quite the character! She's not shy about showing her emotions and takes her sweet time, taking two business days to munch on any new treat. She's clever enough to open the screen door and let herself outside whenever she pleases!

TAPENGA

St. Regis Lake
Age 8, Mixed

This dog is a real character! He thanks his Mama for walks with a cheerful "rahw, rahw, rahw" and insists on Dad sitting in the back seat during road trips. He found his forever home on Thanksgiving night 2016 after being abandoned on the streets of Spokane.

ZERO

Mt. Spokane State Park
Age 2, Belgian Malinois

Meet this fierce French ring competitor who can't resist a game of tug. Despite mama's claim that he has only two brain cells, this pup's playful spirit makes him a lovable goofball.

SAGE

Spokane River
Age 4, Labrador

This cheerful puppy adores going on road trips, bringing along her infectious joy wherever she goes. With a zest for adventure and a playful spirit, Sage makes every journey a delight.

DANTE

Hauser Lake
Age 12, Siberian Husky

In April 2024, this brave dog left our physical world after conquering life with degenerative myelopathy. He brought joy to everyone around him, especially on those magical snow days that he loved so much. His spirit will always be remembered!

JAINEY

Farragut State Park
Age 1, Boxer

Jainey has brought love and light back into the home after the passing of their old dog, Annie. She loves chasing her own tail, bouncing for squeaky toys, and is a generous giver of wet, sloppy kisses.

RUGER

Hayden Lake
Age 2, Labrador

Ruger is obsessed with his emotional support hedgehog stuffie. He can't resist the water at the lake and goes into full-on spin mode when he gets butt scritches.

PEANUT

River of Life
Age 2, Poodle

Peanut has a knack for sensing breakfast time, nudging his human awake for food. On rainy mornings, he loves to stay cosy in bed, but come the weekend, he's all excitement, tail wagging, ready to explore the world!

TAILS FROM . . .
Kuala Lumpur, Malaysia

Known for its iconic Petronas Twin Towers, diverse food scene, and harmonious cultural and religious coexistence.

A DOG'S GUIDE:

1. Relax at Desa ParkCity, where you can explore a large park with a peaceful lake and beautiful trails.
2. Visit Jaya One's The Square or Megah Rise Mall, where you can shop, dine, and enjoy regular pet-friendly events.
3. Discover Gamuda Gardens Central Park, a stunning 50-acre pet-friendly park with tranquil lakes and winding trails.
4. Participate in fun pet-friendly market events and fairs throughout the year.
5. Explore the scenic trails of Bukit Gasing for an adventurous outdoor experience with your dog.

SECOND CHANCE ANIMAL SOCIETY (SCAS)

These photoshoots raised funds for Second Chance Animal Society (SCAS), a no-kill shelter that rehomes animals and promotes responsible pet care in Malaysia.
Visit secondchance.com.my to learn more

JACQUELINE LOH
JACQUELINE LOH PHOTOGRAPHY

Jacqueline Loh is an international award-winning pet photographer based in Kuala Lumpur, Malaysia.
Her authentic work has been featured in national newspapers and vividly conveys the true essence of pets and the heartfelt bond they share with their families. Jacqueline offers on-location, in-studio, and in-home private photoshoots for pets and their families, as well as commercial photography for pet-related businesses and events.
Passionate about animal welfare, she volunteers her photography skills to help shelter animals find their forever homes, and fundraise for shelters.
When not behind the lens, Jacqueline enjoys globe-trotting and making furry friends wherever she goes.

LINKTR.EE/JACQUELINELOHPHOTOGRAPHY

OREO LEE

Sultan Abdul Samad Building
Age 12, Mixed Border Collie

Oreo is a total foodie, always hunting for tasty treats like a Michelin-star chef. With her upbeat vibe, she spreads joy while hiking and running. Though she might resemble a scruffy old rag, she's actually super smart, clever, and bursting with personality!

MIA

Sultan Abdul Samad Building
Age 3, Papillon

Mia is a cheeky, spirited pup who enjoys lively long-drawn debates with her humans. Obsessed with her squeaky duck and her ball, she'll even drop her ball on their heads while they sleep if they're not playing.

PHOEBE

Seri Wawasan Bridge
Age 9, Golden Retriever

Phoebe once 'kidnapped' a baby duckling, taking it for a fun adventure around the park before returning it to its owner. A water enthusiast and great teacher, Phoebe taught all the other dogs in the household to swim.

KING BOBBY

The Kuala Lumpur Library
Age 3, Pembroke Welsh Corgi

King Bobby is a playful pup who adores squeaky toys and sees himself as the king of all dogs. With a charming personality, he has a special fondness for pretty girls.

HULI

Gamuda Gardens Central Park
Age 19, Mixed Breed

Huli is an adventurous dog who used to leap over the fence nightly to patrol the neighborhood. Now older, she can no longer leap over the fence but still makes the occasional attempt! She enjoys up to six walks a day but gets easily frightened by enthusiastic dogs, often seeking refuge at home or hiding in the plants.

QIQI

Gamuda Gardens Central Park
Age 3, Corgi

QiQi is super observant and barks at any changes, like new furniture or clothes on the sofas. As the ultimate guardian, she keeps an eye on strangers and suspicious cars from her lookout spot. Plus, she's a veggie thief who loves sneaking into the kitchen for greens!

HAILEY

The Waterfront, Desa ParkCity
Age 4, Mixed

Hailey, originally from the island of Pulau Ketam, can walk on her hind legs like a kangaroo! She sports a flashy 'gangster' gold chain and knows tons of tricks that she loves to show off.

NOODLE

The Waterfront, Desa ParkCity
Age 5, Chihuahua

Noodle, the adorable dog with really BIG ears, was rescued from the streets of Mexico. She even appeared on The Ellen DeGeneres Show to promote the rescue organization. When her humans moved from California to Malaysia, there was no question: Noodle had to come along!

RISHI

The Waterfront, Desa ParkCity
Age 3, Yorkshire Terrier

Rishi may be tiny, but he's got a huge heart that brings the family together with his unconditional love. During COVID, he was a natural "anti-depressant," and his happy dance while convincing dog lovers for walkies is just adorable.

ROO, ALADDIN AND MAGGIE

Holden Arboretum
Ages 3, 4 and 1, Chorkie, Terrier mix and Miniature Schnauzer

This lively trio is full of energy and curiosity, always eager to explore the world around them. With a keen intelligence, they quickly learn new tricks and commands, making every day an exciting adventure.

TAILS FROM . . .

Lake County, Ohio USA

Known for its beautiful Lake Erie beaches, wineries, and abundant parks.

A DOG'S GUIDE:

1. Enjoy a day at a winery - many have dog-friendly spots and special days for pups.
2. Take a splash in Lake Erie at approved places like Lake Erie Bluffs park.
3. Dine at Ruff Life on the Lake, a restaurant and bar that loves dogs.
4. Explore the 39 Lake Metroparks with over 60 miles of trails, perfect for hikes with your leashed pet.
5. Treat yourself to a pup cup at Fairport Harbor Creamery, where you can find tasty baked goods and ice cream just for dogs.

ONE HEALTH ORGANIZATION

These photoshoots raised funds for One Health Organization, supporting pet owners in need by assisting with veterinary bills to promote loving bonds with healthy pets.
Visit onehealth.org to learn more

KRISTINE LANG
THOUGHTFUL IMAGES

Kristine founded Thoughtful Images during the days of film, although it's now fully digital. The studio began as an all-around portrait and wedding service, but Kristine found that her years of running a successful pet-sitting service in the '90s always made pet portraits her favourite photoshoots.

Ten years of working with a variety of pets, from everyone's beloved dogs and cats to the more unusual 4-foot-long iguana (who needed a daily walk to the bathtub) makes photo sessions fun and relaxing.

THOUGHTFULIMAGES.COM

STANLEY

Blair Ridge Park
Age 3, Bichon Frise

This happy dog is titled in both Flyball and Agility and his favourite thing (other than his mom) is being outdoors. He has a plethora of canine and human friends and is referred to as the Neighborhood Dog.

FRANGELICO

Penitentiary Glen
Age 2, French Bulldog

Frangelico was formerly known as Honey, due to her beautiful golden eyes. She's obsessed with squeaky toys, always on a mission to find and destroy the squeaker. She adores her four siblings and would hate to be the only dog.

EMBER

Lake Erie Bluffs
Age 4, Standard Poodle

This dog is an absolute sweetheart who loves showing off her tricks, especially when it comes to retrieving her leash. She's also a bit of a fashion critic - if you change pants, she insists on inspecting and approving them before you head out!

WINTER

Lake Erie Bluffs
Age 3, Labrador Retriever

Winter "suffers" from too much joy and happiness. In true Retriever form, she loves to play fetch and explores the world through her mouth. Always eager to lend a paw, Winter enjoys helping around the yard.

BETTE

Concord Woods Nature Park
Age 1, Cavalier King Charles Spaniel

Bette is such a cuddler! She's currently practicing to become a therapy dog and loves to play with stuffed toys and chew on bones.

RIVER

Concord Woods Nature Park
Age 7, Cavalier King Charles Spaniel

This active, happy boy loves traveling and camping with his family all over the country. Always up for an adventure, River is also super affectionate.

LUNA

Girdled Road Park
Age 2, Golden Retriever

Luna is a quirky pup who munches on veggies like carrots, lettuce, and cucumbers. She's also a champ at carrying anything in her mouth, even a 10-pound weight! A total Velcro dog, Luna always sticks by her humans' side.

HAVOC

Chagrin River Park
Age 1, Golden Retriever

Havoc is training to be a Service Dog for a disabled Veteran. He loves to entertain himself with a tennis ball for hours and enjoys rolling in fresh cut grass and mud. He once tried Dock Diving, but preferred to be held and float than do any actual diving.

JEDI

Las Vegas Arts District
Age 4, Jindo

Meet brave Jedi, a survivor of the dog meat trade! Despite being an amputee, this little champion is a delightful chaos chaser, bringing joy and energy to everyone around.

TAILS FROM . . .
Las Vegas, Nevada US

Known for its vibrant entertainment scene, with gambling, shows, dining, nightlife, and iconic wedding chapels.

A DOG'S GUIDE:

1. Enjoy a tasty meal with your furry buddy at Lazy Dog Restaurant & Bar, featuring a special menu just for pups.
2. Browse and shop at Town Square Las Vegas for some fun treats.
3. Spend the night at the dog-friendly Cosmopolitan Hotel, where you both can relax.
4. Take a hike up Lone Mountain for some exercise and a beautiful view.
5. Beat the heat and cool off with a splash at Lake Mead during the summer.

HEAVEN CAN WAIT ANIMAL SOCIETY

These photoshoots raised funds for Heaven Can Wait Animal Society, a nonprofit dedicated to preventing unnecessary euthanasia and improving quality of life for pets. Visit heavencanwaitlv.org to learn more

NICOLE HRUSTYK
PAWTRAITS BY NICOLE

Nicole Hrustyk, pronounced "Rustic", has been capturing memories of Las Vegas dogs for their owners since 2004. Her passion for photography started at a young age and her love for capturing the perfect moment continues to grow every day. Nicole takes great joy in seeing her clients light up when they see their final artwork.

With two decades of dog sports and training experience, Nicole is also skilled at keeping her four-legged subjects comfortable and happy during photo sessions, ensuring that they are the stars of the show.

PAWTRAITSBYNICOLE.COM

VIEW

El Dorado Dry Lake Bed
Age 7, Border Collie

This lovable dog adores rolling in dirt and getting filthy. He has the toothiest submissive grin and is 130% dork!

CHARLOTTE

Aliante Nature Discovery Park
Age 11, Bichon Frise

This dog is definitely her own girl, always doing things her way. She adores her daddy the most and can't get enough of treat time.

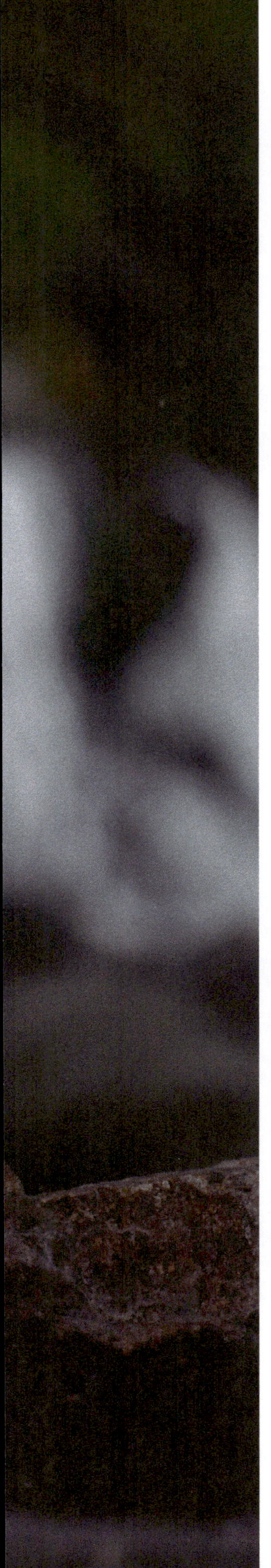

ZERO

Mount Charleston
Age 4, Schnauzer

Zero absolutely loves ice cream! He's also a big fan of all animals, making him the friendliest dog around.

RUBY ROSE

Mountain Crest Park
Age 3, Cavalier King Charles Spaniel/Dachshund

Ruby Rose is a total social butterfly! She adores playing with her feline brother, Rowdy, zooming around the park and definitely loves people more than dogs.

MAE AND ROSE

Floyd Lamb Park At Tule Springs
Age 1, Australian Shepherds

Mae and Rose are two adorable pups with unique tastes - Mae can't resist cheese and loves the ocean, while Rose is all about peaches and cuddles. They both have the cutest wigglebutts and love to strike a pose for the camera!

MAYA AND MYLES

Lee Meadow
Ages 12 and 1, Siberian Husky and Mini Aussie

Maya lives for cheese, especially Kraft American singles. She sometimes sounds like Michael Jackson in a fit of excitement when she arrives at the dog park. Myles loves blowing bubbles while bobbing for ice cubes and has internal alarm clock set for 6:30am everyday, waking his human with approximately 1 million kisses.

LACEY

Doctor Harry B. Johnson Rose Garden
Age 9, Husky

Lacey is a stunning dog who knows she's gorgeous! Super smart and loving towards people, she also has a stubborn side, doing things on her own schedule.

LUCY AND JUNE

Lauf-Schönberg
Ages 2 and 9 months, Australian Shepherds

Lucy has been sucking on her favourite cuddly toy since day one. Her sister June is a quick and eager learner who has never broken a thing. Both dogs share a love for food.

TAILS FROM . . .

Lauf An Der Pegnitz, Germany

Known for beautiful old towns with castles and churches, pine forest hiking trails and local beers.

A DOG'S GUIDE:

1. Stroll through the sandy dunes near Altdorf for a taste of beach fun.
2. Hike to Walberla at sunset for a breathtaking view.
3. Explore the blooming heather fields in late summer around Nuremberg.
4. Breathe in the fresh scent of holidays in the pine forests.
5. Check out the exciting annual sled dog race in Lauf-Schönberg during autumn.

LAURA WOITAS

LAURA WOITAS FOTOGRAFIE

It all started with my first dog, Lotta. I had a photoshoot of her with a dear colleague and after that experience I wanted to be able to do the same.

I wanted to be able to create memories of dogs for people. Over the years, I practiced a lot on my own dogs and then decided to become self-employed in 2022.

With my pictures I try to capture the character of each individual dog and play with a touch of magic and majesty.

LWFOTOGRAFIE.DE

PRIVATE WILDLIFE SANCTUARY

These photoshoots raised funds for a private wildlife sanctuary that rehabilitates native animals and birds for release back into the wild through donations.

BAILEY

Walberla
Age 3, Australian Shepherd/Border Collie

Happy Bailey is a total workaholic, driven by her great will to please. She absolutely loves to swim and dive, making every splash a joyful adventure.

LOKI

Leinburg
Age 2, Mixed

Adorable Loki is full of joy and curiosity, always eager to explore the world despite being a little bit shy.

FLAIR

Lauf an der Pegnitz
Age 8, Airedale Terrier

Flair is all about work and training, always sporting a happy demeanor. She's quite the star in Rally Obedience - it's clear she thrives on the action and enjoys every moment of it!

DINGO

Lauf-Schönberg
Age 7 months, Cattle Dog/Fox Terrier

This dog is super diligent when it comes to learning and mastering tasks. Food is definitely his number one love, but Dingo also can't resist a good cuddle session. It's all about those tasty treats and cosy moments!

NANOOK

Leinburg
Age 2, Australian Shepherd

This dog has a strong instinct to protect his owners, making him a loyal companion. Nanook is also super playful and quite sensitive.

MONTY

Walberla
Age 5, Tibet Terrier

In Tibet they call this breed 'little man' - that suits Monty perfectly. He sleeps with his own pillow or when the family goes to a beer garden, he wants to sit on the bench and be part of the company.

ELLI

Lauf an der Pegnitz
Age 2, Nova Scotia Duck Tolling Retriever

This super well behaved dog also acts like a clown at times. Elli is playful and loves dummies.

LEA AND LUTZ

Leinburg
Ages 7 and 1, Jack Russel Terrier mix

Lea and Lutz make the perfect pair! Lea is very well behaved, always ready for a cuddle, while Lutz brings joy as he acts like a playful little clown.

KIRA

Leinburg
Age 10, White Swiss Shepherd Dog

Kira loves to fetch the ball, but refuses to give it back. She's super sensitive, picking up on her owner's moods, especially when they're not feeling well.

LILY AND HARRY

Prestwold Hall
Ages 5 and 7, Greyhound and Lurcher Cross

Lily is a sweet dog who loves holding hands while she sleeps (for at least 19 hours a day!) Harry loves tennis balls more than anything in the world, but is terrified of insects and seals and hates the word 'Alexa'.

TAILS FROM . . .

Leicestershire, England UK

Known for its rich history, Leicester is home to the remains of King Richard III and the birthplace of Lady Jane Grey.

A DOG'S GUIDE:

1. Enjoy a shopping adventure at the High Cross Shopping Centre, where retail therapy is dog friendly!
2. Treat yourselves at Bark & Brew Coffee Shop, Mountsorrel
3. Experience a fun steam train ride with your fur baby on the Great Central Railway. Travel from Leicester to Loughborough and enjoy the views of charming villages along the way.
4. Take a leisurely stroll around the stunning grounds of Belvoir Castle, which has stood since 1066.
5. Explore Foxton Locks, the longest and steepest staircase of canal locks in the UK.

DRONE TO HOME

These photoshoots raised funds for Drone to Home, which reunites missing dogs with their owners through community support and volunteer efforts.
Visit dronetohome.org.uk to learn more

GEMMA CALDERON

GEMMA CALDERON DOG PHOTOGRAPHY

Hi, I'm Gemma - wife, boss, and mummy to Sofia & Harriet and also our Cocker Spaniels, Rufus & Otis. I'm based in Leicestershire, England and specialise in capturing dog portraits.

While studying photography many years ago, I immediately knew I wanted to be a dog photographer. So began Gemma Calderon Dog Photography!

I love the sense of freedom photography gives me; being out in the woods with my camera allows me to find a sense of escapism, to be liberated and be ME! Away from the daily chores and stresses, it's just me, the dog and my client. There's nothing greater than creating the most beautiful memories.

GEMMACALDERONDOGPHOTOGRAPHY.CO.UK

LUNA

Prestwold Hall
Age 4, Mixed

Luna was rescued from the streets as a puppy. She was a reactive dog, but through hard work she has gone from anti-social to doggy daycare! She loves sprinting through fields and can't get enough of her people and doggy pack.

WESLEY

Swithland Woods
Age 2, Pomsky

Wesley, previously known as Melman, is the most lovable dummy you could ever meet! This over-excited puppy is a true prince, full of sass and attitude. He has been a long awaited addition for his human mum.

JESSIE, ELLIE AND MISTY

Swithland Woods
Age 7, Mixed

Ellie, Jessie, and Misty were born in Koh Chang, Thailand. They are a unique mix of various breeds including: Thai Ridgeback, Jingo, Chow Chow, Akita, Shar-Pei, Shih Tzu, Nordic Spitz, Pyrenean Mastiff, American Eskimo Dog and Polish Greyhound.

FRANK

Prestwold Hall
Age 3, French Bulldog

Frank was re-homed at just 9 months when his original owner couldn't cope with his playful attitude. He is a true performer who delights friends with rolls and tricks. His absolute favourite activity? Zooming for hours on the beach!

WINNIE

Prestwold Hall
Age 2, Staffordshire Bull Terrier

Winnie is an adventurous pup who loves exploring the woods and beach. Super friendly, she enjoys making new doggy friends to run and roll around with. She's incredibly agile and fast, capable of jumping really high!

TEDDY

Prestwold Hall
Age 5, Chow Chow

Teddy, a typical Chow Chow, is as stubborn as they come. His palate is as refined as his personality; he has a love for all things cheese and fish. Fiercely loyal, he takes his protector role seriously, springing into action with a hearty bark at the slightest hint of a visitor.

RUPERT

Prestwold Hall
Age 3, Golden Retriever

Rupert has a stash of stolen socks hidden under the bed. Every night, he curls up in bed with his head on the pillow, and he absolutely loves catching episodes of Bluey on TV.

VENUS

Prestwold Hall
Age 4, Canadian Eskimo Dog

Venus is a rare Canadian Eskimo Dog - there are less than 800 worldwide! As a show dog at Crufts, she thrives in harness work, weight pull and dry land sledding. Proudly, she's one of only five in her breed to earn the Kennel Club bronze good citizen level!

ARLO

Prestwold Hall
Age 4, Cavapoo

Arlo is a total attention seeker and loves to show off his many tricks. He also enjoys going for walks and never misses a chance to stop some doggy ice cream along the way.

ARIA

Long Wood
Age 3, Ragdoll

Meet this adventurous cat who is curious about everything! Although she's an indoor kitty, Aria loves visiting friends and going for stroller walks. A well-travelled companion, she's explored Singapore, France, and the UK, and while catnip doesn't excite her, mum's old office shoes are her ultimate joy!

TAILS FROM . . .

London, England UK

Known for its iconic historical landmarks and cultural institutions like the British Museum, West End theatres, and world-class galleries.

A DOG'S GUIDE:

1. Take a long walk at Hampstead Heath, splash around in the ponds, and enjoy amazing views of the city.
2. Have a pint with your human at a dog-friendly pub, like The Grange in Ealing.
3. Pick up a special memento at the dog-friendly Liberty London department store.
4. Explore Greenwich Market and then stretch your legs with a walk in Greenwich Park.
5. Spend a fun day at Ruislip Lido Dog Beach.

MAYHEW

These photoshoots raised funds for Mayhew, an animal welfare charity enhancing the lives of pets and communities through adoption, veterinary care, and international support. Visit themayhew.org to learn more

CHOHEE COURTOIS

CHOHEE COURTOIS PHOTOGRAPHY

Chohee photographs pets and their people in West London. With a profound passion for capturing the unique personalities of her subjects and the cherished bond between pets and their owners, she has made a significant mark in pet portrait photography.

Her accolades include multiple national and international photography awards. She has an affectionate Pomeranian called Guillaume, and when she's not cuddling with him or doing her photography work, there's a high chance of spotting her at one of the swimming pools in London soaking in her favourite perfume - chlorine.

CHOHEECOURTOIS.CO.UK

WINTER

Buckingham Palace
Age 5, British Blue Shorthair

Winter loves to be hand fed by her hoomans - not for medical reasons, just for being spoilt and a touch high maintenance! A proud Arsenal fan, Winter is a true floofy gooner!

ORLY

Gunnersbury Park
Age 7, Jack Chi

This dog is happiest curled up on Granddad's lap. Born in Orlando and raised in London, Orly found his forever home thanks to Buddies for Life Inc.

TODD

Hampstead Heath
Age 2, Cavalier King Charles

This dog is a cheese-loving goofball who can't resist chasing birds on Hampstead Heath. He's all about the cuddles and gets so excited for attention that he can't help but cry when he's happy!

BRÉAGHA

Hampstead Heath
Age 4, Labrador Retriever

This lovable dog adores cuddles and is absolutely obsessed with the beach. When it's time for a snack, nothing makes Bréagha happier than a tasty cheese on toast treat.

SKYE

Long Wood
Age 2, Boxer

This dog is all or nothing - she's either zooming around at 100mph or snoozing away. If you're sitting cross-legged, Skye will hop in your lap for a cosy hug. She can't stand not knowing what's on the other side of a wall, she'll either jump on top or pop her head over to see.

BARNABY

Hampstead Heath
Age 7, Cocker Spaniel

Barnaby loves going to pubs and tries to enter each one he passes during a walk. His favourite pasttime is lying in muddy puddles - the boggier, the better!

TANGO

Chiswick House and Gardens
Age 8, Border Collie

Tango is an adventurous dog born in Mexico in 2016. He has lived in Bogota, Colombia and London with his family. After seven years as the only pup, he's now a proud big brother to a little human!

ESME

Gunnersbury Park
Age 4, Pug

Esme loves chasing Hoovers and has a refined taste as a part-time cheese connoisseur! She dislikes cats and having her teeth brushed.

ENZO AND FRIDA

Low Cross Wood
Age 1, Neva Masquerade Siberian Forest Cat

Frida and Enzo are very greedy, very naughty, and very cuddly. Frida enjoys affection on her own terms and gives a thorough (and rough), midnight facial. Enzo loves being carried and drapes himself around the necks of his humans while they attempt to cook dinner.

MOLLY

Home
Age 7, Golden Retriever

Molly loves snuggling with her family and is always the first to jump into the pool for a swim. As a certified therapy dog, she enjoys visiting the local elementary school, where she happily meets and brightens the day of all the kids.

TAILS FROM . . .

Media, Pennsylvania USA

Known for its expansive woodlands and the Colonial Pennsylvania Farmstead, which reflects pre-Revolutionary American life.

A DOG'S GUIDE:

1. Enjoy a refreshing pint with your human at Iron Hill Brewery, where dogs are welcome on the outdoor patio.
2. Dine at The Barking Dog Garden Patio for a unique outdoor meal made from fresh, local ingredients right from their garden.
3. Explore the pet-friendly Rose Tree Park, with its grassy hills, picnic spots, gazebo, community garden, and fun seasonal festivals.
4. Go for a hike at Natural Lands Hildacy Preserve, a spacious 55-acre habitat perfect for dogs and their humans.
5. Explore the woodlands with your dog.

ALL 4 PAWS RESCUE

These photoshoots raised funds for All 4 Paws Rescue, a no-kill organization dedicated to rescuing, rehabilitating, and finding loving homes for animals in need.
Visit all4pawsrescue.com to learn more

CAROL ARSCOTT
CAROL ARSCOTT PHOTOGRAPHY

As a rescue photographer, Carol has dedicated her life to capturing images that tell a story of hope and courage. She has a keen eye for detail and an innate ability to capture the essence of a moment.

Her passion for photography was sparked by her love for animals, and she has made it her mission to use her talent to raise awareness about animal rescue efforts. Fundraising is the cornerstone of Carol's pet photography business. In addition to her portrait business, Carol also mentors other pet photographers. She is truly blessed to be able to run a business doing what she loves, while also helping animals in need.

CAROLARSCOTT.COM

MURPHY AND LOLA

Hibernia Park
Ages 6 and 8, Golden Retriever

Lola, a puppy mill survivor, is finally learning to be a dog two years after her rescue. She jumps and runs like a rabbit outside and has just started playing with toys. Meanwhile, Murphy loves his big stuffed carrot but is a bit scared of the cat!

GRAY

Hibernia Park
Age 6, Golden Retriever mix

Gray is a smart dog who is actually 25% boxer (though you wouldn't know it from looking at him!). He knows over 25 tricks and gets into the spirit every Halloween by dressing up as a lion.

ROCKY

Valley Forge National Park
Age 9, Pitbull Terrier/Shepherd mix

Rocky loves taking car rides even if it's just down the street to the park. With his charming brown spots on his ears, dubbed his "Cindy Crawford mole," he's a handsome pup. He loves splashing around in creeks and catching water in his mouth.

LOKI

Home
Age 8, Chihuahua/hound mix

Loki has a unique fetch style, using his paws to catch instead of his mouth. His favourite place to sleep is wrapped up in a fuzzy blanket, on top of a heated blanket - even in the heat of summer! He also loves belly rubs, chicken, and terrorizing the local squirrels.

RUPERT

Ridley Creek State Park
Age 8, English Pointer

Rupert is quite the character! He has a knack for getting skunked and once hitched a ride on the turnpike with a friendly truck driver. When he's not off on adventures, he loves to nose a ball into the pool, swim to retrieve it and repeat all day long.

ROGER

Ridley Creek State Park
Age 7 months, Shih Tzu

Roger, the blind pup, doesn't let his disability hold him back. His favourite toy is a chicken nugget on an elastic band that he plays with daily with his humans. He loves his Mama so much that he keeps her t-shirt with him all day while she is at work.

HARVEY AND ZELDA

Home
Ages 1 and 4, Great Pyrenees mix and GSD

Zelda is totally obsessed with her Kong frisbee and rocks, while Harvey can't get enough of squeaky toys and loves playing fetch solo. They are both true reflections of their respective breeds - loyal, loving, and protective.

MULDER

Hibernia Park
Age 4, Pitbull/Labrador

Mulder is the sweetest, kindest dog who brings joy to his human with his goofy antics. Though he enjoys his lazy moments, his playful spirit ensures there's never a dull day.

HIMS

Ridley Creek State Park
Age 1, Mixed

Hims is a sweet boy who adores meeting new people and has a curious, mischievous side. He loves to run and play, but his ultimate favourite is curling up on the couch for a cosy snooze.

WINSTON

Mehlinger Heide
Age 5, Corgi

Winston was rescued by a kind monk from a meat truck in China. This playful and friendly pup is always ready to entertain, but he's definitely a foodie at heart - he only works for treats!

TAILS FROM . . .

Meisenheim, Germany

Known for its medieval charm, local winemaking and scenic hiking along the Nahe River.

A DOG'S GUIDE:

1. Join the festive Wuffnachtsmarkt Raumbach Christmas market. It's made for pups and their humans and filled with tasty treats, cool accessories, and fun activities.
2. Stroll along the peaceful Nahe River Walk.
3. Discover historical ruins on dog-friendly Disibodenberg Hike.
4. Many local vineyards are happy to welcome dogs, so you can enjoy wine tastings together.
5. Explore various dog-friendly trails at Soonwald-Nahe Nature Park.

LOLA DHONAU
SKELFING ART & PHOTOGRAPHY

My faithful dog Raksha was my original inspiration to specialize in dog photography. I love to photograph all animals outside, in their natural environment - where they can simply be themselves.

I am an animal welfare activist. This means that I am not only passionate about capturing the beauty of animals with my camera, but also about actively advocating for their rights. I feel so lucky to be able to combine these two passions, and to be able to create unforgettable memories for my clients.

SKELFING-ART.DE

WILDTIERHILFE SCHÄFER E.V.

These photoshoots raised funds for Wildtierhilfe Schäfer e.V., supporting wildlife rehabilitation, care, and conservation efforts for injured and orphaned animals in Germany. Visit wildtierhilfe-schaefer.de to learn more

FARRI

Schäferplacken,
Altenbamberg
Age Unknown, Australian Cattle Dog

MURMEL

Raumbach
Age Unknown, Chihuahua

Murmel is an incredibly sweet Chihuahua with a gentle, loving nature. Though she's a bit shy, her quiet charm makes her even more appealing. Always friendly, she loves making new friends, proving that her reserved personality just adds to her cuteness!

HUGO

Bad Sobernheim
Age Unknown, Cavalier King Charles Spaniel

Hugo is a chill pup who enjoys hanging out with his family. Though he can be a bit timid and jumpy at times, he quickly warms up to new experiences. Always the social butterfly, he loves meeting and playing with other dogs!

BONNY AND PENNY

Bad Kreuznach
Age Unknown, Mixed

Bonny and Penny are two adorable shelter dogs who found their forever home. They're super friendly and calm, with gentle temperaments. A little shy initially, these sweet pups are just full of love for anyone willing to take the time to get to know them!

JUNA

Bad Kreuznach
Age 3, Dutch Shepherd Dog

Juna, affectionately nicknamed "Crazy Lady" and "Funny Trampel," is a high-speed noodle of a dog. As a professional Detection Dog, she combines intelligence with energy, yet remains loving and gentle, especially with children and animals.

SOCKE

Wolfstein
Age 1, Corgi

Socke the Corgi is a super cuddly pup with a huge heart, always in tune with everyone's feelings. She's the boss of her pack, playfully ruling over the German Shepherds while thriving on affection from her favourite humans.

BAGHEERA

Mücke
Age 7, Mixed

Baggy, a resilient Romanian street dog, went from a fearful pup to a confident adventurer. After a rough start in a shelter, he now loves hiking, sledding, and exploring the world.

KAIA

Waldböckelheim
Age 2, Mixed

Kaia is a rescue from Romania who brings joy to her family. As the serious one of the pack, she's diligently preparing for her companion dog exam. With a deep bond as a "soul dog," Kaia is always connected with her owner, making her an irreplaceable companion.

MARLEY

Waldböckelheim
Age 2, Mixed

Marley, a 2-year-old rescue from Croatia, is the playful clown of the family. Always full of energy and quirky antics, he brings endless joy and is often seen with a cheerful, smiling face, loving all the pats he can get!

DEXTER

Flinders Street Station
Age 1, Staffy/Heeler

Dexter, a playful pup adopted from Forever Friends Animal Rescue, thrives on fun outings with friends at the park or chasing birds. His love language is most definitely through touch, whether that be cuddling up with on the couch or sharing lots of kisses.

TAILS FROM . . .

Melbourne, VIC Australia

Known for its vibrant food and arts scene, cultural diversity and home of AFL (Aussie Rules Football).

A DOG'S GUIDE:

1. Dive into fun at Brighton Dog Beach, where you can swim off-lead anytime!
2. Treat yourself to a coffee and a puppacino at the Dog House cafe or explore other dog-friendly cafés in the city.
3. Join the Million Paws Walk to help raise funds for animal rescue and enjoy a day out with fellow pups.
4. Explore the vineyards with Gourmet Pawprints in Mornington Peninsula, Yarra Valley, or Bellarine.
5. Enjoy a scenic historic train ride on the Puffing Billy Dog Express in the beautiful Dandenong Ranges, running monthly for you and your humans.

FOREVER FRIENDS ANIMAL RESCUE

These photoshoots raised funds for Forever Friends Animal Rescue, a volunteer-run charity rescuing and rehabilitating abandoned, abused, and sick animals in the community. Visit foreverfriends.org.au to learn more

PAUL TADDAY

PAUL TADDAY PHOTOGRAPHY - PAWS & CLAWS

Based on the eastern outskirts of sunny Melbourne, Paul Tadday Photography - "Paws & Claws" specialises in creating whimsical, character-filled artwork of your furry family member.

My aim is to give you and your pet an enjoyable and memorable photography experience, to design and create artwork that you will have you smiling from ear to ear every time you walk into the room!

There's nothing more rewarding to me than to unveil the final printed artwork to my clients, to see their response when they view the results of their photo session for the very first time.

PAULTADDAY.COM

REGGIE

South Wharf
Age 1, Miniature Schnauzer

Meet Reggie, aka Sir Reginald, the boss of the house! This playful pup loves to snatch socks from the laundry and parade around with them. Reggie is very friendly and greets all dogs he meets with a 'come on, lets have a game of chasey' attitude.

REMI

State Library
Age 6, Border Collie/Kelpie

Remi has over 12 nicknames and responds to them all, but his parents' favourite is 'Silly Pants'. He loves playing hide and seek, swimming, and playing tag with his all of his doggy besties.

STELLA

Royal Arcade
Age 3, Aussie Shepherd

Stella is a well-travelled puppy who's journeyed from Texas to Mexico and now calls Australia home. She's beautiful, loving and very protective of any creatures she considers part of her pack.

THOR

The Shrine of Remembrance
Age 10, Dogue De Bordeaux/Mastiff mix

Thor, adopted in 2022 through Forever Friends Animal Rescue, has made a miraculous recovery from a mast cell tumour regrowth. This talented pup learned to push a skateboard as a complex skill that his 'hooman' needed to pass her Certificate III in Dog Behaviour and Training.

WALTER

Birrarung Marr
Age 2, Lagotto Romagnolo

Walter is a ball-chasing pup who always has a 'teethy' grin thanks to his underbite. He's got a serious case of FOMO. His sister Lola made it into the 2022 book, so he was determined to land a spot in the 2024 edition!

ROCKY ROAD

Federation Square
Age 1, Border Collie/Poodle

Rocky is a soft toy fanatic, especially if they squeak! This food-motivated pup will do just about anything for a tasty doggie treat. He has the most amazing blue eyes and a soft merle coat.

HOLLY AND JESSIE

Victoria Harbour
Ages 11 and 13, Jack Russell Terrier

Holly is a fearless pup, but she absolutely hates balloons since she popped her first one. Jessie enjoys giving herself a full-body rub on the carpet. The two of them often tag along with their mum, a dog photographer, on her fun photography adventures.

MURPHY

Williamstown Pier
Age 2, Labrador

Murphy is a therapy dog who supports assistance dogs, pet dogs and people with disabilities by helping develop handling skills. When she's not wearing her working jacket, she's a complete goofball, enjoying activities like playing with her ball, climbing trees, and swimming!

INDI

Southbank
Age 4, Golden Retriever

The persistent rain during Indi's photo session didn't stop her from taking a spontaneous leap into the Yarra River! She's a caring dog and enjoys walking alongside her elderly grandparent while they use their walking frame.

LUKE

Midland Army Airfield Museum
Age 2, German Shepherd

Luke, the rescue pup with a bit of separation anxiety, has turned into the ultimate loyal companion. Over the last 1.5 years, he's been a fantastic foster brother to 80 rescue dogs and brightens up the days of assisted living residents with his calm presence.

TAILS FROM . . .

Midland, Texas USA

Known for its abundant petroleum and natural gas reserves, proud highschool football culture, and breathtaking West Texas sunsets.

A DOG'S GUIDE:

1. Chill with your furry friend on the patio at Tall City Brewing Co. while enjoying craft beer.
2. Discover the Sibley Nature Centre together and learn about local wildlife and plants.
3. Have a blast at Monahans Sandhills State Park, where you can play in the sand and explore on horseback.
4. Visit Far West Coffee for a unique coffee experience, complete with a puppuccino for your pup.
5. Swing by Fair to Midland for a fun bar stop with beers, puppuccinos, and even a slide, all while supporting local rescues.

MIDLAND ANIMAL SHELTER ADOPTABLES

These photoshoots raised funds for Midland Animal Shelter Adoptables, boosting adoption rates and helping rescue and foster around 2,000 shelter animals.
Visit midlandpets.org to learn more

TASHA SPORT

TASHA SPORT PHOTOGRAPHY

Growing up in West Texas, I can't recall a time when we didn't have a family dog. It began my lifelong adventure with four-legged friends by my side. But it wasn't until after my beloved red heeler, Kate, passed away unexpectedly that I discovered the healing power of a photograph.

As an animal rescue advocate, I've devoted countless hours to helping animals get to safety as a volunteer for several rescue organizations. I realized that another way I could really make a difference and help these animal find their forever homes was through photography. A beautiful first impression will often be the difference between adoption or not.

TASHASPORTPHOTOGRAPHY.COM

WINSTON

Monahans Sandhills State Park
Age 3, Australian Shepherd

Winston is a frisbee and ball fanatic, delighting everyone with his midair spins. He enjoys swimming, but only to his preferred depth. A true social butterfly, just like his mommy, Winston is loved by all who meet him!

CANE

Cactus Mural
Age 2, Corgi mix

Cane, a rescue from the city shelter, sports an adorable grateful look and stunning sky blue eyes that melt hearts. His favourite sound? The freezer opening - no ice cube stands a chance when he's around!

OAKLEY, BLUE, REMI AND PEPPER

Permian Basin Stonehenge Replica
Ages 1, 7, 6 months and 4, Australian Shepherds and Border Collies

Blue is a bossy black and white beauty who wrangles cats and fetches balls solo. Pepper, the chatty Aussie covid pup, loves to gossip, while sweet Oakley, a rescue, is a total heart-stealer. Baby Remi is a regal joy, reminding everyone of the beloved Sadie who started it all.

WYLIE, TEDDY AND SPUD

Ratliff Stadium
Ages 2, 1 and 11, Australian Shepherd, Schnauzer/Yorkie and Beagle

Wylie is an amazing, sweet, and gentle boy who adores his siblings and is his momma's rock. Teddy, despite being deaf and partially blind, shines brightly in everyone's life. Spud, the mischievous beagle, is full of personality and loves being his momma's best buddy.

MAVERICK

Petroleum Museum
Age 3, Husky/German Shepherd

Maverick is a friendly pup who adores everyone he meets. He's quite the chatterbox, always making sure his voice is heard. His mom dreams of getting him trained and certified as a therapy dog to spread his joy even further!

JADA

Sibley Nature Centre
Age 10, Labrador Retriever

Jada was rescued from a shelter in 2016 and became a mom to 13 puppies shortly after. Once they found homes, she was transported 2,000 miles to her adoptive family. In May 2024, they discovered she was in a shelter in Oregon, but now she's back to live as a pampered princess!

JUDD

Wadley-Barron Park
Age 3, Briard

Judd is a big-hearted dog who believes he's a tiny pup! He loves cuddling in his dad's lap while watching TV. At the park, his playful runs have even led people to ask if he's a lion. What a charming and lovable character he is!

ASPEN

Yucca Theatre
Age 1, Corgi mix

Aspen's parents have fostered over 150 bottle baby puppies and he won their hearts when he was only hours old. He loves snuggling on their pillows, often preferring to perch on their heads!

LAILA AND GINNY

Andrews City Hall
Ages 10 and 4, Shitzus

Laila is a sweet rescue pup who's blind but full of love and adventure. Her favourite things? Treats and tennis balls! When she's not munching on snacks, she's looking out for her sister to make sure she's safe and not lost.

TAILS FROM . . .

Mildenhall, Suffolk, England UK

Known for its open landscapes, UK horse racing and Bury St Edmunds, voted one of the best dog friendly towns in the UK.

A DOG'S GUIDE:

1. Visit Bury St Edmunds for a warm, friendly welcome.
2. Explore the vast forests and woodlands, perfect for running and sniffing around.
3. Enjoy the stunning beaches along the Suffolk coastline that stretch for miles.
4. Experience the love for dogs in Suffolk, where you'll always feel welcomed.
5. Take your human to the dog-friendly pubs, a great excuse for a walk together.

NIGEL WALLACE
NIGEL WALLACE PHOTOGRAPHY

I am a UK based dog photographer. It all started when my Border Collie, Darcy, joined our family when she was 3 months old. I found that I would take my camera out on most of my walks with her; taking pictures and creating memories of our time together.

Although I had been a photographer for most of my life, specialising in dog photography was what I really wanted to do. I took early retirement from my day job and started my own business in 2019 as an 'on location' dog photographer. To me, this is not a job - it's a passion of mine and I like to think this comes out in the photoshoot experience and images I produce for my many happy clients.

NIGELWALLACEPHOTOGRAPHY.CO.UK

MILDENHALL GREYHOUND TRUST

These photoshoots raised funds for Mildenhall Greyhound Trust, a local charity in Suffolk that rehomes ex-racing and non-racing greyhounds.

Visit mildenhallgreyhounds.org.uk to learn more

TIG

Bury St Edmunds
Age 3, Pharaoh Hound

Tig may look regal, but he's truly the biggest clown! He adores attention and will demand it by playfully shoving phones away or knocking things over. Running is his favourite pastime, especially when he's with his fellow Pharaoh hounds.

NARU

Felixstow
Age 3, Coonhound

Naru is a pro at scent work and absolutely LOVES treats! She recently became a proud mom to seven adorable puppies. Plus, her bark? It's seriously loud, making sure everyone knows she's around.

JILL

Thetford
Age 5, Border Collie

Jill is a water-loving pup who could splash around all day. She's an awesome swimmer and has a blast jumping in to fetch her toys. Plus, she enjoys playing with her frisbee and taking fun walks in the forest.

CHAPLIN

Cavenham Heath
Age 8, Boston Terrier

Chaplin loves a sunny naps, especially when his butlers move his bed to the perfect spot. He enjoys strutting through Mildenhall woods, sporting leaves as his chic accessories. And let's not forget his hilarious zoomies that always crack everyone up!

BARLEY

Bury St Edmunds
Age 13, Labrador

Barley is a friendly visiting therapy dog who adores cuddles and some good old butt scratches. As a typical lab, he's also a food monster, ready to gobble up anything in sight. His playful and loving nature brings joy to everyone he meets!

BLU

Arneson Acres
Age 3, Cattle Dog/Husky

Meet this charming rescue dog, a delightful mix of cattle dog, husky, and pit bull traits. Blu adores his humans but can't resist stinky treats! Always ready for adventure, he happily joins his family for shopping trips or exploring new hiking trails.

TAILS FROM . . .

Minneapolis, Minnesota USA

Known for its many lakes (11,842 lakes, to be exact), one of the largest state fairs in the US, and the development of Honeycrisp Apples.

A DOG'S GUIDE:

1. Bde Maka Ska Adventure: Take a 3.4-mile scenic walk around the largest lake, perfect for enjoying green spaces and fresh air.
2. Enjoy a leisurely stroll while soaking in the beautiful art near the Walker Art Centre.
3. Explore miles of tranquil walking trails in Theodore Wirth Regional Park.
4. Visit dog-friendly restaurants like Wells Roadside to enjoy a meal or coffee while your dog relaxes by your side.
5. Explore Boom Island Park and walk along paved trails by the Mississippi River.

MINNEAPOLIS ANIMAL CARE AND CONTROL

These photoshoots raised funds for Minneapolis Animal Care and Control, aiding shelter, care, adoption, and responsible pet ownership. Visit minneapolismn.gov/resident-services/animals-pets to learn more

GRACE LIU
GRACE LIU PHOTOGRAPHY

I have had a love for dogs and animals all my life. As a full time student studying physiology, pet photography is a great creative outlet that I have fallen in love with. I started my photography journey in the middle of the pandemic and haven't turned back since.

I am thrilled to be a part of this project and have been a volunteer photographer for numerous shelters and rescues.

GLIUPHOTOGRAPHY.COM

PENNY

Aquila Park
Age 2, German Shorthaired Pointer/ German Shepherd

Penny, a pup from Minneapolis Animal Care and Control, loves tennis balls and Elmo. With big dreams of becoming the Prime Minister of gravity and appearing on The Price is Right, she's definitely got a fun personality and some quirky goals!

BRUCE

Lyndale Park Gardens
Age 4, German Shepherd

Bruce "Batdog" Davis is a total love sponge, craving affection 24/7. This old man in a dog's body groans and yawns loudly when it's time to get up. He earned his name when his tail wagged so hard while singing that it sounded like he could knock a hole in the wall!

MOSES ABRAHAM

Arneson Acres
Age 4, Pit Bull

Moses is a friendly pup who adores other dogs and kitties. He can't stand the cold, so he wraps himself up like a burrito in a blanket. He is convinced that he's a lap dog and will hop onto your knees the moment you sit down!

CHARLIE

Lyndale Park Gardens
Age 8, German Shepherd

This spirited pup adores her ball and hose, but nothing beats her love for her dad and mom! With a sassy personality, she often "talks back" like a husky, and everything is on her terms - snuggles and pets included!

BRINLEY ROSE

Boom Island Park
Age 5, Australian Shepherd

Brinley is a super sweet and shy pup who lights up with a toothy smile when she's excited. Her absolute favourite treat? String cheese!

BELLOW RAIN

Boom Island Park
Age 2, Australian Shepherd

This dog is super smart and really athletic. She loves to swim and play frisbee, making her a fun companion. Every morning, she greets the day with a big "awoooo!" that is sure to bring a smile to anyone's face.

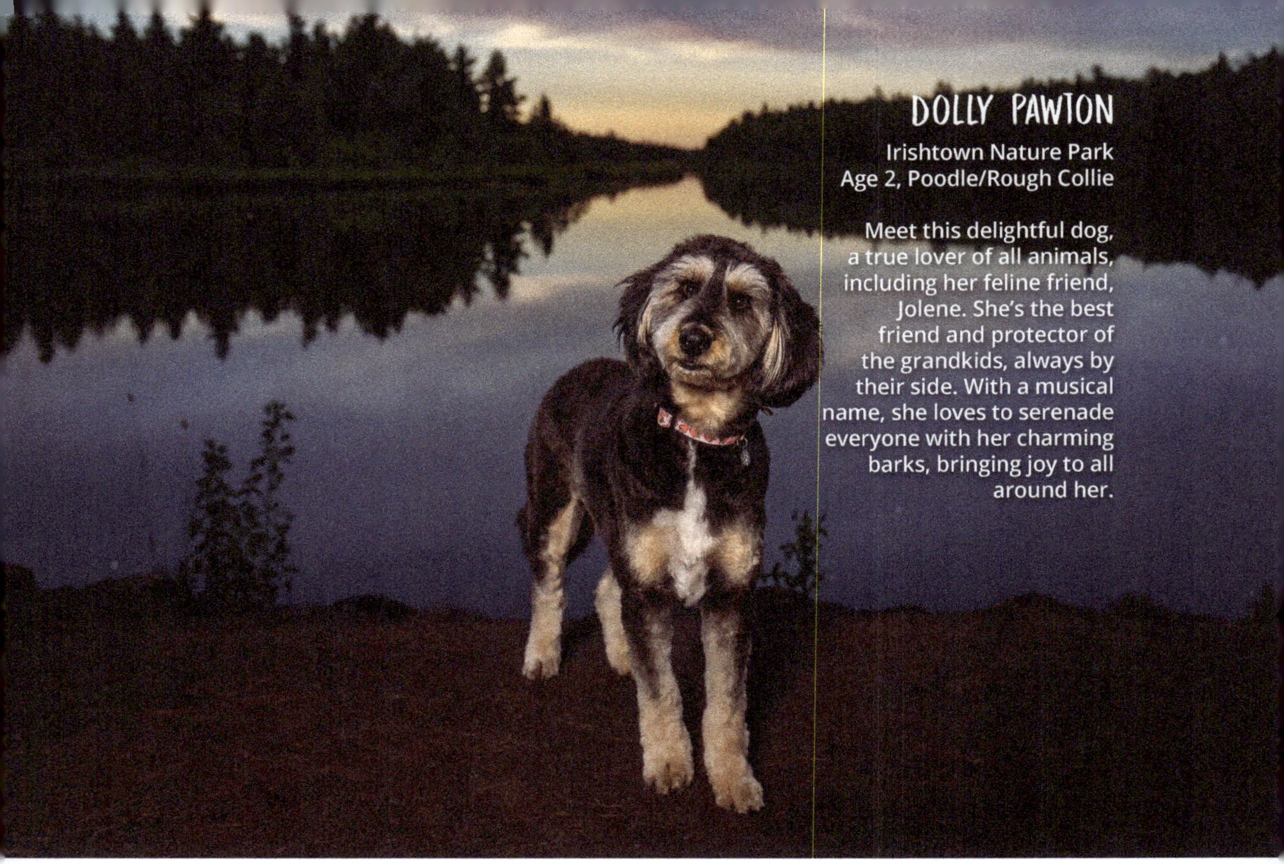

DOLLY PAWTON

Irishtown Nature Park
Age 2, Poodle/Rough Collie

Meet this delightful dog, a true lover of all animals, including her feline friend, Jolene. She's the best friend and protector of the grandkids, always by their side. With a musical name, she loves to serenade everyone with her charming barks, bringing joy to all around her.

TAILS FROM . . .

Moncton, New Brunswick Canada

Known for the giant Tidal Bore wave, being Canada's only officially bilingual city, and the optical illusion of Magnetic Hill, where cars seem to roll uphill!

A DOG'S GUIDE:

1. Get muddy at Hopewell Rocks while exploring the ocean floor during low tide.
2. Enjoy a beer with your humans at dog-friendly breweries, and maybe get a special alcohol-free doggy "beer" from Crafty Beasts Brewing Co.!
3. Discover over 70 km of trails in the city or hop on the TransCanada Trail for more adventures.
4. Treat yourself at LuvPaws Grooming and Bakery.
5. Visit nearby National Parks, but remember to stay on leash, as Fundy N.P. and Kouchibouguac N.P. have bears, moose, skunks, and porcupines.

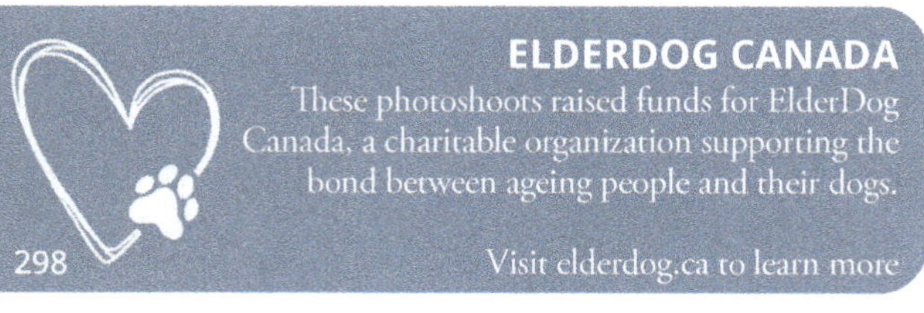

TRACY MUNSON
TRACY MUNSON PHOTOGRAPHY

Tracy's first word was "cat". The cat didn't even like her but was still her favourite family member. As a child, she never dreamed of getting married and having kids. She dreamed of having a koala bear and a monkey. She didn't have imaginary friends, she had imaginary pets. For over 25 years, Tracy nurtured the human-animal bond as a vet tech in Toronto. Now, she is deeply committed to celebrating companion animals with fun and positive photo sessions and believes this is the key to capturing the personality-filled pet portraits her clients love.
In 2018, Tracy relocated to beautiful Fundy Albert to pursue photography full-time. She and her dogs have never been happier.

TRACYMUNSONPHOTOGRAPHY.COM

BAILEY

Local Park
Age 13, Bernese/
Rottweiler

Bailey, a sassy 13-year-old pup rescued by ElderDog Canada, is living her best life after her human passed away - though they planned for her care. With the energy of a 3-year-old and zero boundaries, she's convinced everyone is head over heels in love with her!

WILLOW

Mary's Point
Conservation Area
Age 1, Havanese

This dog has some quirky habits! When she goes potty, she lifts her back left foot a couple of inches. She's mastered the "weave between the legs" trick, but grumbles and rushes for her treat. Not a big snuggler, she loves giving sloppy puppy kisses when you're half-asleep!

RIGGS AND POPPY

Mill Creek Nature Park
Ages 7 and 8 months, Blue Heeler and Australian Shepherd mix

Riggs may act all tough with strangers, but he's a total marshmallow who adores cuddling with his humans and nooking his special blanky. Poppy, the sweetest pup, loves everyone and is set to start agility sports soon. Both are outdoor enthusiasts who join on all the adventures!

CELLO AND NUNA

The Riverfront Trail
Ages 13 and 8 months, Shepherd mix and Shepherd/Husky

Nuna, a rescue from Nunavut, is a bundle of energy who adores cuddling and giving kisses. Her big sister Cello, the most patient pup ever, may have limited energy, but she's always ready to care for Nuna and will do absolutely anything for food!

MR PICKLES AND WAFFLES

Alma
Ages 2 and 1, Panda Pug and English Bulldog

Waffles, affectionately known as Waffy, is a big pushover who happily lets his brother Mr. Pickles walk all over him. They adore their walkies, eagerly anticipate bedtime cookies, and never miss a chance for infinite zoomies!

AVA

Cape Enrage
Age 7, German Shepherd

Ava is her human's best friend and a dock diving champ who enjoys working on obedience. With a family full of police dogs, she sure knows how to keep things exciting and fun!

GRACE

The RCMP Memorial
Age 4, Miniature LH Dachshund

Grace is a CKC Grand Champion Show Dog, but she's got more tricks up her sleeve! She's also a St. John Ambulance Therapy Dog and a social media influencer with her own account, @grace.the.doxie. What a talented pup!

RAYNE, BLUE AND ZIGGY

Abandoned Gypsum Silos
Ages 10, 3 and 7, American Eskimo, Poodle/Pitbull and American Eskimo

Blue, a foster fail from PAW-SBA, taught his family about patience and the importance of animal rescue. Rayne, the energetic Mama Bear, ensures her brothers stay in line. Ziggy, playful and silly, loves to wrestle with his siblings, bringing joy to their home!

KELLIE AND DECLAN

Côte-Sainte-Anne
Ages 2 and 3, Pugs

Kellie was a mischievous escape artist in her youth and once helped her family track down some missing pigs during an escapade! Declan likes to be the last one in at night, waiting for his human to settle in before barking to announce he's finally ready to come inside.

BELLA

Lake Tremblant
Age 8, Labrador mix

Bella is a genuinely free-spirited dog, pensive, strong, and patient. She truly is one-of-a-kind, embodying sweetness and serenity at her very core.

TAILS FROM . . .

Mont-Tremblant, Quebec Canada

Known for its exceptional skiing and snowboarding slopes, and Mont Tremblant National Park.

A DOG'S GUIDE:

1. Explore the hiking trails where you can enjoy nature walks with your human.
2. Stroll around the pedestrian village, a dog-friendly area open year-round.
3. Take a fun pontoon ride on Lake Tremblant, perfect for warm summer days.
4. Stay at pet-friendly hotels like Fairmont Tremblant and Le Westin Tremblant.
5. Join in the excitement at the International Blues Festival, where many events welcome dogs!

ISABELLE GIRARD
ISABELLE GIRARD PHOTOGRAPHIE

Hi! I'm Isabelle. I've always been a follow-your-heart-kind-of-girl. I picked up a camera, pursued curiosity and built my small business in Quebec, Canada. I love dogs... I just love them, so naturally my subjects became hairier and hairier! Feel free to browse my portfolio.

ISABELLEGIRARDPHOTOGRAPHIE.COM

ADOPTION ANIMALE ROSIE

These photoshoots raised funds for Adoption animale Rosie, supporting orphaned animals and connecting them with adoptive homes to ensure their survival.
Visit rosieanimaladoption.ca to learn more

WILLOW

Trails in Mont Tremblant
Age 2, Labrador Retriever

Willow is a goofy, lovable giant who's always on the hunt for new adventures. He loves exploring his surroundings and sniffing everything in sight. And if you mention food? You've definitely got his attention!

WILSON

Trails in Mont Tremblaant
Age 7 months, Weimaraner

This eager-to-please pup is full of personality and ready to become a hunting dog one day. With his spunky, goofy, tenacious, crafty, sneaky, and quick nature, he's bound to keep everyone entertained and on their toes!

CHIYO

Pedestrian Village of Tremblant
Age 8, Beagle

Meet this FUNtastic dog, the ideal partner for agility competitions! With the perfect size for travel, this pup is ready to accompany their human on all adventures, bringing joy and excitement wherever they go.

MAHO

Parc national du Mont-Tremblant
Age 4, Potlicker

Maho is a mixed-breed street dog from Belize with eyes that are almost human. He thrives in various environments and makes an excellent family pet, bringing a unique charm to any home.

MAYA

Pedestrian Village of Tremblant
Age 3, Labrador Retreiver

She's a total velcro dog, sticking to her owner like a shadow. Her eyes are like pools of love, and she'll do anything asked of her, especially if there's a treat in it. It's hard not to adore her!

CHIYO

Pedestrian village of Tremblant
Age 8, Beagle

Chiyo's a social butterfly who adores meeting new people and exploring new places. When things don't go his way, he lets out a howl, but that doesn't stop him from jumping, leaping, and spinning around with whatever toy he can grab!

KENAÏ

Parc national du Mont-Tremblant
Age 10 months, French Mastiff

This gentle giant is a quiet, loving family dog who's always around. His mom can't help but mention his drooling and snoring, but that just adds to his charm!

ZEPPELIN

Monteith
Age 1, German Shepherd

Zeppelin is a water-loving pup who enjoys splashing in his bowl, helping with the garden hose, and playing at the river. He's all about adventures too, from car rides to beach frolics. His name, inspired by a beer, fits perfectly with his family's musical theme.

TAILS FROM . . .

Murraylands, SA Australia

Known for the Murray River (Australia's longest river), the Murray Bridge Bunyip and the Coorong National Park.

A DOG'S GUIDE:

1. Take a walk along the mighty Murray River; the waterfront trails are waiting for your paws!
2. Put on your leash and explore Old Tailem Town, home to over 115 historic buildings, some over a century old.
3. Visit the 1924 River Tavern for a great riverfront dining experience with your human.
4. Enjoy a pet-friendly wine tasting at Kimbolton Wines in Langhorne Creek.
5. Splash around at Lake Alexandrina, a big freshwater lake fed by the Murray River.

FUREVER FARM

These photoshoots raised funds for Furever Farm, a sanctuary in South Australia housing 80 rescued rural animals including sheep, goats, horses, and pigs.
Visit fureverfarm.org.au to learn more

SARINA VELIZ

FUZZ DESIGN

Sarina lives and breathes all things furry and feathered on her farm nestled in the Murraylands region of South Australia. She invites pets and their adoring humans to take part in stunning, one-of-a-kind photography sessions.
Sarina earned accolades and recognition as an award-winning photographer in both local and international competitions. With a degree in Visual Arts, Design, and Photography, she has a knack for capturing the unique personalities of her subjects.
But the work doesn't stop there. She has spent years volunteering in Pets as Therapy programs and dog training. Whether behind the camera or in the community, Sarina's passion for animals shines through in all that she does.

FUZZ-DESIGN.COM

LYLA

Monteith
Age 2, American Bully

Lyla's got three plush pals - Doughie the doughnut, Kenny the chameleon, and Brian the brontosaurus - and she always knows where they are! She seems to read minds, too, running to the back door when a walk or drive is on the horizon. Her excitement is contagious!

RAFFERTY AND ASHER

Monteith
Ages 4 and 1, Papillons

Rafferty is a super smart little guy who showcases his skills like drop, sit, spin, and shake for treats! He's still warming up to Asher, the large, loud newcomer who adores everyone and everything, especially when it comes to retrieving and enjoying new toys.

COCO

Monteith
Age 12, Affenpinscher

Coco is an adorable "Monkey Dog" who is often mistaken for an Ewok. He gets super sniffy when his humans return home, thinking, "Hmm, did they cheat on me? Woof woof!" Coco is a cheese lover by heart and cheesy for his family.

FONZIE, JACQUIE AND ERNIE

Monteith
Ages 2, 6 and 12, Mini Schnauzer, Jack Russell and Maltese/Shih Tzu

Fonzie's super gentle, waking his owner with sweet face pats. Jacquie's the life of the party, always shredding toys and making mischief with the speaker. And then there's Ernie, the sweet old soul who loves sticking close and doing zoomies on the towel post-bath.

ARTY

Monteith
Age 2, French Bulldog

Arty is a lively pup who loves zooming around the house and yard at lightning speed! He doesn't mind getting dirty, digging up the veggie patch and rolling in the dirt. Arty enjoys playing with his doggy friends, Patch and Walt, teasing them to join in even when they're tired.

STITCH

Monteith
Age 1, Maltese/Shih Tzu

Stitch is a playful pup who loves chasing his tail until he gets dizzy! He's notorious for snagging his dad's socks from the laundry, leaving them scattered all over the lawn. But when it comes to treats and food, Stitch's selective hearing magically disappears - he's all ears!

ASKA

Boudevilliers
Age 4, Greyhound mix

Aska is a sweet, sensitive girl who enjoys her walkies, especially sniffing around, but she loves running even more! She adores treats and cherishes cosy moments on the couch with her dog mom.

TAILS FROM . . .

Neuchâtel, Switzerland

Known for its location in the renowned Swiss Watch Valley and its wine festival.

A DOG'S GUIDE:

1. Sniff and hike through the Gorges de l'Areuse, exploring trails and streams.
2. Enjoy a fun cruise on the sparkling waters of lake Neuchâtel.
3. Find a cosy fireplace in nature for a tasty barbecue with friends.
4. Splash and swim in the refreshing lake des Taillères.
5. Discover new sights and smells at the Evologia Parc in Cernier.

LES VIEUX ET LES CABOSSÉS

These photoshoots raised funds for Les Vieux et Les Cabossés, supporting elderly, disabled, or ill animals through donations and handicraft sales.

SOFIA ROTHEN

SOFIA ROTHEN PHOTOGRAPHIE

I'm a dog trainer turned into a pet photographer since 2015. I offer photo sessions for the people that are crazy in love with their dogs, so they can keep memories of their fur babies forever.

Because I'm a dog trainer, I understand that every pup is different. I respect that some need more time or space to be comfortable. My clients also say that I'm super patient.

My favourite place to capture the dog's personality is outside in nature, where they can enjoy their photoshoot and be themselves.

SOFIAROTHENPHOTOGRAPHIE.CH

CHARLY

Valangin
Age 8, Australian Shepherd

Charly is a super playful and energetic dog who's also a bit sensitive. He's super attached to his family and loves to cuddle with them. Plus, he's a natural in front of the camera and will do tricks for treats to show off his skills!

TELMA

Valangin
Age 5, Podenco mix

Telma is a sensitive, affectionate, and funny girl who loves her independence. She enjoys sniffing around and chasing field mice. After a tough start in life, she's now living her best life with her guardian, making every day an adventure!

TOAST

Creux-du-Van
Age 2, Labrador Retriever

Toast is an adventurous pup who loves camping and hiking with his pawrents. He chats with his toys during playtime and enjoys Frisbee, swimming, doing tricks, and getting belly rubs. Plus, he's a big inspiration for his mom Sofia's photography!

PICSOU

Valangin
Age 4, Chihuahua

Picsou has a lot of character, though he can be a bit shy at times. He enjoys the comfort of home, but a glimpse of a cat might just get him outside. When he's indoors, he loves nothing more than cuddling up in his humans' arms

PIXEL

Valangin
Age 5, Pomeranian

Pixel is a loving and calm pup who enjoys walkies, treats, and quality time with his family. His favourite game is searching for hidden toys and treats, but he only runs if his dogdad runs - no exceptions!

STITCH AND OJAÏ

Valangin
Ages 7 and 4, Staffordshire Bull Terrier and Leavitt Bulldog

Stitch is a high-energy girl who loves strutting around with her ball, while Ojaï is more laid-back but a total champ at making funny faces. Together, they enjoy sports with their awesome dogmom, making for a fun-loving duo!

PADAWAN

Cornaux Vineyards
Age 7, Mixed

Padawan loves sipping lake water as an aperitif, paws splashing but avoids swimming. When meeting new, energetic pawfriends, she turns into a total drama queen. Plus, she can't resist the thrill of chasing after cats!

TYLI

Valangin
Age 17, Parson Russel Terrier

Tyli, the fearless and adventurous dog, loves exploring and sniffing around with her brother. Even now, she knows how to make herself heard when she's ready to go home, showcasing her spirited personality and joy for life!

TEPPY, LUNA, OSCAR AND STELLA

Engollon
Ages 12, 10, 8 and 7, Mixed

These four pups are bursting with joy and love hiking with their favourite human. Teppy the intrepid three-legged dog digs holes, while Stella, the rescued rascal, explores to the fullest. Oscar takes it slow and has a crush on Luna, the ultimate escape artist!

ARCHIE

Fonferek's Glen
Age 2, Mixed

This lovable dog is a foster failure, forever bonded to his mom, and they are connected like glue. With a happy demeanor and a touch of sass, he enjoys his days lounging around and taking delightful naps.

TAILS FROM . . .

Northeastern, Wisconsin USA

Known for its stunning natural beauty, vibrant craft brewery scene, and rich cheese production.

A DOG'S GUIDE:

1. Splash and fetch at Point Beach State Forest, where the sandy shores of Lake Michigan are perfect for a fun-filled day.
2. Hike at High Cliff State Park, exploring beautiful cliffs and forest trails with amazing views of Lake Winnebago.
3. Play at the Winnebago County Dog Park in Oshkosh
4. Relax with your human at Fox River Brewing Company in Oshkosh
5. Attend the Green Bay Pet Expo, where you can meet fellow pet lovers, see dogs available for adoption, and enjoy exciting demonstrations!

MISFIT MUTTS DOG RESCUE

These photoshoots raised funds for Misfit Mutts Dog Rescue, which rescues abandoned dogs and finds them loving homes, ensuring no dog goes hungry.

Visit misfitmuttsdogrescue.com to learn more

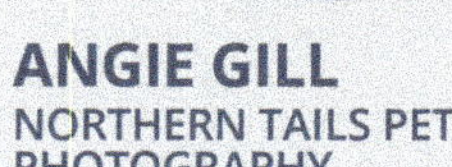

ANGIE GILL

NORTHERN TAILS PET PHOTOGRAPHY

Angie is a passionate and talented photographer born and raised in rural Wisconsin. A lifelong love of dogs and photography laid the foundation for the creation of Northern Tails Pet Photography in 2016.

Specializing in pet portraits, Angie loves forming a bond with each dog she photographs and strives to create portraits that showcase their unique personality and spirit.

Angie is also dedicated to giving back to the animal community. Through volunteer work and fundraising, Northern Tails Pet Photography seeks to make a positive impact on the lives of these amazing animals that have brought so much joy into our lives.

NORTHERNTAILSPETPHOTOGRAPHY.COM

HARPUA

Norbert Rich School Forest
Age 3, French/English Bulldog

Harpua, named after a Phish song about a chubby bulldog, is anything but fat or sweaty! His owners lovingly call him Pua. This lap dog loves being close to his dad, and they both enjoy exploring state parks, especially Peninsula State Park in Door County.

ELVIS

Lake
Age 1, Coonhound/Pitbull

Elvis is an energetic pup who adores playtime! His loving parents often say he has two hearts and no brain, showcasing his sweet nature. While he loves to splash around in water, he prefers to stay shallow and never swims.

DRAKE

Norbert Rich School Forest
Age 10 months, Golden Retriever

Drake is a super energetic dog who adores tennis balls and squeaky toys. His mom can't get enough of the joy he spreads, and he's just a sweet, goofy guy. Plus, he has this hilarious "Toothless smile" that makes everyone laugh!

AURORA

Doty Park
Age 2, Siberian Husky

This sassy and silly husky brings joy to her family by reminding them to appreciate the small things. Confident and outgoing, she adores people and thrives on running, even in freezing cold weather.

RIDOC

Fonferek's Glen
Age 1, Cattledog/Coonhound/German Shepherd

Ridoc is quite the character with his unique markings and long legs. A true velcro dog, he never leaves his mom's side and absolutely loves going to daycare to play with all his doggie friends.

PETE

High Cliff State Park
Age 10, French Bulldog

Pete was adopted by his mom and dad from a rescue in Texas, after a long drive from Wisconsin. This lovable pup is all about giving kisses and nibbling on noses and fingers. He also enjoys catching some Z's while basking in the sunshine.

CHIHIRO

Paine Prairie Woodland
Age 4, Pug

This pup totally thinks she's a kitty, snoozing on the sofa and playing with cat-sized stuffies. A true lap dog, she loves snuggling and curling up between her mom's legs at night. With a bunch of cute nicknames like Chi Chi, Tutu, and Tooties, she's a real sweetheart!

LEIA AND JASPER

Point Beach State Forest
Ages 4 and 3, Pug/Beagle and Pug/Chihuahua

Leia is a regal pug who gracefully avoids puddles and has three different barks. Jasper is a former stray who army crawls when he gets excited. They're both super loved!

SAPHIRA, RAYAH AND SPRITE

Home
Ages 2, 1 and 6, Bull Terrier, Field Spaniel and Bull Terrier

Three fun facts about this gorgeous trio: Saphira can walk backwards on command, Rayah's favourite food is bananas and Sprite was the number 5 Bull Terrier in 2019!

BUCKY

Betsie River Day-Use Park, Thompsonville
Age 5, Golden Retriever/Alaskan Malamute

Bucky is a cheerful dog who loves to swim and has been a wonderful foster brother to 13 dogs over the past two years. Despite being epileptic, his friendly spirit shines through, making him a beloved companion to both humans and furry friends alike!

TAILS FROM . . .

Northwestern, Michigan USA

Known for its stunning natural beauty, over 50 wineries with scenic views of Lake Michigan, and being the "Cherry Capital of the World".

A DOG'S GUIDE:

1. Put on your best outfit for the Northport Dog Parade.
2. Enjoy a splash at Van's Beach, perfect for dogs.
3. Explore the historic Grand Traverse Commons and its shops.
4. Try dock diving at Ultimate Air Dogs during the Cherry Festival.
5. Sip wine while strolling the beautiful grounds of Black Star Farms.

AMANDA LEWIS
AMANDA LEWIS PHOTOGRAPHY

Amanda Lewis is a pet photographer based in Traverse City, Michigan, USA. She has always been an animal person. As a child, when asked what she wanted to be when she grew up, her answer was always "a dog." She now realizes that's not really an option but thinks that being a dog photographer is the next best thing.

After losing her shadow and best bud, Lupin, in 2022, she found purpose in helping other pet parents capture their precious moments with their pets and celebrate their memories in a way they can hold on to forever. She's passionate about showcasing the unique personalities of pets and the magic and joy they bring into our lives.

AMANDALEWISPHOTO.COM

SECOND CHANCE MUSHERS RESCUE

These photoshoots raised funds for Second Chance Mushers Rescue, a sanctuary providing rehabilitation and training for northern breed dogs to make them adoptable. Visit secondchancemushersrescue.com to learn more

PONCHO

Van's Beach, Leland
Age 3, Goldendoodle

Poncho's got a wonky tail that wags to the side, and he's one chatty Goldendoodle! He loves taking all his toys outside, but funny enough, he never actually plays with them out there.

TEDDY

The Botanic Garden at Historic Barns Park, Traverse City
Age 3, Yorkiepoo

Teddy's all about the smiles, especially when his parents come home. He's a road trip enthusiast who believes he should tag along every time they leave. Plus, this clever pup knows a bunch of tricks and will happily kiss his mom on command!

FINNIAN MACDOUGALL

DeYoung Natural Area, Traverse City
Age 3, Miniature Poodle

Finnian is a charming dog who enjoys having his teeth brushed and loves his shower during grooming. His intelligence shines through as he eagerly learns new things, making him a delightful companion!

DOBBY

Antrim Creek Natural Area, Ellsworth
Age 3, Siberian Husky mix

Dobby the house Husky is a total water baby who loves to swim! He's always looking to be as close to his human as possible, and his nickname comes from his resemblance to Dobby the house elf from Harry Potter. Such a cute and cuddly companion!

OLIVE

Bay Front Park, Northport
Age 6, Boxer mix

Olive is currently training for a prosthetic leg, but that doesn't stop her from giving a perfect handshake! She loves nothing more than snuggling up on the couch with a cosy blanket for some quality cuddle time.

ARLO

Antrim Creek Natural Area, Ellsworth
Age 8, Siberian Husky

Arlo, affectionately known as Little Man, arrived at Second Chance Mushers scared and broken but has now become their main lead dog. He hates being left behind, so he tags along with his human on most outings, even if it's just a quick trip to the store.

QUINN

Antrim Creek Natural Area, Ellsworth
Age 2, Siberian Husky

Quinn, nicknamed Queenie, rules her world like the queen she is. Always trying to take charge, she has a strong personality and is definitely a momma's girl at heart.

FREYJA

Antrim Creek Natural Area, Ellsworth
Age 4, Alaskan Malamute

Freyja, the largest dog at Second Chance Mushers Rescue, is a lovable giant who thinks she's small and loves to snuggle up on you. With a big heart and an even bigger appetite for food, she brings joy and warmth to everyone around her!

ZOLA AZUL

Veronica Valley Park, Lake Leelanau
Age 2, Pomsky

Zola, affectionately known as "Little Wolf," has stunning ice blue eyes that captivate everyone. This playful pup can entertain herself for hours on end, making her the life of the party and a beloved companion.

MISS FAME

Paseo Arts District
Age 6 months, Dutch Shepherd/ Pitbull

Once a sickly pup rescued by Free to Live, her sweet face captured hearts. Though initially a "foster dog," she was always meant to be theirs. Now thriving, she enjoys devouring treats, lugging big sticks on walks, and playfully pestering her older sister.

TAILS FROM . . .

Oklahoma City, Oklahoma USA

Known for being the 8th largest metro in the country and featuring historic Route 66, which runs through Oklahome City.

A DOG'S GUIDE:

1. Visit Bar K, recently crowned the #1 Dog friendly bar.
2. Turn your dinner into a pawsome adventure at Picasso Café in the Paseo Arts District! With a special "Doggie Dining" menu, cosy patio seating, and an artsy atmosphere.
3. After a day of exploring Lake Hefner, relax at the lakeside restaurants by the iconic lighthouse.
4. Have fun at Scissortail Park, a 70-acre urban oasis.
5. Hike through Bluff Creek Park, a hidden gem by Lake Hefner with paved and dirt trails through a lush, wooded area.

405 ANIMAL RESCUE AND FREE TO LIVE ANIMAL SANCTUARY

These photoshoots raised funds for 405 Animal Rescue and Free To Live Animal Sanctuary, supporting animal rescue and rehabilitation. Visit 405animalrescue.org and freetoliveok.org

DANI DOMINA

DANI DOMINA PHOTOGRAPHY

As a proud dog mom to three rescue fur babies—Graylee and Oakley, our spirited Pittie mixes, and Moose, our lovable English Cream Retriever—my husband, Chase, and I create the best possible world for them in our Oklahoma home.

With a passion for photography, dogs, and animal rescue, I feel fortunate to merge these interests while serving my Oklahoma community. Capturing the unique spirit of each furkid, I love creating memories that families will cherish forever. I'm also on a mission to make a positive impact and raise awareness for animal rescues in our area; collaborating with local rescues to highlight the beauty and potential of every animal in need of a loving home.

DANIDOMINAPHOTOGRAPHY.COM

KENAI

Scissortail Park
Age 3, Auggie

Kenai is the ultimate adventure buddy, always eager to hit the trails for a hike. He's a high-five expert, ready to share a paw for encouragement or celebration. Plus, his unique charm comes from one ear that never stood up, adding to his lovable character.

JODI

Lake Hefner
Age 5, Australian Cattle Dog

Jodi, a feisty pup rescued at 5 weeks old, has a big personality despite her tiny size. She loves water, tennis balls, and playing keep away, and has a special bond with a 7-year-old boy and her senior Rat Terrier buddy. Smart and beautiful, she's definitely the boss!

MINNI MOO

Wild Horse Park
Age 4, Chihuahua/Labrador

In December 2019, a 9-week-old black puppy with a white star named Minni was adopted in OKC. After a couple of weeks, she became her mom's emotional support dog and best friend, shining bright as the reigning queen of the Adopted Tails household

MYA MAY

The Ponderosa
Age 2, Double Doodle (Labradoodle/ Sheepadoodle)

Mya's first family gave her up after just two weeks, but at 10 weeks old, she found her forever home with Adopted Tails. This happy-go-lucky pup grew into a charming "pretty pony" and loves to lounge on her mom while showering her with kisses.

MARLEE MAPLE

The Ponderosa
Age 2, American Pit Bull Terrier mix

At just 9 months old, Marlee was discovered homeless in Minco, Oklahoma, and adopted in April 2022. Eager to please, she quickly excelled in training. Now a beloved "cow" in the Adopted Tails household, she enjoys chewing nylon bones and patrolling her backyard with a heart of gold!

TITUS

Automobile Alley District
Age 10, Mini American Shepherd/Aussie Cattle Dog

Titus, adopted in 2014, is the ultimate good boy with a big goofy personality. He adores people and loves playing fetch with his squeaky ball. Despite being almost 11, he struts around like a pup and enjoys exploring new places on trips with his mom.

TILLY MAY

Myriad Botanical Gardens
Age 4, American Pitbull Terrier/Cattle Dog

Tilly's a squatty bundle of joy who's obsessed with blueberries! This adorable mix of 19 breeds, mostly larger dogs, is mostly white with a few black spots on her ears. A total people-magnet, she thinks everyone is her best friend and loves kids, thanks to her daycare upbringing.

LOLA AND CHLOE

Oklahoma Barite Mystery by: Haley Spradlin and Matin Alavi, Classen Curve
Ages 8 and 4, Pitbull mixes

Lola, the wiggly butt celebrity of West Hollywood, and Chloe, the professional squirrel stalker, are the ultimate cuddle experts! Always finding the coziest spots to snuggle, these two best buds prove that with a pup cup, there's no such thing as "too cosy" for their happy friendship!

DOLLY JO, ROSEY, SAMPSON, ZERO AND SUGAR

Bluff Creek Park
Ages 10, 13, 10 and 10 months and 2, Chihuahua mix, Staffordshire Cattle Dog mix, German Shepherd mix and Cattle Dog mix

Rosey is the boss of the house, while Dolly Jo charms everyone with her sweet personality. Sampson loves to show off his bones, Sugar jumps like a pro, and little Zero takes it all in with wide-eyed excitement. What a lively crew!

CHARLIE AND COCO

Bodleian Library
Ages 1 and 2, Mini and Standard Australian Labradoodles

Charlie and Coco both come from the same breeder and they share a special bond. Charlie is a cuddly sweetheart who enjoys playing ball, while Coco, quick and clever, excels at football. She's gentle and kind, understanding many words and loving her treats.

TAILS FROM . . .

Oxfordshire, England UK

Known for its rich history and as the home of famous authors, including J.R.R. Tolkien, Lewis Carroll, C.S. Lewis, and Mark Haddon.

A DOG'S GUIDE:

1. Explore 2,000 acres of gardens and parkland at Blenheim Palace.
2. Wander through 160 acres and meet amazing animals at Cotswold Wildlife Park & Gardens.
3. Enjoy delicious burgers and sample local beer at Jeremy Clarkson's Diddly Squat Farm.
4. Foxholes Nature Reserve is perfect for a peaceful woodland walk, especially during bluebell season.
5. If your dog loves water, enjoy a relaxing punt on the river from Cherwell Boathouse.

MIRIAM SMITH
MIRIAM SMITH PHOTOGRAPHY

I was born and raised near the Alps in the Italian countryside. Since I was a child, my life has always been filled with dogs, cats, chickens and rabbits and an incredible love for horses.
I moved to the UK a decade ago, bringing along my two dogs, four cats and two horses. I decided to become a pet photographer when I lost my beloved horses in 2017 and made my job a mission to capture important memories of people's pets.
I am based in the beautiful English countryside between Oxford and Aylesbury, but I travel nationwide and around Italy to follow my pursuit of pet photography. I feel very grateful and blessed to be able to make my passion for pets, my job!

MIRIAMSMITHPHOTOGRAPHY.CO.UK

OXFORDSHIRE ANIMAL SANCTUARY

These photoshoots raised funds for Oxfordshire Animal Sanctuary, which cares for 70-100 mistreated animals daily and rehomes around 500 annually to find forever homes. Visit oxfordshireanimalsanctuary.org.uk

MINNIE AND KIT

St. Mary's Church ground
Ages 4 and 1, Miniature Dachshunds

Minnie is a sassy, loyal, and determined girl who loves cheese and enjoys running and playing ball. On the other hand, Kit is an easygoing, happy pup keen to please, who loves people watching, unstuffing toys, and going on sniffaris. They make quite the fun duo!

SHADOW

St. Mary's Church ground
Age 6, Whippet

Shadow is such a sweet and kind gentleman! He spreads joy as a Pets as Therapy dog, visiting schools and kids in hospitals for cuddles and relaxation. His best buddy is Ariel the cat, who they searched high and low for at rescue centres to find a dog-friendly feline!

POPPY

Market Square
Age 9, Mixed Breed Terrier

This dog loves beach holidays and can often be found chilling at coffee shops. After a successful career as an agility champ, he's now enjoying retirement, soaking up the sun and sipping on pup lattes with his humans. Life is pretty sweet for this furry beach-goer!

MYRTILLE

Rue Crémieux
Age 8, Cocker

This adorable dog is a clingy companion who loves to be by your side! With a hearty appetite for food, he enjoys every tasty treat. Despite being 2/3 blind, Myrtille's joyful spirit shines bright, making him a delightful friend full of love and happiness.

TAILS FROM . . .
Paris, France

Known as the "City of Love" and for its many iconic historic monuments, such as the Eiffel Tower, Notre-Dame Cathedral, the Arc de Triomphe, and the Sacré coeur.

A DOG'S GUIDE:

1. Explore the great outdoors in the Bois de Boulogne or Bois de Vincennes, or if you're feeling adventurous, check out the nearby Rambouillet, Saint-Germain-en-Laye, or Fontainebleau forests!
2. Savor the Parisian café culture at dog-friendly spots like le Café de Flore and le Bouledogue.
3. Treat yourself to delicious goodies from La Casa Del Doggo, the first dog bakery in Paris.
4. Stroll through the picturesque streets of Paris with your owner.
5. Don't miss the Woofest or Planète Chiens in September.

REFUGE SPA DE GENNEVILLIERS

These photoshoots raised funds for Refuge SPA de Gennevilliers, aiding in the rescue and adoption of abandoned animals and supporting ethical campaigns for societal change. Visit la-spa.fr to learn more

GAÉTANE MARCHAND
GAÉTANE LF PHOTOGRAPHIE

I am a 32-year-old French pet photographer living near Paris with my husband, our cat Pesto and our dog Djali. Animals have naturally become my favourite subjects in my journey as a photographer. I love capturing their personality, the joy they bring in our life and the special bond they share with their humans. I believe the role they play in our lives is too often underestimated and I wish to contribute to their recognition as real family members. I shoot natural-light authentic and colorfoul photos, and I am looking for candid emotional moments to immortalize. My pictures come in unique eco-friendly prints, wall arts and albums.

GAETANELF.COM

PRADA

Montmartre district
Age 1, Pomsky

Despite an energetic personality, Prada loves to snuggle - the perfect companion for adventures and lazy days alike!

PIPO

Rue Crémieux
Age 4, Smooth Coat Brussels Griffon

This charming dog may be introverted at first, but once he warms up, his funny personality shines through! He enjoys the company of his two hen friends and loves to play in the water and with scrunchies, bringing joy to everyone around him.

OPPA

Rue Crémieux
Age 1, Pyrenean Shepherd

This lovely dog, adopted from the SPA de Gennevilliers shelter at just 4 months old, is as calm as she is playful. She adores playing one-on-one with her friends, bringing joy and energy to every interaction.

M&MS

Rue Crémieux
Age 8, Shar-Pei

She still looks like a puppy, which often leads people to ask if she is one. After losing her sight two years ago due to surgery, M&Ms has shown incredible resilience and quickly adapted, remaining the sweet and gentle dog everyone knows and loves.

ORKA

Montmartre district
Age 9, Argentine Mastiff/Labrador

This sweet girl was likely a breeding dog before being rescued from the SPA of Gennevilliers in December 2022. She's super affectionate with humans and has the energy and enthusiasm of a typical lively 3-year-old dog.

PIXEL

Sacré-Coeur Basilica at Montmartre
Age 5, Pug

This dog is the epitome of chill - super calm and independent. Despite a laid-back nature, Pixel has become a social media star, charming followers with cool vibes and adorable antics.

OPIUM

Montmartre district
Age 6, Cocker

This dog is a total sweetheart, exuding enthusiasm and a strong-willed personality. While Opium can be a bit stubborn at times, an affectionate nature shines through with both humans and fellow pets.

MIMI AND RUSLAM

Montmartre district
Ages 4 and 10, Chihuahua/Yorkshire Terrier and Chihuahua/Pinscher

Ruslam and Mimi were adopted together from the SPA shelter in Gennevilliers. While they were a bit shy at first, they're super cuddly with their friends. Ruslam is all about balls and squeaky toys, while Mimi is playful and enjoys long walks.

LOLA

Montmartre Hill
Age 6 months, Cavalier King Charles Spaniel

Lola is super playful and really smart, always finding ways to entertain herself and others. She's also incredibly affectionate and loves to cuddle up.

SITKA

Station Square
Age 9, Husky/Great Pyrenees

Sitka, a certified therapy dog through the AKC's TDI program, is soulful, sweet, goofy, and incredibly loving! As he ages, it's vital to create more cool and unique experiences for this delightful pup to cherish together.

TAILS FROM . . .
Pittsburgh, Pennsylvania USA

Known as the Steel City, Pittsburgh has the most bridges in the world (446 bridges!) and is home to several major sports teams like the Steelers, Penguins, and Pirates.

A DOG'S GUIDE:

1. Enjoy delicious ice cream and fresh-baked treats at Salty Paws Pittsburgh.
2. Explore the quirky art at Randyland in North Side.
3. Get festive with pet photos at the annual Pet Photos with Santa event at Petagogy, a local pet supply store.
4. Experience the excitement of PNC Park's Pup Nights, where you can watch the game with special seating and treats just for pups.
5. Unwind at Grist House Craft Brewery in Millvale, where you can relax with a beer and tasty food from an on-site food truck in the dog-friendly outdoor area.

JESSICA WASIK

BARK & GOLD PHOTOGRAPHY

Jessica is an award-winning professional pet photographer who celebrates the joy and love between Pittsburgh pets and their people.

As Pittsburgh's first pet photographer to hold a certification in pet loss grief, she offers a comforting and knowledgeable presence during life's most sensitive moments with an expertise that allows her to connect with her clients and their loyal companions on a deeper level.

Jessica is also a Certified Printmaker specializing in creating luxury artwork that her clients cherish for many years and focusing on natural, candid, and expressive portraits, genuine emotion, and the documenting of joy and love through small moments in time.

BARKANDGOLDPHOTOGRAPHY.COM

THE IZZIE FUND

These photoshoots raised funds for The Izzie Fund, which supports families by providing grants for advanced veterinary care to keep them with their dogs.

Visit theizziefund.org to learn more

TEDDY

Mellon Park
Age 3, French Bulldog

Teddy is a total beach boy who loves digging in the sand, doing zoomies, and even trying to jump into waves! He plays hard and fights naps like a champ, but when bedtime hits, he's out cold. Plus, he adores cats almost as much as the beach!

AUDREY

Strip District Terminal
Age 15, Pit mix

Audrey's a spunky tripod who never lets her missing leg slow her down - she once jumped over her big dog brother! She adores her mom, sunbathing, and sneaking bones from the pet store. And when it comes to treats, nothing beats her love for chicken!

NORMAN

Schenley Plaza
Age 2, Clumber Spaniel

Norman's the kind of dog who instantly loves everyone he meets. He's also a total champ at sleeping and snoring - seriously, he'd win gold if it were an Olympic sport! But watch out, he gets a bit offended if you walk by without giving him some attention.

OLLIE

Mellon Institute Columns
Age 12, Dalmatian

Ollie, a loyal and emotionally needy dog, was rescued by his family at five years old. They adore him just the way he is! Since welcoming twin girls last December, Ollie has been a fantastic big brother, handling all their screams and cries like a champ!

LUNA

North Shore
Age 4, Doberman/Great Dane

Luna is one of nine planet-themed puppies. She's a total diva who loves dressing up for photos and has her own calendar showcasing her outfits, including Julius Caesar for the Ides of March! At night, she snuggles into bed like a human child with her head on a pillow and a stuffie in her arms.

ROUX

Schenley Plaza
Age 2, French Bulldog

Roux loves to settle in with her family on the couch to chew on her vast collection of bones. This adventurous pup excels at hiking and has conquered peaks in Acadia National Park and the Adirondacks. She has no patience for bandanas, bows or tiny birthday hats!

NORMA SUE

Mellon Park
Age 3, Standard Poodle

Norma Sue was almost a show dog, but her puppy underbite brought her home instead. She loves long walks at North Park, happily drinking from human fountains. When she's really excited, she stretches and lets out a stunning howl, which is a rare treat for her family!

DUNCAN

Phipps Conservatory and Botanical Gardens
Age 4, Mini Goldendoodle

Duncan is always smiling and loves being part of the action, joining his humans for their engagement session at the Carnegie Library and their wedding, where "Duncan's donuts" were a hit! He knows how to demand treats, often throwing his ball or licking his lips for them.

COCO

Phipps Conservatory and Botanical Gardens
Age 2, Mini Bernedoodle

Coco has been inseparable from her snuggle puppy since day one, showing off her adorable nurturing side. With Tigger-like bounces and a love for belly rubs, she playfully swats at anyone who dares to stop, as if to say, "Keep those belly rubs coming!"

ARIEN

Maine-New Hampshire Border
Age 7, Belgian Malinois

Arien might seem intimidating, but he's got a goofy side that only his family sees. Not only does he protect them, he is also the guardian of a flock of 16 free-ranging chickens. In his first dock-diving competition, Arien soared an impressive 26 feet and won the whole competition!

TAILS FROM . . .

Portland, Maine USA

Known for its famous Maine Lobster and The Old Port, highlight of Portland, Maine's food scene.

A DOG'S GUIDE:

1. Explore The Old Port, with dog-friendly restaurants and local businesses.
2. Stroll to the iconic Portland Headlight lighthouse, with scenic views, open fields for fetch, and beaches perfect for a refreshing swim.
3. Hike Bradbury Mountain and enjoy the beautiful Maine outdoors with your furry friend.
4. Don't miss Willard Beach, a local favourite for pups!
5. Experience Portland's micro-brewery scene with many dog-friendly spots featuring outdoor seating.

NO BOWL EMPTY

These photoshoots raised funds for No Bowl Empty, a Maine pet food pantry supporting families in need with essential supplies for their pets.
Visit facebook.com/nbe2pfp to learn more

GINA SOULE
GINA SOULE PHOTO

Gina is Maine's only internationally award winning and published dog and pet photographer who exclusively photographs and specializes in pets.

With her years of work in the veterinary world, her experience with animals from all walks of life ensures not only that her client's pets enjoy their time in front of the camera, but that their portraits are truly pieces of art. This attention to detail has also lead to Gina's work gaining international recognition with over 80+ international awards and publications in her short 4 years since first picking up a camera. These include Maine Photographer of the Year, Winner International Pet Photographer of the Year, and two-time GIA award nominee.

GINASOULEPHOTO.COM

CINCH

Northfield Farm
Age 2, Australian Cattle Dog/Blue Heeler

Cinch is the ultimate high-drive dog. Bred to herd, he thrives in various activities like dock diving, tunneling, and hiking. His favourite pastime is daily training for PSA (protection sports) competitions.

LEIA

Cumberland Foreside
Age 5, Border Collie

Leia is a playful pup who loves to run but absolutely hates swimming - she'll only dive in for her cherished tennis ball.

When she joined her family, they took a vote on her name. Their youngest son was adamant she should be named Hobbs, after the comic strip. 3/4 members voted for 'Leia', so they gave her the middle name Hobbs as a compromise. It does get used occasionally!

IZZY

Fuller Farms
Age 7, Mixed

When Izzy was 6 months old, she made the trek from Wynne, Arkansas, to Maine to start her new life; a life full of adventures, treats, and snuggles. She is all about the fresh air and outdoors. She loves hiking, especially if there are rocks and boulders to climb. She loves to see the camper get hooked up, because it means an adventure is coming her way.

ATLAS
Wolfe's Neck State Park
Age 2, Australian Cattle Dog
Atlas is a wild child and the ultimate soul dog! Spicy and eager to learn, he thrives on hiking adventures where his serious demeanor transforms into pure joy. After 20 years of waiting, the moment he held the little puppy with mismatched eyes, he knew Atlas was perfect!

MAKO
Maine-New Hampshire Border
Age 6, Husky/Labrador
Mako is the family's soul dog, rescued from under a porch in Mississippi. This 50% Husky howler has a gentle nature and brings endless love. He's all about adventures, whether swimming, walking, or digging holes in the sand!

POTATO
Hinckley Park
Age 2, Pug
Potato is a peace-loving pug who barks at the TV during battle scenes, especially hating lightsaber fights - definitely a monk in a past life! He waited until 4 months old to come home because he was tiny at birth. Check out his joyful antics on Instagram at Potato_the_Pug1!

BRIGHAM

Mackworth Island State Park
Age 5, Catahoula mix

Brigham loves his peanut butter pup cup from Fielder's Choice in Brunswick, Maine, which makes his eyes light up with joy! Rescued from Baton Rouge, Louisiana, along with his siblings, he's named after his mom's first clinical rotation at Brigham and Women's Hospital.

MÝVATNS ÆSIR

Chandler Brook Preserve
Age 2, Icelandic Sheepdog

Æsir's human claims that his is her "best souvenir"! They met during a trip to Stokkseyrarsel in Selfoss. Æsir (translates to the gods of Asgard) has a goofier personality than his noble name suggests. He is a happy barrel of fluff who enjoys rolling in the grass & chasing squirrels.

SOPHIE

Fort Williams State Park
Age 4, Golden Retriever

Sophie is the ultimate all-American dog, full of personality and affection. She finds comfort in freshly worn shoes, which she lovingly holds. Her favourite toy? Nerf darts! She loves chasing them around and returns them like a pro, holding them gently like a fine cigar.

NEVILLE

Cathedral Park
Age 7, Chihuahua/Pitt
Super Mutt

This dog is probably the softest pup ever! He absolutely loves to run around in the grass or on the beach, and when the sun's out, he can't help but show off his goofy smile.

TAILS FROM . . .

Portland, Oregon USA

Known for its many parks and hiking trails, a vibrant food and drink scene proximity to both the beach and the mountains.

A DOG'S GUIDE:

1. Explore the trails of Forest Park, where you can hike over 80 miles in nature's playground.
2. Join the Doggie Dash with thousands of other pups to support the Oregon Humane Society.
3. Sniff out dog-friendly wineries, breweries, and distilleries.
4. Stroll along the river at Tom McCall Waterfront Park and check out the Saturday Market for yummy homemade dog treats or toys.
5. Enjoy a tasty lunch with your humans at dog-friendly restaurants, some with special doggie menus or even the first-ever doggie food truck!

STREET SAVVY DOG RESCUE

These photoshoots raised funds for Street Savvy Dog Rescue, which rehabilitates abandoned dogs from high-kill shelters and finds them loving homes.

Visit streetsavvydogrescue.org to learn more

KIM HOSHAL
KIM HOSHAL PHOTOGRAPHY

Professional dancer turned professional photographer, Kim Hoshal started off her photography career as a landscape photographer for Arizona Highways and art galleries in Sedona, AZ. While photographing the landscape, she always had her corgi, Max by her side so of course, he made it into some of the images.

After moving to Portland, OR, Kim decided to combine her love for dogs with her love of landscape photography to create Km Hoshal Photography. Now Kim captures images that celebrate your dog and the places they love to roam turning them into works of art that will keep your dog close even when they have moved on.

KIMHOSHALPHOTOGRAPHY.COM

BELLA

Tom McCall Waterfront Park
Age 2, Chow-pomsky

This dog is often described as regal and majestic, and her well-mannered, sweet nature makes her a real charmer. She's the kind of pup who gets showered with compliments from strangers wherever she goes!

SAMMY

Hoyt Arboretum
Age 1, Goldendoodle

This cheerful dog adores saying hi to everyone she meets! She has a special love for water, especially when it sprays her, and enjoys being outdoors no matter the weather - rain, snow, or sunshine, she's always ready for an adventure!

BENEDICT

Slabtown, Downtown Portland
Age 3, Pembroke Welsh Corgi

Benny's a real character! He crashes Daddy's work meetings, trying to chime in despite Microsoft Teams' best efforts. He's also got a knack for turning off phones with his paw. He just might be part cat, as he spends a lot of time perched on the back of the couch, watching the neighbours.

HARLEY

Jenkins Estate
Age 8, Siberian Husky

Harley is a cabbage-loving dog who sports the THICKEST coat around! She's the sweetest thing ever and loves being a couch potato, lounging around 90% of the time.

SIMBA

Pittock Mansion
Age 2, Goldendoodle

Simba is a loving and affectionate dog who brought light during tough times. An adventurous explorer, he enjoys discovering local parks and is always eager to try new treats.

MAGGIE AND OWEN

Rood Bridge Park
Age 7, American Bulldog/Tree Walker Coonhound

These two littermates are the ultimate snuggle buddies, spending all day cuddling together. When they're not napping, you can find them chasing squirrels around the yard, turning their playtime into a fun-filled adventure!

CASSIE AND ROCKY

Forest Park
Age 9 and 5, Terrier mix

Rocky, adopted from a PuppYoga studio, has mastered downward dog but loves licking his mom's face during her stretches. His smart sister Cassie enjoys learning tricks and solving treat puzzles. Together, they have long, hilarious dog conversations about their toys.

LUCA

Home
Age 1, Smoking

This playful cat was adopted from an Asturian shelter and has a zest for life! He loves munching on flowers, climbing to new heights, and rolling over for belly scratches.

TAILS FROM . . .

Principado De Asturias, Spain

Known for its wild beaches, rugged mountains, the classic "Fabada" stew and popular Asturian "Sidra" drink.

A DOG'S GUIDE:

1. Swim at Playón de Bayas, the largest sandy beach in Asturias.
2. Explore various hiking trails, with spectacular landscapes to sniff and enjoy.
3. Visit the city of Gijon, a welcoming destination for dogs.
4. Canoe down the calm, crystal-clear waters of the Sella River.
5. Join the historic pilgrimage routes of the Camino de Santiago, exploring the medieval paths alongside your human.

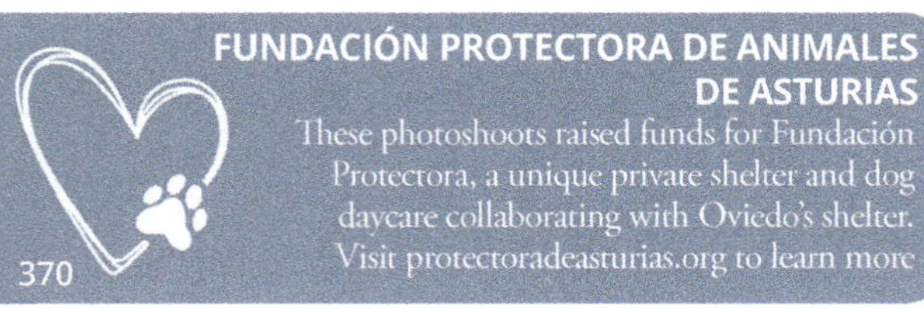

FUNDACIÓN PROTECTORA DE ANIMALES DE ASTURIAS

These photoshoots raised funds for Fundación Protectora, a unique private shelter and dog daycare collaborating with Oviedo's shelter. Visit protectoradeasturias.org to learn more

ALMA GONZÁLEZ

VERDE BONITO BLANCO POLAR

My name is Alma. I live in Asturias, a very beautiful region in the north of Spain. I have always liked animals. My first love was a Siamese cat who unfortunately left us very soon. Shortly after I saw the movie "Gorillas in the Mist" for the first time, and I began to be interested in that magic of photography.

Although it took many years until I dedicate myself to it professionally. I have now happily united these two passions. My photographs are characterized by portraying both the animal only showing its personality; as their relationship with the tutor, capturing the link that unites them. Fusing the basis of artistic photography of animals and lifestyle in his own style.

VERDEBONITOBLANCOPOLAR.COM

DUQUESA

Centro Niemeyer
Age 8, Border Collie/Boxer

This dog shares her home with four cats and is super intelligent and loving. She can be a bit dramatic when she's after some attention, making sure everyone knows she's the star of the show!

ESVA

Parque de Invierno
Age 9, Hound

She was adopted at 2 months old from the "Nueva Vida" shelter in Madrid and is a total 10! This good girl knows 9 countries and is truly the soul of the family. Thanks to her charm, everyone around wants a Hound dog!

IS

Parque de Invierno
Age 10, Australian Shepherd/Border Collie

This dog has infinite patience and has served as a therapy dog for over 25 foster pups. She's a big fan of pizza and melon, making her not just a helper but also a foodie at heart!

RAYO DEL FOURGERON

Guadamía
Age 3, Golden Retriever

This dog is a great life partner, always ready to share affection with everyone. She's so used to the camera that she strikes a pose with ease.

AUDREY

Parque de Invierno
Age 6, English Setter

She was adopted as a puppy from the "Fundación Protectora de Animales de Asturias" and is a very active dog. Growing up with cats and an older adopted dog, she has a friendly and playful spirit that brings joy to her home.

BROWN

Barayo
Age 4, Border Collie

This dog is a bundle of endless energy, always happy to tag along on any adventure. Whether it's running or hiking in the mountains, he's in his element. He has a kind, noble look that melts hearts everywhere he goes.

YOSI

Barayo
Age 5, Parson Russell Terrier

This dog is a total people-lover who gets super excited to see familiar faces. He's a bit stubborn - classic terrier style - but his heart is huge, overflowing with affection for everyone he meets.

FELIPE AND JULIA

Home
Age 4, Mastiff

Two adorable siblings from an unwanted litter in a village in Asturias found their forever home! Thanks to "La Fundación Protectora de Animales de Asturias," these big guys were cared for, and Paola happily adopted them, giving them a loving family they deserve.

RASTA AND NYMPHADORA TONKS

La Laboral
Ages 14 and 3, Jack Russell and Poodle.

Nymphadora Tonks is a playful, tireless poodle full of love, like a giant stuffed animal. Rasta is a tireless grandmother who only thinks about eating. Together, they make quite the quirky duo!

VOLK

Montmorency Falls
Age 6, German Shepherd

This playful pup has an ice cream obsession. He would never sneak food from the table, but would happily steal an icecream cone right from your hand! He loves dock diving, though he often forgets to wait for the toy before making a splash.

TAILS FROM . . .

Quebec, Quebec Canada

Known for Old Quebec (a UNESCO World Heritage Site), the landmark Château Frontenac hotel, and the annual Winter Carnival.

A DOG'S GUIDE:

1. Montmorency Falls Park is a must-see with your dog! Enjoy the stunning 83-meter waterfall and don't miss the exciting suspension bridge.
2. Just 5 minutes from downtown, Baie de Beauport is perfect for a relaxing beach day.
3. Stroll through the historic district of Old Quebec and soak in the city's charm.
4. Île d'Orléans is a lovely day trip destination, with vineyards, orchards, and quaint villages to explore.
5. Discover Parc Linéaire de la Rivière-Saint-Charles, a large urban park along the scenic river.

CHIOTS NORDIQUES

These photoshoots raised funds for Chiots Nordiques, which promotes sustainable solutions through sterilization clinics and supports animal care with a dedicated volunteer team. Visit chiotsnordiques.com to learn more

ANNE-LAURIE LÉGER

BLOOMING DAHLIA PHOTOGRAPHY

My name is Anne-Laurie and I'm a 25yo pet photographer from Quebec, Canada. Known for my artistic style, I really stepped in a new world when I started taking photo 3 years ago. I mainly photograph dogs. Dog portraits, dogs with flowers, dogs in action, some dogs in landscapes... I really find happiness in the variety of the job, in meeting so many different dogs and their humans, discovering new places, developing new skills and learning more and more every day.

My ambitions led me to be a multi-award winning photographer in my second year as a photographer. I'm ready to embrace the Tails of the World project and help some more dogs get the help and the love they deserve.

BLOOMINGDAHLIAPHOTOGRAPHY.COM

ÉMILE

Rivière Saint-Charles
Age 1, Dalmatian

Émile is a bright and affectionate boy who loves running and jumping in the forest. As a puppy, he practiced leaping off the sofa. He's polite, makes friends easily, and can't resist sandals, leapfrog games, or sharing a group kiss!

ANKE

Cap-Rouge River Trail
Age 5, German Shepherd

Anke is an eternal puppy with the biggest heart - so much so that by miracle she managed to recover from dilated cardiomyopathy.

She adores her brother Volk and follows him everywhere. She also believes every animal is her friend, joyfully calling for games with rats and sheep in dog sports.

TOAST

Chutes-Monte-à-Peine
Age 1, Gordon Setter

Toast is a future service dog who's super expressive and a bit dramatic! With a heart full of curiosity and kindness, Toast is sure to bring joy and support to those around.

SKYE

The Jacques-Cartier Beach
Age 1, Welsh Springer Spaniel

Skye is a water-loving pup who dives into lakes, streams, and muddy puddles without a second thought. Her full name is Long Lane Eight Days a Week. She's a master sock thief, sneaking under the table to snag the smelliest socks from her family's little ones.

WILLOW

Delaney Falls
Age 1, Border Collie

Willow is an adorable dog who was born in a stable. He's a hyperactive workaholic who loves herding... with the cats! He's also a multitasking pro, capable of holding two toys in his mouth whilst sliding his bone with his paw. Every week, Willow practices agility with his human and they are hoping to bring home some ribbons.

JINGLE BELLS

Old Quebec City
Age 2, Pembroke Welsh Corgi

She's a once-in-a-lifetime dog, a total drama queen like any good corgi, and her main goal is to make people happy. With her quirky personality, Jingle Bells definitely knows how to steal the spotlight and bring joy to everyone around her.

NOËLLE

The Etchemin River
Age 3, Golden Retriever

Noëlle, named for the season she joined the family, is all about comfort and unconditional love. She thrives in nature, happily getting muddy and fetching balls at the baseball field. In winter, she climbs snowbanks, and in summer, she loves to roll in the grass.

KALEE, NOX, EMMA AND DAISY

Chaudiere Falls
Ages 3, 1, 2 and 4, Border Collies

Daisy, the free-spirited rescue, is her human's heart dog. Kalee, the classic Border Collie, is sensitive, super smart, and reliable. Emma, the little warrior, is very loyal and a great teacher. Nox, the easy-peasy baby boy, is just happy to be happy!

TEEMO

St. Lawrence River
Age 1, Cavalier King Charles Spaniel

Teemo brings joy with playful antics like trying to catch water drops and fetching his ball. His flower-sniffing moments inspire mindfulness, while his adventurous spirit encourages outdoor (sometimes muddy) fun.

TULLAMORE DEW

Historic Oak View County Park
Age 4, Chow mix

Tully fit in with his foster family so seamlessly that they knew he needed to become a permanent member! With his adorable panda bear appearance and constant smile, he brings joy to everyone around him.

TAILS FROM . . .

Raleigh, N Carolina USA

Known as the "City of Oaks" due to the many oak trees that line the streets and named after Sir Walter Raleigh.

A DOG'S GUIDE:

1. Spring Fling at Unleashed Cat and Dog Store is the ultimate dog event of the year, featuring vendors, music, food, raffles, and even a doggie easter egg hunt!
2. West Street Dog is the perfect hangout spot in downtown Raleigh, offering an indoor dog park, bar, trivia nights, and special playtime for small pups.
3. The Umstead Hotel and Spa is a dog-friendly place to stay, complete with cute dog amenities that pamper your furry friend.
4. At Hause of Dogs, you can enjoy tasty doggy ice cream
5. Explore the many parks and breweries around Raleigh.

SECOND CHANCE PET ADOPTIONS.
These photoshoots raised funds for Second Chance Pet Adoptions, a non-profit dedicated to rescuing and promoting responsible ownership for homeless cats and dogs.
Visit secondchancenc.org to learn more

ABBY MORENO

PAWS FUR JOY PHOTOGRAPHY

I'm Abby Mook Moreno, owner of Paws Fur Joy Photography. It fills my soul to use photography as a way to celebrate everything you love about your pets. I started my pet photography business in 2019 when I was recovering from heart surgery. I provide a premier service by incorporating mindfulness and animal reiki into my sessions. I am also a commercial pet photographer.

I love helping busy pet business owners save time and create impactful images that showcase their brand. I spend my spare time with my husband, senior pup Sophie, doing yoga, meditating, drinking coffee, and enjoying nature.

PAWSFURJOY.COM

ACE

Raleigh Little Theater Rose Garden
Age 14, Plott Hound/Beagle

This lively hound is bursting with personality and sweetness! He adores playing with his toys, especially his beloved flower ones, and he still acts like a puppy most days.

TEDDY BEAR

Cary Park Greenway
Age 13, Maltipoo

Teddy Bear loves long walks, solving treat puzzles, and digging. When he's not busy, he's all about snuggling up on the couch to watch TV. He's got his Canine Good Citizen-Advanced certificate and some AKC Trick Dog certifications!

eddy

LUDWIG

Historic Oak View County Park
Age 14, Dachshund

Despite his dimming sight and creaky joints, Ludwig remains king of the world and guardian of order. He's been a constant companion and adoring despot since being adopted from HEART rescue at the age of two.

HALLEY

Historic Oak View County Park
Age 6, Maltipoo

Halley was adopted in 2018 from Second Chance Pet Adoptions and has completed her Canine Good Citizen certification. Now, she's the rock star of the neighborhood dogs, cruising around in the car and enjoying her pupaccinos!

DAENY

Lake Johnston Park
Age 6, Newfoundland

This sweet dog adores attending classes to learn new tricks and commands. She has mastered basic commands and enjoys showing off her impressive repertoire of tricks. With her friendly nature, she loves almost everyone she meets!

HARLEY

Lake Tahoe
Age 6, Labrador Retriever

Harley is a water-loving pup who jumps into any body of water. Every morning, he shows off his sock collection, often bringing up to four from the hamper. He's always ready to greet people with a shoe or toy in his mouth!

TAILS FROM . . .

Reno, Nevada USA

Known for its proximity to Lake Tahoe and the Sierra Nevada mountains and special events like the Balloon Races & Rib Cookoff.

A DOG'S GUIDE:

1. Visit the dog parks to meet new furry friends.
2. Hike along the River at Mayberry Park, Callahan Park, Thomas Creek, or Ballardini Ranch.
3. Dine with your humans at the Wild River Grille with views of the Truckee River.
4. Chill on the patio at The Brewer's Cabinet while your humans sip beverages.
5. Splash around in the water at Washoe Lake and Lake Tahoe's beaches nearby.

LYNICE ANDERSON
WETNOSEFURRTOGRAPHY

After spending 3 decades in Healthcare, I am pursuing my passion for dogs, the outdoors and my new love, photography. I enjoy the challenging technical aspects of making beautiful photos as well as the joy in meeting new pups.

When I am not taking pictures of furry subjects, you can find me on the trails (running, riding and hiking), in the garden or camping with the love of my life and our beautiful chocolate labs Ginger & Sage.

WETNOSEFURRTOGRAPHY.COM

SHAKESPEARE ANIMAL FUND

These photoshoots raised funds for Shakespeare Animal Fund, assisting pet owners with emergency veterinary bills, supporting vulnerable communities in northern Nevada and Florida. Visit shakespeareanimalfund.org to learn more

QUEST

Downtown Reno
Age 2, Border Collie

Quest is an energetic dog who thrives in AKC dog sports like Rally-O, Obedience, and Agility. With a keen fascination for sounds, he loves the cuckoo bird and the Gorillaz' laughter. He has over 80 tricks up his sleeve, including fetching water bottles for his humans and rolling over.

GINGER

Boca Reservoir
Age 7, Chocolate Labrador Retriever

Ginger loves lounging in her chair and watching the world go by. She's super gentle with her toys, still cherishing soft ball from her puppyhood (which she now cleverly hides from her little sister Sage). Ginger will bring a shoe to anyone she meets and "talks" to them as she receives her pets.

SAMMIE
Longford Park
Age 15, Chiweenie

Sammie is a quirky pup who gets a kick out of "killing" squeakers and is an avid bi-directional tail chaser. When there's a kazoo around, you can bet Sammie will join in and sing along!

SAGE

Home
Age 4 months, Labrador Retriever

Sage is a playful pup who jumps off everything like Superman! She's a fan of fresh garden goodies too, munching on apples, raspberries, and more. Sage has loved putting herself to bed in her sleeping kennel since she was 8 weeks old.

WREN

Wheatland Park
Age 2, Akita/Shepherd mix

Wren was rescued by Namaste Akita Rescue Alliance and found her forever home with her foster mom and older buddy Roger. They're inseparable best friends who love wrestling, playing, and cuddling. She's super smart, fast, and an amazing hunter who adores treats!

ROGER

Wheatland Park
Age 7, Akita/Husky

Roger was born in a dump and rescued by Namaste Akita Rescue Alliance. He and his litter mates were all named after the vet team who cared for them. These days, Roger enjoys long walks, swimming, and back rubs. He may not always show it, but he loves Wren.

ALFIE
Hanley Park
Age 2, Labrador Retriever

Alfie is all about playtime! This clever pup aces every command, keeping everyone entertained. He could fetch tennis balls for hours!

TAILS FROM . . .

Saint Louis, Missouri USA

Known as the "Gateway to the West", with its iconic Arch, and home to Ted Drewes Frozen Custard on historic Route 66.

A DOG'S GUIDE:

1. Visit Bar K for pup playtime while adults enjoy food and cold beers.
2. Stroll on Grant's Trail, a 12-mile paved path starting downtown.
3. Catch a CityPark soccer game from the Purina Club box seats with your dog.
4. Explore the Arch National Park and enroll your pup in the BARK Ranger program.
5. Stop by Zoomie's Pet Cafe in the Macklind District for coffee and a tasty Pupsicle.

KRISTI FOSTER
KRISTI FOSTER PHOTOGRAPHY INC

Photographing pets is so much fun for me! I love capturing their personality: some are sassy, some are shy, and some are just so sweet. Every personality brings so much love into our lives! My wish is for everyone to have a photograph that captures that very essence of their furry companion. I have a special spot for both seniors and rescue. I have a foundation that allows families with aging/ill pets complimentary sessions. I also volunteer my time photographing adoptables for various rescues. When I'm not working, you can find me traveling the world with my life partner, hangin with friends, or cuddling up with our feisty Chihuahua Jackson and our oh so sweet & funny Havanese, Ollie Jane.

KRISTIFOSTERPHOTOGRAPHY.COM

HOOTIE'S RESCUE HAVEN

These photoshoots raised funds for Hootie's Rescue Haven, a sanctuary in St. Clair County, Mo., caring for animals needing ongoing medical treatment and finding homes. Visit hootiesrescue.org to learn more

PUCK AND HARRY

St. Louis Art Museum
Ages 5 and 1, Boxer Mix and Pembrooke Welsh Corgie

Puck, a rescue from a hoarder situation, is a total fetch machine and a certified therapy dog. His buddy Harry is also in the works to get certified. Harry is also a climbing enthusiast and an incredible jumper, always ready for an adventure!

EMMIE

Home
Age 7, Morkie

Emmie is a very sweet dog who enjoys cosy movie nights watching the original Star Wars and snacking on cheese and chicken. She's not the biggest fan of her little brother, Archie!

LUNA BLUE AND SUNNY

St. John Manchester UCC Church
Ages 1 and 2, Pembrooke Welsh Corgie

Luna and Sunny are a playful duo who tag along with their preacher mom to the church office. Luna is tough and super smart, while Sunny just loves being cuddled. Together, they bring lots of fun energy that keeps everyone laughing!

ANGEL

The Muny of St. Louis
Age 11, Malshi

Angel truly lives up to her name! This super chill and well-behaved doll loves snuggling on pillows and blankets. She enjoys going outside, but her favourite part is coming back in for a yummy treat!

MOWGLI, CUDDLES AND LOU

August Busch Memorial Conservation
Ages 12, 6 months and 6, Lab/Sharpie, Yorkie and Goldendoodle

Mowgli is a super loving chill dog who enjoys meeting new people and being petted. Cuddles is a lively puppy bursting with energy, while Lou, a retired therapy dog, is a fantastic protector who loves sticking close to his family.

JACKSON AND OLLIE JANE

Home
Ages 12 and 11, Long Haired Chihuahua and Havanese

Ollie is a rescued former breeding dog, who now dances with joy when her family comes home. Jackson, the sassy and stubborn guard dog, takes his job seriously. They share a secret bond of love that they prefer to keep under wraps.

SHUSTRIY

Concordia Seminary Grounds
Age 13, Jack Russell Terrier

Shu is a cancer survivor and total champ. He's a well-traveled pup, having lived in various countries around the world.

TAILS FROM . . .

Santo Domingo, Dominican Republic

Known for being the first city of the Americas, and as a land of happiness and excellent food.

A DOG'S GUIDE:

1. Splash around at the beautiful beaches of Punta Cana and Samana.
2. Enjoy a delicious coffee at El Cafesito in Mirador Sur Park with your furry friend.
3. Explore nature by hiking in Jarabacoa or Constanza.
4. Take refreshing morning walks through the city.
5. Discover the Colonial Zone and savor an outdoor dinner.

FUNDACION EL EDEN

These photoshoots raised funds for Fundacion El Eden, a no-fund charity in San Cristobal, Dominican Republic, housing 30-40 dogs and showcasing their care efforts.

LEYLANI HERNANDEZ
BARKING MOMENTS PHOTOGRAPHY

I'm a pet photographer based in Santo Domingo, Dominican Republic. My work is characterized by being fun, creative, colourful; making the pet the main attraction.

I started my professional pet photography in 2016 because of my pet, Aspen. I adopted him at just 3 weeks old and my goal was to document his journey with me.

Seven years later, I'm working full time on providing the best memories of my clients and their pets. This is the most rewarding feeling I could ever experience and my reason to keep my business going.

BARKINGMOMENTSPHOTOGRAPHY.MYPIXIESET.COM

DIEGO
Mirador Sur Park
Age 7, Golden Retriever
This dog is a multilingual superstar, understanding Chinese, Spanish, and English. He's a total snuggle bug and can't get enough of cosy cuddles. When he's not snuggling, you'll find him happily playing with balls, making every moment a fun adventure!

LILA
Punta Cana
Age 3, Cocker Spaniel
Lila loves beach days, chasing after balls, and playing fetch like a champ. When it's time to chill, she is quick to snuggle up for cuddles. It's all about fun in the sun and sweet moments at home!

LOGAN
Mirador Sur Park
Age 8 months, Labrador Retriever
This dog is all about having fun! He loves playing with balls, soaking up snuggles and kisses, and going for daily walks in the park. Life is a blast when Logan's around!

MILAN

Plaza de la Bandera
Age 2, Australian Shepherd

This dog is all about fun - whether it's playing or going on long walks. He's the ultimate hugger and can't resist the delicious homemade treats his mom makes. Life is good for this furry friend!

PHOEBE

Colonial Zone
Age 11, Yorkie/Maltese

This sassy pup loves to do as she pleases, especially when it comes to enjoying cookies and treats. She adores her mom and cherishes their snuggle time together, making every moment filled with love and fun!

KIRA

Cap Cana
Age 3, German Shepherd

Kira enjoys a refreshing nap on the cold floor. She's a pro at fetching her ball and can't resist her favourite peanut butter treats.

BANDIDO

Mirador Sur Park
Age 2, Mixed

This adorable dog loves to cuddle, making every moment spent together extra special. Bandido enjoys munching on tasty treats and eagerly joins in on family trips.

SHINY

Colonial Zone
Age 11, Golden Retriever

Shiny was the star pet of the Colonial Zone. Loved by everyone, she thoroughly enjoyed her daily walks around the Zone. Truly, she was the happiest dog ever known!

JAKE

St. Barbe Winter Trails
Age 8, Australian Cattle Dog

Jake is a total hero! He acts as a seeing eye dog for his older 'fur-sister' Sydney and has even saved one of her clones from drowning in a frozen river. He's traveled nearly a million miles across North America, helping with mining exploration as a camp dog and sniffing out sulfide minerals.

TAILS FROM . . .

Saskatoon, Sask. Canada

Known for its welcoming prairie spirit and many annual festivals, including the Fringe Festival, Folkfest, the Jazz Festival WinterShines.

A DOG'S GUIDE:

1. Dive into fun at Mayfair Pool's Dog Days of Summer, where pups can enjoy a splash-tastic pool party.
2. Join the Crossmount Cider Company's Dog Paw-ty!
3. Explore the many local dog parks, like Hyde Dog Park and Pierre Radisson Park. For a wild adventure, check out Chief Whitecap Park or Sutherland Beach to splash in the river.
4. Enjoy the summer sun at pet-friendly patios like Cohen's Beer Republic, Leopold's Tavern, or Prairie Sun Brewery.
5. Take a leisurely stroll along the Meewasin Trail, which stretches 80km around the river.

ERIN MCFARLAND
HIGH FOUR PET PHOTOGRAPHY

My name is Erin McFarland and I am the face behind High Four Pet Photography. I live in Saskatoon, Saskatchewan with my husband of 20 years, and our French Bulldog Keiki. I'm short, soft-spoken, but friendly and always positive!

I have won a few awards for my work over the past ten years, however my main focus is not winning prizes, but to preserve the unique personalities of family pets through my eyes. I have so much patience, and a rare ability to bond with all new animals I meet, which makes it easy to truly love what I do.

HIGHFOURPETS.COM

LIVING SKY WILDLIFE REHABILITATION

These photoshoots raised funds for Living Sky Wildlife Rehabilitation, supporting injured and orphaned wildlife until they can return to their natural habitat.
Visit livingskywildliferehabilitation.org to learn

RHONDA

Sutherland Dog Park
Age 6, Lab/Mix

Rhonda was scared of water as a puppy, but now she loves swimming in the river and fetching sticks. She still won't touch a paddling pool though! She's a dignified lady who always crosses her front paws when lying down. Rhonda sometimes howls in her sleep and wakes herself up, and yet she has never once howled when awake!

HARPER

Bus Stop Refreshments
Downtown Saskatoon
Age 3, Mix

Harper absolutely adores playing with her swirl bully sticks and chasing grasshoppers on walks. She always shows her appreciation for her family by wagging her tail after meals and patiently waiting for an invitation to join momma on the couch.

LUNA

Downtown Saskatoon
Age 7 months, Siberian Husky

Luna is an adventurous dog who loves exploring the outdoors, digging holes, and hunting mice. She's quite talkative, especially when it's time to rise and shine! Easygoing and affectionate, Luna captivates everyone with her striking blue eyes while enjoying all the attention she can get.

MORTIMER AND BELLATRIX

Meewasin Trails
Ages 4 and 6, Cavalier King Charles Spaniels

Mortimer and Bellatrix are inseparable buddies who adore walks by lakes and rivers - but are totally freaked out by pools and puddles! They'll open the car window for fresh air during drives and if Mortimer is stuck downstairs, Bellatrix barks to alert everyone.

MANGO

Victoria Skate Park
Age 1, Pug

Meet Mango the Super Pug from TikTok! This talented pup loves to skateboard, scooter, and show off her tricks. Her favourite snack? Mangoes, of course! She has a new baby sister who's her best friend. They tire each other ou with lots of play, then curl up for a much needed nap.

PACINO AND RAVEN

Spadina Crescent Bridge
Ages 13 and 14, Bully/Lab mix and King Shepherd mix

Pacino and Raven proved to be quite the little thieves. Within a week of adoption he took a pound of butter, and she took a whole sandwich! Pacino stays warm with fashionable doggy clothes, and on their first ice fishing trip, Raven stole and devoured her papa's only catch.

KEVIN

CPR Train Bridge
Age 4, Mixed

Kevin, aka "Kevin Eugene Levy", loves the outdoors. He could sit on his patio chair all day. Initially shy, he quickly reveals his sassy and funny side. This curious pup loves exploring and going for walks, always eager to check out the world around him.

SENNA AND ROOSTER

Northeast Swale Nature Preserve
Ages 2 and 5, Border Collie and Lab/Shepherd mix

Rooster and Senna are a dynamic duo who compete in Flyball and frisbee leagues all across Saskatoon! They adore beach days and love to run like crazy. Rooster is a connoisseur of treats and Senna is a collector of toys.

APOLLO, WINNIE AND ATHENA

University of Saskatchewan
Ages 4, 3 and 7, Newfoundlander/Leonburger, Bernadoodle and Irish Wolfhound/Malamute

Apollo is a social butterfly with serious FOMO issues! He loves to be a part of the action, always bringing his stuffie, Sunny the lizard, along for the fun. Winnie loves to give big hugs and Athena, the momma of the group, keeps everyone in line (unless she's got the zoomies!)

TEX

Riddell Beach (Broome)
Age 6, Kelpie/Huntaway

Tex is a charming dog with the most expressive eyebrows, often making him seem like he's questioning your every move. He has a quirky habit of stealing items from strangers' beach bags. He loves to jump on the bed while you're lying down and adopt one of his many crazy, weird sleeping positions.

TAILS FROM . . .

Savannah Way (Broome To Townsville), Australia

Known for its ancient Indigenous culture and diverse landscapes - from colourful red deserts with dramatic rock formations to lush green tropics with waterfalls.

A DOG'S GUIDE:

1. Catch the sunset at Gantheaume Point in Broome - don't forget to look for dinosaur footprints!
2. Explore the rainforests at George Brown Darwin Botanic Gardens and stop by Evas cafe for a tasty treat.
3. Head to Magnetic Island for a tropical escape. A quick ferry ride from Townsville brings you to dog-friendly Horseshoe Bay.
4. Take the Peterson Creek Walk in Yungaburra to explore the Mabi Forest and keep an eye out for Aussie wildlife.
5. Adventure to the Northern tip of Australia at Cape York Peninsula - the only cardinal point you can visit with dogs.

KERRY MARTIN
PUPPY TALES

Photodography™ You'll Adore
Pet Travel & Adventures You'll Dig
Kerry considers dogs very much part of the family so lives this adage to help fellow pet parents create incredible memories of a most pawsome life together. Kerry's Melbourne-based but on the road in Australia for at least the next 2 years. She's known for her seasonal photography, most notably Snow Dogs, & her studio-based Project Dogalogue.

Puppy Tales is a business for good with a mission to make a paw-sitive difference - operating carbon-negative; supporting many local organisations & playing a part in protecting the planet. She's also the founder of the Australian Dog of the Year Awards.

PUPPYTALES.COM.AU

VETS BEYOND BORDERS & AMRRIC

These photoshoots raised funds for Vets Beyond Borders & AMRRIC. VBB deploys experienced volunteer vets and vet nurses to animal welfare projects in desperate need of help. AMRRIC works with remote communities to improve the health of their companion animals. Visit vetsbeyondborders.org and amrric.org

ELPHI

Goomboora Park (Cairns)
Age 2, Chiweenie
(Chihuahua/Dachshund)

Elphi is affectionately nicknamed Golden Eye for her striking eye colour. She loves playing with her soccer ball outdoors and enjoys her daily trike ride. She starts out running alongside, but when she tires, she's popped into the basket.

SASHA AND BANDIT

Lee Point (Darwin)
Ages 6 and 3, Labradors

Bandit, aka Froggy, and Sasha, known as Blondie, are a yin and yang duo. While Bandit is super chilled, Sasha can't sit still. Their fetch game is amusing too - Sasha loves the chase and retrieval, while Bandit prefers to just intercept the ball!

MR LITTLE

Bundilla Beach (Darwin)
Age 4, Miniature Foxie

Mr. Little, the runt of the litter with a cleft palate, beat the odds and thrived! With his quirky twisted nose, he's now the bravest little dynamo. He loves to run and play ball, although fetch isn't exactly his strong suit!

OMEGA, GRAYHAM, TOBY, DAISY AND MERCEDES

O'Keeffe House (Katherine)
Bulldog mix, Camp Dog, Wolfhound/Catahoula, American Staffy/Cattle Dog and Camp Dog

These dogs are "perfect in every way," says their human. Daisy was named for her resemblance to a moo cow. Grayham thinks he is part cat and Mercedes is the ball obsessed one. Omega will make himself comfortable anywhere - including sitting on his fur siblings.

AXLE

George Brown Darwin Botanic Gardens (Darwin)
Age 3, Kelpie/Bull Arab

Axel is adored for his huge ears. The tips flop even though he tries his hardest to hold up them up! He's got a sound effect for everything, from guiding you to his fave spots to asking for cuddles. He's even taught the cat some tricks, like how lying by the fridge gets you fed earlier!

KEIRA

Mindil Beach (Darwin)
Age 4, Siberian Husky/Border Collie

Keira is a total attention hog who soaks up every bit of love she gets. At the beach, she dives headfirst into shallow pools, snorkelling for fish. And during the wet season, she loves chasing after thunderclaps and leaping into the air with excitement!

MERRY AND PIPPIN

Halloran's Hill (Atherton)
Ages 1 and 4, Standard Poodles

Pippin and Merry are named after the Hobbits, in memory of their human's Lord of the Rings loving stepdad. Pippin's favourite trick is standing on his back legs to "Be a bear!" Merry is known as "Miss Destruction", and her humans have to 'Merry-proof' when leaving the house.

NANCY

Lake Tinaroo (Yungaburra)
Age 1, Bassett Hound

Her human's lifelong dream of having a Bassett Hound came true when they learnt of a nearby litter. Nancy was brought home and is a total typical Basset Hound - kind, empathic and extremely stubborn! She loves to carry the biggest stick and then carry it about with her.

SADIE

Palmetum (Townsville)
Age 4, Terrier mix

Sadie is far from ladylike - she's scruffy, sprawls out, rolls in gross stuff, steals food and is generally a bit of a dag! like a true dag! If anyone calls her 'Sadie the cleaning lady', her four-year-old human sibling, Felix, will correct them by saying "no, she is Sadie the pretty lady".

HERSHEY PAWS AND BIGGIE PAWS

Scarborough Bluffs
Ages 3 and 4, Australian Shepherd/Border Collie and Golden Doodle

Hershey Paws enjoys watching the nature channel on the TV and begins his mornings with dramatic stretches inspired by Big Comfy Couch. Biggie Paws is named after the notorious Biggie Smalls. His ears were dyed red for a Clifford inspired "Big Red Dog" look and its been his look ever since! He proudly serves as a therapy dog for the Ontario Health Partners Therapy Dog Program.

TAILS FROM . . .

Scarborough, Ontario Canada

Known for the scenic 100 meter cliffs of Scarborough Bluffs, Guild Park's artistic heritage, and the tranquil Rosetta McClain Gardens.

A DOG'S GUIDE:

1. Take a scenic walk at the Scarborough Bluffs, where the stunning cliffs rise from the lake like a natural cathedral.
2. Dive into the fun at Rouge Beach, part of the Rouge National Urban Park, for a refreshing swim.
3. Visit the Common Good Beer Company, a dog-friendly spot where you can relax with your human.
4. Hike the Doris McCarthy Trail for beautiful lake views and a chance to spot wildlife.
5. Hang out at R.C. Harris Water Treatment Plant, where there's plenty of green space and the beach starts nearby, perfect for off-leash swimming.

JUST PAWS ANIMAL RESCUE

These photoshoots raised funds for Just Paws Animal Rescue, an all-volunteer, foster-based program caring for dogs in home settings within the Greater Toronto area.
Visit justpaws.ca to learn more

TERRI JANKELOW
TERRI J PHOTOGRAPHY

I am a pet and family photographer based in the city of Toronto, dedicated to celebrating the irreplaceable bond you share with your beloved pets.

My goal is to provide awesome images that encompass the joy and love that your dog gives to you, and to create stunning pet portraits that not only adorn your walls but also warm your heart every time you glance at them. Whether it's a playful puppy, a shy dog or a senior, I strive to capture their individual personalities in every shot.

Drawing from years of experience in dog training, I bring a deep understanding of canine behaviour to every session. And this enables me to handle dogs of all temperaments and ages.

TERRIJPHOTOGRAPHY.COM

OREO

Meadowvale Conservation Area
Age 15, Maltese/Shih Tzu

Oreo might be a senior dog, but she's still a spunky little girl! She recently lost her lifelong companion, which has been tough for her as she's still grieving.

ASTRA

R. C. Harris Water Treatment Plant
Age 2, Mini Golden Doodle

Astra is a sweet and friendly dog who has made tons of friends in the neighborhood, connecting her family to the community. Due to severe allergies, her human was sure owning a dog was out of the question. After babysitting a friend's dog without any reactions, they were overjoyed to be able to welcome Astra into the home.

ENCORE

R.C. Harris Water Treatment Plant
Age 13, Bichon/Shitzu

Encore, named after the lottery, is one lucky pup! She doesn't even realize she's a dog and gets pretty annoyed when anyone tries to steal her "cute" spotlight.

SADIE

Scarborough Bluffs
Age 3, Jackapoo

Sadie's human has two sons and male cats, so was determined to have a female dog. Out of the four puppies born in the litter, only one was female. It was meant to be! Sadie joined the family and became a beloved companion and true best friend for the semi-retired empty nester.

LYDIA

R.C. Harris Water Treatment Plant
Age 9, Terrier mix

Lydia was adopted from a friend who was moving and has been inseparable from her new family ever since. This curious, excitable, and cuddly diva taught her humans how to care for her and they look forward every day to serving her every need! She has deepened t relationship to each other and to all living beings.

GIMLI

Birkdale Ravine
Age 1, French Bulldog

Gimli's human had first pick of the litter and so has been named Gimli since she was just 3 weeks old! She's convinced all people should pet her immediately. Her cute tongue often gets caught out of her mouth thanks to her teeth.

LUCY LU

Guild Park and Gardens
Age 2, Havanese/Poodle

Lucy Lu is a sweet dog with warm hazel eyes that radiate calm and understanding. She's playful and always up for an adventure, but also knows how to comfort her humans when they're feeling low. Lucy Lu truly embodies the pure, simple love that pets bring into our lives.

CASEY

Birkdale Ravine
Age 2, Poodle/Jack Russell Terrier

Casey, affectionately known as Quesadilla, arrived from Mexico as a Just Paws foster and captured her foster mom's heart instantly! Now training to be a service dog, she shows a natural kindness towards other fosters and cats.

LEXI

Birkdale Ravine
Age 3, Australian Shepherd/Mini Poodle

Lexi is a total joy for her family and has helped the daughter conquer her fear of dogs. She brings shoes when they come home and dances happily for visitors. But watch out - if she doesn't like the walk route, she'll just lie down and refuse to move!

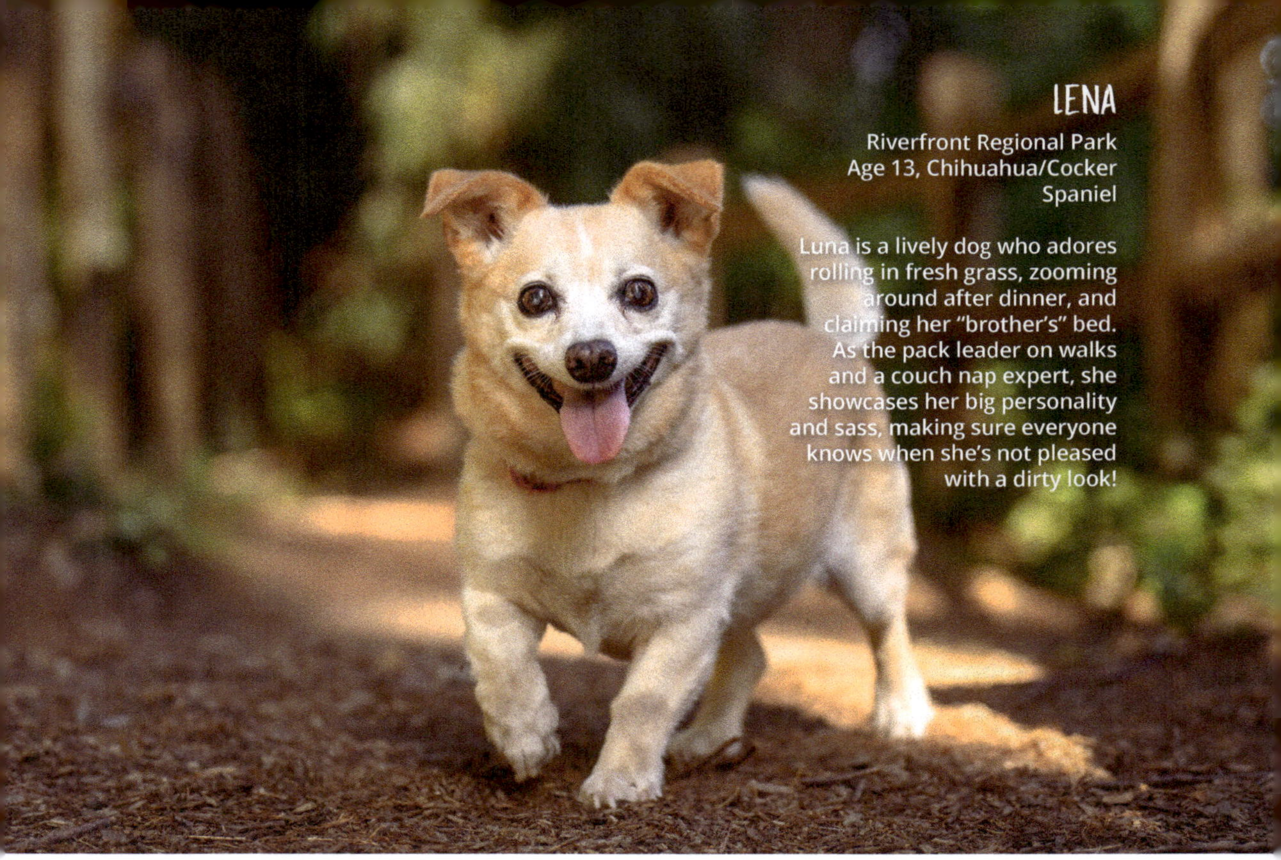

LENA

Riverfront Regional Park
Age 13, Chihuahua/Cocker Spaniel

Luna is a lively dog who adores rolling in fresh grass, zooming around after dinner, and claiming her "brother's" bed. As the pack leader on walks and a couch nap expert, she showcases her big personality and sass, making sure everyone knows when she's not pleased with a dirty look!

TAILS FROM . . .

Sonoma County, California USA

Known for picturesque vineyards, farm-to-table dining experiences, and majestic coastal redwoods.

A DOG'S GUIDE:

1. Dive into fun at Spring Lake's "Water Bark" event, helping raise funds for dog-friendly parks and trails.
2. Join the "Yappy Hour" at Mutt Lynch Winery, where you can enjoy wine and fun activities while supporting local service dog organizations.
3. Take a dip at Doran Beach in the new off-leash dog park.
4. Chill out with a craft beer at Russian River Brewery, where dogs are always welcome in the outdoor area.
5. Attend St. Francis Winery's "Blessing of the Animals" event each October, supporting local animal charities.

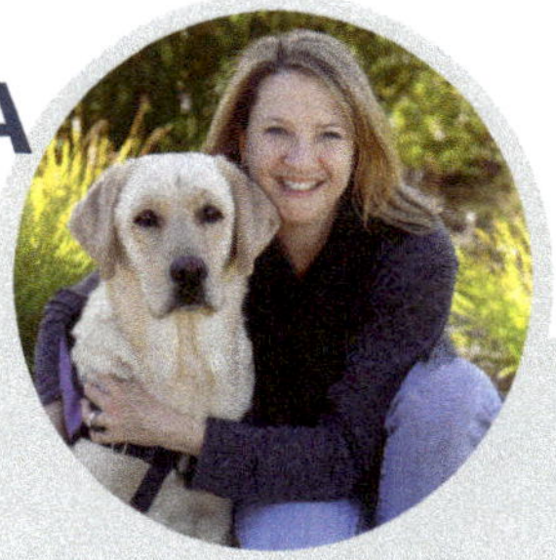

HEIDI ADLER
HEIDI ADLER PHOTOGRAPHY

I'm an educator and award-winning photographer based in the heart of Sonoma County Wine Country. Nothing brings me more joy than capturing beautiful images of dogs in breathtaking locations amidst the hills, vineyards, and the California coastline.

From the irresistible breath of a puppy to the comforting presence of a senior dog enjoying their golden years, every pet holds a special place in our hearts and homes. Pets are family, and it's my honour to create beautiful, lasting artwork that celebrates the connection between pets and the people who love them.

HEIDIADLERPHOTOGRAPHY.COM

ICY AND MAHINA

Dillon Beach
Ages 2 and 3, Pit Bull Terrier/GSD and Bernese Mountain Dog

Icy and Mahina are living their best lives together! Icy is super smart, has been an important part of 17 foster dog experiences, and loves to run and explore. Sweet Mahina adapted very well to living in a home after being confined in a cage for most of her entire life. Now she helps other puppy mill mamas adapt to home life as a foster dog.

REMINGTON

Armstrong Woods State Natural Reserve
Age 6, Chihuahua/Shar Pei

Remington is the sweetest, most loving dog ever! He and his brothers were discovered in a box outside a liquor store as tiny pups. This happy little guy loves playing, snuggling, beach trips, and walks in Armstrong Woods. He has the cutest wrinkles and his massive smile says it all! He is the happiest little guy who is loved more than anything.

DILLON

Dillon Beach
Age 4, Terrier/Chihuahua

Dillon is a fun-loving dog who adores her family, car rides, hikes and playing with her ball and toys. Her favourite outing is a trip to Dillon Beach, where she feels totally relaxed by the ocean!

LG, OLIVER AND MOOSE

Spring Lake Regional Park
Ages 6, 5 months and 7, Labrador Retriever

LG, the gentle service dog, brings comfort to everyone she meets and once even saved a baby bunny! Oliver, the water-loving pup, would probably be a fish if he wasn't Oliver the dog. He adores his sisters and snores louder than thundering elephants. Meanwhile, Moose loves his person, tolerates everyone else, hates water and believes he's the best lap dog ever.

SCOOTER

Ragle Ranch Regional Park
Age 7, Chihuahua

Scooter, a brave and feisty pup, was tossed in a dumpster as a newborn due to her missing front legs. Luckily, some kids found her and took her to the Humane Society of Sonoma County. Now, she's a friendly little dog who adores kids and other small dogs!

GRETA

Spring Lake Regional Park
Age 2, Xoloitzcuintli

Greta loves snuggling under the blanket, often snoozing long after her humans rise. She charmingly cocks her head to one side when spoken to and delights in watching TV, especially when dogs or other animals are on screen.

LUNA

Campbell McKinney Vineyards
Age 9, Husky/American Eskimo

Luna is a beach-loving pup who enjoys swimming and rock climbing like a little goat. With her unique split-colored eyes - brown on top and blue on the bottom - she's a standout. She enjoys agility, trick training, and dock diving, especially if treats are involved!

MILLIE AND BARLEY

Bohemian Flowers & Farmstead
Ages 2 and 12, Labrador Retriever

Millie loves coastal camping, doggy daycare, and making silly noises when she sniffs something fun. Her sister Barley is a total sweetheart who adores treats, snuggling, and showering her parents with kisses. The sisters have a blast together and love each other tons!

GUTHRIE

Duncan's Landing
Age 2, Australian Cattle Dog/Pit Bull Terrier

Guthrie's got the best ears in town, showcasing all sorts of emotions. He's a frisbee-fetching, grass-rolling, hay-digging pro! He makes sure to take a lap around the local brewery to greet his favourite people before his humans settle down. He loves to see and be seen!

JUJUBA

Parque Campolim
Age 10, Mixed

This resilient dog survived canine distemper and was returned twice before finally finding her forever home. Her new family soon realized that while they thought they adopted her, in fact it was Jujuba who had rescued them.

TAILS FROM . . .

Sorocaba and Alumínio, Brazil

Known as the "Manchester Paulista" of Brazil due to its booming textile industries and home to the country's most famous "Coxinha" dish at Padaria Real.

A DOG'S GUIDE:

1. Explore Chico Mendes Park in Sorocaba, a vast area with trails, lakes, and diverse trees where you can connect with nature.
2. Visit Praça do Campolim, a family-friendly park featuring two lakes, a walking track, and an outdoor gym, perfect for pets.
3. Stop by Santa Crema for pet-friendly coffee and snacks.
4. Get a bath for your furry friend at Auteliê, the top pet store in Sorocaba.
5. Enjoy delicious meals with your pet at Oca Burger, a welcoming spot for both of you!

AATAN SOROCABA

These photoshoots raised funds for AATAN Sorocaba, supporting a shelter with around 300 animals, many needing specific treatment and care.
Visit aatansorocaba.com.br to learn more

FERNANDA CERIONI

FOTOGRAFIA PET

With 10 years of experience, Fernanda is a pet photographer based in Alumínio, Brazil. At the age of ten, she first encountered photography through her family's analogue camera, beginning her journey by taking pictures of her dogs.

She offers a variety of session types, including studio shoots, outdoor or at the pet's home. She also provides themed birthday sessions complete with decorations and a pet-friendly cake in her studio.
Her mission is to immortalise the beauty of pets, capturing the emotional bond between them and their families through portraits and candid shots, and delivering the cherished narratives of their lives, enriching their hearts with precious pet memories.

FERNANDACERIONI.COM.BR

DORINHA

Parque Campolim
Age 3, Mixed

There was no mischief in the ho before Dorinha arrived. Now the little thief using her paws like hands to snatch bread off the table, and no bin is safe from her curiousity. Mischief definitely found a new home when Dorinha moved in!

JOAQUIN

Parque Campolim
Age 5, Mixed

Joaquin is part dog, part cat and full gentleman. He has the sweetest smile any pup could sport.

AIMÊ

Parque da Biquinha
Age 6, Cavalier King Spaniel

This dog wins the hearts of everyone with her sweetness and affection. She's super smart and always ready to shower her humans with love and kisses. Honestly, it's impossible not to smile when you're next to her!

AVELÃ

Parque Chico Mendes
Age 3, Mixed

This playful pup is very expressive; her look says it all! Her favourite game is playing with balls and she is happiest when snuggled on her mother's lap.

ALICE

Associação Atlética Alumínio
Age 7, Mixed

This adorable, needy girl loves being around people and soaking up affection! She snores cutely while sleeping and brings joy to her family. As the daughter of a photographer, she beams with happiness during photo sessions in the studio, always ready for her close-up!

CACAU

Parque Chico Mendes
Age 5, Shih Tzu mix

This dog is a total foodie - everything tastes good to her! Her smile when her humans come home is the best part of the day.

LOLLITA

Paço Municipal
Age 8, Maltese mix

Lollita is a genius girl and a natural leader with impressive hunting skills.

PIPPOCA

Paço Municipal
Age 5, Mixed

This dog is a big eater who never turns down food. She's super affectionate with everyone and has a chatty personality, always ready to talk.

PRETA PRETINHA AND TOBIAS HENRIQUE

Villa Flora
Ages 6 and 5, Mixed

Tobias joined the family as a pup, while Pretinha came along later as almost an adult. Pretinha especially loves humans and insists on saying hi to everyone who walks by! They are an active, playful and inseparable duo, they always need to be around each other.

YELI

HAWS Schallock Centre for Animals
Age 3, Golden Retriever

Yeli was meant to be a hunting dog, but instead spends her time doing fun dog sports like agility. Always ready to give 110%, her favourite activity is swimming.

TAILS FROM . . .

Southeastern, Wisconsin USA

Known for its beer, including Pabst, Miller, Schlitz, and Blatz, and as the birthplace of the Harley-Davidson company.

A DOG'S GUIDE:

1. Chill at the public beer gardens in summer or visit a dog-friendly brewery anytime.
2. Enjoy running on dog-friendly beaches by Lake Michigan or try Stand Up Paddle Boarding in the lakes.
3. Treat yourself to doggy ice cream at Salty Paws in Bay View.
4. Hike the Ice Age Trail, a scenic adventure over 1,000 miles across Wisconsin.
5. Grab a coffee at Colectivo, where there are great patios for dogs.

HUMANE ANIMAL WELFARE SOCIETY SCHALLOCK CENTER FOR ANIMALS

These photoshoots raised funds for HAWS Schallock Centre for Animals, promoting adoptions and education in a unique sanctuary setting. Visit hawspets.org/schallockcenter to learn more

NADIA HALL
BARKING DOG IMAGES

Nadia Hall is the owner of Barking Dog Images, and dogs are her passion. Years ago, when she wasn't training or competing with her dogs, she discovered that she loves to photograph them. Now, she wants all pet parents to have beautiful memories of their pets frozen in time. She is known for her dreamy outdoor portraits, capturing human and pet relationships, and her nationwide coverage of dog sport events.

Nadia believes that...
Dogs belong in the bed;
Meals are meant for sharing;
Our pets are our babies;
Dog training should be fear-free;
Adopt or shop responsibly;
Our lives are better with pets in them;
You can NEVER have enough photos.

BARKINGDOGIMAGES.COM

PIPPIN

Ice Age National Scenic Trail
Age 2, Mixed

Pippin was a foster fail within a week of bringing her home. After battling Parvo as a puppy, she's been a loyal companion through her mom's chemo and several cancer surgeries - talk about a true fighter and best friend!

ELLIE

Whitnall Park
Age 1, Mixed

Ellie's dad is a police officer. He found her stuck under a police car after being abandoned by her abusive previous owners. It was love at first sight. These days, Ellie enjoys playing fetch with balls and squeaky toys and loves exploring new walking trails to admire nature.

PORTER

Black Cat Alley
Age 4, Border Collie

Porter is quite the athlete, competing in multiple dog sports nationally with his mom. He loves playing dog disc and swimming with his Golden Retriever sisters.

TOTO

Milwaukee Art Museum
Age 14, Chihuahua mix

Toto is a lovable dog who was adopted from a Florida shelter. He is a true people magnet, always attracting attention and adoration. Although not a fan of winter, he loves basking in the sun, napping with his favourite duck plush, and chasing after balls in the yard.

JOURNEY

Estabrook Park
Age 4, Husky

After the loss of a pet, Journey's mom was looking for a volunteer opportunity at the local shelter. It was there that she m Journey - it was meant to be. Journey loves hiking and camping with his humans. His favourite place is anywhere along the lakeside or afternoon at a park.

JYN

Grant Park Beach, Lake Michigan
Age 6, Australian Shepherd

Jyn totally saved her mom's life during the stress of completing medical school and residency through the pandemic. Together, they've competed in multiple dog sports, even performing at the Wisconsin State Fair, and have gone on awesome multi-day backpacking trips together.

REMI

Lannon Quarry
Age 5, American Foxhound

Remi was found tied to a picnic table outside in the cold Indiana winter. She was rescued and adopted by her forever mom in 2020. Together they have tackled training challenges and now they compete in dog sports together. Remi's favourite thing to do is sniffing anywhere new.

AMELIA GENE

Lapham Peak State Park
Age Unknown, Mixed

Amelia Gene is a spirited three-legged dog who loves to hike and be with her people. She was flown from Alabama to Wisconsin for emergency amputation surgery by a kind pilot named Gene, which is how she got her middle name.

MAVERICK

Kettle Moraine National Forest
Age 1, Mixed

Maverick was Texas stray, covered in fleas and dirt. Now he's totally beloved, and his favourite place to be is playing in the yard at his grandma and grandpa's house. His best characteristic is that he always tries to cheer up his mom after a hard day at work.

ARI

Dufferin Islands
Age 11, Pomeranian

Ari is the life of the party, always sure to be the loudest in the room! This attention-loving pup thrives on being the centre of focus, but remember, Ari doesn't work for free - treats are a must for any performance!

TAILS FROM . . .

St. Catharines, Ontario Canada

Known as "the Garden City" and filled with fruit, vegetable and flower farms.

A DOG'S GUIDE:

1. Explore The Commons in Niagara on the Lake, where you can run and play off-leash.
2. Treat yourself and your furry friend at Bench Brewing Company in Lincoln, where the "pup plate" offers a tasty mix of doggie-safe fruits, veggies, and chicken.
3. Join the fun at the Muddy Paws Wine Festival at Featherstone Winery each June.
4. Visit Port Dalhousie, a dog-friendly spot bustling with pups.
5. Hit the trails in Niagara, like the Bruce Trail, for beautiful walks and hikes with your family and pets.

TAILS OF THE NORTH DOG RESCUE

These photoshoots raised funds for Tails of the North Dog Rescue, a charitable organization providing loving care for dogs in need through dedicated fosters and volunteers. Visit tailsofthenorth.ca to learn more

KIM LEARN
TWO SAINTS PHOTOGRAPHY

Hi I'm Kim. I've lived in the Niagara Region for over 30 years. I've always loved photography and picked up a camera at several different times throughout the years .After a few university degrees and several jobs I finally discovered a passion a for pet photography. What I love about dogs and photography : dogs are authentic, natural and just plain incredibly joyful to be around. It's really hard NOT to live in the present moment while in a dog's company. I can't think of a greater pleasure than photographing dogs and creating beautiful pieces of artwork for pet parents. Dogs are amazing. They deserve to be celebrated in a Huge way!!!

TWOSAINTSPHOTOGRAPHY.CA

EEVEE DE LA BRISE

Niagara On the Lake
Age 2, Pyrenean Sheepdog

Eevee is a Pyrenean Sheepdog, an ancient herding breed known for their hyper-vigilance and agility. She's super loyal to her loved ones and thrives in any activity that keeps her on the move!

FRANKIE

Hamilton, Cherry Hill Gate
Age 1, Chihuahua/ Dachshund

Frankie is a super social pup who makes friends wherever she goes. She kicks off her day with cosy morning snuggles, enjoys tackling puzzle toys, and loves being held like a baby while getting belly rubs.

MARELY, MIA AND MAX

13th Street Winery
Ages 10, 6 and 6, Tea Cup Poodle and Maltese mix

Marley loves being the boss and much prefers to be carried than walking these days. Mia adores toys and will cry like a baby when she wants something. Max has priceless human-like expressions and snores while napping during grooming sessions.

KASIA

Cherry Hill Gate
Age 5, American Eskimo and Pomeranian mix

Kasia is a friendly and social dog who loves making new friends wherever she goes. Not only a pretty face, this little pup is also an accomplished sport dog. She excels in sports like Agility, Hoopers, and Rally Free. Kasia is a smart pup is always eager to learn!

LEO

Fort Erie farm
Age 9, Boxer/Springer Spaniel

Leo is the ultimate momma's boy and named after her zodiac sign. His favourite spot to snooze is his cosy teepee.

DEXTER

Lakeside Park Beach
Age 12, Belgian Malinois Shepherd

Dexter is a big sucky boy and totally a toy-aholic! He's humans reckon he is the "best boy of all the best boys out there!"

MIA

Dufferin Islands
Age 1, Hound mix

Mia is a cute little troublemaker who chews everything. Valuables have to be placed up high and out of Mia's reach. She loves to lay by her parents' feet while they cook and once the food is ready, she lays her head down on their lap, looking up with her pretty brown eyes.

COWBOY AND TARA

Niagara Parkway
Ages 12 and 6, Chesapeake Bay Retriever and Black Lab mix

Cowboy roamed the streets before being rescued. He loved fetching giant sticks and was a beautiful boy inside and out. Tara is also a rescue dog, and a huge cuddle bug. She loves to swim in a Niagara river with the geese. She sneaks in a kiss whenever she can!

SAMI

Balls Falls in Lincoln
Age 2, Saint Bernard

Sami is a joyful dog who absolutely loves mud and water! She often tries to catch fish whilst swimming. As a therapy dog, she delights in meeting new people and exploring new places, spreading happiness wherever she goes!

MOXIE

Ramshaw Rocks
Age 5, Staffordshire Bull Terrier/Pug

Moxie is a lovable pup who adores kisses, cuddles, and plenty of food. She enjoys walks, especially on the beach or anywhere with water. Her human says that "adopting Moxie is the best decision I have ever made!"

TAILS FROM . . .

Staffordshire, England UK

Known for its namesake dog breed, the Staffordshire Bull Terrier and as the historic centre of ceramics with renowned brands like Moorcroft and Wedgwood.

A DOG'S GUIDE:

1. Discover the beautiful gardens at The Trentham Estate.
2. Stroll through the woods and splash in the stream at Biddulph Country Park, followed by a visit to The Hideaway for dog biscuits and doggy ice cream.
3. Try a refreshing dog beer or snack from The Dogs Dinner menu at The Mainwaring Arms in Whitmore.
4. Join in on scent sports like Mantrailing or Barn Hunt with Constellation Dog training.
5. Gain confidence in the water with hydrotherapy swim sessions at K9 Hydro Care, which also offers a shop for all your doggy needs.

LUOSKO GERMAN SHEPHERD RESCUE

These photoshoots raised funds for LUOSKO German Shepherd Rescue, aiding abandoned dogs in need of a second chance, regardless of age or medical conditions. Visit luoskogermanshepherddogrescue.org

KATIE ANDERSON-PALMER
ADVENTURE PAWTRAITS

I'm Katie and I'm the face behind Adventure Pawtraits, capturing dogs in the great outdoors in the beautiful county of Staffordshire and surrounding areas. It means the world to me to use my creativity and skills to give dog parents the most beautiful memories of their fur babies.

I live in the countryside in a little village in Staffordshire with my Husband and my two dogs, Nala and Arlo. My Portuguese Water dog, Nala, is my biggest inspiration and best friend. I love the spirit she has for life and adventures and the impact that has on me and my passion for the outdoors. Our Wirehaired Vizsla, Arlo is very young and still learning the ropes, he fits in with our family perfectly.

ADVENTUREPAWTRAITS.COM

SYLVIE

Ramshaw Rocks
Age 1, Bedlington Terrier mix

Sylvie is a speedy little dog who loves chasing her ball like a tiny racehorse! She's incredibly loyal, always keeping an eye on her humans during walks. With her Bedlington spirit, she's both stubborn and hilarious, constantly plotting to sneak socks from the laundry basket!

RALPHIE

Mow Cop Castle
Age 1, Cavapoo

Ralphie didn't have the best start to life - he was attacked by another dog at four months old and needed spinal surgery to save his life. Despite that, he's still such a friendly boy and loves to play with other dogs! Super friendly and playful, he even gets shy dogs to join in. He enjoys agility work, but if you ask him to jump through hoops, you better make sure the reward is worth the effort!

MOXIE

Mow Cop Castle
Age 11 months, Sprocker

Milo is a cuddle-loving pup and is so happy to be picked up. He's totally food obsessed, sneaking anything left out, from salt bowls to lemon drizzle cake! He tags along everywhere - he's even on the tube to Buckingham Palace and he loved the bustling crowds.

RALPHIE

Apedale Country Park
Age 2, Mixed

Ralphie's human found him as a beat up little stray pup in Goa, India. He was brought back to the UK, where he enjoys long walks and a life filled with love.

KEVIN

Mow Cop Castle
Age 1, Golden Retriever

Kevin is the smartest goofball. One minute he's learning new tricks, the next moment he's jumping around like a Kangaroo! He has a beautiful ability to sense stress; immediately approaching his human for a cuddle if they're having a hard time at work.

RATCHET AND SPANNER

Mow Cop Castle
Ages 5 and 8 months, German Shepherd and Sprocker

Ratchet and Spanner are rescue pups who adore water and mantrailing. Ratchet joins his human on 10km runs and has climbed Snowden twice. Adding Spanner to the mix was interesting. Ratchet spent the first two days ignoring her, now they are the best of friends!

ROCK AND IVY

Barlaston Downs
Ages 1 and 2, American Bull Terrier mix and Rottweiler

Ivy and Rock are two adorable rescue pups. Ivy was dumped in Cyprus as a puppy, while Rock was saved from the pound right before being euthanised. They're both food mad, love tug balls, and have their own quirky personalities - Rock is goofy and Ivy warms up with treats!

FINALI AND KIARA

Ramshaw Rocks
Ages 4 months and 9 months, Red Fox Labrador and Golden Retriever

Finali is named from the film 'Ready Player One' and Kiara is named from 'The Lion King 2'. Kiara adores her ball and greets guests with random gifts like slippers and toys. Finali loves barking and growling at the TV, no matter what's playing!

TODD

Apedale Country Park
Age 1, Longhaired Dachshund

Todd is a shy pup with a big heart who adores belly rubs and his beloved crinkly elephant!. After losing their dog Woody to cancer, Todd brought joy and a zest for life back into the home, reminding them that life is very special.

SOL

Maroochydore, Boat Houses
Age 1, German Shepherd

Meet this extra-large pup with an even larger heart! He's a playful character who brings joy and laughter wherever he goes - like Chandler Bing! Always ready for mischief, cuddles and tail wags.

TAILS FROM . . .

Sunshine Coast, QLD Australia

Known for its pristine beaches, laidback vibes and diverse landscapes of mountains, beaches and rainforests.

A DOG'S GUIDE:

1. Sniff out a hike at dog-friendly Mt Ninderry.
2. Get your paws sandy at our dog-friendly beaches.
3. Check out the Noosa Pet Expo by the river.
4. Hire a boat on Noosa River for a sunset adventure.
5. Explore Wild Horse Mountain lookout for stunning views of the Glass House Mountains.

SUNSHINE COAST ANIMAL REFUGE SHELTER

These photoshoots raised funds for Sunshine Coast Animal Refuge Shelter, supporting rescue efforts, community assistance, desexing programs, and education for over 45,000 animals.
Visit sippycreek.com.au to learn more

COURTNEY BENNETT
COURTRAITS PHOTOGRAPHY

Courtney is a pet photographer based on the Sunshine Coast, Australia. Since a child, she has always had a love for photography, specifically landscape photography. When she volunteered at an animal shelter, she started taking the adoption photos for the cats and dogs and found a whole new passion and love for photographing pets.

Courtney combined her passion of the outdoors with pet photography to create whimsical, pet portraits within the Australian landscape. She has two dogs; Willow and Luna who are her greatest inspiration. Having recently lost her senior dog Patch at the age of 20, Courtney makes her mission to ensure pet owners have beautiful memories with their loved ones.

COURTRAITSPHOTOGRAPHY.COM

SADIE AND SIMBA

Beerwah Forest
Ages 3 and 6, Samoyed and mixed

Sadie and Simba - aka the land seal and the lion - are the best of friends. After being diagnosed with Osteosarcoma, Simba has been through a leg amputation and six rounds of chemo. With Sadie as a supporting sister, these two adventure and live their life to the fullest.

PINK

Noosa
Age 2, Shiba Inu

Pink is very sweet with a dash of sass. Her hobbies include devouring dried pork snouts, long walks on the beach and making you feel awful for not sharing your dinner.

HADLEY

Noosa Lake Webya
Age 2, French Bulldog

This dog has always been a water baby, even swimming in his water bowls as a pup! Now a pawfessional model, he's strutted his stuff for plenty of pet apparel brands. Fun fact: he's the only one in his litter with those striking light green eyes!

WINSTON

Caloundra
Age 4, Rottweiler

Winston is a gentle, goofy boy who's always changing people's opinions on big dogs. He loves his family, enjoys playing with his ball, munching on snacks, and snuggling up for some cuddles.

BOLT

Lake Webya, Noosa
Age 4, Great Dane

Bolt, the giant lap dog, is known for his graceful yet powerful stance. With an irresistible charm, he captures the hearts of everyone he meets.

HAMISH

Wild Horse Mountain Lookout
Age 8, Dalmatian

This pup will do anything for a treat, earning him the nickname "the tap" thanks to his epic drooling. His biggest adventure to date was walking his mum down the aisle and being the ring bearer at his pawrents wedding .

MARSHMALLOW

Caloundra
Age 5, Pembroke Welsh Corgi

Marshmallow is an Instagram famous doggo who will perform all the tricks for treats. He tends to wake up at ungodly hours and beg to play with the hose water.

WILLOW

Noosa Botanic Gardens
Age 3, Australian Shepherd/Kelpie

Willow is a typical working breed who enjoys learning new tricks and thrives in dog sports like tracking, agility, and noseworks. Her favourite pose, the delightful Sit Pretty, showcases her playful spirit and eagerness to impress!

DOTTI AND MAGGIE AND MABEL

Ben Bennet Park
Ages 4, 1 and 4, Cocker Spaniels

Dotti is sunshine in dog form and Maggie is the most energetic, loving and curious girl. Mabel is the little wildflower, who keeps her humans on their toes - but honestly, they wouldn't have it any other way!

LOUIS

Humber Bay Park West
Age 3, Wheatamix

Louis is a kind soul who loves everyone, captivating hearts with his charm and warm spirit. This delightful mix of Wheaten Terrier, Miniature Schnauzer, and Poodle greets each new friend with a wagging tail and playful energy, spreading joy wherever he goes.

TAILS FROM . . .

Toronto, Ontario Canada

Known for the CN Tower, part of one of the most recognized skylines in the world, and as host of the huge Toronto International Film Festival.

A DOG'S GUIDE:

1. Attend Woofstock, the largest dog festival in North America.
2. Enjoy the waterfront at Lake Ontario, with off-leash Cherry Beach and opportunities for canoeing or sailing.
3. Watch an epic sunset together at Riverdale Park West, perfect for those picturesque moments.
4. Take a stroll through the Distillery District, a pedestrian-only area filled with cobblestone streets, shops, and outdoor cafés.
5. Explore Graffiti Alley, a dog-friendly spot showcasing vibrant murals and street art for cool Instagram photos.

KAREN WEILER
POSH PETS® PHOTOGRAPHY

Karen Weiler of Posh Pets® Photography is an award-winning animal and pet photographer based in Toronto, Canada. She spends most days photographing the urban dogs and cats in the beautiful city she calls home.

However, when not photographing other people's pets, she and her husband toil tirelessly for the benefit of Panda and Baxter, the two rescue kitties who live quite a charmed life now in their forever home.

POSHPETSPHOTO.COM

FETCH + RELEASH DOG RESCUE

These photoshoots raised funds for Fetch + Releash Dog Rescue, a volunteer-run organization dedicated to saving and rehoming dogs in need. Visit fetchandreleash.ca to learn more

MURPHY

Humber Bay Park West
Age 7, Cockapoo

Murphy's has an adorable crooked smile and is super vocal while resting, which makes for some pretty funny moments. His most random trick is that he knows how to conga!

ROSSEAU

Yorkville
Age 5, Golden Retriever

Rosseau is a ball obsessed dog who has totally mastered the art of professional begging. His humans say that he is "the cutest, bestest boy around!"

OPAL

Hotel X
Age 5, Scottish Fold

Opal is a rescue from the Toronto Humane Society who lives with Osteochondrodysplasia. She has a dog-like personality and is extremely adaptable and well-traveled. She's also loving, always wanting to hang out and play with her humans and occasionally her dog buddies.

OAKLAND

Stanley Barracks; Hotel X
Age 6, American Staffordshire Terrier mix

Oakland is a special pup who has donated blood nine times to help save other dogs. She's a rescue dog who adores all pets and has lovingly assisted in raising several litters of foster kittens.

FREYA
Humber Bay Arch Bridge
Age 5, Rescue mix

Freya is a happy foster failure and known as the world's laziest dog! Despite being a total medical lemon with multiple health issues, her family loves her to bits and thinks she's absolutely perfect!

TILLIE

Hotel X
Age 10, Australian Shepherd

Tillie coaches rowing in the Toronto harbour every morning. By day, she either hangs out in the office as a legal assistant or catches some Z's on the couch.

TOFU

Sunnyside Park
Age 8, Pomeranian

Tofu might not look like it, but he's a big adventurer! This curious pup has lived in four Canadian provinces, seen the Northern Lights, and two total solar eclipses. With his adorable smile, he never fails to get "aww"s during walks, brightening everyone's day!

ODIE

Sunnyside Park
Age 3, Jack Russell Terrier mix

Covered in distinctive wiry scruff with prominent eyebrows that Odie fancies give an air of sophistication. A svelte athlete who loves to leap and play chase with larger dogs at the park, Odie is proudest when prancing alongside the family.

THUMPER

Sunnyside Park
Age 5, Northern Mutt

Thumper is a real foodie who insists on having his strawberries quartered and leaf-free. This Toronto pup loves weekend mornings spent sniffing out the best coffee shop snacks. Thumper has never met a baby he didn't like and is a likely baby-napping suspect.

HENRY

Ann Morrison Park
Age 9, Chihuahua mix

Henry is a 14 lb cuddle bug who adores people! Always the life of the party, he's easy to carry around but also loves to run like the wind. Despite recent health challenges, Henry remains his happy, loving self. His resilience is inspiring, spreading joy even during vet visits and treatments.

TAILS FROM . . .

Treasure Valley, Idaho USA

Known for the Sunnyslope Wine Trail, with 19 wineries along winding country roads and patchwork farmlands.

A DOG'S GUIDE:

1. Visit Boise River Greenbelt, a 25-mile, tree-lined pathway perfect for walks along the Boise River.
2. Play at Together Treasure Valley Dog Island, a 5.4-acre off-leash park in Ann Morrison Park.
3. Enjoy Huckleberry Dog Park in Nampa, with trails, grassy areas, and a misting station to keep cool.
4. Amity Dog Park is fully-fenced and even has a swimming pond.
5. Shop at D & B Supply, a pet-friendly store stocked with everything you need for a happy life in The West!

SHANNON EDNEY
SHANNON EDNEY PHOTOGRAPHY

Award winning pet portrait photographer Shannon Edney's internationally acclaimed work has graced numerous magazine covers and adorned print and digital advertisements globally.

With an ability for capturing perfect expressions and subjects bathed in unique lighting, Shannon crafts portraits teeming with artistry, destined to be cherished for generations.

SHANNONEDNEY.COM

BOXER LOVERS RESCUE

These photoshoots raised funds for Boxer Lovers Rescue, a nonprofit dedicated to rescuing, rehabilitating, and rehoming Boxers in the Pacific Northwest. Visit boxerloversrescue.com to learn more

SOPHIE

Indian Creek Plaza
Age 7, Boxer

Sophie was rescued as a pup after being hit by a vehicle. Now she's a "Foster Auntie", helping raise two litters of foster puppies and she is very protective of her Pomeranian brother (even when he's being a pest). She has an adventurous spirit too and has travelled across the country!

MACK JANE

Indian Creek Plaza
Age 3, European Boxer

Mack Jane loves to adventure - whether it's riding in the side-by-side, camping, swimming, or cuddling, she enjoys it all and even puts herself to bed when tired at the end of the day. She's a princess with personality, who makes sure her humans know exactly what she wants!

MARLEY

Indian Creek Plaza
Age 13, Lab/GSD

Marley is a spry senior who loves walks, cooler weather and claiming her spot on the bed. Affectionate and social, she enjoys belly rubs and the company of other dogs - though she prefers them as admirers rather than playmates!

MCCOY

Ann Morrison Park
Age 7, Pittie mix

McCoy is a lovable 56-pound mix of silliness and sweetness. Despite a tough past on the streets of Stockton, CA, he's now a devoted bestie who adores car rides, playtime, and cuddles, showcasing his bright spirit and resilience. He truly knows how to steal hearts!

PIXEL

Indian Creek Plaza
Age 4 months, Border Collie

Pixel was a surprise addition to the family, choosing her human at just 4 weeks old, and it felt like fate since her dad is a littermate of their beloved Snix. Known as "Baby Doll," she adores snuggles and is an A+ puppy class student with a heart-melting gaze.

DEMPSEY

Indian Creek Plaza
Age 8 months, Boxer

Meet Dempsey, the goofy Boxer pup with a flashy brindle coat and a playful spirit! A proud BLR alum, he was born after his mom was rescued. His forever family couldn't resist his charm and now he enjoys endless adventures with them!

COOPER

Indian Creek Plaza
Age 2, Boxer

He may be 82 lbs of muscle, but Cooper's real strength is his heart. Despite initial anxiety after being rescued, Cooper learned to trust again and quickly became a beloved family member. He's a whip-smart boy who lives for adventures like road trips and hikes with his humans.

PENNY

Indian Creek Plaza
Age 6, Border Collie

Penny is such a unique beauty, with her fluffy, lilac merle coat. After herding for two years, she transitioned to a service dog due to an eye condition. Now happily retired in Idaho, Penny enjoys a peaceful life filled with morning walks and evening cuddles with her human mom.

RYDER

Indian Creek Plaza
Age 8, Boxer

Ryder is full of energy and joy, known for her gazelle-like jumps. She loves running at top speed, hiking and peanut butter. She's less keen on baths and the UPS truck driver. Strangers can't help stopping to compliment her stunning looks.

HERA

Andselv
Age 4 months, Collie Retriever mix

This dog is a total character! She loves to stand up paddle board and hilariously sounds like an old man when drinking water. When she runs at full speed, watch out - walls and people are no match for her unstoppable energy!

TAILS FROM . . .

Troms, Norway

Known for its awesome mountain scenery, camping culture, and breathtaking views of the Northern Lights.

A DOG'S GUIDE:

1. Hike the Sherpa Steps in Tromsø with your dog, then take in the view at the ski resort cafe.
2. Leave your pup at the hotel and experience a thrilling dog sledding tour under the winter sun or Northern Lights.
3. Join the "Tromsø Canicross og hobbytrekkhund club" for weekly training runs or races with your furry friend, open to all skill levels.
4. Treat yourself to ice cream while enjoying the beautiful sandy beaches of Sommerøya with your dog.
5. Camp in Senja and wake up to breathtaking mountain views, with amazing hiking trails to explore together.

NOR DOG

These photoshoots raised funds for Nor Dog to evacuate, feed, rehome, and rehabilitate animals affected by the war in Ukraine. Visit nor-dog.org to learn more

KATIE GYLTNES
VILL FOTO

Hi, my name is Katie and… I am a dog addict! I am an Service Dog Trainer turned dog photographer. My main passion in life is capturing the beauty of our furry friends on camera. In 2021, I established my photography business here in Norway, Vill Foto.

Currently I have 5 dogs, 3 retired huskies, who are living out their days lounging on the sofa and cuddling with the kids, and two puppies (one husky and one collie mix) who are partners in crime and my go-to dog models.

I love capturing dogs doing what they love in beautiful outdoor surroundings. That includes anything from skijoring or dog sledding in the mountains to running free in the forest.

VILLFOTO.COM

ONYX

Øverbygd
Age 8, German Shepherd

Onyx is a total character! Just like Buck from "The Call of the Wild," he loved his first sled dog experience so much that he broke down the fence to join the team again. Normal activities didn't impress him, but running with the huskies made his eyes shine!

PAGLA

Målselva river
Age 9, Irish Setter

This adorable dog has a quirky habit of sitting like a human on the sofa and her favourite food is vegetables! She absolutely LOVES hiking and exploring the great outdoors.

ZELDA

Elverum
Age 3, Finnish Lapphund

This sneaky pup isn't allowed in the bed, but she ninja creeps in once everyone's asleep! As a fantastic guard dog for the cow farm, she keeps watch, but her weird favourite snack? Cat poo!

OLLIE AND FREDERIKE

Setermoen
Ages 10 and 2, Cairn Terrier

Ollie is a star in obedience competitions, transforming from the laziest dog at home to a lively performer in the ring! She even tells time, reminding her owner when it's dinner time. Meanwhile, Frederike, a bundle of energy, keeps things exciting with her love for tennis balls.

RIEKKIS

Rundhaug
Age 6, Australian Shepherd/New Zealand Huntaway

This adventurous dog loves to sit on the quad bike and is trained to herd reindeer. In the summertime, Riekkis delights in picking and munching on delicious blueberries from the forest.

ATHINA, BIANCA, CORNELIA AND CONRAD

Storholmen
Ages 8, 4, 2 and 2, Bernese Mountain Dogs

These beautiful, hardworking dogs love their family and brings joy and energy to every day.

FALK

Målselv
Age 4, Flat Coat Retriever

This dog is a real character! He struts around with the owner's mobile phone like it's his job, tries to befriend everyone - even a grazing reindeer - and can't resist jumping into any car that pulls up. He's just all about making friends and having fun!

PLUTO

Ersfjorden
Age 2, Border Collie

This dog is a total lapdog who could chill in a lap all day. He's a bit of a klutz, having had plenty of accidents, so soft toys and reminders to "use his eyes" are a must. Surprisingly, he's super chill, except for his fear of cats from a distance!

SOL

Råvatn
Age 6 months, Alaskan Husky

This adorable dog sports one blue eye and one brown eye, and she absolutely LOVES treats - seriously, she'll do anything for food! She's also a fantastic nanny, playmate, and cuddle monster for the baby twins, making her an irreplaceable part of the family.

BONNIE

Picacho Peak State Park
Age 14, Shar Pei mix

This sweet dog was rescued from an abusive situation and has blossomed into the protective old lady of the house. She adores her human and furry family, especially looking out for her mom, ensuring everyone feels safe and loved.

TAILS FROM . . .

Tucson, Arizona USA

Known for having 300 days of sunshine each year, and being a UNESCO-recognized city of gastronomy, due to their commitment to preserving the culture of Sonoran Mexican food traditions.

A DOG'S GUIDE:

1. Hit the trails! Explore one of Tucson's many pet-friendly hiking paths on a sunny day.
2. Cool off in A/C and find your pup's next favourite book at Bookman's.
3. Join the fun at Woofstock in April or Dogtobefest in October, hosted by The Tucson Dog Magazine.
4. Take a drive to Mt Lemmon for a change of scenery and stroll through Summerhaven Village with your pup.
5. Visit the MSA Annex for shopping, tasty bites, a great coffee while reading, or enjoy a locally brewed beer with a friend.

CANDICE EATON
C EATON PHOTOGRAPHY

I picked up a camera for the first time in years as I headed to Alaska for a bucket list trip, and, as I did, I learned how to use it after getting home from that trip. I started my journey as a pet photographer by going to the shelter where I adopted my best friend Buddy years before on the weekends and photographing the adoptable dogs when they were out on their walks.

Then, one day, after playing weekend warrior for a few years, I decided to leave my corporate job as a product development scientist and start my pet photography business. Now, I am Arizona's favourite pet photographer, and I couldn't be more excited to be a part of this project.

CEATONPHOTOGRAPHY.COM

OLD SOULS ANIMAL RESCUE AND RETIREMENT HOME

These photoshoots raised funds for Old Souls Animal Rescue, supporting geriatric and special needs animals with care and companionship. Visit oldsouls.org to learn more

LUCY

Picacho Peak State Park
Age 4, Pitty mix

Lucy is a semi-truck dog who has traveled more of the US than most people! Adopted during COVID from a tire shop in the middle of nowhere, this wiggly wiggler spreads happiness wherever she goes.

ANNIE

Catalina State Park
Age 2, Sheepadoodle

This sweet dog can be a bit shy at times, but she truly loves to cuddle with her favourite humans. When she's not snuggling, she enjoys chasing lizards in the yard.

ARCHIE

Sweetwater Preserve
Age 6, Terrier mix

This lovable pup may have short legs, but he has a huge heart! He adores his sister Bella and follows her everywhere like a shadow, and when the sun shines, you can find him splooting happily on the patio.

BRUCE

Picacho Peak State Park
Age 2, Cane Corso

Bruce is named after Bruce Banner for his giant paws that "Hulk smash" everything. He may be big, but that's just more dog to love!

OAKLEY
Catalina State Park
Age 3, Goldendoodle

This Instadog is a local celebrity, snagging the title of Humane Society of Yuma's Pet Star of 2023. His favourite thing in the world is a tennis ball.

BELLA

Sweetwater Preserve
Age 6, Pittie mix

This sweet dog was rescued as a stray puppy and totally picked her family at a pet supply store. She's a social butterfly, loving every human and dog she meets, and even helps her mom at their doggy daycare, greeting new pals and making sure everyone has a great time!

PRINCE

Sweetwater Preserve
Age 14, Cocker Spaniel

Quirky Prince always eats exactly half of his food, leaving a straight line between the eaten and uneaten half in the kibble. He knows the names of all his toys and was an avid squirrel hunter in his younger years.

CHUNK

Picacho Peak State Park
Age 10 months, Old English Bulldog

Chunk is totally obsessed with her tennis ball. She is jealous of anyone who might be getting treats when she isn't!

BO

Kesselse heide
Age 1, Cavalier King Charles

Bo is a lively pup who's always cheerful and full of energy. She adores playing with her best friend, the cat Lauke, and has a special bond with human kids who absolutely love her. Her playful spirit and loving nature make her simply irresistible!

TAILS FROM . . .
Zandhoven/Antwerp, Belgium

Known for "Antwerp Handjes" cookies, its status as the "Diamond Capital of the World" and housing the world's largest coffee warehouse.

A DOG'S GUIDE:

1. Treat yourself to delicious cookies and pupcakes from Sweet Bea's Barkery.
2. Unleash your energy at a dog playground.
3. Experience the ultimate dog bar tour with a food truck offering everything from dog-friendly beer and wine to tasty daily meals and desserts like cupcakes and donuts.
4. Capture your paw-some moments by having a statue made of your paw at Bodycasting Jessy in Zandhoven.
5. Join the fun at the annual Antwerp Dog Festival where you can walk, play, enjoy yummy snacks, and discover unique accessories.

CINDY VAN OSCH
PAWS AND MEMORIES

Cindy is a dog photographer based in Zandhoven, Belgium. After more than 7 years of experience, Cindy became a professional photographer in 2019. She has endless patience and never force a dog to do something they are uncomfortable with.

Hi! I'm Cindy, married, mom of 3 beautiful children, dog mom, passionate photographer, founder, manager, content creator and more at Paws and memories. Your story together with your four-legged friend, a period that is so precious, but also flies by too quickly. With a memories for life photo session I can freeze time, so that you can relive this period again and again. I create a lasting memory that you can cherish all your life.

PAWSANDMEMORIES.COM

THERAPIEDIER VZW

These photoshoots raised funds for Therapiedier vzw, supporting therapy animals that assist in therapy practices and improve social contact and daily life for individuals.
Visit therapiedier.be to learn more

MILA

Zandhoven Bos en Heide
Age 8, Mixed

Mila, an 8-year-old mixed breed dog, boasts a heart-shaped marking on her flank that mirrors her loving personality. She is Bloom's loyal best friend and plays an important role in the training of future canine-assisted therapists. Mila helps students with her patience and warm presence, making her indispensable in the learning process.

BELLA

Zevenbergenbos Ranst
Age 2, Cavalier King Charles

Bella is a happy and enthusiastic pup who loves cuddles and playtime. Her friendly nature makes her a social butterfly, quickly befriending everyone, both humans and animals. With her big, expressive eyes and soft coat, she radiates love and coziness.

VOLA AND PRINCESS PIPPA

Kesselse heide
Ages 2 and 8, Border Collies

Princess Pippa and Vola are the ultimate best friends. Their wild adventures include running, playing, and exploring together. With Pippa's wisdom and Vola's youthful energy, they're always ready for whatever fun comes their way!

BLOOM

Kesselse heide and Zandhoven bos en heide
Age 2, Mixed

Meet Bloom, the ultimate cuddler! She spreads love everywhere and rocks her modeling gigs for Paws and Memories. Bloom's best bud is Mila, and together they're an adorable duo that no one can resist.

OMER

Zandhoven bos en heide
Age 2, English Cocker Spaniel

Omer is a total rascal! Just like his "human" Mamie, he is also a bit of a stress chicken, but that only makes him cuter. Despite his antics, he is a real cuddle bug, always ready to shower you with love. His mischievous eyes and soft fur make him irresistible to everyone who meets him.

JESSIE
Geelong, Australia
Photographed by Caitlin J. McColl

THE FINE PRINT

DISCLAIMER
All dogs were under effective control and on leash when required by local law or safety. Leads have been removed digitally from the final images.

TAILS OF THE WORLD
PET PHOTOGRAPHERS FOR ANIMAL RESCUE

www.ingramcontent.com/pod-product-compliance
Lightning Source LLC
LaVergne TN
LVHW081341100325
805572LV00007B/34

* 9 7 8 0 6 4 8 4 5 1 9 5 2 *